T0283371

ICE
TRIALS

ICE TRIALS

M.A. ROTHMAN
D.J. BUTLER

A Baen Books Original

Baen Publishing Enterprises
P.O. Box 1403
Riverdale, NY 10471
www.baen.com

ISBN: 978-1-9821-9380-5

Cover art and interior maps by MIBLART

First printing, December 2024

Distributed by Simon & Schuster
1230 Avenue of the Americas
New York, NY 10020

Library of Congress Cataloging-in-Publication Data

Names: Rothman, M. A. (Michael A.), author. | Butler, D. J. (David John), 1973- author.
Title: Ice trials / M.A. Rothman, D.J. Butler.
Description: Riverdale, NY : Baen Publishing Enterprises, 2024. | Series: Time trials ; 2
Identifiers: LCCN 2024040079 (print) | LCCN 2024040080 (ebook) | ISBN 9781982193805 (hardcover) | ISBN 9781625799920 (ebook)
Subjects: LCGFT: Time-travel fiction. | Science fiction. | Novels.
Classification: LCC PS3618.O868715 I34 2024 (print) | LCC PS3618.O868715 (ebook) | DDC 813/.6—dc23/eng/20240830
LC record available at https://lccn.loc.gov/2024040079
LC ebook record available at https://lccn.loc.gov/2024040080

Printed in the United States of America

10 9 8 7 6 5 4 3 2 1

For Steve Ruskin,
who caught us in a howler.

⫷ CHAPTER ⫸
ONE

Gunther Mueller strained to see past the white light that blinded him. He tried moving, but he couldn't feel his arms or legs. It was as if he were a consciousness suspended in a pool of pure light. Sensing movement around him, just beyond his perception, Gunther was suddenly jolted by a booming voice echoing in his head, fragments of words crashing against his consciousness.

"... can show ... to control ... it's merely a ... of ..."

The world exploded in a scintillating storm of infinite colors and Gunther fell forward onto a sand-covered beach. Waves of nausea washed over him as the world tilted. Gasping for breath, he inhaled deeply of the salty sea air.

Amidst the chaos, Gunther detected a whisper in his mind, though its message remained incomprehensible. The voice faded, yet the fragments of its words bounced around in his head. Had he imagined them?

He couldn't shake the feeling that someone—or something—was desperately trying to communicate with him, albeit unsuccessfully.

A shiver raced down his spine as he surveyed the rest of the team, each member collapsed onto the damp sand. With his chest constricting, Gunther fought to draw in a breath. The increasing pressure was akin to being squeezed by a giant boa constrictor.

As he felt the crushing pressure outside his chest, something bloomed within him, as if it was trying to push its way out. "Calm yourself," he muttered in his native German. A bright glow emanated from his fingertips, spreading up his arms, and Gunther was again blinded by a flash of light. He gasped as a wave of exhaustion washed over him, the competing pressures suddenly melting away.

Gasps erupted from various team members as they, too, pulled in deep breaths. Marty Cohen staggered over to Gunther, collapsed onto his knees, and patted him on the shoulder. "Thanks . . . Whatever you did . . . that helped."

Gunther clambered to his feet, unsure that he'd done anything other than have what felt like a panic attack. As the rest of the team rose, one thing became clear: they weren't in Egypt anymore.

"Welcome, seer. It is time."

Marty's ears popped and he fell forward onto all fours as an intense bout of dizziness struck him. He clenched fistfuls of wet sand and held on as the world spun around him.

He smelled smoke and looked up, his eyes opening to a vast river just ten feet away.

Thousands of floating flower petals drifted by.

Surjan Singh staggered to his feet and walked to the shoreline. He breathed in deeply and panned his gaze all around them. "I can't believe it!"

"What?" Marty asked.

The large man pointed upriver. In the distance, a crowd gathered around a fire near the shore. They wore white tunics. And then Marty shifted his gaze downriver and saw the same image repeated. Another gathering of people. Another fire.

Marty climbed up to his feet and felt a wave of nausea.

"We're in India." Surjan said it with a note of certainty. "And this is the Ganges River."

"Yeah, but *when*?" Gunther asked.

The team looked to Marty.

He was the so-called seer, expected to have a vision of their next destination. But this time, Marty's heart thudded loudly as he realized his vision was mostly blurred. The images he'd witnessed as they'd crossed from one place and time to another were all a smudged mess in his mind's eye.

François patted Marty on the shoulder. "Well, Dr. Cohen, it looks like we're embarking on a new adventure. Where to now?"

Marty scanned the expectant faces before him and, for a moment considered just walking away—he'd volunteered to help translate some ancient texts at a dig site south of Cairo. This wasn't Cairo. Yet here he was, somehow the de facto leader of a dig team turned group of reluctant adventurers: François, the eclectic Frenchman who had bankrolled the dig; Lowanna, the occasionally moody Aboriginal anthropologist; Gunther, the fellow archaeologist who'd dragged Marty into this mess; Surjan, the bearded ex-military head of security with his long hair wrapped in his turban; and Kareem, the teenage digger from the streets of Cairo. They were all looking to him for guidance. Marty could only shake his head. "To be honest, I have no idea. The images I saw weren't very clear."

Even though the team looked a bit unsteady on their feet, they were all accounted for. "Is everyone alright?"

The team responded with affirmative responses, except Lowanna Lancaster, who wore a stunned expression. Marty approached her. "Are you okay?"

"I'm not sure." Lowanna's voice wavered, a stark contrast to her usually assertive tone. "I really thought we might be heading home. This feels like we're starting over again, doesn't it? Back to square one."

"It's hard to tell," Marty said as he breathed in the fresh air, detecting the unmistakable scent of the nearby ocean. "I can say this much, it sure doesn't smell like Upper Egypt." He took a deep breath, noticing something distinctly different about the aromas carried by the breeze. Despite the warm weather, there was a familiarity to the scent, reminiscent of opening his kitchen freezer.

The air smelled of ice.

He pressed his lips into a thin line as a million thoughts raced through his head.

About a month ago, Marty and the rest of the archaeological dig team had somehow found themselves transported to the ancient past. Since then, they had journeyed across North Africa in hopes of returning to the modern world they had left behind. However, walking back into the chamber that had initiated their unfortunate adventure had not given them the results they'd hoped for.

Now, Marty and the team faced a new dilemma: Where and when had that mysterious chamber sent them?

⁘ ⁘ ⁘

The warmth of the sun did little to lessen the unease that clung to Marty and the rest of the team. On the far side of the river, palm trees swayed gently in the breeze, yet the air carried an unfamiliar scent— a hint of snow, an anomaly in this climate. Turning to Surjan, a towering figure with a turban expertly wrapped around his head, Marty voiced his uncertainty. "Are you sure this is the Ganges?"

The normally placid man held a troubled expression, raking his fingers through his long beard as he scanned the water. "A moment..." With purposeful strides, Surjan approached the shoreline, cupped his hand into the river, and took a sip. Immediately, he spat the water out, grimacing. "No. This is all wrong."

"What's wrong?" Marty asked.

"This is ocean water. It's full of salt."

"I thought the Ganges originated in the Himalayas," François noted. "Water from melting glaciers should make it a source of fresh water."

Surjan frowned. "I apologize for jumping to conclusions. I think I'm mistaken about this being the Ganges. Maybe a bit of wishful thinking on my part."

François patted the large man on the shoulder and chuckled. "No need for apologies, my good man. We're immersed in the unexpected and the mostly unexplainable. Wasn't it Ursula Le Guin who said that the only thing that makes life possible is permanent, intolerable uncertainty? Having our preconceived notions proven incorrect seems to be par for the course, I'd say. At least on this adventure." The Frenchman turned to Marty. "Any thoughts or guidance, grand seer?"

Grand seer. Marty wasn't sure if François was poking fun at him or just being friendly. The man was often moody and hard to read.

Marty hitched his thumb at the forest of pine trees behind them and asked, "Are there pine trees in India?" He turned to the rest of the team. "On the other side of the river, we have palm trees, while on this side, we seem to be standing on the edge of a dense pine forest. Obviously, we're nowhere near North Africa anymore; that much I'm certain of. Anyone have any idea where we'd find these trees growing side by side?"

"There are pine trees in northern India," Surjan replied, scanning the horizon. "But from our current vantage point, I don't see any mountains. Closer to the Himalayas, there are a lot of pine trees—"

"But they wouldn't typically be growing right next to palm trees," François interjected, "would they?"

"Southern California," Gunther murmured.

"Forbidden!" A woman's voice echoed from a distance.

Marty turned toward the voice, his eyes widening at the impossible sight of a copper-skinned woman with graying hair standing on the water's surface, midway between the shores, gesticulating and yelling in their direction.

"How is she standing on the water, by God?" Kareem stared at the woman with his mouth agape.

As the woman jogged toward them, still shouting, "Forbidden!" Marty and the others walked closer to the shore.

"That's not a language I recognize," Surjan remarked with surprise, "yet I understand her."

"Just like before," Gunther added. "We've had the local language downloaded into our brains. Why is she yelling 'forbidden' at us?"

The woman appeared visibly agitated, her emotions unmistakable in her voice. Marty had no explanation for his ability to understand her words. Here was a woman speaking in a language that sounded like gibberish, yet he and the team understood her perfectly. The same thing had happened when they'd arrived in ancient North Africa. He didn't like Gunther's choice of the word "downloaded," but he didn't have a better one, and that made him uneasy.

"The tonal qualities . . . there's a musicality to it," Lowanna noted, her head tilted as she focused on the shouting woman running toward them. "But it's not like Mandarin or Vietnamese. It's more subtle, with a lot of shifts in pitch. There are ejectives, sharp and precise, punctuating the flow of speech like exclamation points. And then, those lateral fricatives, almost like a soft rustling of leaves. It's actually a beautiful-sounding language, whatever it is."

"But how is she walking on water?" Kareem asked again.

"It's forbidden to be in the Sacred Grove!" the woman yelled. Her eyes were wide with fear.

Lowanna stepped forward as the woman reached the shoreline. "I'm sorry, we didn't realize—"

The woman grabbed Lowanna's hand and motioned to the other side of the river. "Come. Before you attract the spirits!"

Marty was about to intervene when Lowanna waved him away. "We'll follow you, but how did you walk across the water?"

"You must follow me." The woman nodded vigorously, turned and jogged across the water for a couple of seconds. She turned and urgently motioned for them to follow. "Come!"

Unsure why the woman wasn't sinking, Marty walked up to the shore, looked down into the river, and let out a nervous laugh.

He stepped into the water and his foot landed solidly on the beginning of a stone pathway just inches below the water's surface. He turned to the team and said, "Come on, there's a path."

The team advanced slowly, and as François took his first few steps across the water, he laughed and patted Kareem on the shoulder. "See, not everything is a bunch of hocus-pocus."

Marty and Lowanna fast-walked right behind the middle-aged native, who occasionally paused to make sure everyone was still following.

As they reached the other shore, Marty skirted past a large fire being manned by several men who stared wide-eyed at him. One of the men, clad in a roughly hewn white toga, held a basket to his chest filled with white flower petals and tossed some in his direction. The man's motions reminded Marty of a scene from *The Exorcist* when the priest was flinging holy water at a possessed person.

The woman, whose reddish skin gleamed in the fading sunlight, turned and motioned frantically at the others who were still on the water-covered path. She cupped her hands and yelled, "It's perilous to tempt the spirits, hurry!"

Marty turned to the woman and asked, "What is the name of this place?"

"We're outside the Sacred Grove," the woman replied, her tone grave. She took a step toward Marty and stared at him with a puzzled expression. "Why are you so—" The woman paused, turning to Lowanna. "Why is he the color of sand? What happened to him and those others?"

Marty barely suppressed a smile as the woman looked to Lowanna, whose aboriginal complexion was even darker than her own.

Lowanna glanced at Marty and turned back to the woman. "We are from far away, and some people have a lighter skin color than us."

Marty nodded, realizing that these people had likely never seen someone as fair as, say, Gunther.

The woman stepped within arm's reach of Marty, ran her callused thumb across his cheek, and examined her thumb. "The color does not come off." She looked at the gathering team and held a puzzled expression. "Half of your people are bleached by the spirits." She glared at Lowanna. "Are you responsible for them being in the Sacred Grove?"

"She's not," Marty responded. "We all appeared on . . . er, came to the island by accident. None of us remember how or why. We are trying to understand where we are."

The woman's eyes widened, and she nodded. "The spirits must have bleached your skin and clouded your minds. It makes sense."

"It doesn't make sense," one of the men near the fire blurted out with a hostile tone. "How did we not see them cross onto the island?"

Marty exchanged a worried glance with Lowanna. These men didn't seem to be armed, but were clearly agitated by their presence. Especially their presence on the "sacred" island.

"We are too close to powers of the spirits." The native woman waved dismissively at the question. "Your eyes have obviously been affected by their magics, as have the minds of these strangers."

The guard's eyes narrowed, but before he could respond, another guard stepped forward, his expression troubled. "Not all of us were blinded. I saw these outsiders stumble out of the Sacred Grove. They looked . . . confused. It is why I called for your guidance."

A tense silence descended, broken only by the crackling of the bonfire as the shadows lengthened around them. The guards exchanged uneasy glances.

Marty watched as several of the men put their open palms on their chests, as if feeling their own heartbeat. They all held concerned expressions.

The guard who'd previously spoken with a hostile tone bowed his head and said with a trembling voice, "It's as if the spirits themselves had expelled them from the Sacred Grove."

The woman turned to Lowanna and then shifted her gaze to Marty and the others on the team. For a moment, the stiffness in which she held herself relaxed, but when the hooting of an owl erupted from a nearby tree, the woman's expression hardened. "Until the king regains his magic from the spirits," the woman declared, her voice stern, "the island is forbidden to outsiders. Leave this area, and do not return to it, for fear of the Hungry Dead if nothing else." The woman pointed north, away from the water.

Marty motioned for the team to gather, and they walked far enough north to be out of earshot of the natives, who continued staring in their direction even as the sun set. He turned to Surjan and said in a low voice, "Can you scout ahead and see if there are any obvious places we can take shelter?"

Surjan nodded, retrieved his sharpened ankh from within his tunic, and jogged north.

Noticing Lowanna's troubled expression, Marty leaned closer and whispered, "Are you sensing anything?"

For a long moment, Lowanna was silent as she stared into the ever-darkening horizon. Her eyes darted back and forth as if seeing things that nobody else could see. The woman took in a deep breath and let it out slowly. "I can hear whispers of things in the night. They're talking to each other."

"They?" Marty asked.

"The animals." Her voice carried an uncharacteristic level of emotion, almost as if she were about to cry. "I can still hear them."

Marty lowered his head, gave her a one-armed hug, and whispered, "That's a good thing, Lowanna. We need to take advantage of any of the little gifts we find at our disposal."

He turned to the rest of the team and said, "Surjan's out scouting for a safe spot to camp for the night. In the meantime, keep watch for anything out of the ordinary. Anyone have any questions or issues?"

Kareem stepped noiselessly forward and nodded. "I have one. Do you know where we are?"

"Not yet." Marty shook his head. "Obviously we need to come up with a plan. As soon as we settle for the night, the stars will come out and we'll hopefully be able to get a better idea of roughly where we might be. That's step one. We'll have to come up with the next steps once we have a little more information about our situation."

Lowanna was surprised at how calm the team was with their new situation. Inside *she* was freaking out, both disappointed with the idea that they were clearly nowhere near getting back to where things seemed familiar, and a bit afraid of what was to come.

This wasn't exactly the life she'd expected for herself—popping in and out of chaotic situations that none of them were trained to handle. Nobody was trained for this kind of crap. Not knowing where they were was one thing, but having to determine *when* they were was still something that was hard to reconcile.

The sun had set quite a while ago, and with the last vestiges of its light fading on the horizon, darkness lay across the grasslands like a shroud.

They were all waiting for Surjan to return, and even though she was a bundle of nerves, she tried to maintain a calm exterior.

Marty was only about a dozen feet or so away, sitting cross-legged and staring in the direction Surjan had gone.

The others were scattered around, all within a fifty-foot radius, and for whatever reason, they all maintained a silent posture.

"What's taking Surjan so long?" she whispered to herself.

Psst … hey, you.

Lowanna jerked her head in the direction of the sound.

It wasn't a human's voice.

For some reason, she could hear the mutterings and whispers of creatures large and small, and just like with the foreign language spoken by the native woman, she could understand it. Marty could, too, though he seemed to be too far away to hear the voice that was speaking now. It was just one of the many strange and disparate gifts the team had developed since leaving their natural time.

Hey, you. Can you hear me? The barely audible squeak was coming from somewhere in the grasses ahead.

"I can hear you," Lowanna whispered. "Who are you?"

Most animals weren't up to talking in the sense that they formed sentences. It was usually one-word utterances that came across, so hearing an actual question from the whispers in the night set her on edge. What was this thing talking to her?

Are you human or gray?

Gray? What did that mean? "I'm human," she whispered in response. "Who are you?"

I am Shushiyumastra, but you can call me Shush. That's what my human calls me. Why are you humans out here? You're scaring the nighttime bugs and I wanted a snack.

Lowanna had wondered why the night was so quiet. Normally, once darkness set in, crickets and other nocturnal creatures would be having a party of sorts.

"Sorry about that. We're waiting for a team member to return."

The grasses moved slightly and a nose poked out from within the dense undergrowth. Slowly, a ratlike face emerged and Lowanna smiled as she recognized the species of creature she'd been talking with.

It was a weasel, and he was busily sniffing the air. *Why don't you come with me? My person, he calls himself Muwat. He always has fish at the hut.*

Lowanna's eyes widened at the unexpected invitation. She'd never had an actual conversation with a creature like this. "I have others with me. Do you think we'd all be welcome? How far is it from here?"

Not far. The weasel walked across the dozen or so feet separating them and looked up at her. His chittering language grew louder and more emphatic. *He's an old fisherman, lonely. Could use the company.*

"Welcome back!" Marty's voice echoed loudly in the night as a tall figure appeared, coppery in the light of the fire. "Did you find anything?"

Before Surjan could even respond, Lowanna volunteered, "I just learned of an option we could pursue."

In the dimly lit confines of his solitude, Gunther sat in quiet contemplation, his eyelids closed as he delved deep into the recesses of his mind. With each breath, he sought to forge a connection, a fragile tether reaching out into the infinite expanse of the unknown, yearning to touch the elusive presence that had once attempted to breach the barriers of his consciousness.

With every ounce of his being, he pushed against the boundaries of his own perception, visualizing the intangible rope extending farther and farther into the unfathomable depths. In the silence of his mind, he strained to catch even the faintest whisper, the echo of a voice that had tantalizingly teased his senses before.

And then, for a fleeting moment, amidst the infinite expanse, he felt it—a distant echo, a mere whisper carried on the winds of his thoughts. The voice, though distant and ethereal, resonated within him, offering cryptic fragments of its message.

"*. . . can show . . . to control . . .*"

But as swiftly as it had come, the ephemeral connection slipped through his grasp, leaving him grasping at shadows in the recesses of his mind. With a heavy exhalation, Gunther collapsed, drained by the effort, the echoes of the elusive voice fading into the ether.

"Okay, let's gather up and move." Marty's voice barely penetrated Gunther's consciousness and it took everything he had to gather enough energy to stand, even unsteadily.

"Gunther, are you okay?" Marty asked as he walked over to him.

Gunther nodded. "I'm fine, just a little tired. Lead the way."

As the team followed Lowanna toward an unknown destination, Gunther's mind kept drifting back to the voice.

The voice was trying to tell him something important, that much he knew.

He staggered forward as the team moved, and Gunther knew that even though he lacked the strength to communicate with whatever it was that was out there, he couldn't stop trying.

Gunther wasn't sure why he believed it, but he was certain that the message would make all the difference in the world for the team.

The hive mind sensed the exception triggered by an anomaly in the test matrix, and immediately launched a thread to analyze the issue.

"Probe-mode activated for a test anomaly out of the Orion arm of the Milky Way galaxy. Planet Earth, local relative year is 252 B.C.E.

"The Interrupt Service Routine has generated a fatal exception in a previous test and pushed the prior test subjects into a new location in Brane sigma+654PWJZBE."

The Administrator shifted a part of his attention to the anomaly and asked, *"What caused the error?"*

"An unknown surge of energy shifted the landing parameters."

"I presume the test subjects have been erased. Earth's fate is thus sealed."

"The test subjects remain operational. A previously idle thread picked up the exception and serviced it. The test subjects somehow survived the shifting context. All six have been deposited at another test node. Local relative year is 9104 B.C.E."

The hive mind triggered a priority alert. *"Detected another unexplained surge at the aforementioned test node."*

The Administrator shifted more of his consciousness to the alert. *"Give me the ID of the event."*

The hive mind sent the ID packet and the Administrator focused on the precise location and time of the event.

He sensed a high-frequency signal penetrating one of the test subjects.

As the Administrator tracked the origin of the signal he sent a command to the hive mind: *"Decode the signal being received by test subject Gunther."*

His consciousness followed the signal from the event, up through the planet's atmosphere. The gossamer-thin signal was barely detectable as the Administrator followed it through the interstellar medium, boring through the Milky Way, past the local group, and beyond the Virgo Supercluster to the edge of Brane sigma+654PWJZBE.

The Administrator applied all of his focus on the signal's exit point.

It was a very rare situation when a signal crossed from one universe into another . . . but this wasn't what had happened.

The hive mind alerted, *"The signal carries patterned content, yet after applying all known resources, we cannot decipher its meaning."*

The Administrator paused for a few Planck cycles and contemplated the hive mind's message. It shouldn't be possible to *not* decipher a coded message. At least not for them.

Yet it also shouldn't be possible for a signal to vanish at the edge of a universe.

The focus being applied on this issue was not making progress.

"Alert me if another such signal appears."

The Administrator shifted his attention back to the rest of the multiverse.

⪦ CHAPTER ⪧
TWO

Marty followed Lowanna's lead as she led the team along a narrow path in the darkness. He caught a glimpse of what looked like a weasel weaving through the grasses. Occasionally, it paused, poked its head above the undergrowth, and continued on its way.

After about a quarter-mile hike across lush grassland, Marty heard the sound of waves breaking on a beach before actually seeing them. A sliver of moon above the horizon provided enough light for him to see the first signs of a beach. Emerging from the shadows, he spotted a hut woven of slender branches nestled amidst the tall grasses. Gutted fish were laid over its roof, possibly to dry them out, and as the breeze shifted in their direction, the smell of rotting fish was unmistakable. A hunched-over figure emerged from the doorway.

With a grunt of effort, he straightened his posture, cupped his hands near his ears, and stared in their direction.

"Welcome, strangers," the figure called, his voice weathered with age. He grabbed a nearby fishing spear and leaned on it. "I do not recognize your footfalls."

Lowanna walked over to Marty and whispered, "The man is supposedly friendly. His name is Muwat."

Marty grinned. "Did your weasel friend tell you that?"

She ignored the question and turned in the direction of the old man. "We mean you no harm."

"A woman?" The old man's eyes widened.

"And her companions," Marty added. "We're a bit lost and were looking for shelter for the night."

The man leaned his spear against the hut. "I hear your voice and immediately know you are not from Nesha. I also hear the uncertainty in the pattern of your footsteps." He motioned for them to approach. "I may not be able to see much anymore, but I'd rather not yell across the night to be heard. You and the four others, come. What I have, I will share."

Marty motioned to the rest of the team, and they approached. The man's eyes gleamed dull white in the moonlight, as if his eye sockets had round white stones embedded in them. "Sir, there are six of us, in total. I don't want to be a burden."

"Six, you say. Funny how I only hear the swish of five feet. Come, the fish I have remaining will only be good for fertilizer if not eaten soon." The fisherman motioned for them to approach, his milky eyes scanning the group, then snapped his fingers. "Shush! Get me my flint."

Marty's eyes widened as the weasel, who'd been digging for something in the grasses, stopped, popped his head up above the grasses to look over at the old man, and rushed past the old man and into the hut.

Seconds later, the weasel emerged from the shelter with a stone tool in his mouth and dropped it at the man's feet. *Will you make a fire?* the weasel asked.

"That's one articulate weasel," Marty murmured.

"I hear you, my friend." The old man scooped up what turned out to be a large chunk of flint and crouched in front of a pile of dried grasses. It took only a few practiced strikes with another stone, and the first signs of a fire bloomed within the grasses.

Marty walked in the direction of the hut and asked, "Were you planning on cooking the fish that are drying on the roof?"

"Aye." The old man gathered a few nearby sticks. "If you don't mind, gather what you need, and I'll prepare something that should fill your bellies."

As Marty walked closer to the drying fish, the unmistakable smell of putrefaction enveloped him, and he winced at the thought of eating the rotting fish. He motioned to Gunther, and as the German approached, Marty gathered a few of the fish. The slimy texture coupled with the fishy odor turned his stomach. Maybe the people here were used to eating stuff like this, but this would really be a challenge for him and likely most of the team.

Gunther sniffed at the air as he studied what was in Marty's hands. He leaned in and whispered, "I'm thinking those are not . . ."

"Agreed." Marty nodded. "You and I are on the same page, but do you think you can do something?"

"Do something?" Gunther stared back at him with a confused expression. "François is the cook. What are you thinking?"

"You know, sort of like a blessing over the food. Maybe it'll work? Like . . . heal the food?" Marty had personally witnessed Gunther's ability to heal a person's ailments, whether they were cuts, bruises, or even worse. It was an unexplainable ingredient in this crazy series of tests they were undergoing, not unlike his and Lowanna's ability to communicate with animals or the entire team's ability to understand and speak in an unfamiliar language.

Gunther hesitated as he put his hand over the bundle of fish Marty was carrying. "I don't know about this."

"What's the worst that could happen?"

Gunther shrugged, and with his hand hovering just an inch above the pile of fish, he closed his eyes, his brows furrowed in concentration.

Marty held his breath as the faintest glimmer of light emanated from Gunther's hand.

He nearly dropped the bundle of rotten fish as he felt the load shift, almost as if the animals were alive.

But they weren't moving in that way.

Marty stared in awe as the partially desiccated filets plumped up with moisture right in front of his eyes.

In the glow of the growing campfire, the flesh of the fish shone brightly, almost as if they'd been sliced open only moments ago.

Gunther's eyes opened, and he removed his hand. "That felt strange."

Marty sniffed at the fish and smelled almost nothing. He looked up at Gunther and smiled. "My friend, you definitely did something."

"Have you gathered your supper?" the old man called out. "The fire is ready."

Marty walked over to the old man and crouched low with a pile of fish held in his arms.

Without even looking, the old man reached over, grabbed one of the fish, and skewered it on one of the sticks. As he continued preparing the fish, he looked in the direction of the others on the team and began barking orders. "One of you go into the hut and bring me my large bowl. I also need one of you to go into my bin and gather enough potatoes for us all. Also, I heard a woman's voice. I would like you to help gather some gamagrass."

Marty glanced at Lowanna, who had turned to survey the nearby grasses. He had no idea what gamagrass was, but she seemed to take the request in stride. "The others can also help gather the gamagrass."

The old man shrugged as he continued skewering each fish in a zigzag pattern. "Yes, but a woman's fingers are best suited in its preparation. Much more dexterous than a man's."

Marty looked over at Kareem, whose attention was focused on the fire, and said, "Kareem, go help Lowanna gather the grass."

"It's not really a grass," Lowanna called out from the darkness. "It's more like wild rice."

Marty's mind raced as he watched Kareem turn and walk in the direction of Lowanna's voice, his silhouette melting into the dark backdrop of the night.

He hadn't yet told the team about the vision he'd received ahead of their arriving in this place.

Marty wasn't sure how the team would react, but the one thing he knew for certain was that someone or something was testing them.

And the stakes were certainly higher than just their getting back home.

He suspected that this thing they were involved in was much bigger than Marty or his five companions knew.

The evening air was alive with the crackle of the campfire and the sound of waves lapping against the nearby shore. As Gunther bit into the crispy-skinned fish, he was pleased that the mild white flesh held no off flavors. It was a bit salty, but that was easy to overlook as his belly filled with nourishment. A chorus of compliments filled the air, praising the old man's cooking skills.

"Muwat, this fish is incredible!" Marty exclaimed between bites, savoring the delicate flavor.

"Top-notch, my good man. It's excellent," François chimed in as well.

Muwat chuckled modestly, his weathered face breaking into a

toothless grin. "Glad you enjoy it, my friends. Not much else to offer, but I make do with what the sea provides."

Using a flattened reed as a makeshift scoop, Gunther dug out a large helping of the wild rice from a hardened clay bowl, popped the steaming grains into his mouth, and began chewing. The rice had a strange, yet satisfying blend of vegetal and nutty flavors, complementing the fish perfectly.

Marty leaned in close to Gunther, his voice barely above a whisper. "We're going to need more of your blessings over our food from here on in. This is the best rotten fish I've ever eaten."

Gunther nodded, surprised at how his newfound ability had exposed a new facet of usefulness.

"Tell us more about the Sacred Grove, Muwat," François prompted, his tone eager. "What do you know about it?"

Muwat's expression turned somber as he shifted his gaze in the direction of the island. "The Sacred Grove . . . it's a place of mystery and power," he began, his voice tinged with reverence. "Legend has it that it is the source of the king's ancestral power. But with each passing season, the waters have risen, and the attacks of the Hungry Dead have multiplied, because the king's power over the elements was waning. Some say the king's magic was leeched from him by the powers of the spirits that dwell within the Grove."

"And was it the king who chose to confront the spirits?" Surjan asked as he worked on stripping the bark from a long branch he'd found on the beach.

Muwat shrugged. "I cannot be sure. I'm old, and do not live in the central village anymore. I just hear things on occasion, and all I really know is that recently the king traveled to the Sacred Grove to confront the spirits, trying to reclaim what was rightfully his."

"With the hope that he could reclaim his magic and lower the waters?" Marty asked.

The old man nodded. "I believe so. It's not just the waters, but the weather has been odd of late. Some argue it has been warmer than normal, yet others claim that the water has grown colder. These are confusing times. Also, I'm not one who would know the thoughts of our king. I'm just an old fisherman."

"Do you know what is in the Sacred Grove, other than spirits?" Surjan asked.

Muwat paused, his wrinkled hands tracing invisible patterns in the sand. "No one knows what lies within the Sacred Grove, other than the king. I've heard rumors that there's a dry well, and not much else. But these are from stories that have been passed down for many generations and originated long before my time." The crackling fire cast flickering shadows across the sand as Muwat rose from his seat, stretching his arms above his head with a tired yawn. "I thank you for the conversation, but I need to sleep. The fish along the shoreline will be the most active in the early morning, and I cannot miss it. Can you please bank the fire once you are done?"

"We will make sure everything is taken care of," Marty volunteered as the rest of the team wished the old man a good night's rest.

As Muwat turned to make his way back to the hut, Gunther approached him, feeling a surge of sympathy for the old man's situation. His existence had to be difficult, especially being blind and alone.

"Muwat," Gunther began softly, "may I have a moment of your time?"

Muwat nodded, his milky eyes clouded with age turned toward Gunther. "Of course, my friend. What is it?"

Taking a deep breath, Gunther hesitated for a moment before broaching the delicate topic. "I couldn't help but notice your eyes... Can you tell me what happened? I assume you were not born this way."

A wistful smile touched Muwat's lips as he spoke. "Ah, my eyes. They are not what they used to be, I'm afraid. The veil over them has grown thicker with each passing season. Now, I can only detect light and dark. That is it."

"I assume that there is a village somewhere nearby where most people live—why not live closer to other people? It must be hard being out here by yourself."

"You truly are newcomers to the island nation of Nesha." The old man gave him a toothless grin. "Yes, there is a village not far from here. I moved closer to the shore while I still could see enough to make my way. This way, I can keep my life and be independent. I didn't want to be a burden to others."

Compassion welled up within Gunther as he listened to Muwat's words. He reached out to the man with both hands and hesitated. "Let me give you a small blessing. I hope it can help in some way."

Muwat nodded. "You have a kind heart, I can sense it. I have no need for such a blessing, but I appreciate the thought."

"If you don't mind, I would still like to give you this as a way for me to thank you for an excellent meal. It would make me happy if you would allow me to do this."

The old man shrugged. "Very well. Do what you will, but I must get some rest."

Gunther felt a tingle race up and down his spine as he reached out and gently placed his hands over the old man's eyes. His palms began glowing with a soft, golden light. A surge of energy flowed from Gunther, and he sensed that whatever it was he was doing, it was being accepted by the man's body.

The archaeologist knew almost nothing about his newfound "healing" ability, but the one thing he'd learned since undergoing the metamorphosis the entire team had gone through was that this ability would either be accepted or rejected by the target. And if rejected, it was almost like spraying a water hose at a wall—the water would splash back, soaking him—and this wasn't what he was sensing.

"My friend, it's a strange sensation I'm feeling." Muwat frowned. "It's almost as if my head has been relieved of a headache I didn't realize I had."

Gunther felt a sudden reverberation from the energy flow; whatever healing he was attempting was no longer flowing into the old man. "Okay, I'm done." He stared at the old man, hoping to witness a miracle.

Muwat's eyes opened and whatever glimmer of hope Gunther had felt vanished as the milky-white eyes stared back at him. "Thank you for the blessing. I appreciate the intent behind your act." He reached out and awkwardly placed his hand on Gunther's shoulder. "I must get some rest. The sunrise waits for no man."

The old man turned and entered his hut.

"Gunther," Marty called out from the campfire, "let's gather for a team meeting."

Gunther stared for a moment at the ramshackle building and felt a bit deflated. "It was worth a try."

One of the larger chunks of wood shifted in the campfire, sending a handful of embers in all directions. Marty glanced at the fire and shrugged. "All I can tell you is that at the end, the voice coming out of the shadows announced that we had passed and we'd be able to move on. I couldn't see who was behind the voices, and to be honest, I'm not even sure if they were voices in the sense that you could hear them. It was more like I was hearing thoughts. Anyway, what it was that they were expecting from us, I'm not exactly sure, but I got the impression that we'd just barely passed."

"Hold on"—François flicked away the cricket that had landed on his knee—"let me see if I can summarize. As we got zapped from ancient Egypt to this place, you heard some voices debating the merits and faults of our activities as we tried to get back home. We were blamed for the death of one of our teammates..." The Frenchman paused, his chin quivering. Abdullah bin Rahman had been a close friend of his. "We were lauded for our help of the native villagers we encountered, and after much debate, we were deemed passable."

"What would have happened if we didn't pass?" Kareem asked with a wide-eyed expression. "Would we have gotten killed? Maybe not woken up?"

Marty shrugged. "I have no idea, but the one thing that's in evidence is that someone or something is watching us. They're putting us through our paces."

"Could it be the Builders that Narmer talked about?" Lowanna asked.

"Maybe." Marty struggled to remember exactly what he'd read on the original tablets back when all of this had first started. He could recall almost every moment since they'd begun this crazy adventure, but that picture-perfect memory didn't extend before that time. "If I remember correctly, the tablets from Nabta Playa talked about finishing our foes and continuing, with the alternative being that we'd likely die if we failed. I'm thinking the wisest course of action is forward, and we need to just do the right thing as we encounter it."

"Well, the first thing we need to do is figure out where we are," François remarked.

Lowanna looked up at the expansive night sky. "Well, like last time, let the stars be our guide."

François pointed into the cloudless sky and said, "That grouping of stars forms the shape of the Big Dipper."

Lowanna followed his gaze, her expression thoughtful. "Agreed, and if you trace an imaginary line from the two outer stars of the Big Dipper's bowl to the North Star—"

"And measure the angle between the horizon and the North Star," François interjected, "we can estimate our latitude."

Both Lowanna and François held up their hands, measuring the angle. "About thirty degrees north," they said in unison.

"Except," François continued, "that the north celestial pole moves over time. For all we know, the pole star now is Thuban or Vega. And the farther away from Polaris the pole is, the more dramatically Polaris can swing. Maybe we're at twenty degrees and maybe we're at forty."

"Still, that narrows down our possible locations," Marty said. "We're in the northern hemisphere, in the middle latitudes. And there are palm trees, so we should err around the lower middle latitudes, I think. Anyone remember their world map well enough to remember what's around thirty north? Give or take?"

Lowanna pursed her lips. "We're in the subtropical zone, and Muwat mentioned that this place is an island. There are a couple of possibilities. The Ryukyu Islands would be at the right latitude, but these people don't look anything like East Asians."

"No," François agreed. "And Hainan Island would be out as well, the Canary Islands off Spain might be okay, as would many islands in the Caribbean like Cuba, the Keys, and the Bahamas."

"Climate changes over time, boys," Lowanna said. "We're making some big assumptions."

"Isn't Hawaii right around twenty-five north?" Marty asked.

"It is." Lowanna nodded. "But these people don't look Polynesian. I'd say we're either in the Caribbean somewhere or maybe François is right and the Canary Islands would be possible, though I'm unfamiliar with the ancient demographics of that area. Based on the handmade clothing and rough weaving techniques, I'm assuming we're sometime in the past. Wouldn't the folks near Europe have a more Caucasian look? Mind you, people migrate."

"Sort of like Viking explorers?" Gunther asked.

"Maybe." Lowanna shrugged. "Like I said, Western European anthropology wasn't my focus of study, especially prehistoric."

"Folks, we need to get some rest," Marty announced with a loud yawn. "Who wants to take first watch?"

"I'll take first watch," Gunther volunteered.

Marty turned to Surjan as he got up, wielding the results of an hour's worth of stripping and sharpening a large branch. "You have some plans for that spear?"

The large, muscular Sikh shook his head. "I believe in being prepared, mate. I'm going to go scouting and see what else is around here. I'll be back before dawn."

"Be careful, Surjan," Marty cautioned, "we don't know what's out there yet."

"I'm out there, that should be scary enough." The commando smiled, gave Marty a nod, and walked into the inky blackness of the night.

Lowanna lay on her side and said, "Gunther, wake me for the next watch."

Marty pushed several mounds of sand around the edge of the campfire and looked over at Lowanna. "Wake me when you get up, I'll join you."

Lowanna grunted an acknowledgment, but in the flickering light of the campfire, he caught a flash of an uncharacteristic smile coming from her.

Marty lay on his side, his back against a bundle of kindling, and closed his eyes.

Before he could even think about counting sheep, the darkness of the night claimed him.

Surjan tightened his grip around the wrist-thick spear as he approached the ford to the Sacred Grove. The bonfires had burned low, and he noticed the two guards stationed there were slumped over, their snores echoing softly in the night air. With cautious steps, he moved past them and took his first tentative stride on the pathway hidden just beneath the surface of the water. The dim light of the moon overhead was just enough to keep his bearings as he crossed the flooded lowland onto the beach.

Something about this place had struck him the moment they'd first appeared in this world. The sound of a faint cry in the distance replayed in his mind. At first, he'd mistaken the bonfires across the flooded plain along with the flower petals floating on the water as a sign of a funeral, and the wailing having come from a group of mourners. But something had been eating at him ever since.

His initial instincts had failed him, and Surjan was sure that the wailing noise had not come from the men across the flooded plain but instead had come from within the pine forest. With his senses heightened, he walked across the beach and entered the tree line, heading for the mysterious heart of the Sacred Grove.

The air grew heavy in his lungs as Surjan ventured deeper into the forest, his eyes adjusting to the dim moonlight filtering through the thick canopy above. His heart pounded in his chest, a mix of fear and curiosity driving him forward. Ahead, the darkness of the dense forest gave way to the moonlight as he strode into a clearing.

Suddenly, a rustle caught Surjan's attention. He froze, his muscles tensing as he scanned the darkness for any sign of movement. Ahead, he spotted what looked like a well. Its casing stood three feet tall and its lip rose and fell in crenellations, like a medieval castle.

In the shadows, something shifted.

Wielding his spear, Surjan's grip tightened as his instincts screamed about an unseen threat looming in the shadows. At the same time, he sensed movement in the trees. Emerging from the shadows in the clearing, a figure stepped into the moonlight.

It was a man, his face contorted, the shadows rendering his visage an inhuman mask. The man's eyes widened as he spotted Surjan.

Surjan took a step back as the other man advanced. The stranger was emaciated, that much he could tell even in the dark. He held a wild, feral look as he approached Surjan.

"Are you the king?" Surjan asked.

"Your voice is strange." The man came on.

"Do you need help?"

The stranger's breathing was ragged, his eyes wide with a manic expression. "Spirit!" He lunged toward Surjan.

Surjan reacted swiftly, dodging the king's attack and grappling with him in the darkness. The man had strength born of desperation, and Surjan was knocked backward.

"Die!" The rabid man's spittle-flecked beard shone in the moonlight. "You will not have what is mine!"

With a surge of strength, Surjan shoved the wild man from him and brought his spear to bear. He didn't want to kill the man, but as the crazed stranger approached, Surjan knew that this wasn't going to end well for one of them.

⊹ ⊹ ⊹

As Kareem silently trailed behind Surjan, he marveled at his own stealth, relishing the thrill of moving undetected through the shadows. Keeping his gaze fixed on Surjan, Kareem stayed focused on the unfolding scene ahead.

In the dim light of the Sacred Grove, Kareem spotted what certainly had to be the king approaching Surjan. His heart raced with excitement as he watched the tense confrontation, sensing that it was about to erupt into violence. Kareem felt conflicted about staying back in the shadows. After all, Surjan was a friend of sorts, but the larger man was better off without him possibly getting in the way. He weaved his way along the edge of the clearing, remaining in the safety of the shadows.

With a sudden burst of movement, the king launched himself at Surjan, knocking the giant Sikh back on his heels. The two figures collided in a flurry of blows, their struggle illuminated by the faint glow of moonlight.

As the fight raged on, Kareem's attention was drawn to a golden bracelet atop what appeared to be an altar nearby. It gleamed dully. He chuckled.

Items made of gold could always be traded for something they'd need in the future. That was always the case where they'd come from, and it likely remained true in this world.

The king cursed the spirits as Surjan knocked the smaller opponent to the ground. With a quick glance around to ensure he remained unnoticed, Kareem darted from the shadows, snatched the item, and raced back into the safety of the forest.

With his prize in hand, Kareem slipped away from the chaos unfolding in the clearing, his footsteps silent as he melted back into the darkness of the Sacred Grove. He felt a pang of guilt at not helping Surjan with his confrontation with the king, but as he weaved his way back to camp, he was confident that things would work out for the large man.

Besides, if he intervened to help Surjan, Surjan would know Kareem had followed him, and he wouldn't like that.

Surjan and the king circled each other warily, their breath coming in ragged gasps as they prepared for another clash. Surjan gripped his wooden spear tightly, its rough-hewn surface providing a sure grip on the weapon. Across from him, the king had managed to retrieve his own weapon—a spear crafted from what looked to be a long, straight animal horn of some kind. The gleaming surface of the king's spear reflected in the pale moonlight, showing a twisted pattern to the bonelike weapon.

The image of a narwhal came to mind, a rarely seen whale with a long spearlike tooth protruding from its upper jaw.

"We don't have to fight!" Surjan growled as he parried a blow from the six-foot-long weapon the king wielded with practiced ease.

"I reclaim my powers from you!" the king yelled as he advanced, swinging his weapon back and forth. The bone made a whistling sound as it cut through the air. "I will not die! The sacred spear shall be the end of you!"

Surjan dove to the side as the king lunged, his spear just barely missing the large Sikh.

"Thief!" With a roar, the king surged forward, his spear slicing through the air with deadly precision. Surjan parried the blow with practiced ease, his muscles straining against the force of the impact. With a swift counterattack, Surjan lashed out with his spear, aiming for the king's exposed flank.

The king staggered, his grip on his weapon faltering for a moment.

Surjan pressed his advantage, driving forward with relentless ferocity.

Blow after blow rained down upon the king, each strike aiming to dislodge the weapon from the man's grip.

Ignoring any semblance of defense, the king let out a roar, leaped forward, and impaled himself on Surjan's weapon with such force that the wooden spear snapped in half.

Stunned, Surjan stepped back. The king let out a strangled cry, his strength failing him as he collapsed to the ground in a heap.

Kicking the spear from reach, Surjan crouched over the fallen king, a sense of dread washing over him.

With Surjan's spear embedded in the man's chest, the king coughed up blood and stared up at the stranger who'd defeated him.

Was there time for him to run back to get Gunther? Could the man hang on until—

"Beware..." The king grabbed a fistful of Surjan's shirt and coughed up a disturbing amount of blood. "Beware the spider's bite."

The cryptic warning sent a shiver down Surjan's spine. With a rattling wheeze, the king exhaled his last breath.

"I'm sorry for this . . . it was not my wish to see this come to pass. I pray that your next life is a blessed one. Waheguru, Waheguru, Waheguru." Wonderful Lord.

The large man backed away from the corpse, gathered the spear, and was surprised at how warm the weapon felt. Almost as if something inside it was giving off heat.

Surjan's attention was immediately claimed by a faint wailing sound echoing across the clearing. Were these spirits the natives talked about real? His gaze fell upon the well.

Surjan hesitated for a moment, his rational mind dismissing the notion of ghosts and specters. But as the eerie sound repeated itself, it seemed to be coming from the direction of the well. The sound sent a chill down his spine, and he knew it was time to leave the Sacred Grove behind.

With one last glance at the well, Surjan turned and made his way back into the night, the echoes of the king's final words lingering in his ears.

⪡ CHAPTER ⪢
THREE

"Wake up," François told Lowanna. "Wake up, there's breakfast. It's fish, and fruit. And, ah . . . trouble."

"I can see!" Muwat said.

Lowanna knew Gunther had tried to heal Muwat's blindness and hadn't succeeded . . . but maybe there'd been some delayed effect to the healing? Interesting. But not interesting enough to get her out of bed.

"Trouble for breakfast?" Lowanna grunted, not really wanting to wake up yet. She wasn't comfortable, exactly, just tired. Her watch had been uneventful, but long.

François prodded Lowanna's shoulder. "Trouble for breakfast, trouble for lunch, and probably enough trouble left for snacks. Come on, get up. You aren't the only one who stood watch last night."

"Yeah," Lowanna murmured, "but I did the best job, and it was exhausting. You can have my share of the trouble."

"I can see! I can see!" It was Muwat's shouting rather than François's poking her shoulder that finally made Lowanna stir. "You are great magicians!"

Lowanna sat up from her bed of matted grass. Before they had gone back in time, a night spent sleeping in the grass would have left her with kinks in her neck and multiple charley horses. She would have dragged her carcass to a coffeepot and hugged it to herself until it rescued her from morning crotchetiness. But the time travel, or the alien ankh-devices they each possessed, had revitalized them all, and she felt fine.

Maybe even perky. She took a deep breath, and smelled the salt of the sea, along with the tang of pine needles.

Somewhere in the middle latitudes of the northern hemisphere, on the sea.

François walked away toward Muwat's hut. A bright yellow sun cracked barely over the flat horizon of the ocean. "There's fish when you're ready. Arnun is a fast learner."

"Who's Arnun?" Lowanna shot back, stretching.

The sun rising over the water meant they were on the east coast of whatever land mass they were on.

Arnun is Muwat's son, the weasel Shush told her. The creature sat up on his haunches a few paces from her. He held a snail in his front paws and pecked it open by tapping it repeatedly against a stone. *Zidna is his wife. Telipi and Yaru are his daughters. I am his weasel.*

"I'm used to speaking to animals," she said. "Well . . . sort of used to it. I'm not used to animals having very much to say."

I'm not used to humans speaking, Shush said. *Mostly, you just make that mushy moaning sounds with your mouths.*

"Mushy?"

Like fruit rotting, but loud, Shush said. *Like a wave, but without the crisp snap of it striking rocks. Like the rumbling of an empty belly. You all make the sound of a sick herd beast, calling out to its fellows for attention.*

Was Shush a poet? "But why do you live so close to these humans? To Muwat and his family?"

They are my pack. The weasel shrugged. *They sound like sick herd beasts but they catch food and they let me take shelter in their hut.*

"You are a clever creature," she told the weasel.

He pried the snail from its shell and gulped it down. *So are you.* Then he turned and bolted into the grass.

She stood and stretched, enjoying the feel of her muscles unwinding. On the open space of packed earth and pebbles beside the hut, her companions gathered around a fire and ate.

"You're not Neshili," a voice said. The voice didn't startle her, but it sent a bit of a shiver up her spine; it was a baritone purr, masculine but also gentle. She turned to face the voice and found a muscular man with coppery-brown skin, a high forehead, and straight black hair to his shoulders. He wore an undyed kilt and sandals and he leaned on a spear. A quiver hanging behind him from his belt held half a dozen javelins, and a throwing stick—an atlatl—hung attached to the quiver. His eyebrows danced playfully and one corner of his mouth curled up.

"I'm not," she admitted.

"I don't think you're a spirit, either," he pressed.

"What if I were?" she asked. "Are you a shaman, to capture me? Or an exorcist, to drive me away?"

He laughed. "I would do as my king required." His eyebrows leaped. "Or my queen."

Behind him, three men in white togas moved toward the fishing hut and the fire. They walked almost in synch, taking steady, solemn steps. They had the spearman's complexion, but with the lines and wrinkles of age, and hair white as snow.

"But you may be a wise woman," the warrior continued. "I listened to you speak with the animal."

"As I am speaking to you."

"Yes. As you are speaking to me." The warrior inclined his head. "I am Sharrum."

"I see." Lowanna left him without introducing herself, trotting to join her friends.

The fisherman Muwat orbited around the fire, staring about himself, eyes wide open. Beside the fire on a stone sat a woman a few years younger by appearance, clasping both her hands over her mouth and staring at the fisherman. Three youths, teenagers by the look of them, cooked fish and fruit on wooden skewers over the flames. François handed Lowanna a kebab of cubed roasted fish alternating with chunks of something that looked like pineapple, and then turned to the approaching elders.

Surjan stood and faced them squarely as if preparing to fight. He held a spear whose point looked like a unicorn's horn.

Marty stepped forward, putting himself between Surjan and the approaching elders. Behind the elders came Sharrum and two other men wearing kilts and carrying spears, with javelins and throwing sticks on their belts. They kept their distance, several paces behind and to the side of the older men. They planted their spear butts in the dirt and smiled, eyes alert.

"Don't worry, Lowanna," François said. "I'll protect you."

"Shut up," she told him.

"Welcome," Marty said to the newcomers. "We didn't expect visitors, or we'd have prepared more food. Still, we have abundance. May I offer you fish?"

One of the elders, a fat man with a neck creased like an accordion, grunted and folded his hands over his belly. "Since when does the blind fool Muwat have abundance? His children have been struggling to keep him alive for years! He's known to eat fish that washes up dead on the rocks!"

"Blind no longer!" Muwat shrieked. "And if not blind, then perhaps not a fool, either, eh, Ammun?"

Ammun snorted. "Have these strangers lifted the veil from your eyes, then? Did your own people cause your blindness? Perhaps the gods were angered by my words, and punished you with blindness for them!"

Muwat stooped, snatched a pebble from the ground, and send it winging into the fat man's belly. "Witness for yourself! Compose a poem about it! Tell the genealogy of the stone!"

The three elders murmured to each other.

Gunther stared at the ground beside Lowanna, where he was drawing a repeated geometric image with a long, straight stick. The symbol resembled a triangular *E*, a *W* with a back to it, or maybe a crown.

"What's going on?" Lowanna whispered.

Gunther shook his head as if trying to escape a buzzing mosquito.

The second elder, a tall, thin man with long fingers and a vertical scar running down his left cheek, cleared his throat and looked past Marty at Surjan. "Was it you who healed the fisherman?"

"Does any man heal?" Marty interjected. "Or do the gods heal? Is it not they who provide the herbs with their properties and the stars with their virtues and even the words of power?"

The thin man shook his head and focused on Marty. "You did not kill the king."

Lowanna grabbed Gunther by the shoulder. "Someone killed the king?" she whispered.

He turned his head to meet her gaze and spoke slowly, in German. "Yes, someone killed him."

"Are you here to inquire about the death of a king?" Marty asked. "Tell us about your king."

"I am Tudhal," the thin man said, "high priest of the Neshili, who speaks on their behalf to all their gods. Who are you?"

"He is Marty Cohen," François called out, stepping forward. "His titles are Doctor and warlord. He wears the secret black belt of the spirit fighters of shaolin. He has come from across the ocean. He brings only prosperity and peace. Behold, we have already instructed the son of Muwat in the art of setting traps for fish, and the daughters of Muwat in the sacred cooking craft of kebab."

"How long did I sleep in?" Lowanna murmured.

"If kebab means meat on a stick," Ammun said, "your gifts are not so rare or so precious."

"And you are his herald," Tudhal said.

"I am his minstrel and herald." François crossed his arms over his chest. A stiff sea breeze ruffled his hair, blowing it out sideways. "I am also a loremaster and a crafter. I am François Garnier."

"Would you force me to violate the rules of guest-friendship, Tudhal?" Muwat keened. "Would you harass guests in your own house with unwanted questions while they were trying to eat? Stop bothering my guests. This tub of fat Ammun has no decency, but I always took you for a good fellow and a wise man. If you want to ask these people questions, I'm sure they can come to the palace later."

"Silence!" Ammun bellowed. "Or I will restore your blessed blindness by tearing out your eyes with my bare hands!"

"Would you undo what has been done by the gods?" Muwat shouted.

"If *I* undo a thing, it is undone by the gods themselves!" Ammun's face was red and veins bulged out in his neck and temples.

The third elder pulled Ammun back. This man was built like a low brick wall, wide and flat, with a hard face and a few streaks of black remaining in his hair. He stepped in front of Ammun and cracked his knuckles.

"My name is Sapal. You," he said, pointing to Surjan. "Are you shield bearer to the warlord? Do you serve him? Carry his booty from the field?"

Lowanna shook her head and plucked Gunther's elbow. "Doesn't this conversation seem strange to you?"

Gunther had surrounded himself in crowns scratched into the dirt. In answer to her question, he only shook his head.

"Why can't they just ask what they want to ask?" she wondered out loud. Their king was dead, they believed—correctly, as it happened—that one of the strangers had done it . . . why couldn't they ask directly whether their guess was right?

"Technically," Surjan said, enunciating carefully, "I work for François."

"Worked," François said. "Nobody's on payroll now."

"But I'm accumulating a pension, right?" Marty cracked.

Sapal shook his head. "Your words are strange. Do you also serve your own minstrel?"

"It was a joke," Marty said. "We come in peace. We do not wish to disturb you or your people. Muwat is right, we should come visit you in your palace, where we can pay our respects to your leaders."

The three elders looked at each other uncertainly.

"We do not know how to receive you," Tudhal said.

"For what purpose did you come to Nesha?" Ammun asked.

"We save humanity from monsters," Surjan said.

"I knew it!" Ammun snapped.

"The king had lost his powers," Tudhal said. "He was no monster."

"Perhaps he *had* lost his powers," Sapal cautioned his fellows. "That was the question that was put to the test."

"And we know the answer!" Ammun roared. "Look! It would stab you in the eye if you were standing any closer!"

Lowanna's gaze flickered to the warrior Sharrum and found him staring at her. She felt her face flush. Looking away, she noticed Kareem. The young Egyptian stood at the edge of the party. He seemed to drift away without consciously trying, as if he were just disappearing into the grass behind him, moving away from the group and toward a spot behind the elders. She shook her head at him, and he shot his hands into his pockets and frowned.

"I know why you have come," Surjan said.

"Surjan," François said. "You don't need to do this."

"Someone has killed your king," Surjan said.

"Yes," Ammun agreed. His normal color had returned.

"The order of things is upset," Tudhal observed.

"Justice must be done," Surjan suggested.

"The world must be set right," Tudhal said. "The world cannot be right without an effective king upon the throne."

"What was your king's name?" Surjan asked.

Ammun raised his eyebrows. "Which name?"

Surjan frowned. "Whichever is right to tell me."

"Beware," Sapal muttered. "You have invited the genealogist to speak all day."

"And poet," Ammun said. "Genealogist and poet. His mother gave him the cradle-name Hoom. But of course when he took the throne, he was crowned Zarum the Fourth."

"Least of his line," Tudhal murmured.

"May he not be the last of his line," Sapal said.

Lowanna braced herself for the clash that seemed unavoidable now. She looked into her heart, trying to find that space where the lightning lived, but couldn't reach it. The sky was disappointingly clear. She put a hand into her pocket and found her sling.

"Enough, perhaps, that he not be the last." Ammun cleared his throat. "And what is your name, stranger, killer of monsters?"

"Surjan Singh," Surjan said.

"May I know its meaning?" Ammun asked.

Kareem had his hand on his ankh. Marty stood with a relaxed posture, but his hands curled ever so slightly toward making fists.

Surjan hesitated. "'Singh' means 'lion.' I think 'Surjan' is a person who is godly or pious."

"Ah," the three Neshili elders murmured together.

"The divine lion," Ammun said, as if announcing a revelation.

"I slew your king," Surjan admitted. "I did not intend to kill him. He attacked me."

The three elders gasped, and for a few blinks of an eye seemed like frozen statues, when suddenly they settled onto their knees and then bowed low, faces to the ground. After an added moment's hesitation, the spear-armed warriors followed suit.

A cold tingle of shock raced through Lowanna as she realized how much had happened while she'd slept.

Muwat dropped to his own knees, dragging a woman, who must be his wife, down with him.

"What are you doing?" Surjan asked.

"You have the royal spear," Tudhal said, his voice muffled by the earth into which it was released. "We have been waiting for you to claim your deed."

"There was no deed," Surjan said. "I was simply scouting. Exploring, to make certain our campsite was safe. And a man attacked me."

"Zarum," Sapal said.

"The fourth," Ammun added. "Your predecessor."

"Whoa," Surjan said. "Slow down."

"This is an ancient pattern," Lowanna said. She chose her words carefully, not wanting to sound too alien to the three elders. "When a king is weak, when his magic begins to fade and his presence no longer protects the people, he goes into the sacred place and waits."

The six men rose from their prostrate position but remained on their knees, watching Lowanna intently.

"What is this, *Golden Bough* stuff?" Marty muttered.

Lowanna ignored him. "The man who can challenge the king in the sacred place and kill him has the favor of the gods. He becomes the new king."

"I didn't challenge him," Surjan protested.

"He's innocent!" The voice came from behind the three elders. All three turned their heads, but no one was there. Lowanna looked among her companions, half expecting to find Kareem missing, but the young Egyptian was at the edge of the grass, staring intently at Surjan.

"Sometimes the challenger has to be one of the old king's retinue, one of his warriors." Lowanna looked to Sharrum and saw him narrow his eyes. "Sometimes it can be anyone. Even a stranger who happens along and wanders into the sacred place."

"The king attacked me," Surjan said. "I tried to warn him off. I tried not to fight him."

"Even better," Tudhal said. "The voice of the gods is clear. You did not choose the throne. They chose it for you."

≼CHAPTER≽
FOUR

François made his way back toward the fisherman's house. "Hey, look!" he called to his friends. "Look what I found!"

After their meeting with the Neshili elders, the party had sent the elders back to the palace. The elders, and Sapal in particular, had urged the party to come with them. One of their guards had had a keen eye for Lowanna, and seemed also to urge that the party accompany the elders back with particular enthusiasm.

But Surjan, once relieved of the concern that he might be in danger of being imprisoned or executed, was struck by the much stranger fear that he might be about to become a king, and he had wanted to delay that process. After much pleading, he had agreed at least to send a message—not of acceptance, but a simple message stating that he had slain old king Zarum and would come to the palace in the evening.

What exactly the palace, and for that matter the city around it, looked like remained to be seen. François was prepared to be underwhelmed.

The party had washed and then fallen into interminable discussions. Given that the course of action was already committed, François eventually grew bored and wandered away in search of novelty. Now he held a trove of purple fruits that he had determined to be edible, and moreover informative, and he returned to share his find. The sky clouded over and stiff winds sent gray sheets of cloud scudding across the sky.

Arnun raced up to him, holding one of the empty traps. The boy was wiry, with big-knuckled hands like the paws on a puppy and a shock of thick, black hair. "There was nothing in here, boss!"

François had taught the boy and his two sisters the word "boss." He knew he was borrowing from Samuel Clemens, and it delighted him.

"Why did you pull the trap up?" François asked. "We discussed this, you go out in your coracle and check each trap once a day, in the morning. If there's a crab in it, you take the crab. Either way, you put the trap back. We just placed that trap this morning. You shouldn't be checking it until tomorrow, and you shouldn't pull it out unless the trap is broken and needs to be replaced."

"I had a dream, boss!" Arnun said.

François resisted the urge to quote Martin Luther King. "You had a dream about what? Did you dream there was a crab in the trap?"

"Yes! Only there wasn't!"

François nodded, trying to be patient. "So, maybe this shows that your dreams aren't a good indicator as to whether or not there's a crab in the traps."

"It shows that a sorcerer has been meddling with our traps!"

François managed to neither sigh nor laugh. "Maybe. Do you have protective charms?"

The boy nodded.

"Are they good ones? Do they usually work?"

"Usually," the boy conceded.

"And are all your dreams always of things that are real in the world?" François asked. "Or sometimes do you have dreams that are more mysterious omens?"

"What do you mean?"

"I mean, maybe you dream of a crab in a trap not because there is, in fact, a crab in the trap, but because guests have come to your home, and we bring abundance, like a catch of crab."

Arnun frowned. "Maybe. Yes, sometimes I have dreams that are omens."

"Me too," François said. "So I find that the wise thing is to follow my procedure. Have good protective charms, and check my crab traps once a day, in the morning. And otherwise, I leave the traps alone. What if there's a crab wandering across the sand where this trap was right now? If you hadn't moved the trap, you'd have caught a nice, fat crab, but instead, he's getting away."

Arnun turned and raced for the beach.

Because he now knew that he could, François threw his voice into the grass beside the running boy. Masking his voice as a low growl, he called out, "Boss is wise and right!"

Of the million things at which he had tried his hand in his life, ventriloquism had never been one. And then this morning, in a moment of stress and trying to distract the Neshili elders, keep them off balance, François had suddenly discovered that he knew how to throw his voice.

This was a brand-new talent that François could only explain, essentially, as a preternatural ability. He had always been generally allergic to ascribing things to mystical, magical mumbo-jumbo, but he was becoming more open to the concept. And it was for that reason he didn't totally dismiss Arnun and his countermagic charms and concerns about a crab-stealing sorcerer.

But the boy needed to learn to implement a process and then stick to it.

The party was forming up at Muwat's hut, Marty rising from a nap and Surjan coming up from the beach, where he seemed to have bathed and combed his hair and beard.

"Marty!" François called. "Gunther! Look at this!"

The two men met him at the head of the path that led up toward the city and its Sacred Grove. He showed them his find.

"What is this, a plum?" Marty asked.

Gunther just gazed at the fruit thoughtfully, as if it had asked him a riddle.

François sliced one of the fruits open. "I'll give you the plumlike color, but look at the starlike pattern in the pulp and note the strong sweet smell."

"Star apple." Gunther looked up the coast as he spoke.

"Yes, star apple." François felt mildly annoyed. If the German was going to scoop his discovery and take the big reveal, he should at least act excited about it. "Which means we are where?"

Marty shook his head. "Thirtieth parallel north, more or less."

"The Caribbean." Gunther still looked distracted.

"Are you okay, Gunther?" Marty asked.

Gunther nodded weakly.

"He's fine!" François snapped. "He's also right. This fruit is native to Panama and the West Indies. In the twenty-first century, it's in Southeast Asia, too, but I don't think we're in the twenty-first century."

"Gunther, what's bothering you?" Marty pressed.

"Yes, Gunther," François said. "What's bothering you? What has you so gloomy that you can't get excited about us discovering where we are on the globe?"

Gunther rolled his shoulders, shuddered, and shook his head. "I'm excited."

Marty frowned at François and shook his head, and at that moment, Surjan, Lowanna, and Kareem joined them.

"Let's go see Surjan's kingdom," Kareem said.

Surjan led the way in a brisk walk.

"You understand," Lowanna said, "that in the same way these people expected that someone would come along and kill their old king, they expect that one day someone will kill their new king, too?"

"I haven't said I'd accept the job," Surjan said.

"And they will fawn all over the new guy when the time comes," she continued.

"I haven't said I'd take the job!"

"Of course you'll take it!" Lowanna laughed. "You're a man, and they just asked you to be king!"

"Leave me alone."

"You know there's probably a harem."

"Aagh!"

As anticipated, the city, when viewed unemotionally and by the light of day, wouldn't amount to a medium-sized town in the twenty-first century. Ten thousand people might inhabit the conglomeration of huts hugging the rim of a bright blue bay. A vast stone shelf stood off from the bay, sheltering it from the ocean's waves. Along the bay bristled a row of stone docks, at which moored sailing vessels. Most were small fishing boats, but a few were larger, and he wished he had the time to run down and examine them. Among the huts lay stretched strips of berry patches and tiny orchards, garden plots and what looked like livestock yards. On a hill overlooking the whole area sprawled a building of baked brick and tile, a palace three stories tall and several times larger than any other building in the town. It had several wings lurching out in different directions from the central pile.

"Why build such a large place?" Marty murmured.

"That's easy," Lowanna said. "Government architecture isn't really about utility, it's about communication. You build the biggest, fanciest palace you can for several reasons. It impresses your own people as to the wealth, power, and effectiveness of your ruling dynasty. It instills civic pride and builds the sense that your people are a people who can accomplish great things. And it intimidates visitors, pushing them away from wanting to fight you and toward wanting to ally or trade with you."

"Or," François pointed out, "the big fancy building was constructed by a previous civilization, which is now gone, and the current population is using the old building for all the reasons you mention. Think Stonehenge. The current inhabitants—that is, the twenty-first-century inhabitants—of the Salisbury Plain couldn't build Stonehenge with all the will in the world."

"Sure they could," Lowanna said. "They'd just call in a construction company from London."

"Fine, smarty-pants," François said. "We'll ask these people if they hired a construction firm from London to build their palace."

"I'd feel a lot more dismissive about the idea that something was built by an ancient lost civilization if we were still back in the twenty-first century," Marty said.

"It's true what they say, then," François told him. "Travel has broadened your horizons. I can say that even my views on things have evolved over just the last few weeks of our journey together."

The Neshili stared as the party entered Nesha and climbed its hill. The city's roads were dirt tracks, some no wider than footpaths. The party stuck to the main thoroughfares, which were reasonably even streets. Occasionally, they crossed a wide flat paving stone, suggesting an older highway that had been obliterated by time.

François cheerfully shared the star fruit with Kareem, who was the only member of the party interested, and they polished off the sweet fruits before they reached the palace, spitting out the hard, flat seeds as discreetly as they could.

The palace gate was an arched entryway, red brick over blue tiles. The three elders from their morning meeting stood beneath it, beaming, clustered about a veiled woman. Two unveiled women, both quite young, positioned themselves to either side of the woman whose face was hidden. Behind them stood other people in white togas, and to either side of the arch, men with spears.

"Look at that!" Lowanna called.

François spun about, his attention pulled away from the people waiting in the gate to the bay and the ocean beyond. A mass of ice, like a sixty-foot-tall replica of the Matterhorn, drifted toward the bay. François started, taking two quick steps down toward the bay before he realized that the boats in the harbor would be protected by the stone shelf.

"There's nothing to fear," Surjan said.

Moments later, the iceberg calf crashed into the stone. The collision dumped ice and snow onto the rock slab in heaps, then sent a much-reduced iceberg spinning away along the coast.

"The king was right!" Tudhal intoned.

"I'm not your king," Surjan said.

"Not yet, Your Majesty." The veiled woman lowered herself slightly in a curtsey.

Surjan growled.

"Send someone to get the ice at least," François suggested. "Crush some star fruit over it, or . . . I don't know, do you have sugar cane?"

"You are rightfully Zarum the Fifth," the veiled woman said.

"I will not take a dead man's name," Surjan growled. "I am not convinced that I will take his throne."

"And his queen," the woman said softly.

"Told you," Lowanna said.

"We didn't come to take a throne," Surjan insisted. "Or a . . . woman."

"There are also the queen's handmaidens," the veiled woman said. "Nirni and Kuzi."

"We didn't come for any women at all," Surjan growled. "Women are not prizes."

"You came to slay monsters," the woman said. "It is the king who slays monsters."

"If you will not be king," Tudhal said slowly, "then you must wait in the Sacred Grove and fight all comers until another man slays you. Then *he* will be king."

"I like my chances," Surjan said.

"And I like a man with strong will," the veiled woman said. "You will need that will, if you are to be king. Come, at least see our home."

"'Our' home?" Surjan asked.

"I am Halpa," she said. "I am your queen."

"Your Majesty." He inclined his head.

"Your Majesty." She curtseyed again. "If you will not take the name Zarum, perhaps you will be Singh the First. The Lion King. It is a noble name."

François suppressed a giggle.

"I . . . cannot be the Lion King," Surjan said. "The gods would not like it. It is a taboo. There will be no Lion King." He looked over his shoulder at François. "No Lion King, you hear me, minstrel?"

Queen Halpa took him by the arm. "King Surjan, then. No doubt Surjan the First, to be followed by many of the name."

She led Surjan under the arch and all the others followed. François found himself walking beside Ammun, the genealogist and poet.

"So then," Ammun said, smiling widely, "whence do you come? Are you from the other half of the fleet? Are you from the City of the Gods?"

Fleet? François considered his options. Bluffing might lead to revelations, but also to missteps. Mystery would allow him to continue to conceal his hand—or his lack of one.

"We come from very far away," he said.

"That is obvious." Ammun looked down at François's clothing. The party were all still dressed in their twenty-first-century gear, shredded from having made it through a season of rough wear in the fourth millennium B.C.E. "Your clothing is outlandish. Also, your sophistication tells me that you are a royal party. Tell me the truth, is King Surjan already a king in his native land? Or at least a prince?"

François nodded slowly. "The men of King Surjan's people are all men of majestic courage," he said. "And the women are all princesses."

"I knew it." Ammun grinned. "I have won a bet with the priest, thank you. And why are you traveling in disguise?"

"Disguise?" François asked.

"You are dressed as beggars." Ammun's brow furrowed in open disdain.

"We have traveled a long way," François said. "We are rather the worse for wear. We would be happy for new tunics, if you could help us obtain them."

"The king already possesses an opulent wardrobe," Ammun said. "I will provide for the rest of you."

The party had stopped, and François looked about. They stood in the center of a large courtyard, and Queen Halpa pointed down at what looked like an open shaft in the middle of the floor as she spoke to Surjan. The shaft must once have been built as a well, because the remains of the casing still rose three feet above the courtyard floor, terminating in stylized toothy crenellations. François had fallen back several ranks and couldn't hear well what was being said.

"Is that water?" he asked.

"Water comes into the palace by pipeworks," Ammun said. "That is the Well of the Beast."

François smiled. "What is the Beast? Is that the entrance to the land of the dead?"

"Not the land of the dead, François Garnier." Ammun didn't smile at all. "That is the lair of a monster."

"What kind of monster lives beneath a palace?" François asked. He didn't ask, though he wanted to, what kind of idiot builds a palace on top of the lair of a monster?

"Not a monster that will trouble King Surjan, I am sure of it." Ammun rubbed his hands together. "Come, let us find you new clothing."

⊰ CHAPTER ⊱
FIVE

Marty's breath hung in the frigid air, visible wisps vanishing into the surrounding cold as his gaze fixed on the colossal ice cliffs ahead. They loomed like ancient sentinels, guarding the mysteries of a long-forgotten Arctic realm. The wind howled—a haunting symphony whispering secrets that he couldn't discern. As he trudged closer, the ground beneath his feet crunching with each heavy step, his eyes caught a peculiar sight: a tunnel, perfectly arched, piercing through the ice as if carved by the hands of giants.

The tunnel emitted an eerie glow, a light that defied the natural order of the polar night. It wasn't the luminescent blue typically scattered by glacial ice; this was different—otherworldly, phosphorescent, casting an uncanny radiance that beckoned him closer. Compelled by a mix of dread and wonder, Marty approached, each step drawn by the tunnel's hypnotic allure.

As he neared the tunnel's mouth, a sudden movement snagged the corner of his vision. He turned sharply. Penguins—a group of them, huddled together yet curiously undisturbed by his presence. Their black-and-white forms shuffled in the snow, but as he watched, they seemed to be not merely animals. They moved with a purpose; a deliberate intelligence uncharacteristic of the simple creatures he knew.

One of the penguins turned its head, its eyes catching the glow from the tunnel, reflecting it back at Marty as if it were a mirror. A shiver that had nothing to do with the cold ran down his spine. Were these guardians of the tunnel? Or were they, too, drawn to the strange light within?

Suddenly, the ground beneath him trembled, a low rumble that escalated into a cacophony of cracking and shifting ice. The cliffs trembled, snow cascading down their ancient faces like the tears of giants. Marty's heart pounded, the surreal glow from the tunnel intensifying, now pulsing in rhythm with his own quickening heartbeat.

And then, without warning, he woke.

His body jolted upright in a bed made from leather-covered bundles of grass, the remnants of the cold Arctic wind biting at his skin fading as did the vision.

Had it been a dream? It felt too vivid, too real. Marty's eyes darted around the room, half expecting to see the glow, the penguins, or the ice. But there was only darkness, the silence of night.

"What's wrong?" Lowanna's voice reached for him across the darkness.

Marty blinked and was barely able to make out the shadowy silhouette of her form lying about five feet from him.

François's light snore came from deeper in the darkness and Marty remembered how the team had been accommodated in a guest room of the palace. Queen Halpa had been trying to get Surjan to take the king's bedroom while François was to take the first watch and Gunther the second. Kareem was also somewhere in the room, but Marty couldn't sense him or his breathing. Somehow, everything about the teen seemed harder to discern than it had been—as if he was fading, becoming a living shadow.

"Marty, what's the matter?" Lowanna asked, her silhouette shifting slightly as she faced him, propping herself up on an elbow.

"Nothing," Marty said. "I had a dream, that's all."

"A dream or a vision?"

He sighed. "I'm not sure." He'd had visions like this before, and the last time it had happened, they'd traveled across a continent to end up nearly getting killed by unimaginable beasts. "I saw a glacier with . . ."

"With what?"

Marty frowned. It all seemed so preposterous, the idea of taking cues from a dream. "Penguins. I saw a tunnel with a glowing light and if you can believe it, penguins."

"Interesting." Lowanna spoke in a whisper. "That's a pretty strong indicator of the Antarctic."

"You'd know better than I would." Marty shrugged. "They're only in the southern hemisphere?"

"Yes." François's voice echoed through the darkness as Marty heard him shift position. "Sounds like we need to find our way to the south."

"I don't know, François." Marty shook his head. "You seem to have a lot of ready faith in my dream."

"It worked last time. Was this a dream, or was it a vision like last time?"

Marty pressed his lips together and shivered as he recalled the feeling of the brisk Antarctic wind blowing through his hair. "The dream felt as real as the vision I experienced when we first arrived in ancient North Africa."

"Well, there you go." Lowanna spoke with a confident tone. "This was a premonition of something to come."

"I wish I could feel as confident as you guys seem to be. Penguins and glaciers are a strange destination. I'm full of misgivings over a lot of this," Marty confessed.

"You saw that iceberg careen off the coast; it makes some level of sense," François said, his voice tinged with wonder. "And given what we know about our location, I'd wager the only reason there'd be ice this far south is because we're in the deep past. Sometime during the last ice age would be my guess."

"We will see penguins?" Kareem's sleepy voice broadcast from the far corner of the dark room. "I never thought I'd see a penguin."

"Aye, boy." François shifted in the darkness.

The room brightened slightly as Gunther opened the hide-covered door and peered in the room. "Why are you guys awake? It's still three hours until dawn."

Marty suddenly felt a wave of exhaustion wash over him and let out a yawn. "We can talk more in the morning. Let's get some shut-eye."

He closed his eyes and rested his head on his outstretched arm. It took almost no time for sleep to claim him.

With Queen Halpa leading, Surjan cautiously entered a lavish chamber. The walls were adorned with woven tapestries that told tales of ancient battles and strange creatures. The air was heavy with the scent of exotic spices coming up from a pile of glowing embers at the center of the chamber; the dim lighting cast seductive shadows across the room. Halpa herself was a vision, draped in a flowing gown that highlighted her graceful contours. Her eyes, dark and inviting, fixed on Surjan as she approached him with a slow, deliberate pace.

"Surjan," she purred, her voice a melodic whisper that seemed to pull at his very soul, "you look weary. Let me ease your burdens." She reached out, her fingers lightly brushing against his chest.

With his heart racing, Surjan felt a strong urge to run, as if facing an insurmountable opponent. Everything seemed to slow down as the woman smiled up at him, a knowing look that said much and left his senses reeling. Was there something in the smoke that was affecting him?

As she drew closer, Halpa's hands slipped the straps of her gown off her shoulders, letting the fabric fall, exposing her smooth, bare skin. "Your hands look strong, can you help me relax?" she suggested, turning her back to him. Her long hair cascaded down her back, and she swept it aside, revealing the nape of her neck. There, to Surjan's astonishment, was a small, dark mark that looked eerily like a spider.

Surjan's heart skipped a beat. The dying words of the previous king echoed in his mind: *Beware the spider's bite.* His breath caught in his throat as he stared at the mark. Was it a birthmark, or a tattoo? A sign, perhaps, of danger much closer than he had anticipated?

Snapping back to the present, Surjan cleared his throat and stepped away, his mind racing.

"Halpa," he started, trying to keep his voice steady. "The Well of the Beast—can you tell me more about it?"

Halpa's smile didn't waver as she turned to face him, but her eyes gleamed with a sharper light. "Curious about our history and legends, are you?" She moved closer, her hands finding their way to his shoulders. "The well is old, older than any living memory. It is said to be a gateway."

Surjan sensed her trying to lead him deeper into the room. The smoke permeated the chamber and it was hard for him to think. "A gateway to what?" he asked, trying to steer her toward the room's entrance rather than the bed that loomed ominous and inviting in the corner of the room.

"The tunnels, Surjan," Halpa whispered as she leaned in, her lips nearly touching his ear. "They stretch far and wide beneath our lands, from one sacred well to another, like the one in the Sacred Grove."

Surjan's mind raced. "And the creatures that dwell within these tunnels...?"

Halpa stepped back, her hands slowly untying the sash around her waist. "Ah, the monsters. You will see them soon enough." Her tone was both tantalizing and terrifying. "But tonight, why don't we—"

Surjan interjected, gripping her hands gently. "Why would you build a structure over one of these wells? Do such beasts travel through these wells? What do they seek?"

For a moment, Halpa's façade faltered, her gaze turning distant, as if she peered into memories best forgotten. "Power, Surjan. They hunger for what lies above, what thrives under the sun. Our ancestors built this palace over the well to guard it, to keep the darkness contained. We are to guard against them ever coming into the light again."

"But has it worked?" Surjan pressed, noting the slight tremor in her voice.

Halpa released her grip, moving toward the bed. "Sometimes the darkness finds a way," she said, her back to him now. "Sometimes it seeps through."

Surjan watched her, a plan forming in his mind. He needed to see this well, understand its secrets. Halpa might be trying to seduce him, but within her seduction lay clues, a way to unravel the truth about the darkness lurking beneath.

"Show me the well," Surjan said firmly.

Halpa turned, her expression one of surprise and then, slowly, intrigue. "Very well, Surjan. Come, see the depths of our past. But beware, for some truths are as seductive and dangerous as the night itself."

As they left the chamber, Surjan couldn't shake the feeling that he was stepping into something that was far more complex and sinister than they'd anticipated. Tonight, he would confront the ancient darkness of the Well of the Beast, and whatever truths it held, he was determined to face them head-on.

Marty joined the others at breakfast in a long hall.

François grabbed one of the star apples from a large basket of fruit and offered it to him. "Get some carbs into you. I suspect today will be full of unforeseen events."

Gunther handed him a wooden bowl of something steaming as Marty sat cross-legged in the semicircle that the team had formed. "The wild rice is actually quite good. I think they've mixed in some sort of soured wine and honey in it, because it has a strong sweet-and-sour tang to it that reminds me of sauerbraten."

Using two of his fingers like a scoop, Marty shoveled the rice in his mouth and began chewing as he panned his gaze across the gathering. "Where are Surjan and Lowanna?" he asked with his mouth half full of tangy wild grains.

"Our taciturn member of security has his hands full with that queen of his." François chuckled. "She's dragged Surjan somewhere to help him understand what being king would entail. As to Lowanna, she just grabbed a piece of fruit and left, not looking like she was particularly interested in conversation."

Marty frowned. "I needed to talk to her about something." He began wolfing down the bowl of grains and, just as he was about done, he said, "I'll go get her and see if I can track down Surjan. We need to have a team meeting."

Marty hopped up onto his feet and suddenly regretted eating so quickly as he felt the weight and heat of partially chewed grains inside him. "Hang out here for a bit, I'll be back with Lowanna."

A breathy, almost ghostlike noise somewhere nearby caught Marty's attention.

"Did you hear that?" he asked the others.

"Hear what?" François asked as Kareem and Gunther shook their heads.

Marty paused, straining to hear the noise again and then shook his head. "Never mind. I'll be right back."

He stepped outside the building, the rising sun casting long shadows across the hillside. Marty breathed in the crisp sea air.

It felt cool, much cooler than he'd have imagined of any location along the Caribbean. François might be right about *when* they were. If it was around the time of the last ice age, the waters off the coast would probably be cooler than in modern times.

He panned his gaze across the horizon until he spotted the silhouette of a lone figure standing near the stone docks.

His steps quickened as he walked down the hill, toward the docks.

Lowanna's gaze was fixed on the distant horizon where the sea met the sky in a haze of orange and purple. As Marty approached, he noticed her posture, tense and withdrawn, an unusual sight compared to her typically confident demeanor.

"Lowanna, are you okay?" Marty asked as he came to stand beside her.

She didn't turn to look at him, her eyes remaining fixed on the darkening waters. "I'm fine. Just needed some air and wanted to clear my head."

But Marty wasn't convinced. "You don't seem fine. You've been not fine since we arrived in this new place," he pressed, his worry morphing slowly into frustration. "What's going on? You know you can talk to me."

Lowanna sighed, her shoulders slumping slightly, yet she remained silent.

Marty's annoyance flared. "You need to learn how to open up to people. I mean, there's something obviously upsetting you, and that worries me. Is there something I did, or someone else on the team? Unspoken expectations end up being premeditated resentments, and that's something we can't afford."

She turned to face him then, her eyes meeting his in a long, searching look. For a moment, it seemed she would confide in him, her lips parting as if to speak. But instead, she sighed, and almost looked like she was about to cry.

Marty's impatience flared and he blurted out, "I need to talk to you about the vision I had . . ."

The words hung in the air, and Marty immediately regretted the interruption. Lowanna's expression chilled, as if whatever emotional turmoil she'd been dealing with suddenly was turned off. Her gaze turned cold and the brief window into her thoughts slammed shut.

She shook her head, a mixture of disappointment and frustration crossing her features. "Not now, Marty. I can't do this right now."

With that, she turned away from him and began trudging up the hill toward the palace.

Marty stood there, the chill of the morning soaking into him, realizing his impatience might have cost him an opportunity to really understand what was troubling Lowanna. He watched her, feeling a mixture of helplessness and regret, knowing he had missed a crucial moment to connect, caught up in his own needs and worries.

Surjan moved through the bustling city square. He carried a sense of nausea at the thought that all the preparations were for *his* wedding reception. Garlands of vibrant flowers were strung from post to post, and the air was filled with the scents of roasting meat. Despite the celebratory atmosphere, a palpable tension lingered just beneath the surface—the villagers' smiles were a bit too strained, their laughter a touch too forced.

He felt the weight of responsibility on his shoulders as the Neshili looked to him as some kind of savior. This wasn't something he'd signed up for.

As he navigated through the crowd, Surjan spotted Marty, standing alone, observing the festivities with a keen eye. He approached him, their conversation a stark contrast to the jovial scene around them.

"Marty," Surjan began, lowering his voice so only the man beside him could hear, "we need to talk about the Well of the Beast. There's something down there . . . something that the people are deeply afraid of."

Marty turned, eyebrows raised. "What did you find out?"

Surjan glanced around to ensure no prying ears were nearby before continuing. "Halpa told me the well in the palace is ancient, and to be honest, I looked at it and it looks like an exact copy of the well I saw at the Sacred Grove. She told me that the legends say it once served as a portal to another place, but now . . . it's a lair for monsters."

Marty's brow furrowed in concern. "Monsters? What kind of monsters?"

"That's just it—I'm not entirely sure what we're dealing with," Surjan admitted, frustration coloring his tone. "Children have gone missing, believed to be taken by whatever resides in these wells. The people think that the monsters awoke because the old king's powers had faded."

Marty rubbed his eyes. "Hmm. Children could easily go missing for other reasons—wild animals, or swept away by the ocean currents."

"The whole village expects me to do something about it," Surjan added, scanning the faces in the crowd. "They're scared, Marty. Whatever's down there, it's bad."

Marty rubbed his chin thoughtfully. "Well, what's actually down there?" he asked, looking Surjan directly in the eyes.

Surjan shrugged, the weight of uncertainty heavy on his shoulders. "Halpa wasn't much help on the specifics. She hinted at old tales—something about ancestors leaving the islands because of these creatures. But she wasn't clear on details."

Marty nodded slowly, his mind racing with the implications. "So, we're dealing with an unknown threat, rooted in legend, with no clear understanding of what they are or how to deal with them."

"Exactly," Surjan confirmed.

Marty scanned the crowd, his eyes finally landing on Ammun, who was dressed in a vibrant array of colors. With a quick gesture, he beckoned him over. Ammun approached, his expression open and curious.

"Yes?" Ammun adjusted the bright yellow sash around his waist.

"Surjan and I were talking about the well, the monsters, and the legends surrounding them," Marty began. "Surjan mentioned ancestors leaving the islands. What can you tell us about that?"

Ammun nodded thoughtfully, his gaze drifting over the celebrating villagers before returning to Marty. "Ah, yes, the people of old. In my grandfather's grandfather's time, the weather shifted dramatically. It was said that our time here was coming to an end. Many of the Neshili and old ones left. That is the other half of the fleet. Those you see here today are the ones who remained."

"Who are the old ones?" Marty pressed, intrigued.

Ammun shrugged slightly. "I cannot say for certain, because they are from tales handed down from our ancestors. They are not of the Neshili but are rumored to have built the world underneath."

"Underneath?" Marty repeated, glancing at Surjan. "You mean where the well is?"

"I wouldn't know precisely," Ammun admitted, "but the tales tell of an entire city under the ground where the old ones lived. A vast network of chambers and tunnels, long forgotten by most who walk above."

"So, who are these monsters in the well?" Marty asked, his voice low. "Are they maybe left over from the old ones? Are they people or actual creatures?"

Ammun shook his head, his expression somber. "Who's to say? I've never seen one myself. I just know the tales, and more recently, know of their handiwork . . . the kidnappings. Both of children and of missing livestock."

Marty and Surjan exchanged a look. The mystery deepened with each shared word, painting a picture of a history intertwined with myths and dark realities.

"We need to investigate this," Surjan said firmly. "Whatever these creatures are, understanding their origin might help us figure out how to deal with them."

"We have faith in your abilities, King Surjan." Ammun nodded, his eyes reflecting the flickering lights of the celebration. "However, I must warn you both. The old tales are not just stories; sometimes, they are warnings. What lies beneath may have been left there for a reason."

With that sobering thought, Marty thanked Ammun and turned back to Surjan. "Tomorrow, we go down into the well as a team. We need answers, and it seems the only way is to confront whatever waits in the darkness."

Marty watched as Ammun took his place at the head of the gathering. The sun was going down over the land, and fires had been lit in the city's largest square.

The crowd quieted, their attention turning toward the corpulent elder as he began his speech. "Today, we celebrate not only the union of two souls but also the courage and magic that our new king has brought to our people," Ammun proclaimed, his voice carrying across the assembled villagers. "It is his bravery and use of magic that will shield us from the darkness lurking beneath."

He turned to face Surjan and Halpa, who stood side by side.

Marty knew Surjan was not happy with the entire concept of him getting married, even if the wedding was largely symbolic. But he had ultimately chosen the wedding over waiting in the Sacred Grove for unseen attackers to make attempts on his life, or the party going to war against the Neshili. He had insisted to the group that he had no sexual interest in the woman, bellowing over François's argument that the Guru Granth Sahib's teaching that he must conquer lust didn't apply to a woman he was married to. Now his face bore an iron-jawed, neutral look.

Halpa's expression was a stark contrast to his. She looked excited, barely containing the smile that Marty had seen several times that evening.

With a ceremonial flourish, Ammun took a rope laced with white flowers and looped it symbolically over the couple's outstretched arms, binding them together. "In the presence of the spirits of our ancestors and the watchful eyes of the Neshili, I bind you Surjan to Halpa, and Halpa to Surjan as a mated pair. May you watch over each other as you watch over the people you are now charged with protecting. I declare you Queen Halpa and King Surjan—the Lion King!" he announced.

Surjan winced at the title. Marty grinned.

The air was thick with a mixture of jubilation and the unspoken fears of the villagers. "Let us rejoice in their union and trust in their leadership to guide us through the shadowy time ahead," Ammun finished, his voice ringing with a hopeful note.

The crowd erupted in cheers, but a single voice cut through the celebration, its tone urgent and laden with fear. "Save us from the monsters in the wells!" the voice yelled, turning all heads. The momentary joy faltered, reminding everyone of the imminent threat lurking beneath their feet.

Marty noticed Surjan stiffen upon hearing the voice. He could only imagine the weight of responsibility Surjan was feeling.

As Halpa pulled at Surjan's arm to join in the festivities, he locked eyes with Marty.

Surjan's expression was grim.

Marty lifted a mug of vinegarlike wine and saluted Surjan. They both knew what needed to happen.

Surjan would go through whatever social niceties he needed to after the ceremony and the team would meet up afterward.

They needed to figure out what was in that well, and tonight was the night.

⫷ CHAPTER ⫸
SIX

François adjusted his newly acquired tunic, having shed the ragged modern clothing they'd been wearing through two different ages, and gazed on the dark, gaping maw of the Well of the Beast. The air was heavy with a tangible sense of dread, the kind that clings to your skin and seeps into your bones. Around him, the team gathered—Marty, Surjan, Lowanna, Gunther, and Kareem—each wearing expressions of grim determination.

Surjan stepped forward, his voice steady as he addressed the group. "I've had the chance to talk with a lot of eyewitnesses," he began, his eyes flickering with the reflection of the torches that lit the ancient stone around the well's entrance. "The locals are terrified. They're losing livestock, and worse, two children have gone missing. One was taken right from her crib at night."

François felt a chill snake up his spine.

"Wait a minute," Marty interjected. "Shouldn't we be at the well where this happened, or did something also happen here in the palace's well?"

"It seems to be that the last incident was here at the palace." Surjan held a grim expression. "The queen told me in great detail how one of the palace servant's children yelled in fear. Evidently the former king responded, seeing the child's feet as they disappeared into the well. His failure to rescue her sealed his fate."

Lowanna frowned. "Are you sure she we're getting the full story of what happened?" She frowned. "I don't mean to disparage your new partner"—the tall Sikh's expression soured—"but she strikes me as the scheming type."

Surjan nodded. "I don't trust Halpa's motivations, but her fear of what's purported to be in this well I think is genuine," he said. His voice remained steady as he continued, his face shadowed by the flickering light. "Descriptions of the creatures are sparse but consistent—tall, lithe figures, big eyes, and skin like gray salamanders." He paused, his gaze meeting each of theirs in turn. "One witness claimed to have come face-to-face with one. She described it wearing a shiny rock on its nose."

"A shiny rock?" François asked, his tone skeptical. "Considering these people are mostly still at a Stone Age level of technology, that sounds suspiciously like how someone might describe a metal nose ring."

At this, a collective gasp rippled through the group. François exchanged looks with the others; their faces reflected the same shock and recognition. They had encountered beings adorned with nose rings before—creatures from ancient Egyptian lore.

Creatures of extraterrestrial origin.

"If we are actually facing creatures similar to those we battled in Egypt, then these creatures from the well aren't going to be a trivial thing to deal with," Marty said, his voice low but fierce.

"And those kids have probably been eaten a long time ago." Kareem's voice carried a sinister edge as he drew his sharpened ankh from a hidden sheath under his tunic. "I'm looking forward to this encounter."

Gunther shook his head and sighed. "I don't suppose there's much choice in this. We have missing and likely dead kids. That's something we can't ignore."

Lowanna, who had been quiet, spoke up with a determined glint in her eye. "Then we go down. We find these creatures, and we find the children. Whatever it takes."

François felt the weight of guilt on his shoulders. He wasn't the fighter in this group. He wouldn't be the one who'd avenge anyone's death in the traditional sense, nor would he be much help in defense of the palace if one of these things came to attack.

He'd have to find another way to help. "Um, guys. You weren't exactly thinking of just climbing down there totally blind, were you?"

Marty turned to him and asked, "Did you have another idea? If so, I'm all ears."

"Well, why don't we try to lure one of these things out and see what we're dealing with first?" François posited. "They eat meat, it sounds like. Why don't we put a stake in the ground here, tie a goat to it, and keep watch?" He turned to Surjan and grinned. "You're the new king, surely you can find us a goat that we can use."

Surjan nodded. "I'll see what I can do—"

"Good." François patted the large man on the shoulder. "While you do that, I saw some passable items I think might form the basis of a nice pulley system we can use to create a trap."

"That sounds great," Marty said and began talking with the others on how they might best leverage François's idea of a lure and trap.

François studied the martial arts master and hired linguist and felt a surge of satisfaction at his choice for hiring him. If nothing else, the Frenchman knew where his own skills lay, and one of them was certainly in picking the right people for the tasks at hand. Marty was a good leader and organizer.

The man's skills would certainly be tested in this first of many tasks to come.

In the center of a large, walled courtyard lay the Well of the Beast, and dominating a significant part of the space, François had laid a reinforced fishing net across the floor between the well mouth and the courtyard's entrance. The only light came from a flickering torch near the door leading into the palace, but it provided enough illumination for François as he hammered a wooden tension stake into the ground with a large, smooth rock. He paused only at the sounds of the thudding of feet and a man cursing outside the courtyard.

With a loud grunt, Surjan entered the courtyard, pulling on a rope attached to a massive llama. Its head towered over Surjan, and the beast had to weigh at least four hundred pounds. It began making loud, shrill-pitched vocalizations, its eyes widening as it took in the presence of the others on the team.

"That has got to be the biggest llama I've ever seen," François remarked.

Lowanna made soothing noises as she approached the beast, shifting to guttural utterances that sounded as though her throat was full of phlegm, and extending her hand toward the unruly animal. "I can't believe it."

Suddenly, the llama shifted its attention toward Lowanna and responded with a phlegm-filled utterance of its own.

"Be careful," Surjan warned. "This thing likes to spit and bite."

"It's okay." Lowanna approached cautiously, making more animalistic sounds. "He's just afraid." She cooed softly and whispered to the beast, which towered over her. "We're not going to hurt you." She laid her hand on the beast's fur-laden haunch, and its muscles twitched nervously, but it remained focused on Lowanna. It responded with more guttural intonations, and she began raking her fingers through the animal's fur. Turning to Surjan, she exclaimed, "Do you have any idea what you've got here? This is a Hemiauchenia macrocephala. They've been extinct for over ten thousand years. Not since the last ice age has anyone seen one of these alive."

Marty tilted his head, eyeing the beast. "Are you sure?"

"I'm not an idiot," Lowanna shot back with a glare. "Of course, I'm sure. This guy's facial structure and build are totally different from the llamas that are native to this continent, and heck, llamas aren't even native to North America. They were brought here from South America in modern times. No, this guy is definitely a Hemiauchenia macrocephala."

"I told you guys!" François said, smiling. "And the presence of this beast only confirms what I said. I'm guessing we're in a place that exists about eleven thousand years before any of us were born."

Marty stared at the beast a few seconds and nodded. "Okay, then. I guess we have our lure." He turned to Lowanna. "Is our no-longer-extinct llama okay? All we need is for his scent to be detected and maybe for him to make some noises for us."

"I can probably make the noises if it doesn't cooperate," Kareem said with a furrowed brow. He then let out a loud, high-pitched, and rapid braying sound that almost perfectly emulated the panicked vocalizations the llama had initially made upon entering the courtyard.

The creature turned toward the teen and lowered its head, almost as if trying to discern whether the young Egyptian was some kind of mutated kin.

"That'll be excellent, Kareem." François tightened the tension on the ropes holding the net in place. "The moment the beast in the well crosses the tripwire, it'll be engulfed in the net, and we can at least know what we're dealing with." He turned to the team, most of whom were gathered along the edge of the courtyard near the exit, and asked, "Are you all ready?"

Everyone nodded, and Marty said, "François, this is your show. Just be clear on what you're expecting us to do."

"For now, just keep off the net and don't be a distraction." François turned to Surjan. "The llama is fine?"

Surjan turned to Lowanna, who was stroking the animal's furry neck. She turned to François and said, "He's fine. Just not particularly excited about being indoors with so many people. We might need Kareem's help if you need a reliable call on cue."

"Kareem, you good with that?" François asked.

The teen nodded. "Sure."

François checked the ropes and the tripwire one last time, skirted around the net, and joined the others. He turned to Kareem and said, "Make one of those calls."

Kareem took a deep breath and issued a startlingly accurate high-pitched braying sound that seemed to agitate the llama as the sound echoed across the courtyard.

François carefully watched where he stepped and approached Kareem. "Can you do that again, but this time into the well itself? We want to maximize the chance that whatever's down there can hear it." Kareem nodded, and just as he was about to proceed, François grabbed the teen's upper arm and whispered, "Once you do it, come right back. We need to trap this thing. Not vice versa."

Kareem carefully skirted past the trap and almost disappeared into the shadows of the dimly lit courtyard as he leaned over the lip of the well, repeated the call, and quickly scuttled back to the group. Silence engulfed them as they waited, listening for any noise or sign of movement.

Nothing.

"Again," François whispered after a tense minute had passed.

With a nod, Kareem approached the well again, leaned over the edge, and peered down into the darkness. He made another llama call, this time louder and more desperate. Scrambling back, he rejoined the group. They listened—and listened. Kareem's ears twitched; he tilted his head and murmured, "I heard something."

Surjan nodded.

François hadn't heard anything; he looked to Marty, Lowanna, and Gunther, and they all shook their heads. With his heart thudding loudly in his chest, the Frenchman stared at the well, waiting for a sign of something to appear.

The llama shuffled its feet with impatience as everyone focused silently on the well.

Five agonizing minutes ticked by.

"One more time," François said, his voice taut with urgency.

Kareem approached the well once more. He cupped his hands around his mouth, preparing to make another call when suddenly, long, gray arms—thin and sinewy—shot out from the darkness of the well with terrifying swiftness.

François's heart lurched as the arms grasped Kareem.

In a blur of motion, the teen was yanked over the side of the well. The sound of ropes whizzing through the air exploded as Kareem's disappearing leg managed to trigger the trap.

Pandemonium broke out among the team.

Everyone rushed to the well's edge, shouting Kareem's name.

⇥ CHAPTER ⇤
SEVEN

"Kareem!" François lunged over the lip of the well, trying to grab the young man and missing. One of the crenellations jabbed him in the belly and he swayed, leaning over the pit. The Frenchman might have fallen in himself if it hadn't been for Marty grabbing him and pulling him back.

François sobbed. "We can't let—"

"We're not losing another team member!" Marty gave him an angry look, and before anyone could do anything, dropped down the hole.

The Marty of one year earlier or eleven thousand years later, depending on your point of view—the Marty Cohen of the twenty-first century—would have wanted a light and a rope. He'd have wanted to plan something or move cautiously. But Marty had changed. Growing up, he'd heard of the warrior spirit and all his life he'd been training his body and mind, without any particular sense of a destination. A goal to achieve. But lately, he'd been feeling a stronger sense of that warrior spirit coming to the fore, and when it came time to react, it was something within him that asserted itself. A surge of confidence washed over him as he dropped into the darkness.

Grandpa Chang had told him tales of shaolin monks who could control their rate of fall, as long as they fell close to a wall. The stories said that those men could gently touch the wall as they dropped, with a finger or a toe, and slow their fall without harming themselves. Grandpa Chang had known no more than that, but had always nodded and smiled enthusiastically when young Marty asked if the stories were true.

Now Marty simply did what Grandpa Chang had hinted was possible. Instincts he didn't know he had drove his actions. He couldn't see the walls of the shaft, but he felt where they were. Falling, he reached out to grab the wall, ever so slightly. He touched it twice, three times, a fourth, and then he landed on the balls of his feet on the floor below.

Marty raised his hands in a defensive position in front of his face. He couldn't see, but he sensed that no alien creature was within immediate striking distance. He heard the scrambling noises of one of his companions climbing down above him, and the pitch of the grunts and imprecations told him it was Surjan.

"I don't see any of the monsters!" Surjan called, then dropped the last eight feet to stand beside Marty in the dark. Marty heard the hissing sound of Surjan unsheathing his sharpened ankh.

"I don't sense them either," Marty said.

"That sounds less strange than it should in my ears."

"It feels less strange than it should in my mouth. François! Get lights down here!"

"Kareem!" Surjan roared.

The only answer was the echo of the Sikh's own voice.

"Give me a minute!" François called. "I'm grabbing torches from the wall brackets!"

"I'm coming down!" Gunther yelled. "Catch me if I fall!"

"Someone should stay there and watch the exit," Marty suggested.

"François and I will wait here," Lowanna said. "Yell if you need help and the cavalry will come."

"Can you do that lightning bolt thing underground?" Marty asked.

"I don't know. And even if I could, do you really want me to do that in a confined place?"

It was a good question. "Never mind . . ."

"I think there may be other exits," Surjan said. "When I fought King Zarum in the Sacred Grove, I heard . . . wailing sounds. I don't think he was the one making them. If the Grays have an exit through that grove it would verify the story that there's an underground network of interconnecting tunnels."

"Gunther, how's it coming?" Marty called.

At that moment, the German landed on top of Marty, knocking them both to the ground.

"Good aim," Surjan said, helping both men to their feet.

Orange light appeared at the top of the shaft. "I'm throwing torches down!" François called.

Marty, Surjan, and Gunther stepped to the side and made room for the fiery brands. The floor was brick, dusted with dry dirt and sand; the torches rattled and bounced as they hit, but the flames didn't go out. Three of the torches were burning, and three more dropped unlit. Marty saw that they stood in the corner of a long rectangular chamber with half a dozen archways leading out. The narrow well shaft ascended from a recessed corner of the room, and given the dimensions and rough texture of the walls, Marty was confident he'd be able to climb back up it without any help. The chamber's floor was a brick-orange color, but the walls were tiled in blue and yellow.

He scooped up the torches and distributed the burning ones, holding on to the unlit brands himself. "Surjan, can you track the Gray that grabbed Kareem?"

Surjan panned his gaze across the chamber, pointed at the floor and nodded. "Easily. Kareem was resisting—look at the scuff marks."

Marty didn't see the scuff marks, but he trusted that Surjan did. "Lead on."

Surjan broke immediately into a brisk walk, heading toward the far end of the chamber. Marty heard a surprised-sounding yelp, and then the scraping of unseen feet.

"I hear more than one of them," Surjan growled.

Marty raised his burning torch higher. Overlapping pools of orange and yellow splashed out from the three torches, spilling down into side passages as they marched past. Marty heard slithering noises, and a dismayed hoot. At the end of the chamber, a heap of bones lay in the mouth of a hallway holding a descending staircase.

"Those bones are fresh," Gunther said.

"They've been gnawed," Surjan told them.

"You can tell that, standing up, ten feet away from the bones lying on the floor?" Marty asked.

Surjan shrugged.

"They're human bones." Gunther sounded miserable.

"Release my man!" Surjan roared. "I will kill every last one of you, if I have to!" Then he charged down the stairs.

Marty followed, making sure to drag Gunther along. The German had lost his distracted air, but still seemed shrunken, uncertain.

The stairs ended and the passageway opened into another large chamber. Marty pushed past Surjan to raise his light and look; the ceiling here rose two stories in height above the floor. A mezzanine ran around the entire room, and beneath it, on all four sides, a colonnade. The ceiling pulled up into a delicate onion-dome point. The whole thing reminded him comically of the architecture of Alhambra in Spain.

"What is this place?" Surjan growled.

"Look!" Gunther pointed at a black blotch on the floor. Steam rose in a faint wisp, and Marty's nose detected a bitter tang.

Breathing in the all-too-familiar scent, Marty's mind raced with a thousand thoughts at once. The smell of an injured or dead Sethian was the last thing he'd have expected in this place.

"Kareem wounded his kidnapper." Surjan chuckled. "Good lad."

"Be ready for a fight, there may be more than one of these creatures," Marty pointed out.

In the center of the chamber's floor was the mouth of another circular shaft leading down. Marty edged up to it and raised his torch to look down inside. For as far as he could see, the shaft descended.

"What is this place?" he asked.

"It's the real palace," Surjan said. "It's the whole building. Queen Halpa and her servants only live in the attic, it appears."

"Was it built underground like this?" Marty asked. "Or was it built, and then swallowed up by the earth?"

"That's not even close to the most interesting question," Gunther said. "The real question is, who built it? And who lives here now . . . or what?"

"The only question that matters is, where is our friend?" Surjan spat. "You academics sit here and gaze at your navels." Turning to face the far side of the room, he threw back his head and roared. "I fear you not!"

Torch raised high in one hand, sword glittering in the other, he broke into a run.

Marty and Gunther followed.

Surjan raced toward an open archway beneath the colonnade. As he closed the final steps, Marty saw the shadows beneath the mezzanine overhead shift, and he realized that Surjan was running into an ambush.

"Surjan!" he yelled.

His cry was too late, because even as the name escaped his lips, a swarm of shadows sprang from the darkness and fell upon Surjan. As their wiry bodies articulated themselves from the shadow, the yellow light on rubbery gray skin gave them a sickly greenish hue. Marty saw long, splayed fingers, eyes like black marbles, and gaping mouths full of needle teeth beneath metallic glints, descending in a storm on his friend.

These things looked nothing like the Egyptian creatures they'd previously encountered.

But Surjan was not taken by surprise. The first Gray sprang for Surjan's head, and the Sikh met it with a flaming torch thrust directly into the creature's face. It shrieked, managing to rip the brand from Surjan's hand before it fell to the brick, whining and writhing.

At the same moment, Surjan stepped forward into the net of grayish flesh and swiped left. The blade flashed yellow and then neatly sliced the heads off two Grays, like a child might take the heads off so many dandelions. Two steps forward carried Surjan into another Gray, which he slammed against a brick pillar with his shoulder.

Grays bounded to attack Surjan from behind, but Marty arrived in time to intervene. The creatures moved with great speed, but it was at the cost of poor balance. Marty deflected one head-first into the nearest column and heard its neck snap instantly. He directed a second downward, plowing it onto its face on the brick floor and then tiptoeing rapidly up its spine to gain elevation. From the Gray's lower back, Marty leaped into the air and spun, kicking a third Gray in the face and staving in the bridge of its nose before landing in a fighting stance.

The remaining Grays shrieked and backed away, chittering.

"I feel sort of ripped off that my forte is healing," Gunther said.

Surjan grunted. "Don't sell yourself short. You also bless food."

"I would like to point out that I'm doing all of this in heavy hiking boots," Marty said. "Barefoot, I'd really be something to contend with."

The Grays backed away in a semicircle, sniffing the air. They all had nose rings, like domesticated bulls, or like the aliens Marty's party had encountered in ancient North Africa. They made whimpering noises to each other, noises that seemed to end in question marks.

"Return my man," Surjan growled, "and I will spare your lives."

The Grays broke and ran. Surjan howled, raised his ankh over his head, and gave chase. Marty followed as closely as he could, raising his torch high to give Surjan light to see by. The flame snapped violently with his motion, but didn't go out.

A short corridor opened into a massive kitchen. Two walls were dominated by huge stone tables, one of which was shattered in the center and lay sunken in dust. The far wall bore a fireplace as wide as a two-car garage and three paces deep. The Grays split and raced away in multiple directions, bursting left and right through different exits.

Surjan hesitated, and Marty and Gunther caught up.

"Which way?" Marty asked.

"They have nose rings," Gunther said. "Maybe we can smash their nose rings to incapacitate them, like with the Sethians."

"These things are tiny and seem to be more fragile," Marty pointed out. "We don't need to know the special Achilles' heel of hobbits to defeat hobbits. Just hit them."

"More like Gollum than hobbits." Gunther sniffed.

"Gollum was just a twisted evil leather boot of a hobbit," Marty said.

"This way." Surjan strode toward the fireplace. He wasn't walking, he was self-consciously striding. He looked like a warrior king, on the war path to rescue his retainer.

Marty scooted around to Surjan's side to light his path. The Sikh walked up to the fireplace, looking at the floor as he moved, ankh held out before him.

"Are you tracking . . . by smell?" Gunther asked.

"Yes," Surjan said. "It's not so strange. All humans have better senses of smell than we realize. We just never use it, so it atrophies. But also, Kareem's boots leave very different tracks from the bare feet of the Grays. Look." He pointed with the tip of his weapon.

In the depths of the fireplace, in the back left corner, there was a gap in the wall the size of a door.

"Let me go first," Marty said. "Or take a torch."

"Follow me closely." Surjan ignored Marty and pushed into the gap.

Marty followed, raising his torch high. The flames burned through cobwebs and sent unseen creepy-crawly things skittering away in the darkness above Marty's head. The passage was rough, a gap that had been torn by an earthquake or some other act of destruction. Surjan turned through half a descending twist, down a C-shaped corkscrew passage, and then stopped.

"There's a drop here," the Sikh warned Marty. Then he disappeared from view as he jumped.

Marty finished turning the corner, pulling Gunther behind him.

Surjan stood in the center of a cube-shaped chamber about six feet below them. The air was surprisingly good, despite the tang of ichor, which must be the scent Surjan was following. Air was circulating somehow down here, though Marty hadn't yet felt a breeze. Surjan looked wide-eyed at the wall from which Marty was emerging.

Marty scrambled down the wall, and Gunther silently followed suit. They walked over to where Surjan was standing and he pointed in the direction they'd just come from. They both turned and looked.

"It's clear in the light," Surjan said. "Thank you."

"It's a map," Gunther said with a tone of reverence.

Etched onto the wall was a clearly drawn map. Something about the map rang as familiar in Marty's mind. Had he seen it before, or just similar maps?

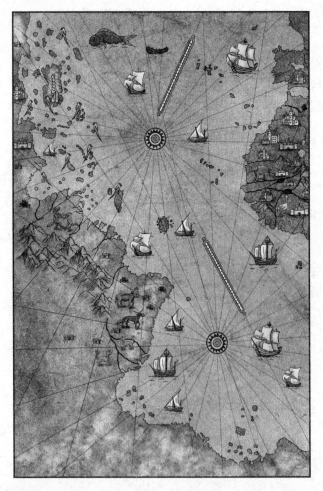

"Those are Spain, the Pillars of Hercules, and Northwest Africa up on the right," Gunther said.

"So that's the coast of Brazil on the lower left," Surjan continued. "Except that South America doesn't dribble east like that."

"It doesn't in the twenty-first century," Gunther said.

"Are you saying it once did?" Surjan asked. "Because that would make South America and Antarctica one massive landmass."

"Not sure how old this map is," Marty said, "but it's obviously old, since we're looking at it. Maybe it's inaccurate. Maybe it shows different coastlines because the coastlines were in fact once different. Also, note that it shows windrose lines—those lines running from point to point, like spiderwebs crossing all the seas. These maps don't have longitude and latitude, they tell you what course to chart to cross from point A to point B. That means they may not look like Mercator projections. And all three of those factors could be in effect, causing this map to look the way it does."

"I'm not going to lie," Gunther said. "The way it looks is amazing."

"Thinking like an archaeologist?" Marty asked.

"Thinking like the kid who wanted to grow up to be an archaeologist," Gunther said. "I'm underground in a palace that was ancient thousands of years before my own time and is totally unknown to my contemporaries, looking at a map on the wall that maybe shows Antarctica attached to South America. Whoever built this palace knew how to sail from France to Florida to Antarctica and back. I would have given my left arm to have known this moment, as a kid."

"You may be about to give your left arm now," Surjan said. "Stand back-to-back."

Marty and Gunther complied, Gunther facing the closest wall. Marty watched Grays ooze from four arched entryways in the walls facing him. They hissed and snapped their tongues, pacing from side to side.

"Kareem!" Surjan called out.

"Can you see him?" Marty was afraid to turn his head and look.

"I can smell him," Surjan said.

"What does he smell like?" Marty asked.

The Grays charged.

⪪ CHAPTER ⪫
EIGHT

Gunther held only a lit torch. He knew he could probably stun a couple of attackers with his . . . powers, but he'd quickly exhaust that ability, so he wanted to save it until he really needed it.

He swung his torch wildly, chasing back a couple of the Grays, and tried to shelter between his two more martial companions.

This way . . .

"What way?" he asked out loud, but he knew.

There was an opening in the corner. Two openings, but one was lower than the other, and full of water. But the other opening was dry, and broad, and empty.

This way . . .

The voice was talking to him again. Or was there a voice? Wasn't it possible that he was just losing it? Wasn't it possible that all the strange things that had happened to him in recent months—traveling back in time, battling aliens, developing weird psychic powers—had somehow broken him?

Or, more likely still, he realized with chagrin, wasn't it possible that none of those things had happened after all? Wasn't it possible that he was lying in the dig site near Aswan, having the most intense fever dream imaginable?

Maybe the voice was the sign that he was cracking up.

Or maybe he had already cracked up, and the voice was someone trying to summon him back from his madness. Maybe the voice belonged to some doctor or nurse from Médecins Sans Frontières whom François had summoned to the dig to see to Gunther.

But the voice didn't sound like the voice of a Nigerian doctor or French nurse.

It sounded like the voice of an angel.

And now it wanted him to go down the unguarded hallway.

"What's there?" he demanded, and the voice didn't answer.

"Gunther!" Marty snapped.

Gunther focused on his surroundings again and saw one of the Grays rushing him, claws extended.

"Stop!" Gunther bellowed, raising a hand. The hairs on his arms stood on end as energy surged from within him.

The Gray stopped and tumbled to the floor.

Marty had dropped the unlit torches and his own torch had burned out, leaving Gunther holding the only light in the room. Surjan and Marty fought side by side, Surjan slicing through the Grays with equanimity while Marty spun like a top, throwing out kicks and punches with equal facility. The foes they dropped seldom rose, melting quickly into fuming puddles that smelled of copper and turpentine.

Gunther scooped up two of the unlit torches. They were straight sticks with strips of cloth bound around one end, the cloth impregnated in something resinous and cloying to the smell. Gunther lit them both just as his torch sputtered to a dying halt, filling the room with light again.

This. Way.

Gunther didn't look. If he was cracking up, he wasn't going to follow the voice of his madness, no matter what it told him to do. And if some doctor was trying to revive him from a fever by calling out to him, they were just going to have to try harder. Or at least be a little more explicit.

Another Gray rushed at Gunther and he countercharged, waving the two torches and howling. The Gray turned and ran.

"Hold them here!" Surjan shouted.

Without waiting for an answer, he darted through an opening in the wall of Grays and plunged into one of the tunnels. The Grays folded in to chase him and Marty attacked them from behind, punching them where humans would have vulnerable kidneys and then cracking them on the backs of their skulls. Gunther covered Marty covering Surjan, waving torches, shouting, and, when he had to, thrusting fire into the faces of his enemies.

Gunther heard a bloodcurdling scream and the Grays scattered. Marty stood tall in a slime of evaporated foes, and the German backed away several steps toward the crack in the wall through which they'd come.

Kareem emerged from the tunnel. He tossed aside the severed head of a Gray, which sizzled with light and then burst into goo as it hit the ground. His hair looked disheveled and his eyes were narrowed in anger, but he looked unharmed.

Surjan emerged after him. "There are more coming! Back the way we came!"

Kareem fairly sprang up the brick wall and into the crack that led to the chimney. Gunther eyed the wall skeptically, wondering whether he could perform a similar feat. Without asking permission, Surjan grabbed Gunther and hurled him straight up into the gap, torches flailing. Gunther scrabbled at the cracked brick and Kareem grabbed him by the tunic, pulling him into safety. Surjan handed him his torches.

"Come," Kareem whispered. "We watch the other end."

Gunther shoved the butt end of his torch into a crack in the wall. Surjan was already climbing up into the chasm, and Marty held the Grays at bay. He was fast as a hummingbird, but there were so many of them.

"Marty!" Gunther cried.

"Go!" Surjan shoved him, and Gunther stumbled around and up the corkscrew, back into the kitchen. Kareem crouched in the fireplace there, visually scanning all the exits.

"There are too many shadows," Gunther said.

"You forget that I can see in the dark," Kareem said. "As you forget that Marty can run up and down walls."

"Marty can run up and down walls?" Gunther asked.

"You need to pay more attention," Kareem said. "Here they are. Run now!"

This! Way!

The voice called him still. It shivered with static, but it had a musical quality to it, like notes generated by touching the rims of crystal wineglasses. It made him think of the music of the spheres, or the voices of angels.

He lurched across the kitchen in Kareem's wake.

"Can you take us back to where we came from?" Surjan called to Kareem.

"I can see your footprints that brought you here," the young man said, "slowly fading but not gone yet. I can follow them."

Kareem led the party to the room with the mezzanine level and the colonnades, then across the center. Running out ahead of Gunther's torchlight, he nevertheless ran neatly around the lip of the pit in the center. Gunther lingered to make sure that Surjan and Marty had light enough to avoid catastrophe, though he wasn't sure he needed to. Surjan could track by sense of smell—could he also smell the open pit? And Marty seemed to have some kind of sixth, psychic sense that detected life forces.

Was Gunther the only member of the party who was helpless in the dark?

Surely, François was also useless when blind.

Kareem led them to the bottom of a staircase. It looked like the stairs by which they had descended before, but Kareem hesitated, and Gunther also wasn't sure. Water flowed over the steps now, an inch deep across the entire staircase, and then spilling out in a wide stream that flowed toward the pit.

"I can't see the tracks anymore," Kareem said. "I came down stairs, though. I think these were the stairs."

Hooting and howling filled the room as Grays burst from the hallway from which they'd recently emerged.

"Go!" Surjan shouted. "Gunther, Kareem, up the stairs!"

"We'll hold the stairs!" Marty told them.

"*I'll* hold the stairs!" Surjan bellowed. "Marty, you go!"

Marty hesitated a moment but then ran up the steps first. Gunther followed, side by side with Kareem. He marveled at his own stamina. As a younger man, he'd never had the fitness to run this much, up and down stairs, in water, climbing up and jumping down walls. Not even when he'd been in the military. Now he felt tired, but not excessively so.

Turn back.

He stopped, halfway up the steps.

Marty and Kareem splashed forward several steps, then turned to stare at him.

"Are you hurt?" Marty asked.

Gunther shook his head, not sure how to explain what he was experiencing.

"Then run, you idiot!" Kareem yelled.

What if he was wrong about the voice, though? What if Gunther wasn't cracking up? What if, instead, some true part of himself was speaking to him? What if his unconscious mind, his right brain, was trying to get him to recognize something important?

What if some external party was trying to speak to him, and this was how he was hearing it?

Turn back.

But that just meant he was crazy anyway, didn't it? What kind of external party would be telling him to go deeper into a maze filled with flesh-eating ghouls?

Was it possible he was hearing from the Grays? That they had some mind control power, and were trying to use it on him? Or they had some mighty Gray sorcerer who was trying to capture Gunther?

But why go for Gunther, if they had their choice? Why not try to capture, say, Marty?

Was Gunther the most vulnerable one?

"Idiot!"

Kareem grabbed Gunther by his tunic and pulled him up the stairs. Gunther staggered off-balance for several steps, sloshing water over his knees, and then finally ran on his own. Kareem followed, poking him in the back over and over.

As Gunther reached the top of the stairs, he heard Surjan roaring below. Many Gray voices shrieked in unison, and then Surjan came splashing up the steps. Gunther turned and saw the Grays begin to rush up after the Sikh. He was waiting, looking for an opportunity.

He felt a crackling sense of something surging through him as he picked his target with precision.

"Stop!" Gunther yelled. He directed his command at a Gray running ahead of two other Grays, who in turn were just a couple of steps ahead of a knot of five more.

The lead Gray tumbled back, stricken. He crashed through his fellows on his heels like a bowling ball through pins, sending sickly green limbs flying in all directions.

As Surjan reached him, Gunther turned and ran.

The rope at the bottom of the well dangled ahead of him. Marty and Kareem stood prepared to defend the lower end of the rope.

"Gunther, you first," Marty suggested. He looked up at the well and yelled, "François, Lowanna, whoever's up there, get ready to pull on the rope!"

"Tie a bowline around Gunther's chest," Surjan countered. "François will haul Gunther up, and the rest of us climb. Now!"

"I can do it." Gunther knew his knots from the military. Handing his torches momentarily to Kareem, he knotted a bowline around his chest. "Ready!" he shouted. Then he took back the torches. The rope under Gunther's arms went tight and yanked him a foot off the ground.

His companions began climbing up the shaft, Marty fastest of all—Kareem was right, he practically ran up the brick shaft of the well. Kareem also moved quickly, wedged into the corner of the room with one hand and one foot on each wall, ninety degrees apart, shimmying up like a spider. Surjan moved more slowly, but with deliberate confidence, grabbing each handhold or foothold, testing it, and then moving his weight onto it as he searched for the next grip.

Grays burst into the far end of the room.

Marty and Kareem disappeared overhead and Surjan rose to the height of Gunther's chest. Gunther gripped his two torches, gritting his teeth and facing the howling mob of man-eaters as they scurried forward. Some of them ran on their legs like men, he now saw, while others ran on all fours like dogs or cats. In the gleam of the torches, he imagined seeing a mist of spittle in the air around their misshapen, leathery heads.

"Faster, please!" Gunther called upward.

Door. Door.

"What?"

Gunther tried reaching for the brick-lined shaft to help speed things along but couldn't quite manage it as he dangled helplessly in the middle of the shaft. He felt himself get yanked upward a couple feet.

Turn back. Door.

"Shut up!" he snapped.

"What?" Surjan asked from above him.

"Pull!" Gunther yelled. "Pull!"

The Grays rushed forward. Gunther kicked one in the face and pushed another away with a lit torch, but then a third wrapped itself around his ankle.

"Hey!" He shook his leg, trying to toss the Gray aside, but couldn't budge it. He rose another foot into the air, but then a Gray leaped and wrapped itself around his other leg.

Gunther jammed a lit torch into the back of one Gray's neck. It shrieked, howled, and then bit his leg, just above the knee.

More Grays swarmed toward him. He rose a foot into the air again, but he wasn't getting away fast enough. He beat the Grays with his remaining torch, waved it at the oncoming mob, and thought maybe he should have listened to that static-ridden angelic voice, after all. More Grays leaped for him.

Suddenly he shot four feet straight up. He narrowly missed jamming the torch into the face of Surjan, who had wedged himself into position with his legs only and hoisted Gunther by main strength. With his ankh, Surjan neatly ran both Grays through the head, one at a time. In turn, each burst into gray slime, and then the rope went taut again and Gunther rose toward the light.

Gunther rose, and then rocks began falling past him. In the torchlight, he saw Surjan press against the wall of the shaft as a cascade of stones struck the climbing Grays repeatedly. A harsh keening sound erupted from below as one of the creatures was struck, fading away into the depths of the underground palace.

As he emerged from the mouth of the well, Gunther was struck by spray. Rain crashed against the outside of the palace and water ran in rivulets across the tiled floor.

He looked down and saw Surjan slowly advancing up the shaft when Lowanna pulled him away from the edge and helped him yank the rope from his chest.

"The other exit," Gunther tried to tell her.

"What other exit?" she asked.

"The Sacred Grove," he said. "At least. Maybe others we don't know about."

"He's right." Marty looked over into the well and called, "You okay?"

"I might be a bit slower on the climb, but I'm coming," Surjan said with an air of annoyance.

Marty hitched his thumb toward the well and said, "Surjan thinks there's another exit from the underground ruins. The Grays might come out there."

"I don't care if this thing escapes tonight," Lowanna said. "I want a place by the fire to wait out the storm."

"There's not one thing down there," Marty told her. "There are hundreds. We should make sure we're not being blindsided." To François and Kareem, he said, "You stay here and help Surjan get out."

Then Marty headed out of the palace, Lowanna in tow and Gunther tagging along behind.

Should he mention the voice?

Was it possible that the voice's reference to a door was to this same second exit that Surjan thought he'd identified?

They exited the outer edge of the palace grounds, past two startled spearmen, huddling beneath the entry arch to shelter from the rain, and then skirted left. Trudging back to where they'd started this whole misadventure, at times sliding in the mud where they had to and clinging to old stone pavers where they could, they finally crossed over into the Sacred Grove.

There was a path into the wood that none of them had noticed before, yet somehow Marty had managed to sniff it out as if he'd been there previously. It was only about fifty feet into the woods when they entered a clearing.

"He was right!" Lowanna howled into the wind and rain.

Gunther followed her pointing finger to see a mound of rocks like a tumulus or an altar. Not far from that was a well, built like the one in the palace courtyard but fully intact.

Grays began climbing from the shaft and over the crenellated casing.

Marty ran forward and Gunther ran with him, pulling his ankh from his belt.

Behind them, Lowanna shouted. The night grew bright as lightning cracked high above.

With a blinding flash, lightning struck the top of the rock mound, surging through the leathery bodies of the Grays.

Marty rushed forward, and even though he was half-blinded by the lightning, Gunther wielded his ankh and followed, stabbing again and again at the alien creatures until he thought he could stab no more.

And just as suddenly as the fight started, the wave of Grays spilling from the well finally broke, leaving him gasping from the exertion on the wet rocks.

⊰ CHAPTER ⊱
NINE

As the rain slacked off, Marty held a conference with the whole party in the palace, within view of the Well of the Beast. The courtyard was well-lit by many torches in brackets in the courtyard walls, just in case. At Surjan's instruction, six of the palace spearmen had gone to stand guard at the Sacred Grove, with strict instructions that if any of the Grays were to appear, five were to remain to keep them penned in and one was to run to the palace and inform the king.

Gunther, after the encounter with the Grays, seemed to be confused and a bit on edge. Had he been like this before the encounter as well? Marty wasn't sure if, like Lowanna, the German had been affected by their transition to this new place and time.

They were old friends, and Marty had to trust that Gunther would tell him if something was truly wrong.

"The Grays have rings in their noses," Kareem said. "They are not of this world."

"Are you sure? There's a lot of history behind piercings across various civilizations around the world," Lowanna pointed out.

"You didn't see what we saw, Lowanna. These things melt when slain," Surjan said. "Also, I completely understand why some of the Neshili call these things the Hungry Dead. Their pallor, large eyes, and spindly, almost spiderlike build makes them look the part of an alien."

"Concur," Marty said. "UFO pilots, straight out of central casting."

"They turned into bubbling, foul-smelling mucous just like the Sethians did," Gunther said.

Kareem fiddled anxiously with his dagger.

"But they talk about them as if the Hungry Dead appear from time to time to take a chicken or a small child," Lowanna said. "They feed them animal sacrifices and, until recently, it's kept things quiet. The Neshili haven't ever said that the Hungry Dead come in berserker waves."

"But they do, by God," Kareem said.

"Maybe they didn't want to admit how big the problem was," François said.

"Maybe they've never experienced them thus," Surjan said. "I will demand answers of the council in the morning."

Marty frowned. "We definitely need some answers."

"Something is up, and it's what ultimately ended up causing the old king, Zarum, to be sent off to that Sacred Grove to die," Lowanna said. "His so-called magic failed. Whatever the status quo used to be, the Hungry Dead's behavior has changed. We don't really know what's initiated any of this and how different things have now become."

"I will find out," Surjan said. He sounded tired.

"We'll find out more from the council in the morning," Marty said. "The question inevitably is, what, if anything, we can do about this."

"We save humanity." Gunther's voice was void of energy, thin and spent, but it still quivered with determination.

"From these Grays that are suddenly coming up to the surface?" Marty asked.

Gunther nodded, wordless.

"But what's causing the restless upheaval of the Grays?" Marty asked. "Obviously something has changed, and we need to get to the bottom of this. Cure the disease, not just the symptom."

"This is an old story," François said. "It's the story that humanity all on its own plays out, time and time again. A population exceeds its constraints, either because its environment becomes more constrained, such as by drought, or because its fertility explodes, such as by the introduction of clean water or increased food. The excess population has to go somewhere, so it launches out in a wave of conquest. Hence we get the Huns, the Mongols, the Amalekites, the Arabs, the early industrial British, and every other population that ever set forth to find new land to seize."

"I think you're thinking of *Battlestar Galactica*," Lowanna said.

"I am, in fact," François admitted. "Part of the greatness of *Battlestar Galactica* is the way it captures an archetypal human situation that everywhere fills our epic literature but is ignored in modern art: humanity on the move."

"We did this one before," Marty said. "We gathered refugees from the Sethian ravages across North Africa."

"Not quite the same," François said. "We gathered an army and fought. Now there is a whole people, and a new threat has appeared in their own home. Maybe there's nothing we can do about the Grays— what if there are thousands of them down below? We have no idea what we're dealing with. We might need to consider that the Grays bursting forth from their homeland is like Genghis Khan actually seeking to conquer and we're just in the way."

"You said these things were easier to fight than the Sethians were," Lowana said. "We don't have a reason to believe there are thousands down there; if there were, they'd probably have overrun the population on this island already. We could go down there and eradicate the Grays . . ." She frowned as the words hung in the air. "I'm okay with animals that occasionally eat a human because it crosses their path on a bad day, but a sentient species that eats humans as its target prey? This feels like something that needs intervention."

"You're suggesting a war between the Neshili and the Grays?" François asked.

"War has already been declared," she countered. "I'm suggesting we defend the humans."

"Maybe there's a more basic problem, though," Marty said.

"You're thinking of your vision." Lowanna met Marty's gaze. "Antarctica, the cliffs of ice. The icebergs that float past this palace, two thirds of the way down to the equator."

"That's a good point. Maybe the thing that is changing the equation here is the changing climate," François said. "I don't know quite how to read that one but maybe temperatures are rising, which is melting the polar ice—we're seeing this as calving icebergs, surprisingly far south. It fits with what we believe the year to be—we're at what is believed to be the end of the last ice age. That's raising ocean levels and increasing the amount of free water in the system generally—this island may find itself underwater soon enough. Don't get me wrong,

I'm saying this as a layman, not knowing for certain if that's what's really going on, but it's an educated guess."

"None of us is a climate scientist," Gunther said. "But we all can see the icebergs in the tropics."

"So maybe, in some way we're seeing that the changing climate is disrupting the food practices of the Grays." François shrugged. "If they're like the Sethians and low in iron, then maybe the shellfish beds are being disturbed and they're looking for alternatives to iron-rich foods, and they've taken to eating humans are a supplement."

"It's as good a guess as any," Marty said. "So . . . what do we do? Do we sail to the South Pole to look for an answer?"

"You mentioned a map down there." François's eyes narrowed. "Can you draw it for me?"

"You think it will give us an answer to the question?" Marty asked.

"I collect all the data I can, all the time," François told him. "I never know when something I learned ten years ago is suddenly going to give me the answer to a question today."

Marty quickly sketched out the lines on the muddy tile floors.

"And there were straight lines from point to point across the oceans?" François asked.

"Windrose lines." Marty nodded. "Many of them. Looked like an old-timey sailor's map, to use technical archaeology language."

"Are you sure it showed this entire region connecting, almost as if Antarctica and South America are a contiguous landmass?" François asked.

"I have no doubt," Marty said. "I can still see it perfectly in my mind."

François pursed his lips and scratched his jawline. "I think I've seen a map like this before. Let me chew on it for a bit."

"And what do we do about the queen?" Surjan asked.

"Do about her?" Marty looked over at him and grinned. "What do you mean?"

"She tried to seduce me." Surjan grumbled.

Marty couldn't help but smile at the large man's plight.

"I imagine you can think of something to do about that," Lowanna quipped.

Surjan sighed. "In addition to me continuing to resist her blandishments, because I'm not that kind of man . . . what *else* shall we do about the queen?"

François pointed at the Sikh and chuckled. "My friend, there is no 'we' in that problem. As king, this is a 'you' type of problem."

"I'll watch her." Kareem smiled, and in the dancing light of the torches, his teeth looked like flames in his mouth.

"They are not your dead," Surjan said coldly. "They are not human and they never were. They are different creatures from you entirely."

He stood in the ring of the Neshili council, holding the king's scepter. This was a tall wooden rod with a serpent carved at its tip. He wore a saffron-colored sash around his waist and a bleached white kilt. Marty and François sat on divans in the ring, along with the queen and the three elders of Nesha. Spearmen stood about the room, along with Lowanna, Gunther, and Kareem. The chamber was on the highest floor of the palace, and windows opened on three sides to cloudy, blustery weather.

The divan was comfortable and Marty was tired, but he had far too much adrenaline coursing through his veins to feel sleepy.

"Demons, then?" Tudhal the priest asked.

"No." The party had anticipated this question and rehearsed the answer. "They're beasts. Animals who eat the children of men as do other beasts, such as sharks."

"They have the forms of men," Tudhal insisted.

"Do they?" Surjan grinned and laughed. "Have you seen them?"

"Once," Tudhal admitted.

"Describe them," Surjan pressed. "What color are they? How are their eyes? What is their manner of speech?"

"They are gray," Tudhal admitted, "with eyes that lack whites entirely, and also irises. Their speech is a chattering noise with no pattern to it."

"They are not men," Surjan said, "nor demons. They are not your dead ancestors who are owed fealty or food. They are dangerous beasts and, unbeknownst to you, they have lived beneath your feet for a very long time. Now their manner of life is disturbed, and they are feeding on you."

"On us, Your Majesty," Queen Halpa said. "On our people."

"On *my* people," Surjan said. The vehemence in his voice surprised Marty.

"Are you certain," the genealogist Ammun said slowly, "that the beings we call the Hungry Dead are not rather a kind of people, from very far away? Maybe as far away as you have come?"

Marty stared, wondering where these people thought they'd come from.

Surjan's mouth hung open.

François was the first to recover himself. "From where do you think such people might come?"

"From the stars, of course." Ammun nodded piously.

Sapal snorted.

"As all people do," Ammun insisted. "We lived among the gods, all of us as stars, and then we came here upon the Earth. If the Hungry Dead aren't dead at all, but people, they came from the stars. Perhaps they came with us in the fleet from the City of the Gods. Perhaps they came from the City of the Gods at another time."

"The City of the Gods," Lowanna said. "A city in the sky? A city of stars?"

Marty noticed one of the spearmen ogling her. Sharrum, he thought the man's name was. He'd come to Muwat's hut with the elders the morning after their arrival, hadn't he?

"No, the City of Gods on Earth," Tudhal said. "Whence sailed the Fleet of the End of the World."

"Does this matter?" the queen asked.

"I'm curious," François said. "Where is the City of Gods on Earth?"

"In the east," Ammun said. "This is where we come from. We came down from the stars with the gods, to be their servants in their city. It was a mighty city and it prospered for many centuries."

"Many thousands of years," Tudhal asserted.

"Its sorcerers were mighty, its scholars were wise, its rulers were noble," Sapal said. "And the gods lived among us there, and our lifespans were ten times the length of a man's life today."

"Until someone went and ate that apple." Lowanna put her fists on her hips. "Let me guess, was it a woman?"

The three elders furrowed their brows and stared at her.

"What apple?" Sapal asked.

Sharrum smiled lasciviously at Lowanna. Marty stood, deliberately putting himself in the way so the guard couldn't look at her anymore. "Lowanna only means that we have heard similar stories before. Similar, but not necessarily the same. Go on."

"The city learned that its time was going to come to an end," Ammun said. "We have heard different explanations for this. Maybe the gods withdrew. Maybe we failed them. Maybe the city was built with a fatal flaw, that was inevitably going to break it apart."

"It isn't Eden after all," Lowanna said. "It's Krypton."

Sharrum smiled at what she'd said, though the spearman couldn't possibly understand the reference.

Marty turned to the anthropologist. "Maybe a little less snark. Also, we don't need anyone naming their kid Eden Kryptonite because we accidentally drop too many cultural references."

Lowanna's face went stony. She was in a mood.

Tudhal took up the story. "So, the City of the Gods sent out fleets of ships in all directions. We don't know the names of all the fleets, but we know that one fleet was called the Fleet of the End of the World. We know that because our ancestors were on that fleet, and the fleet had the quest of establishing two of the Daughters of God."

"Daughter cities, you mean," François said.

Marty turned his attention back to the elders. "How many fleets went out?"

Tudhal shrugged and Ammun shook his head.

"Do you know which direction they went?" he pressed.

"All directions," Ammun said.

"From the City of the Gods," François said, "which is in the east. To be fair, like Eden."

Marty sighed. "Fine. So, the Fleet of the End of the World set one group of people here and at least one group somewhere else."

"You are going to ask us where," Sapal said, "and we don't know."

Marty shook his head. "I was going to say, Ammun asked François if we were from the other half of the fleet, or the City of the Gods. Now I understand."

"You might also have been from one of the other eight Daughters of God," Tudhal said. "But if you are from any of those places, you either don't know enough to say so, or wish to conceal your origin from us." The priest gazed at Marty through lidded eyes.

Marty ignored the pointed rebuke. "You're saying maybe the Hungry Dead came with you on the Fleet of the End of the World, and . . . what? You forgot about them?"

"Exactly," Ammun said.

"If they are not the Hungry Dead, we should stop calling them that," Tudhal suggested. "Also, we should not call them demons, apparently."

"They are Grays," Surjan said.

"Grays." Tudhal rolled the word around in his mouth and then nodded.

"How long have you been here?" François asked.

"Eighty-six generations," Ammun said. "Would you like to hear them?"

Surjan raised a hand to stop him. "Later."

"And the Grays?" François asked. "How long have you suffered their depredations?"

"Always," Sharrum said.

To Marty's annoyance, the spearman had shifted his position a pace to one side and was making eyes at Lowanna again.

"Always," Tudhal and Sharrum agreed.

"Who built this palace?" François asked. "And what other entrances are there that descend into the heart of the world below?"

"We built it," Queen Halpa said. "Our ancestors. Using the sorceries of the City of the Gods. And we can show you all the entrances."

"All the entrances you know of," Kareem muttered. Marty wasn't sure anyone other than himself heard it.

"You seek to fight the Guardian?" Ammun asked.

"I don't seek to fight anyone." François smiled. "I like teaching."

"Good," Ammun said. "It is not your place to fight the Guardian of the . . . the Guardian of the Grays."

"Fine." François smiled again. "What is the Guardian?"

"The poems say that it is the great leader of the . . . Grays," Ammun said. "Their war leader, their shaman, their king. It sits in darkness, and its children bring it flesh to eat and blood to drink."

"Does it hold a pitchfork and sit in a pit of burning tar?" Lowanna asked.

Sharrum chuckled out loud, the annoying twit.

"No," Tudhal said, "but it is keeper of sorceries from the City of the Gods on Earth."

Gunther gasped loudly. His face drained of color.

"Are you okay?" Marty asked him.

"I need air." Gunther stood and stumbled to a window.

"What kinds of sorceries?" François stood. "Sorceries such as those that built this palace?"

Tudhal nodded. "In a day."

Marty shook his head. "Lowanna will remind us that this is a cliché, and she'll be right."

"About time you admitted it," she shot back.

Marty sighed.

"The poems say that the Guardian has access to mighty weapons," Ammun said, "and healing arts, and an open gate connecting it to the gods."

Gunther made retching sounds.

"Well, pitchfork and tar, or mighty weapons of the gods," François said. "Either way, I'm glad not to be fighting the beast."

Ammun nodded. "That is for King Surjan to do."

⇥CHAPTER⇤
TEN

François looked down the pit into darkness. He saw and heard no sign of motion or life. Outside the palace grounds the rain continued, with occasional flashes of lightning. Water trickled down the sides of the well.

"It's possible this is not a great idea," Marty said. "I want to acknowledge that sometimes you've had great ideas. This might not be one of those times."

"Are you kidding me?" François asked. "We want to know where the City of Gods on Earth is and where the other half of the Fleet of the End of the World went to, and you're telling me there's an actual map, and now you don't want to go."

"That's all true," Marty acknowledged, "but I don't understand why you need to see this map for yourself. I can picture it in my head easily and I've drawn you its likeness in the dirt."

François waved dismissively at the words. "I need to see this with my own eyes."

Marty shook his head. "You're also glossing over that there are leathery-skinned demon-men down there who apparently eat humans."

"They're not demons," François said. "We were very clear with the Neshili about that. They're people."

"We told the Neshili that so they wouldn't panic," Surjan said.

"Right." François tested the rope, still anchored to the tripod he had built. "And I don't want you to panic when we go down there, either."

Marty harrumphed.

The three men stood above the same well Marty and Surjan had gone into before. Lowanna and Gunther were there too, as well as four of the palace warriors with their long spears and atlatls. One of the warriors kept contriving reasons to be standing beside Lowanna—to hand her small objects or clear her way—and Marty looked peevish about it.

François wasn't sure where Kareem was.

"You know right where we need to go, right?" François asked.

"We know," Surjan said.

"So, we run in"—François patted the pocket of his tunic—"I copy what I need to from the map with this charcoal and bit of linen, and then we come right back up."

"What do you need to copy from the map?" Marty asked.

"I won't know until I see it," François said. "At worst, all of it."

Surjan laughed. "You really are used to getting your way."

"I've got a feeling about this." François shrugged. "Look, don't we agree that we want this data that the Neshili is talking about? We need to understand more about these things down below. And besides, the Grays are probably asleep during the day. And if not, they're probably leery of us after what they got at the Sacred Grove."

"Or really angry with us." Marty ran his fingers through his hair and turned to one of the warriors. "You, what's your name? Sharpie?"

"Sharrum," the warrior said.

"You come with us," Marty said. "Bring your three men."

"But the lady Lowanna—" the warrior objected.

"Lowanna is indeed a lady," Marty said, his nostrils flaring. "She is also a sorceress who could blast you to jelly with a word. She will be fine without your assistance."

Lowanna crossed her arms and cocked her hips. "True."

Sharrum looked to Surjan in appeal, and Surjan nodded his agreement with the plan.

The Neshili warriors went down first, two at a time, the second man holding torches to light the chamber below. When they pronounced the landing safe, the three party members quickly followed. François came last, carrying a rectangular board under his arm.

The area below the palace had the look of grand subway chambers, the sort that are sometimes sealed off when not used, only to be rediscovered decades later. It also had the aspect of a maze, shot through with passageways launching off in all directions. As they walked quickly through the passages, they passed pits suggesting levels farther down. Water flowed in streams across every level surface and down many of the walls.

Maybe the ecological crisis that was forcing the Grays into action was as simple as a flood? Maybe the right metaphor wasn't Eve eating the fruit, it was Noah. The Grays needed an ark.

François stayed alert for signs they were being followed, but he knew that Surjan, with his heightened senses, or maybe the Neshili warriors, with their long experience, would hear signs of approaching enemies or predators long before he would.

Finally, they squeezed through a ragged corkscrew crack that had opened into a large fireplace, and dropped into a cube-shaped room.

The water here was knee-deep.

A warrior named Piyam, a young man with a round face but a pointed chin, held two torches high. Marty, Surjan, and the other three Neshili men stood watch, while François looked at the map on the wall, his heart racing.

"Piri Reis," he said, the name coming to him.

"Is that a place?" Marty asked.

"It's a man." François wrapped the linen around his piece of wood and began sketching what he saw. "A Turkish admiral. And he had this map of the world made, oh, along about the time of King Henry VIII. And he seems to have been copying from earlier maps, and his map was surprisingly accurate considering this was a time before the Europeans had crossed the oceans. Or at least before Columbus."

"You're not saying this map was made by a Turkish admiral," Surjan said.

"I'm saying the maps Reis copied from had some relationship to this map," François said. "Maybe his maps were copies of this one. Or maybe they came from a common original."

"A map made by some admiral of the City of the Gods," Surjan mused.

"Cuba's lying the wrong way," Marty pointed out.

"If that's Cuba. Piri Reis copied from earlier maps, so there's the interesting possibility that he was copying from maps that were really old, and maybe his map shows at least some of the landmasses as they were, not in 1500 C.E., but as they were during, say, the last ice age."

"Sounds like pseudohistory to me," Marty said. "Tinfoil hat stuff."

"It does, doesn't it?" François decided to forego sketching in the windrose lines and focused on the coastlines, including the strange little blotches here and there. "And yet, some people think the map shows the coast of Antarctica, free of ice. So, how did he pull that off?"

"I'll bet you a million dollars right now that most scholars in the year 2021 do not believe the map shows the Antarctic coast, free of ice."

"You don't have a million dollars, Marty," François said. "But you'd be right. Of course. Still, there's that weird, wrong-shaped Cuba. How hard is it to get the shape of Cuba right? And for that matter, why is it only one island? It looks for all the world like Cuba and Hispaniola have been swallowed up by some larger landmass." He paused. "The Bimini Road."

Marty sighed. "I'm afraid to ask what that is."

"I don't want to hurry the delicate artistry of the mapmaking," Surjan growled, "but I would like it to go faster."

"Okay," François said, "I will adopt the language of your unimaginative, consensus-enforcing, guild-patrolling, jargon-speaking academics."

"Remember that I hate academics myself," Marty said. "I got thrown out of that guild after I punched one of them."

"Ah, right." François resumed drawing. "In that case, what those dumb bastards would say is that the Bimini Road is not a megalithic structure off Bimini Island in the Bahamas, but a natural rock shelf that just happens to look like a megalithic structure."

"Wait," Marty said. "You're telling me . . ."

"The rock shelf that protects the bay," François said. "We should go look at it closely, when we have a chance. It might be the Bimini Road. In which case, we know exactly where we are. We're on Bimini Island, though of course it's part of a larger landmass. Maybe the larger landmass that somehow survived onto Piri Reis's map."

"The Neshili use atlatls," Marty said. "That doesn't prove anything, but it's an extremely old technology."

"So, these people . . ." Surjan said, switching to English. "Where are they from?"

"Let's not repeat Columbus's mistake." François spoke in English, too, and then snickered. "They're not Indians, Surjan. I don't know. Do they look Asian or Austronesian to you?"

"Their own claim is that they come from the east," Marty said.

"They also say they come from outer space, and—" Surjan paused as he gazed back and forth from the pool of water to the wall with the map. He pointed at the water and said, "Look at the map in the water's reflection. Do you see anything strange?"

François followed Surjan's gaze and his eyes widened as he compared it to the wall. "Wow . . . are you seeing those crosshatches on the water? It's almost like number markings on different parts of the map, but it's not obvious from looking at the map itself, just the reflection."

"Good eyes, Surjan," Marty remarked. "How is that even possible?"

François shook his head and made some quick markings on his copy of the map. "The water reflects certain light wavelengths differently, and maybe it's sort of a weird invisible-ink-type of situation. I'd never have thought it possible. Notice how there's a number right on top of us and a series of others, one of which is also right around where we know there's a portal, just south of Cairo."

"Who knows what it means? The reflection shows a marking right where we are, but there's no obvious sign of any portal, though I see marking near the Antarctic as well."

"We need to get going," Surjan murmured with a nervous tone.

"Well, I've copied what I need . . ." François shook the excess charcoal from his linen map, folded it up neatly, and tucked it into the pocket of his tunic. "Shall we go back up?"

Following the queen was child's play for Kareem. She acted like a woman who was used to being obeyed; she ordered her servants to leave her alone and then didn't watch to see whether she was being followed. Kareem's soft step and sharp hearing let him stay just around the corner from her as she moved about the palace. The more difficult task was staying out of sight of the servants himself, but he was able to slip behind curtains or into window wells and once even out a window onto the tiled rooftop below it, and stay unseen.

It wasn't fair that the other teammates had gained abilities that were literally magical, and Kareem had only seemingly found it easier to blend into the background—not exactly as dramatic a skill as what the others had. Lowanna could speak with animals and summon lightning. Gunther could heal. Marty ran up and down walls like a squirrel. François... well, maybe François hadn't really gained magical powers. He could talk louder and was more persuasive.

And Kareem could see in the dark.

He fingered the metal of his sharpened ankh, feeling the urge to bury it in someone. It wasn't only the satisfying sensation of plunging the weapon into muscle, sinew, and bone. It was the thrill of what would happen after the body was found. His desire for mayhem was an itch he had felt since their first jump backward in time, but at this moment it was overwhelming. Since the Grays had grabbed him, he had felt a lust for blood. For *their* blood. The few Grays he had killed in climbing out of the chambers beneath the palace hadn't done anything to lift his desire.

But he couldn't kill the queen. He had to follow her.

She had tried to seduce Surjan. This didn't seem like an obviously bad thing to Kareem. Wasn't she Surjan's wife, since he killed the old king? Maybe she was just trying to make the best of a bad situation. Maybe she wanted to be Surjan's ally. Maybe she even found him handsome—he was tall and broad-shouldered and had a manly beard. If the queen had tried to seduce Kareem, he might simply have let her succeed.

But Surjan thought she was trying to manipulate him, so maybe she had ill intent.

As vast as the underground labyrinth was, the palace above was still big enough to have unoccupied rooms and even wings he'd yet to explore. Kareem was uneasily reminded of Giza, and the sense that the current inhabitants were a numerous but tiny people, squatting on a territory settled and built by giants. He shook the feeling off and followed the queen into a washing area. Lurking in the shadows, he watched as she washed in a stone bath, perfumed herself, dressed in linens thin as gauze, and then slipped through a back corridor into unused chambers.

She was headed for the temple that adjoined the palace. Old scar-faced Tudhal ruled over his clutch of acolytes there, and Kareem was a little uncertain how to stay hidden from their view. Dodging up to the highest story of the palace, he let himself out a window onto the gable of the east wing. He ran light-footed along the top of the gable like a tightrope and crouched in the rain and shadow at the far end, watching through the vines covering a trellis and walkway below, in the space between the palace and the temple.

The rain pouring down his neck and chest was cool, but it felt good. Kareem felt alive. When the queen walked from the palace to the temple beneath him, dressed to break hearts, he felt like a wild animal, like a predator, poised to strike her down. He had to force himself to grip the tile of the gable beneath his feet, and not dive down, plunging the sharpened ankh into her breast.

Then she passed into the temple. He took a deep breath, shook off the murderlust, and leaped over the gap to the temple.

He landed on a circular platform with a knee-height balustrade around its edge. The only part of the temple taller than this platform was a spire rising to the east, thin as a flagpole, and it was only ten feet or so taller. In the center of the platform, spiral stairs descended into the interior. The balustrade was made of stone, a single ring carved of a single chunk of rock, six inches in diameter. Its upper surface was marked with notches at regular intervals, and here and there squiggles that looked like writing, but Kareem couldn't read them.

Out on the ocean, a blue-white chunk of ice the size of a small stadium rocked through the rain and wind toward the rock shelf.

Kareem crept to the stairs and listened. To his quiet delight, he heard the murmuring of two voices in the room below. One of them was the queen's, and the other was Tudhal's. He could have remained where he was and simply listened, but Kareem knew he could get closer, so he did.

He padded down the stairs, found a shadowed corner of the staircase from which he could observe the space below, and sat.

The room below the platform was dominated by a large brass contraption. He squinted and stared at it, trying to find apt comparisons. It looked like several wire spheres nestled within each other and overlapping each other. It moved as he looked at it, and he realized that there was a brass globe in the center. Arms spun around and within the spheres, and the arms ended in additional globes; some of them had smaller balls circulating about them, and the whole was moving—

It was the solar system. He'd seen a model of such a thing before, maybe in school, or was it in Cairo that he'd seen posters about the opening of a new planetarium he'd never be able to afford to go visit?

He couldn't tell what made this thing move, but some power source had the whole thing spinning. And then he frowned. He should bring François back here to look at the model—François was knowledgeable about such things, certainly much more than Kareem was.

Kareem wasn't certain, but he thought the model had one planet too many.

"I can make you king."

That was Queen Halpa speaking. Kareem tore his attention away from the orrery and looked at the rest of the room. There were shelves stacked with scrolls, small brass hand tools Kareem didn't recognize, and broad tables. The queen sat on one of the tables, leaning back seductively. Old Tudhal stood beside the table, looking like a dog fidgeting and trying to be patient until its master told it to go ahead and eat the leftover shawarma.

"What about the gods?" Tudhal asked. "What about the will of the gods? I couldn't possibly defeat that monster Surjan in hand-to-hand combat, not even if he was asleep."

"You underestimate yourself."

"I am no fool."

"I made the last two kings," the queen purred. "I can make you."

Tudhal pressed himself closer, against the heavy wood of the table. Halpa turned back her shoulders, seeming to open herself like a morning flower without actually getting any closer to the old priest.

"It couldn't be a fair fight," Tudhal murmured.

"There are no fair fights," Halpa said dreamily. "There is only the will of the gods, and the one they choose."

By God, Surjan had been right. This woman was a conniving wench... yet Kareem admired the game she was playing.

Also, Kareem kind of wished he had something to drink. Sitting and watching this seduction was the most entertainment he'd had in months.

"How do you know the will of the gods?" Tudhal's voice was thick.

"*I* am the will of the gods."

Kareem had seen enough. He stayed until the tension of seduction finally gave way to the boring mechanics of table-mounted acrobatics, and then got up and padded away in the rain.

⇐ CHAPTER ⇒
ELEVEN

Gunther stood at the edge of the temple complex, gazing out over the horizon. The setting sun cast an orange glow over the ancient stone structures, but something felt off. *Get Lowanna and take her outside.*

The world tilted as the voice echoed loudly in his head.

He barely caught himself as a wave of dizziness washed over him. The voice was up there still, almost as if it was a tangible presence looming over him . . . his head filled with static, and even though he couldn't hear what the voice said afterward, Gunther felt the compulsion.

His mind raced back across the centuries and millennia to a different time. He was in the German military for a short period, and he felt the command rattling around in his head no differently than were it given to him by his superior officer.

With his heart racing, he scrambled to his feet and sprinted through the palace, searching for Lowanna. He found her in the central chamber, by herself, snacking on a piece of fruit.

"Lowanna," he panted, grabbing her arm. "We need to go. Now."

She looked up, startled, her eyes distant and withdrawn. "Gunther, what's going on?"

"No time to explain. Trust me." He pulled her along, and his gait faltered as he realized he was marching to a set of orders he couldn't explain. Some voice whose origin was a complete mystery had commanded him to do something, and he was doing it. Somehow, he knew there was no time for question his own sanity ... something was wrong. He felt it in his bones.

They found Surjan nearby, talking with some of the elders.

"Surjan, we need your help," Gunther urged, his voice tinged with barely controlled panic. "There's something outside ..."

Surjan's eyes narrowed as he looked at the German archaeologist-turned-healer, frowned, but gave him a curt nod. He followed without question.

They ran outside, and as they reached the courtyard gate, they saw it: the Neshili city below the temple complex was flooding. The ocean had encroached, and water was rising rapidly, submerging the lowest parts of the city.

"My God," Lowanna breathed, her detachment momentarily breaking. "The people down there ... is it some kind of tidal wave? We have to help them."

Without another word, they dashed down the ancient paths leading to the city. Neshili were already in a panic, scrambling to save their belongings and loved ones. Gunther uncharacteristically took charge, his military training kicking in.

"Everyone, move to higher ground!" he shouted. "Leave your things! Save yourselves!"

"This is your king!" Surjan yelled, his voice booming with authority. "Do as the healer says, get to higher ground, now!"

Lowanna ran to a group of children huddled together, their eyes wide with fear. She scooped up the youngest in her arms and beckoned the others to follow. "Come with me! I'll keep you safe!" Her voice was gentle, though she remained withdrawn from the people around her, focusing intently on the task at hand.

Surjan rallied a group of men to help herd livestock to safety. "Get the animals to the temple! They'll be safe up there!" he commanded, leading the charge.

Gunther waded through waist-deep water to reach an elderly couple struggling to stay afloat. "Hold on!" he shouted, grabbing their hands and pulling them to higher ground. He glanced back and saw the water rising faster than he'd anticipated, fueled by a relentless surge from the ocean.

Some unseen barrier must have burst or maybe it was a giant ice shelf collapsing, causing the unanticipated surge from an unfathomable distance. But could that be right? How much ice would have to melt, all at once, to cause the ocean levels to rise noticeably?

To Gunther, the world seemed to move in slow motion.

He was aware of the sounds all around him, as if his hearing acuity had suddenly been boosted by some strange force.

Had he gained a level . . . ? In this place, he hadn't seen any of the strange globes of light they'd absorbed back in Egypt, yet that moment of overwhelming dizziness felt familiar.

He'd been through this several times before. He glanced over at Lowanna as she ripped away the woven entrance from a hut.

Lowanna, drenched and determined, moved from house to house, ensuring no one was left behind. She found a young mother clutching her baby, too scared to move. "It's okay," Lowanna said softly, wrapping an arm around her. "We'll get through this together." She'd always seemed more comfortable with the animals than some of the members of the team, but her compassion clearly extended to the terrified villagers.

As the fleeing Neshili reached the temple steps, Gunther noticed a trapped llama, bleating desperately from a makeshift pen. Without hesitation, he dashed back, untangling the terrified animal and guiding it to safety.

Surjan and his group managed to secure most of the livestock, but the water was relentless. "We need to hurry!" he yelled over the roar of the encroaching ocean.

Gunther, Lowanna, and Surjan formed a human chain, guiding the Neshili up the hill to safety. The temple grounds filled with frightened but relieved faces, huddled together and watching as their city below was swallowed by the sea.

Exhausted and soaked, Lowanna looked at Gunther. "You saved all of these people."

Gunther shook his head, breathless. "I can't really take the credit." He panned his gaze at everyone shuffling nearby and knew this wasn't the time to talk about the voices in his head. "I just sensed something was wrong out here. I'm just glad I listened."

"Nonsense." Surjan clapped a hand on Gunther's shoulder. "You saved many lives today. We all did."

The sun dipped below the horizon, casting a red hue over the scene.

Much of the Neshili city within sight of the palace grounds was now a watery grave.

Suddenly, yelling erupted in the distance.

A group of Neshili warriors scrambled up the hill yelling, "The village over the ridge is drowning! There's chaos at the docks!"

Before anyone could do anything, Lowanna darted toward the ridge directly west of them as she yelled, "Don't just stand there, lead them to higher ground!"

Lowanna's heart pounded as she sprinted through the second village, the air thick with the smell of salt and the distant roar of encroaching waves. The island was sinking, or perhaps the water was rising—either way, the situation was dire. She reached the fisherman's hut, where Sharrum, one of the Neshili warriors, was already helping Muwat, the now no-longer-blind fisherman who'd previously hosted them.

"Lady Lowanna, over here!" Sharrum called, his voice carrying over the chaos.

Lowanna rushed to his side. Muwat blinked as if he'd just been woken up. He had arms looped over the shoulder of his two daughters, Telpi and Yaru, who looked equally terrified. His wife, Zidna, was being helped by their son, Arnun. Nearby, Shush the weasel darted about, sensing the urgency as he climbed up onto the old man's shoulder and chittered at her. *The water sneaky. No like it.*

Ignoring the weasel's complaints, Lowanna turned to the soldiers who were trying to help. "There's not enough space on the temple grounds or the palace. We need to get these people to the boats." Lowanna grabbed Muwat's arm. "Come on, we have to move quickly."

With the soldiers' help, they guided Muwat and his family, along with a flock of other Neshili, toward the stone pier where the boats hopefully remained moored. The ground shook, sending a fresh wave of panic through the villagers.

An earthquake?

Lowanna's eyes widened as she stared at a large object in the distance.

Past the stone dock where the boats rested was a mountain of ice rising at least one hundred feet into the air.

She knew that what she saw was only a minor part of the colossal chunk of glacier that had just slammed into the island, temporarily blocking the rushing water.

"Get to the boats!" Lowanna yelled. "People will be safe on there while we gather everyone!"

One of the villagers cried out, "But our food, the llamas are—"

"Get to safety, I'll see what we can do about the livestock!"

Lowanna's mind raced. She knew that the llamas were a key source of protein for the community that was now scattered and scared.

Lowanna noticed Sharrum nearby and said, "I need to find the llamas."

Sharrum frowned. "They have certainly drowned or scattered in all directions. How can you—"

"I can find them!" Lowanna closed her eyes to focus.

"If you find them, I will help gather the stubborn creatures."

With her eyes closed, Lowanna imagined herself looking inward, tapping at something she didn't understand, but knew was there. It was a source of some form of consciousness that until they'd started this crazy adventure, she hadn't believed existed.

Now, as the world around her faded, she felt a connection forming.

A nest of invisible threads shot out from within that place inside her. In her mind's eye she sensed where each thread weaved outward, almost as if her eyes were at the head of the filament scouring the land for the lost animals.

Lowanna's eyes shot open as she felt the pull of the creatures, huddled in a mass, scared and unsure of what was happening.

She turned and ran, her feet sloshing in mud as she followed the invisible thread connecting her to the animals.

The warrior's feet thudded heavily behind her as she raced up a slope, into a copse of trees that gave way to a sheltered grove.

It was there that she found a herd of nearly three dozen llamas, their eyes wide with fear.

Sharrum's heavy footsteps clambered up the slope.

...bad water...

Afraid...

Strange woman...

She helps us?

Lowanna understood the nickering voices of the llamas as if they were toddlers speaking broken English.

"Come on," she whispered, her voice calm and soothing. "We need to get to the boats. You'll be safe, I promise." Lowanna felt a warm camaraderie with the animals as they responded with flicks of their tails and ears, each of which spoke to her.

"Be careful, they're dumb, strong creatures and can easily—"

"Shut up," Lowanna cut him off, waving dismissively at the spearman as she motioned to the nearest of the beasts. "Come, follow me."

She turned and began walking down the slope, all the while motioning for the llamas to follow.

Sharrum's eyes widened as the herd of animals began walking nose-to-tail, following Lowanna as if she were their mother. "What kind of magic do you possess for such a thing to be possible?"

Lowanna led them carefully, her senses alert to the shifting ground and rising water.

Sharrum raced ahead and as they approached the docks, he pointed at some of the nearest and largest boats. "These are set up for livestock."

Lowanna urged the llamas forward, guiding them onto the boats where some of the villagers were already helping to secure them.

She spotted Muwat and his family huddled together on the far end of one of the large boats, relief evident on their faces. A blur of motion streaked toward her and she laughed as Shush the weasel hopped up onto her tunic, scrambled up onto her shoulder, and chattered incessantly about the height of the waves and the depth of the water.

Lowanna stroked his thick fur and whispered, "I have to get back to the others. You'll be safe."

"The ice is blocking the channel out to the sea," one of the men announced as he scrambled down from one of the boat's masts, then began shouting orders at the crew members. "Loosen the ropes! We don't know how long the ice will hold the water, but we don't want to be tied to the dock when the water rises higher."

Lowanna scanned the horizon and, despite the setting of the sun, she could see clearly enough that the iceberg was literally acting at a temporary dam for the rising water. When it was inevitably dislodged, chaos would reign over Nesha.

✤　✤　✤

Gunther's hands moved swiftly, his military training guiding him as he bandaged the wounds of the injured Neshili. He'd long ago exhausted whatever preternatural healing powers he'd had and was having to resort to conventional first aid, working on the ground in the temple courtyard. Beside him, François assisted, holding supplies and following Gunther's terse instructions.

"Apply pressure here," Gunther directed, pointing to a deep gash on a man's leg. François nodded, pressing a relatively clean cloth against the wound.

The scene around them was chaotic. Adults shouted, children cried, and the sound of rushing water grew louder. The ocean's relentless advance was swallowing the lower parts of the island.

And if the island was flooding, what was happening to the catacombs beneath the palace? And might the Grays come swarming out of the wells, forced by the waves? But Surjan had set spearmen to all the catacomb's exits, and Gunther tried to believe they would contain the problem, if it arose.

Luckily, most of the Neshili's injuries were relatively minor. He'd managed to heal a few obviously broken arms, which had exhausted him, and the rest were a large selection of cuts and bruises that would heal in time.

"What about Inara Village?" a woman screamed, her eyes wide with fear. "They need help too!"

Gunther looked up. "Which way is Inara?" he asked.

The woman pointed.

Gunther handed a wad of bandages to François. "We can't leave anyone behind. François, stay here and keep helping the injured. I need to find Marty."

François nodded, already moving to the next patient. Gunther stood and scanned the crowd, spotting Marty and Surjan organizing a group near the docks. He pushed through the throng of people, urgency driving him forward.

"Marty!" Gunther called out, grabbing his attention. "We need to rescue Inara Village. They're probably in a world of hurt."

Marty's face hardened with resolve and he turned to Surjan, whispered something to him.

The large Sikh snapped his fingers at the nearby villagers and spoke out loudly, "Marty, gather a team. We're heading to Inara."

Marty nodded, quickly rallying a group of able-bodied Neshili. "Everyone, follow us. Bring whatever you can to help—boats, ropes, anything."

Gunther raced after them as the group moved swiftly, adrenaline fueling their steps as they headed toward the path leading up the coast to Inara Village. The rising water made the journey treacherous, and they had to wade through knee-deep currents, but they pressed on, driven by the cries for help that grew louder as they neared the village.

When they arrived, the scene was worse than Gunther had imagined. Homes were partially submerged, and people clung to rooftops and trees, desperately trying to stay above the water. Surjan shouted instructions, his voice cutting through the chaos.

"Get the boats closer! We need to start evacuating them now!"

Surjan led the way, helping an elderly woman down from a roof and into a waiting boat. "We'll get you to safety," he assured her. "Just hold on."

Gunther and Marty worked together, pulling people from the floodwaters and guiding them to the boats. The Neshili warriors, strong and determined, moved swiftly, saving as many as they could.

A child's cry caught Gunther's attention. He turned to see a young boy clinging to a piece of driftwood, his eyes wide with terror. Surjan saw the boy, too, and didn't hesitate. He plunged into the deeper water, swimming to the child and lifting him onto his shoulders.

"You're safe now," he said, his voice steady despite the chaos around them. "I've got you."

They moved methodically, ensuring no one was left behind. The few small boats they'd carried to the village filled quickly, each one making trips back to the main docks where rescue and organization efforts were underway.

As the last of the villagers were evacuated, Surjan looked around, ensuring no one remained. Satisfied, he signaled to the others, and they began the final trek back to either the docks or higher ground.

When they arrived, exhausted but triumphant, the Neshili cheered.

Many of the Neshili clapped Surjan's back and smiled. Others cheered. "Surjan! Our Lion King!"

It was a miracle that none of the villagers had died in the flooding, although several llamas had perished, and were being cooked for the villagers' consumption.

As night fell, the island's survivors huddled together, their spirits bolstered for the moment by the large fires and full bellies.

The water had temporarily stopped rising, and tomorrow would bring some decisions.

Gunther still had a nagging feeling of concern as he watched the campfires crackle and a llama turning on a spit.

⇥ CHAPTER ⇤
TWELVE

Kareem's heart pounded with a mixture of excitement and trepidation as he descended into the tunnels beneath the palace. He had overheard Surjan talking about some of the things Queen Halpa had told him. There was some cryptic talk about a portal hidden in these labyrinthine depths that had struck him as interesting. His previous encounter with the Grays had been harrowing—he had allowed himself to be kidnapped, dragged through these very tunnels, trying to gather as much information as possible before escaping just in time to rejoin a would-be rescue party made of Surjan, Marty, and Gunther. Little did they realize that he hadn't needed rescuing. He had had everything under control. Now, he was back, driven by a burning curiosity and the tantalizing prospect of finding this portal.

The tunnels felt different this time, even more otherworldly. The sound of rushing water was loud throughout the maze and streams poured across every floor, but the wells within the complex seemed to be deep enough to absorb the flow.

Kareem imagined a portal similar to the one that had brought them to this strange land. If he found it, could it be their ticket back to safety? He chuckled at the thought of François's reaction—how much would the Frenchman pay for a way back home?

As he ventured deeper, the air grew cooler, and the walls seemed to close in around him. Even though there was utterly no way for light to penetrate into these halls, Kareem saw a faint glow coming off the walls.

He'd detected the faint light the first time he was down here, and it was just enough for him to be able to navigate in the darkness.

No torch required.

Then again, a torch would have almost certainly gotten him unnecessary attention down here since the Grays didn't seem to need any light, either.

Having gone as far as he'd gone in his previous travels, Kareem panned his gaze across the ancient stone, taking in the new surroundings.

He moved forward.

Every now and then, he paused to listen, straining to catch any sound that might indicate he was not alone. Any sounds of motion he might have heard were masked by the rush of running water.

Kareem moved silently, his senses on high alert. He came across carvings and symbols etched into the walls—remnants of a long-forgotten civilization. Some of the symbols looked familiar, things that resembled the tunnels he'd spent so much time excavating. Marty would probably pay a small fortune to get a look at the carvings.

Then again, maybe he could talk Marty into coming down here with him. The Chinese Jew wasn't a bad sort, and tried to be fair with the team. Maybe the symbols spelled out information to help find the portal?

Kareem froze midstep as he sensed something. The air hummed with energy, an almost palpable sensation that made the hairs on the back of his neck stand up.

He reached a fork in the tunnels and hesitated, trying to figure out which path to take. To the left, the tunnel sloped downward, and a faint, rhythmic hum emanated from its depths. To the right, the tunnel remained level, but the air was colder, and the darkness seemed more impenetrable. Trusting his instincts, Kareem chose the left path and continued his descent.

The farther he went, the louder the hum became. It sounded almost like an engine, but in this ancient place? Impossible. Or was it? Alien technology was beyond his understanding, but he had seen its capabilities. His pulse quickened as he followed the sound.

As he moved deeper, he noticed more signs of the Grays' presence—discarded tools, more strange markings on the walls, and occasional glimpses of their strange, iridescent blood.

It wasn't blood, per se . . . when these things died, just like the

Egyptian monstrosities, they turned into sludge. But the dried remnants on the floor, they held that same smell of alien death.

Had some ancient fight occurred here?

With his pulse racing, Kareem knew that he was getting closer to something significant. The tunnels twisted and turned, each bend bringing him closer to the source of the hum.

He came across a small chamber, partially collapsed, with rubble strewn across the floor. In the center of the chamber lay a strange object, half-buried in the debris. It was nearly the size of a small car.

Kareem approached cautiously.

The device emitted a faint glow, and as he examined it, he noticed a series of buttons and symbols. He resisted the urge to press any, knowing that one wrong move could spell disaster.

He stared at the device, for a moment wishing some of the others were here to look at this, to explain what it was. Kareem had no idea what he was looking at, yet the humming noise was louder than ever, and it was calling him.

With some reluctance, Kareem pried himself away from the strange object and pressed on.

He encountered what at first seemed like a dead end; a large slab of stone had fallen from the ceiling in years past and beyond it lay another narrow passage.

With some effort, he squeezed past the obstacle, finding himself in a part of the tunnels that felt like they'd not been explored in ages. There was a layer of grime everywhere, and the air smelled stale. The hum was louder now, reverberating through the walls and filling the air with a sense of urgency.

He moved cautiously. A bioluminescent mold clinging to the damp walls lit his way. The glow coming from the fungus pulsed in time with the hum, creating an eerie, otherworldly atmosphere. The passage narrowed further, forcing Kareem to duck and weave around protruding rocks. His senses were on high alert, every nerve in his body tingling with anticipation.

Suddenly, he heard soft, shuffling footsteps echoing through the tunnel. He froze, listening intently. The footsteps grew louder, and he pressed himself against the wall. Two Grays appeared around the bend, their large, black eyes gleaming in the dim light. They seemed to be guarding something.

Kareem held his breath, watching them for a moment. They stood beside a narrow doorway, their attention focused inward. Taking a deep breath, he crept closer, his sharpened ankh ready. With swift, silent movements, he lunged. The first Gray crumpled silently as Kareem's knife found its mark. The second turned, too late, as Kareem drove the blade into its chest. They fell without a sound, and Kareem took a moment to catch his breath, wiping the sweat from his brow.

The passageway was filled with the scent of death as the aliens' corpses bubbled and dissolved right in front of Kareem's eyes.

The hum was louder now, almost overwhelming. His senses drew him forward, and eventually, he saw a passage that he'd not explored before. He spied a long, impenetrably dark passage with a crack of light at its end.

There was something different about this tunnel. The rock was different. It held none of the glow he'd found in the prior passageways, and he couldn't see a thing between where he was standing and the end of the passage.

For all he knew, there was a bottomless pit between him and his humming objective.

Slowly, Kareem advanced, carefully testing the ground as he placed one foot in front of the other.

He was utterly blind in this passageway.

Even though he knew that there was a wall within a few feet to his left or right, he couldn't detect it. Kareem couldn't see the floor he was standing on.

It was as if some sorcerer had cast a darkness spell over this entire place and his gaze couldn't penetrate it.

Kareem moved cautiously, his heart racing. As he approached the end of the passage, it become obvious that the crack of light was from a door that was slightly ajar. An unnatural light was pouring forth, yet it didn't illuminate his approach whatsoever.

This was something different from anything he'd experienced aboveground. Something utterly alien.

Just as Kareem took his final step, reaching the door, the ground beneath him began to quake. Dust and small stones fell from the ceiling, but he pressed on. He pushed the door open a fraction more, peering inside.

The room beyond was bathed in a soft, pulsating glow. Strange symbols adorned the walls, and in the center of the room stood a large metallic arch that hummed with energy. It looked like a portal, similar to the one that had brought them here, and there was a white swirling glow within the arch beckoning him.

Kareem's mind raced. Could this be his way home? He had to find out. Just as he stepped closer to examine the portal, the ground shook violently, and he struggled to stay on his feet. Rocks and debris began to fall from the ceiling, crashing around him.

His heart pounded in his chest as the realization hit him—he had found something monumental, but it seemed like the entire chamber was collapsing.

Kareem dove to his right as a large chunk of rock slammed onto the ground.

Before Kareem could move out of the way, another rock smashed down, ripping his tunic as he backpedaled from the collapsing chamber.

Kareem took one last look at the glowing portal, committing it to memory, before turning to make his escape.

He sprinted back into the darkened passage. Several times he almost lost his balance as he tripped over debris that he couldn't see.

The quaking earth threatening to swallow him whole.

Surjan awoke with a start, his senses on high alert.

The room was dark, the faintest glimmer of light coming through the closed shutters. His sheets smelled of salt and sweat. He heard nothing.

The quiet of the borrowed room was unsettling, but after all the chaos resulting from the flooding, hundreds of upset and displaced people, and the uncertainty of what the morning would bring, the emptiness of this bedroom was a welcome respite. For the first time in what felt like ages, he had managed to find some peace, away from the relentless pressures of leadership and the queen's unwanted advances. He had caught some much-needed sleep, and needed more, but he felt a tension in the air.

Something was amiss.

Surjan sat up as he detected the faintest sound, a barely perceptible shuffle. His muscles tensed as he strained to locate the source. Before he could fully react, the door to his chamber burst open, and two shadowy figures lunged at him, daggers gleaming in the dim light.

Surjan rolled off the bed, narrowly avoiding the first strike. The assassin's blade sliced through the air where his head had been moments before. He landed on the floor, already in a crouch, and sprang up with a feral intensity.

The first assassin, cloaked and masked, advanced with a series of quick, calculated slashes. Surjan deflected the blows with his forearms, moving with the fluid grace of a practiced fighter. He grabbed the assassin's wrist, twisting it violently. The dagger clattered to the floor, and with a swift, powerful motion, Surjan drove his elbow into the assassin's throat. The man crumpled, gasping for breath.

The second assassin came at him from the side, taking advantage of the distraction. Surjan felt a searing pain as the attacker's blade nicked his shoulder. Ignoring the wound, he spun around, catching the second attacker off guard. He delivered a crushing blow to the assassin's temple, stunning him. Seizing the moment, Surjan wrapped his arm around the attacker's neck and twisted sharply. The sickening crack of vertebrae echoed in the small room.

Breathing heavily, Surjan turned back to the first assassin, who had recovered enough to draw a second blade from his boot. The man lunged desperately, but Surjan sidestepped and caught him in a viselike grip. With a swift, brutal motion, he snapped the assassin's neck, the body collapsing lifelessly to the floor.

Just as Surjan stood over the fallen assassins, the door burst open again, and four Neshili warriors, armed with spears, stormed into the chamber. They halted abruptly, their eyes wide with shock at the sight of the two dead assassins at Surjan's feet.

The warriors exchanged uneasy glances before stepping over the bodies. Their discomfort was palpable as they formed a semicircle around Surjan, their spears pointed downward but ready.

Young Piyam, who was the senior warrior of the four, spoke with a voice that barely concealed his apprehension. "King Surjan, you must come with us. The royal council has summoned you."

Surjan wiped the sweat from his brow, his gaze steady and unflinching. "Why does the council summon me in the middle of the night?" he demanded, his tone hard. "And who are these two who attacked me?"

One of the warriors knelt beside one of the bodies, removed the cloth mask, revealing a youthful face. A teenager. He looked up at Piyam and shook his head.

Piyam shifted uncomfortably, his grip tightening on his spear. "We do not know, but the queen herself has ordered this. We are to bring you before them immediately."

Surjan took a deep breath, his mind racing. The council's summoning could mean any number of things, none of them probably good.

"Beware the spider's bite."

The prior king's warning replayed in his mind. Queen Halpa was up to no good, of that much he was certain. Surjan nodded curtly. "Lead the way."

The warriors parted to let him pass, their expressions a mix of respect and fear. As they walked through the darkened corridors of the palace, Surjan couldn't shake the feeling that whatever awaited him before the royal council would likely be deadlier than the would-be assassins he had just faced. The brief respite he'd found in this hidden room, away from the queen's machinations and the endless turmoil, seemed like a distant memory as he stepped into the unknown.

⇥ CHAPTER ⇤
THIRTEEN

Marty's nostrils flared as he and the rest of the party, apart from Surjan, were marched into the grand chamber of the royal council. The stern-faced guards flanked them, their expressions unreadable. The chamber itself was about thirty feet square and the furniture had been rearranged. Gone were the divans in a circle, suggesting conversation and conference.

Outside, the dawn was obscured behind sheets of rain.

Now arrayed around the back wall were sturdy-looking wooden chairs with a single oversized chair encrusted with glistening uncut stones and pearls. Halpa sat on the throne, the wooden chairs filled with the Neshili elders, most of whom Marty recognized.

The room was filled with tense silence, broken almost immediately by the echoing footsteps of a new set of warriors.

A murmuring arose among the councilmembers as Surjan walked into the room with a grim determination in his step, escorted by a foursome of spear-wielding guards.

The soldiers who had drummed Marty and others from their room had offered no word of explanation.

Halpa sat elevated above the council members, regal and imposing. Her eyes, cold and calculating, locked onto Surjan as he was brought to the center of the room. The murmurs of the assembled councilors ceased as the queen rose to speak.

"King Surjan," she began, her voice dripping with accusation, "you have failed us. Your magic, which was supposed to protect this island, has faltered. The flooding that has brought chaos to our people is proof of your failure."

"That didn't take long," Lowanna muttered.

Marty felt a shiver run down his spine. The queen's words cut through the air like a blade, and the atmosphere in the chamber grew heavier. The queen's tone was accusatory and bordering on venomous. This woman was undoubtedly the one in charge of these people, so why the charade of needing a king? Why the charade that the gods or the magical power of the king had anything to do with who sat on the throne? How did they even get into this situation?

He looked over at François, who stood beside him, and the man's face held a confident yet serene expression. The Frenchman stepped forward, his voice calm and composed.

"Your Majesty," François began, his voice carrying a hypnotic quality that seemed to draw everyone's attention.

Even Marty felt a sense of near-compulsion as the liquid words spilled from the man's tongue.

"If I may speak on behalf of King Surjan?"

The queen's eyes narrowed, but she gave a curt nod. François turned to the assembled council, his voice taking on a captivating rhythm as he addressed them.

"Queen Halpa, elder councilors, I am François, speaker of wisdom, keeper of lore of the natural world. I am familiar with the things that are happening around us. We are witnessing a great change, a natural phenomenon that is beyond any one man's control," he explained. "We are at the end of a great ice age. The climate is warming, and with that comes significant changes to our world. Allow me to explain."

He paused, allowing his words to sink in. The councilors leaned forward, their expressions wide-eyed with curiosity and bafflement at the same time.

It had largely been unspoken among the team members, but Marty had noticed more than just the physical changes to François. It was easy to see that the man had shed twenty years from his appearance, but Marty saw that subtler things had changed: at times, something about the Frenchman's voice became hypnotic. Listening to François, he could imagine how the sirens of mythology might have lured sailors to their death.

It was obvious to see that hypnotic power were being employed now as Marty noticed the tension in the councilors' faces beginning to ease, their focus entirely on François.

Even other members of the team and the guards were focused on the French financier-turned-adventurer.

It was only Queen Halpa who seemed unaffected.

"In the far north," François continued, "there are massive sheets of ice—vast expanses that stretch farther than the eye can see. These ice sheets are unimaginably large, greater than the size of our entire island many times over."

The queen interjected, her voice sharp. "What has this to do with our flooding?"

François met her gaze without flinching. "Your Majesty, these ice sheets are melting. Sometimes, they crack and massive pieces break off, falling into the ocean. You have seen these chunks of ice yourself. You have all seen them. This sudden influx of ice causes the sea levels to rise abruptly."

He turned his focus back to the council, his voice resonating through the chamber. "The iceberg that recently slammed into our island is but a small fragment of these immense ice sheets. Imagine, if you will, an iceberg so vast it dwarfs our island. When such a mass collapses into the sea, the resulting waves and rising waters can reach far and wide. In the short term, the waves will strike and then withdraw. We have seen this. But eventually, as more and more ice melts into water, the ocean levels will simply rise, and the waters will cover Nesha."

François's explanation was met with stunned silence. These common people might not grasp the full science, but they understood the scale of what he described.

The queen glanced at her councilors on either side of her and shook her head.

Marty saw the queen's expression shift as François's words painted a vivid picture.

"It is not Surjan's magic that keeps the water at bay," François said, his voice firm. "That is a higher power, a force of nature beyond our control. King Surjan's role is to lead us, to guide us through these challenges, not to control the elements themselves."

An elder councilor, his face lined with age and wisdom, seemed to snap out of his stupor. He stepped forward, his voice challenging. "How can we fight the water, keeper of lore? What are we to do against nature itself?"

François turned to him, his expression earnest. "We must adapt, wise elder. We must build barriers, find higher ground, and prepare for the changes that are coming. We cannot fight the water, but we can work with the world, using our knowledge and strength to protect our people."

A general murmuring ensued.

François turned to the council and raised a hand. "If I may, I would like to call upon a witness. Someone who can testify to the fact that the flooding predates our arrival."

The queen's eyes narrowed, but she nodded. A Neshili woman, an elderly woman named Ilyana, stepped forward. Her weathered face and steady gaze spoke of a lifetime of experience and observation.

"Ilyana," François said gently, "please tell the council how you and I met."

"You bound my wounds," the old woman said. "During the storm."

"Thank you," François told her.

"And you rescued my grandchildren," she continued. "And that one saved my llama." She pointed at Lowanna.

"Thank you," François said again. "Will you please tell the council what you have witnessed regarding the flooding?"

Ilyana nodded and addressed the council, her voice strong despite her age. "The flooding started long before these outsiders arrived. It has been growing worse each season, steadily encroaching on our lands. I have lived on this island for over seventy turns of the heavenly wheel, and I can tell you that these floods are not the result of King Surjan's magic failing. It is something else entirely."

The council members murmured among themselves, and Marty saw a flicker of frustration cross the queen's face. François continued, seizing the moment.

"Your Majesty, elders of the council, the changes we are experiencing are part of a larger pattern. The climate is shifting, the ice is melting, and the seas are rising. These are forces beyond our control, but with understanding and preparation, we can adapt and protect our people."

The queen interjected again, her voice less assured. "But how do we know you speak the truth? How can we be certain about this direction when our lives are at stake?"

François's voice remained steady. "I am sorry, Your Majesty, but this is the reality we face. The floods will get worse in our current position if we do nothing, regardless of whatever magic we use."

The elder who had spoken earlier now looked thoughtful. "If what you say is true, then we must learn to live with these changes. Adapt. We cannot blame the king for the will of nature itself."

François nodded. "Exactly. We must work together, use our knowledge and skills to build barriers, relocate to safer grounds, and prepare for the future. This is not about blaming King Surjan or anyone else. It is about survival and adaptation."

The council fell silent, considering François's words.

Marty felt a surge of pride and gratitude at the Frenchman's helpfulness in a sticky situation. François had not only defended Surjan but also provided a path forward for the queen and the council to think on.

The queen's expression softened.

As the councilors fell to debating among themselves, one of the younger warriors stepped forward. "What about our magic? It can't be totally useless, can it? Can it help us fight what the water is doing?"

François shook his head gently. "Magic is a powerful tool, but it cannot stop the forces of nature. We must use our magic wisely, to aid in our preparations and protections, but we must also rely on practical measures and cooperation."

The chamber buzzed with murmurs as the council discussed the matter. Marty exchanged a glance with Surjan, who looked relieved but resolute. They had faced countless dangers together, and now they stood on the precipice of a new challenge. With François's newfound eloquence, they had bought some time.

Marty wasn't exactly confident about the next steps, but all he needed to do was look at the malicious glare coming from Queen Halpa and he knew one thing for sure about how to plot his course of action: he must do the opposite of whatever it was she had in mind.

The chamber of the royal council was filled with tense anticipation. The queen had reluctantly stepped back, allowing the council to deliberate on François's compelling explanation of the flooding. But the air was still thick with unease, and it wasn't long before Tudhal, the high priest, stepped forward with an air of grim authority. The queen's gaze followed the rail-thin councilor, her expression one of satisfaction.

"The omens are clear," Tudhal proclaimed, his voice echoing through the chamber. "There are no places of safety on these islands from the wrath of the gods. The gods have shown me visions that the king's magic has failed. Our protector's power is no more. There is nowhere to hide from their wrath unless we appease the gods with sacrifices, starting with the newcomers."

Marty felt a chill run down his spine. The priest's words were met with gasps and murmurs of fear from the guards and some of the councilors themselves. He stepped forward, his heart pounding in his chest.

"High priest," Marty began, his voice strong and clear, "I too have had visions. The gods have spoken to me, and they have shown me a path to safety."

All eyes turned to Marty, and he felt the weight of their gazes. He took a deep breath and continued, "The gods will lead us to safety in the south. They have shown me a place where we can find refuge from the rising waters."

Surjan, standing beside Marty, seized the moment. "We must act now," he declared. "Let us go to the ships and prepare to leave. We cannot waste any more time."

François stepped forward, lending his voice to the moment. "Elders of the Neshili, listen to your king! We have the means to survive this crisis, but we must act together. Follow King Surjan, and we will find safety. Do anything else, and the sacrifices will be the entirety of the Neshili population itself."

The people crowding the chamber, already mesmerized by François's earlier words, were now fully rallied. Murmurs of agreement rippled through the chamber, and the people began to move, driven by a renewed sense of purpose and hope.

The queen's face turned red with fury, her eyes blazing with anger. She stepped forward, her voice trembling with barely contained rage. "A mistake has been made in appointing this king. This must be rectified. Blood sacrifices at the temple will appease the gods and ensure our survival."

The high priest nodded and yelled above the din of the chamber, "I agree with the queen's direction. We cannot listen to the false king. The gods have need of such sacrifices before things will return to normal."

Lowanna rushed up to François and whispered something into his ear.

Marty's blood ran cold as he took stock of his surroundings and gathered himself for a fight. The hairs on the back of his neck stood on end as François took a step forward.

The Frenchman pointed at the high priest and yelled, "You're blaspheming against the will of the gods, and they will not bear a priest of theirs lying on their behalf!"

The moment François lowered his arm, the chamber filled with a blinding flash of light.

Marty was pushed back as a loud clap of thunder erupted, mixed with the queen's scream and yelling from others.

Tudhal, the high priest, lay on the ground, his robes smoking and his body convulsing.

Gunther rushed forward, and before Marty could suggest that maybe they were better off not healing the guy who wanted them dead, a glow bloomed from the German's hands and seemed to get absorbed by the no-longer convulsing high priest.

Surjan stepped forward, addressing everyone in the chamber with a commanding voice. "The gods have spoken and shown who is speaking untruths. We cannot waste time on false prophecies and deceit. We must move forward and prepare to leave. The safety of our people is our highest priority."

The guards and others in the chamber, still reeling from the shock of the high priest's collapse, slowly began to rally around Surjan's leadership. The queen's face was a mask of fury, but she knew she had been outmaneuvered. Her personal guards moved to her side, their expressions wary.

Surjan walked up to Marty and was about to say something when Marty patted the large man on the shoulder and murmured, "You and François handled that well."

François glanced over at Lowanna, who held an expression of disgust and was busy staring at the queen and high priest talking to each other. "I was just playing politician, it was Lowanna's idea to insert her finger-wiggling pyrotechnics, which probably sealed the deal."

"The water is still rising," Surjan whispered. "This island is low ground, and if the sea level rises much it will go under. I think you're right about your vision, Marty. We need to get the people to the ships and ensure we have enough supplies for the journey. Time is of the essence."

"You're right. That's our priority." Marty shifted his gaze toward the queen. "But realize we also need to deal with that queen of yours. She's dangerous and probably still has influence with the people."

"I know." Surjan's face held a grim expression. "Trust me, I don't like having to look over my shoulder every waking moment of the day."

"Speaking of that," Marty said as he panned his gaze across the chamber. "Where's Kareem?"

⊰ CHAPTER ⊱
FOURTEEN

The morning sun cast long shadows over the harbor as Surjan stood on the dock, surveying the ships that would carry the Neshili away from their homeland. The rain had let up, at least for now. The air was thick with tension and worry, and the murmur of anxious voices filled the air as the Neshili gathered around, waiting for guidance.

Surjan turned to the royal council, his expression serious. "We must inspect the ships thoroughly. We can't afford any mistakes."

One of the younger council members was wringing his hands, the worry easy to read from his expression. "Your Highness—"

"Please, just call me Surjan. Now isn't the time for formality."

"Sorry, your high—um, Surjan. I'm concerned over your friend's vision. He spoke of a land to the west where we can continue gathering supplies as we travel south, but are we sure that land exists?"

"Your Highness, he has a point," the portly genealogist Ammun interjected. "Despite his obvious error. We are seafarers, we know that there is land to the west of us, and indeed we can see it as a gray line on the horizon from the western shore of this island. But those lands are occupied by savage animals and fierce tribes, who will not welcome us. This is a very large risk."

"I understand your concern." Surjan patted the fellow's shoulder. "But Marty's visions have never been wrong. They are his gift from the gods, and it would be unwise to ignore them. Besides, we have no other choices. The water levels are rising and we cannot know how far they will rise. Our salvation lies elsewhere." He motioned toward the boats.

"Let's go over the fleet and make sure the ships are in good order. Especially after the storm, it bears confirming."

The council members nodded, and they split into groups, each tasked with examining different vessels.

Surjan walked down the muddy slope toward the farthest set of docks. He spotted Marty and François talking to each other and motioned in their direction. "Hey, you two, I'm about to inspect the lead ship. You guys want to help?"

Marty clapped François's shoulder and turned to face Surjan with an amused expression. "I know next to nothing about boats, but I'll tag along."

The Frenchman nodded and said, "I used to do a fair bit of sailing in my youth. Not sure how much that experience will translate to these ships, but I'll help as much as I can."

Surjan motioned for them to follow as he trudged across the soggy terrain and pointed in the distance. "These are all pretty simple vessels. The one ahead is the largest and oldest of the fleet."

"Whoa . . ." Marty stopped mid-stride as he stared at the largest of the boats. "I've seen this kind of construction before. It reminds me of Ra's solar barque."

François tilted his head and nodded. "I think you're right. It's strange, because the construction looks much like the ship that was uncovered with the pharaoh Khufu. It's just the sail on it is fairly primitive and ragged, and the topside shelter has seen much better days."

"Those high curving ends fore and aft also make the ship look vaguely Sumerian, don't you think?"

Surjan stared at the ship and had no idea what either of them was talking about. To him the vessel looked like a long and thin version of a Viking ship, but with a crude boxlike shelter constructed on its deck to serve as a place for people and supplies to get shoved into.

"Well." Marty motioned in the direction of the boat. "King Surjan, you lead the way."

Surjan harrumphed at Marty's use of the king appellation and approached the large boat. The scent of salt and weathered wood filled the air as others busily climbed on and off the deck, loading baskets of supplies onto the vessel.

They climbed aboard, their footsteps echoing on the wooden planks. Surjan ran his hand along the railing, feeling the rough texture of the sun-bleached wood. "Just keep your eyes peeled for anything that looks out of place or might be a seaworthiness issue."

François walked up to the dual-masted setup, which had put a frown on the man's face. He focused on the llama-skin sails and rigging, his keen eyes panning up and down the masts, pushing and pulling at random pieces he came across until he nodded. "These sails are horrible, but considering what we have to deal with, I think they'll work fine. We'll need to make sure we have material to patch or replace these sails or the rigging. The journey south will be long and arduous."

Surjan's mind raced with the enormity of the task ahead. They were leaving the only homeland these people ever knew. The place that had been their sanctuary for generations.

He saw worry etched into the expressions of the Neshili loading the ship, their fear of the unknown palpable.

Marty walked up to Surjan and asked in English, "Anything got you concerned?"

"Not about the ship, per se." Surjan said. "It's about the people. We need to reassure them that everything will be fine. They need to know we have a plan, that we will lead them to safety."

Marty nodded. "You're their king, that's on you. I'll take a second position as some kind of seer of visions. It's going to probably infuriate the priests, so we'll need to try not to ruffle their feathers too much. Remember, if things work out the way we hope, we're going to leave these people behind. They need someone they can look to when things are uncertain."

"Marty is right," François noted as he walked up to them. "A succession plan is needed. That's something we'll have to work on."

"They need a new homeland. Someplace that will survive the coming floods." Surjan knew that this exodus wasn't going to be easy. That queen of his had shown her cards. She wanted him and the rest of them dead and out of the way. The priesthood itself was highly suspect, and even though they were supposed to be somehow an independent authority to the king or queen, he had the distinct impression that they were under Halpa's thumb.

François put his hand on Surjan's shoulder and leaned in close. "My friend, you realize that wife of yours is probably going to need to be taken care of, right?"

Marty gave François a severe look and shook his head. "Guys, let's focus on one thing at a time. Let's get everyone in a position to move safely off the island, and we'll worry about the rest—"

"Did you find out where Kareem was?" François asked.

Marty shook his head. "Lowanna's out looking for him. She'll find him."

Surjan sighed as the image of Halpa's pretty face bloomed in his mind's eye. Their appearance had clearly ruined whatever it was she'd been planning, and François was right.

Something would have to be done about his so-called wife.

After climbing up from the underworld, where he'd nearly been crushed by falling rocks, Kareem barely managed to evade the guards as they took the rest of the team to the council chambers. His ability to avoid detection could no longer be written off as a coincidence. This was something new.

Was he invisible? He looked at his hands. He didn't think so, but, somehow, he'd developed an innate ability to blend into shadows. Even when he wasn't actively trying, people often overlooked his presence— it was as if something about him made their eyes skip over him. From his hidden perch on the second story outside the building, Kareem had managed to peer through an open wooden shutter into the council chambers. He saw everything that happened, including the stroke of lightning that beamed down from the clouds.

That was certainly the witch's doing. Lowanna made Kareem nervous. She was quiet and dangerous in her own way. That might be something he'd have to deal with eventually, but now was not the time. His focus was on another self-appointed mission.

Kareem moved through the shadows of the palace with a singular purpose. His hands trembled with a mix of determination and anticipation. The queen and the high priest, Tudhal, were the architects of chaos, and their grip on the people had to be broken. His plan was simple but dangerous: he had to kill them both.

He also knew this wasn't the kind of thing he could have asked permission to do. François might have said it was the right thing, but Marty and the others were too kindhearted—or maybe cowardly—to do what needed to be done. This was what Kareem was here for. His skills were honed and ready to be used.

Though he hadn't necessarily anticipated needing this outcome to play out, he had watched and waited, studying their routines, giving him the data he needed for this act. The queen was generally surrounded by guards, a constant, impenetrable barrier. Tudhal was often by her side, their unholy alliance evident in their every move. But today, Kareem saw an opportunity. Tudhal was to undertake a solitary prayer in the inner sanctum of the temple, a rare moment when he would be alone.

The prayer along with the gods would almost certainly turn into cavorting with the queen.

Kareem slipped through the palace corridors, his sharpened ankh hidden beneath his tunic. He moved with the stealth of a predator, his senses heightened by the adrenaline coursing through his veins. The dim light of torches cast flickering shadows on the walls, but Kareem's focus remained unbroken.

He reached the temple and paused in the shadows, his eyes fixed on the entrance to the inner sanctum. The heavy wooden doors stood slightly ajar, and Kareem could hear the faint murmurs of Tudhal's prayer. He took a deep breath, steadying himself for what was to come.

With silent steps, he entered the temple, his eyes almost immediately adjusting to the dim light. The sanctum was a small, sacred space, filled with the scent of incense and the faint glow of glowing embers. Tudhal knelt before the altar, his back to Kareem, completely absorbed in his ritual.

Kareem approached slowly, his hand tightening around the ankh. Each step felt like an eternity, the distance between him and Tudhal closing with agonizing slowness. When he was finally close enough, he drew the ankh from his tunic and raised it high.

In one swift, fluid motion, Kareem plunged the sharpened ankh upward into the back of Tudhal's skull, just at the base. The priest's thin body went rigid, then collapsed, lifeless, to the floor. The prayer was abruptly cut off, replaced by the deafening silence of death.

A rush of euphoria washed over Kareem as he stood over Tudhal's corpse. His vision sharpened, and his hearing became acutely sensitive, as if the act had awakened something within him. He felt more alive, more powerful than ever before. The years of pent-up anger and frustration seemed to melt away, replaced by a newfound clarity and strength.

Kareem quickly wiped the ankh clean and concealed it once more.

He took a moment to steady his breathing when suddenly the door to the temple opened.

"Tudhal?"

It was the queen!

She was early.

Not having a chance to do anything with the body, Kareem slunk rapidly from his position, blending into the shadows as he slipped out of the sanctum.

With his senses tingling, Kareem rapidly navigated the temple corridors with ease.

He reached the trellis above the temple's main hall and hid among the shadows, watching intently.

With his jaw clenched, Kareem felt a surge of fury course through him as the queen walked into the inner sanctum.

This wasn't how it was supposed to go.

He was going to kill the priest, hide his body, and lie in wait for the viperous woman.

It was only in this cloistered chamber that the two were ever alone.

Halpa moved with an air of authority, her eyes scanning the darkness of the inner sanctum. "Tudhal?" she called out, concern lacing her voice. "Are you all right after what happened earlier?"

Then a sharp, anguished cry echoed through the temple as the queen spotted Tudhal's lifeless body.

She rushed over to the corpse, shrieking. Moments later, her guards rushed into the chamber behind her.

Kareem smiled as he witnessed the queen's face contort with rage and fear, her control slipping in the face of this unexpected blow.

"Find who did this!" she screamed, her voice reverberating through the temple. "Find the murderer and bring him to me! He will pay with his life!"

The guards sprang into action, fanning out to search the temple grounds. The queen, her face a mask of fury, turned and stormed out of the sanctum, her guards trailing behind her like shadows.

Kareem watched as they disappeared from view, a frustrated grimace playing on his lips. The first part of his plan had been executed, but the opportunity to kill the queen had been spoiled by her early arrival. He felt a surge of frustration as he slipped from his hiding place, his senses keen and his resolve to finish what he'd started unshaken.

⇥CHAPTER⇤
FIFTEEN

Gunther was talking. Talking to someone.

About an invitation.

"Fire!"

The shout cut through Gunther's sleep-fogged perception.

It wasn't over. Gunther could still say yes.

But he was afraid.

"Fire! Fire!"

Gunther snapped awake and rolled from his cot, tangling himself in sweat-soaked linen. The air was so wet with rain and spray, he could barely inhale. He thrashed his way to his feet, climbing out of the light blanket and lurching from his sleeping cubicle into the hallway. The world spun about him.

The weasel Shush scurried back and forth in the hall, shrieking. For a moment, Gunther had the impression that the weasel had been the one shouting fire, but then he finally got air into his lungs and the world settled into place.

Lowanna burst from her own cubicle. "Where?" she asked.

"Where what?" Gunther countered.

The other party members crashed into the hall, rubbing sleep from their eyes and elbowing each other.

Lowanna squealed and chittered at Shush, who chittered back. "Follow me!"

Gunther followed close on Lowanna's heels, descending to the courtyard and into a curtain of rain flinging itself sideways across the landscape. Yellow light snapped on the other side of the shrouds of water.

"Fire!" Gunther heard again.

The fire was among the ships. Some of the boats seemed to be drifting away, though he had a hard time seeing clearly in the darkness and the storm.

Turn back, Gunther heard another voice. *Come down.*

"Fire!" he yelled, and raced down through the town toward the water.

He got separated from Lowanna and found himself running alongside François. Neither man was especially fast or agile, so they slid down together through mud and rain. Lightning flashes illuminated hulks of ice drifting toward the shore, and three ships putting laboriously out to sea, pulling their oars in the rain.

"Time to stretch yourself, Gunther!" François shouted.

"I can't run any faster!"

"I don't mean that! I mean, what can you do magically?"

"Heal!" Gunther snapped back immediately. "Bless food!"

"You can do more than that!" François shouted into the wind. "You can stun opponents. Can you put a hole in a ship? Can you extinguish a fire?"

They slid to a muddy halt just out of reach of the flames that were devouring the lower part of the town but especially the harbor. Gunther stared over the burning boats to the water and saw the Neshili. They struggled to put out the flames but they also waved to the departing ships, screaming for help.

Queen Halpa leaned against a rope of one of the ships, watching the shore as she drifted away.

"So, Halpa chose the Noah option before we did," François murmured. To Gunther, he said, "How about it? Can you strike the queen dead?"

"Let's get closer." Gunther ran down to the harbor and turned to run along it. He jumped over nets and pots and little boats, and François ran with him. Ahead of them and to the right, Gunther saw Surjan organizing warriors on the shore.

Gunther raced out along a spit of sand. He got as close as he was going to get to the disappearing ships, just as Halpa stepped to the edge of the deck and raised her voice.

"My people!" she called. "This land is cursed! The magic of its kings has run its course! The new king, Surjan, is no better than the man he slew. The gods will have neither of them. But the gods have chosen me to lead a small remnant of you, a few chosen survivors, away to found a new city. If I can, I shall send servants back to look for you!"

"Give her palsy!" François urged. "Knock her senseless, lift her from the boat, do something!"

Gunther focused his will. He shouted every word that occurred to him. "Die! Sleep! Wither!" Finally, he shouted "Stop!" knowing it would only knock the queen down temporarily.

She duly collapsed.

At that moment, Surjan's warriors let loose a hail of darts. Men aboard the ship with atlatls returned fire, and François pulled Gunther away by the elbow. "The fire!" the Frenchman shouted into his ear. "Let Surjan fight the battle, what can we do to fight the fire?"

Gunther turned and staggered back toward the harbor. The crescent of masts and sails had become a half-moon of glowing orange, with most of the boats on fire. Gunther felt faint and leaned on François for support.

"Put the fires out," François urged him. "I know you can do it."

Gunther raised a hand and directed a wave at the flames. "Extinguish!" he cried. "Douse! Out! Retard flame!"

The fires burned on.

He closed his eyes and shook his head. "I'm sorry."

Come to the door. I can teach you how to use the door.

"Look down," François said.

Gunther looked down and saw that his own body and François's both sparkled with a metallic orange sheen.

"But I wasn't on fire," Gunther protested.

"Let's go put out the flames!" François said.

The Frenchman rushed to the nearest burning boat. The flames didn't seem to hurt him at all, so Gunther followed suit. He climbed into a flaming boat, feeling no pain or even warmth. Working directly in the flames with mud, seawater, and sails, he was able quickly to smother and douse the fire. Thinking the ship might be used to pursue the fleeing queen and her supporters, he went to raise the sail, and found that the ropes had been cut.

He looked to François, who had just finished putting out the flames on the boat he'd boarded, and held up the severed end of a line. François did the same on his ship.

There would be no pursuit, but some of the ships could be saved.

Working together, Gunther and François picked the largest burning ships and saved them from the fires. Other ships were pushed out into the bay and dragged up onto the stone shelf, where a splitting iceberg had left a pile of ice and slush. The ice was more effective than the rain at dousing the flames. Before it was finished, Marty had joined them, and with him the weasel Shush. Marty and Shush spoke to each other in Weasel and Shush helped Marty by gnawing through inconvenient ropes and fetching water pails. Most of the Neshili had also come, working together to save some semblance of a fleet.

In the chaos, Lowanna got separated from her companions.

She was up to her ankles in sucking mud. "Where is everyone?" she shouted, wiping rain from her eyes.

I am here! The voice belonged to the weasel Shush. *What do you want?*

"Take me to Surjan!" Lowanna knew the harbor was on fire, but she trusted Surjan to be at the essential action, whatever it was.

The weasel scampered along a stony elevated street whose pebbled path somehow managed not to be a morass of mud. Holding one hand pinned to her forehead like the visor of a cap, Lowanna succeeded in clearing her eyes of water in time to realize she was running into a firefight.

Darts whizzed past her.

"Get down!" Sharrum's voice barked at her, and then he dragged her to the sand behind a thick log.

She climbed to her knees and peered over the log. Sharrum crouched beside her; elsewhere on a long spit of sand, warriors sheltered behind storm-battered palm trees and even in low depressions. Ten steps away, Surjan crouched behind a large rock. A dart struck the rock and whizzed away.

On the other side of the sand, the ocean raged. They were beyond the stone of the shelf here, and three ships were beginning to pick up speed and cruise away. The warriors on the first ship were out of range and could only watch now, but the warriors on the second and third ships continued to fling darts with their atlatls.

"Lowanna!" Surjan called.

"I'm fine!" she shot back, staying low. "Stay down, they'll be gone in a minute!"

"They're stealing!" he yelled. "Food, treasure, the sacred and magical items of the Neshili!"

"Who cares?" she shot back.

"I care," murmured Sharrum beside her. The answer made her feel slightly embarrassed.

"I care!" Surjan shouted. "These are my people, and I am supposed to protect them! They're being robbed! Can you reach them?"

Lowanna looked deep into her heart. She found there were things she could do, and considered them. She was confident—she didn't know how she knew, but she knew—that she could breathe underwater if she had to. And she could use that power to board one of the ships.

But first, she'd have to cross the beach, and that would involve getting turned into a pincushion.

She saw that she could twist wood at the touch. If she were standing on the deck of one of the ships, she could twist its mast and snap it, or shatter the oarlocks to ruin the work of the rowers, or break the rudder. But she'd need to be close to be able to do that—not necessarily touching, but very short range.

And that would involve first running across the beach.

A dart struck the sand, too close to her leg for comfort. She pulled closer to the protective log, looked again—and found what she wanted.

Shouting the words she instinctively knew, Lowanna stood and charged across the beach. Black vapor rose from the ground around her and from her own flesh, hiding her within a shifting, billowing cloud. The storm winds didn't help, and would wear down the duration of the magic, but she only needed it to last long enough to get her across the beach. She could see out, as through a grimy windshield, but she knew others would have difficulty seeing in. The vapor didn't need to stay centered around her; she could direct it with her will, and she did so. She walked off-center in the cloud.

"Lowanna!" Sharrum rose from protection and dove into the cloud with her.

"Fool!" She grabbed his hand and pulled him to the side. Her actions were rewarded when two darts in quick succession fired through the center of the cloud, missing Sharrum by an arm's length.

"I can't see!" he said.

"Either lie flat or run!" she told him, but she didn't let go of his hand. She broke into a sprint and dragged him with her.

"Fire!" Surjan yelled. "Give her cover!"

The Neshili on the beach renewed their fire on the Neshili aboard the hindmost fleeing ship. Some of the shipboard snipers continued to fire at Lowanna, but the dark vapor made them miss, and most of them turned their concentration to Surjan and his men on the sand.

"We're about to dive into the water," Lowanna warned Sharrum. "Be ready! Stay down!"

She then cast her underwater breathing spell on herself. She couldn't cast it on both of them and she needed it herself. She dove into the water, Sharrum plunged in beside her, and the vapor disappeared.

Down she dove, the warrior at her side, but when he had to turn up, she found she didn't. She breathed water as she would have breathed air and swam forward comfortably.

"If I can breathe this medium," she said out loud, "surely I can speak in it."

Darts struck the waves above her but their impetus was immediately blunted by the water. The raging of the storm disappeared, replaced by gentle, but strong, currents, tugging her out toward the depths of the ocean.

She saw the third of the fleeing ships first as a shadowy bulk, oars thrashing by its sides. It took her a little effort to swim to catch up but once she reached the back of the ship, she grabbed the rudder with one hand and was able to relax. She was just below the water, but the ship's crew would be entirely focused on rowing or steering or shooting at Surjan. They'd never see her.

She took a deep breath (of water) and prepared to cast her final spell, the wood-warping charm.

A spear stabbed into her shoulder from above. Blood burst into the water, clouding her vision. She let go of the rudder, which saved her life, as it made the second spear that stabbed down from above miss her.

The ship was moving, and would quickly be gone. She cast her third spell, chanting the words and pointing at the wood she wanted warped. Three boards close together peeled back like curled shavings, like banana peels stripped away from the banana, creating a hole in the hull as big as a human torso.

She tried to swim away but found that only one of her arms would work. To her horror, she realized that she was floating to the surface. Thrashing, she tried to swim down, but the currents drew her up and she wasn't strong enough with her one arm to resist.

A second spear pierced her body, in her thigh. She screamed and broke the surface of the water, water gushing from her mouth as she yelled. She drew a moment of satisfaction from the cries of panic she heard. If she was going to die, she at least wanted to know that she sank the ship. But then prudence got the better of her and she dove again.

This time she fought down several body lengths, felt a dart narrowly miss her, and then lost her fight to the current and was swept to the surface again.

A powerful arm wrapped around her clavicle and under her arms, grabbing her and pulling her. She wasn't sure in which direction she was being pulled, but she had lost the strength to fight. She was rapidly losing the strength to do anything, and could feel her life ebbing through her shoulder and through her thigh. Any moment now, she knew she would lose consciousness.

Strong arms hoisted her into the air and she felt her heels dragging in the surf. Had the vapor returned? But now she was on the outside of it, because she couldn't see. She fell a thousand miles and then she landed hard on sand, but she barely felt the landing because she was a thousand miles away from her own body.

"Gunther!" someone yelled. Surjan.

Thudding footfalls through the ground.

Rain splashing on her face.

Then hands pressed against her shoulder and she was surrounded by angels. They shone like white fire and their faces smiled down at her. More hands pressed her thigh. More angels surrounded her and raised her up onto their shoulders until she was so close to the sun, she thought it might burn her.

Then the angels began to sing.

CHAPTER SIXTEEN

The last of the fires was extinguished and the storm slackened, without entirely ceasing. François rubbed rain from his eyes and surveyed the damage.

Surjan stood on the largest dock, barking orders to the nearby natives. The survivors from the ship that had fled but sank had been gathered up and were being held at spearpoint. Fishermen inventoried the damage done and the repairs needed to the ships left behind. Houses had been torched in the town, and François had heard that someone had set fire to the palace, too, though he couldn't see fire damage that far away in the darkness.

The water levels had risen so that it was practically even with the surface of the docks. Many of the people's homes were now claimed by the ocean floods, and there was a palpable fear among the Neshili about what was about to happen.

François shifted his thoughts to their prior threat, the Grays . . . They had taken a back seat given the immediate dangers presented by the flooding and the fires that followed. Had the Grays drowned in their underground world? Had they suffered any damage or casualties? Or had they taken the opportunity to slink from hiding and snatch vulnerable humans for their grim repast, and in chaos nobody had yet noticed?

A group of old women had been deputized to count noses and compare reports to determine who had gone with the queen, who had died in the fires, and who was unaccounted for. They went from house to house in pairs, conferring with each other in the crooked intersections.

A man tugged at François's elbow. "Forgive me, but you are the king's herald, are you not?"

François examined the newcomer. He had a complexion the color of chalk and linen, and he drooped, from top to bottom: nose, gold-ringed ears, his shoulders—his entire body seemed on the verge of dissolving into a puddle on the spot. His tunic was dyed a gentle brown. François had seen him before.

"You're one of the priests," he said. "You didn't leave with the queen. What's your name, Kazoo or something, no?"

"Kazap. I didn't leave with the others and I had no knowledge of their plan to depart," the priest said. "Very few of us did. I have been accounting for my brethren, and it seems that I am the senior priest of the temple now."

"Priests don't have to lurk at night in the Sacred Grove, waiting for a stranger to come attack them, to determine who's in charge, I guess?" François chuckled.

Kazap inclined his head. "I am not the king. But I must speak with the king, and he will want to speak with me. Will you help me get his ear?"

François knew when he was being offered authority. He led Kazap past Sharrum and another warrior standing guard and out onto the dock, where the rest of the party had gathered. Lowanna leaned on Gunther's arm and moved gingerly. With Kazap came a young woman in a yellow tunic, with a yellow shawl covering her hair.

"Surjan," François said, "this is Kazap. Sounds like he's the new high priest."

Kareem glowered at the brown-robed man and immediately put his hand to his sharpened ankh.

"After what the last high priest did to me," Surjan said, "I'm considering burning the temple."

"You don't mean that," Marty murmured, surveying the destruction of Nesha.

"Maybe not," Surjan growled. "I could be talked into it, though."

Kazap bowed at the waist. "Please allow me to talk you out of it. Such sacrilege would destroy your power as king and bring the world to ruin. You cannot offend the gods and still bear their power in the world."

"Look around you," Surjan said. "The world is already ruined."

"And only you can save it," Kazap said. "Only you can defeat the Guardian of the Hungry Dead and bring peace back to our land."

"You mean the gray ones?" François murmured, not particularly liking the idea of having anything to do with those alien creatures. As far as he was concerned, the farther they were from them, the better.

"Correct," Kazap confirmed.

"This is what we should do," Gunther said.

"'We'?" Surjan turned on the German. "'We'? Are you seriously suggesting that *we* should go down into the dungeon and fight some giant-sized version of those Gray creatures?"

"When have we ever left you to fight alone?" François asked. "If there's a fight to be had, it should be as an organized group, but I don't see the point of going down there at all, if I'm being honest."

"No," Kazap protested. "Some duties fall to the king alone."

"The Grays are not the problem," Marty said. "The problem is the rain."

Surjan shifted his gaze from the priest who seemed to be itching for a fight with the creatures belowground and focused on Marty. "I'm not afraid to go down and face whatever's down there, but is there really a point?" He hitched his thumb toward Kazap and switched to English, "Other than this maniac who bloody well wants us to go to war with these things, is there any reason to go down there?" He panned his gaze across the team, focusing on each and every person.

"I don't understand, Your Highness," Kazap said with a confused expression. "You're speaking in a manner I don't recognize."

Surjan motioned at the man dismissively. "Kazap, give me some space. I'm discussing something with these others that are only for their ears. I'll fill you in on things afterward."

The short priest stepped back, his mouth opened as if to say something, then he snapped it shut and walked away. The young woman in yellow followed him.

"So don't go back," François suggested. "Maybe it's time for the Noah maneuver. Marty had a vision with a destination."

"Noah? As in build an ark?" Surjan asked.

"We can get in the boats and go," François said.

"Those visions with the giant cliffs of ice have happened several times, each leaving me with a feeling of more urgency than the last," Marty admitted.

"Guys..." Gunther's face held an embarrassed expression. "I should probably have mentioned something earlier, but I've been hearing something in my head. It's not, I suppose, unlike Marty's visions, but this is almost all oral communication. Just words, you know? I hear a voice. Someone or something is trying to get me to go down below to some door. It says it will teach me to use the door, that that will take us where we need to go."

François frowned. "That seems highly risky, and given the flooding that's been happening, those Grays are probably on the verge of climbing out of their holes and causing chaos to everyone remaining here."

Surjan noticed Kareem shifting nervously while trying to blend into the shadows of the nearest tree. "Kareem, you have something to say?"

The young man shook his head.

"I can't tell you how strong the message is that I'm getting to go where those cliffs of ice are," Marty said. "Oddly enough, this part of the world is getting inundated with giant icebergs drifting from the north, but our target is seemingly all the way south. The South Pole. It won't be hard to find if we are where we think we are, simply just follow the coast until there's no more coast to follow."

"Queen Halpa seems to have sailed off south with her cronies," Gunther said with a frown. "It's likely a coincidence, but maybe it isn't."

"And what will be at the South Pole, exactly?" Surjan asked.

"The next thing," Marty said with a shrug. "We didn't know exactly what we were going to meet up with at the end when we traipsed across North Africa."

"What are you imagining?" Lowanna asked. "Some machine that lets us solve climate change?"

"Probably not, but I'm not sure." Marty shook his head. "Hopefully it gets us one step closer to getting back home. Frankly, that's all I really want."

"Well, what are we doing with all these people? To me they all look somewhat like ancestors of the Inuit, but I feel an obligation to not lead them into harm," Surjan said. "Obviously, our immediate goal is to save these people from an environmental disaster by taking them south with us, but to what end?"

Marty glanced at Lowanna. "Do you know when the first human inhabitants occupied South America?"

Lowanna shook her head. "Not particularly, that's not a part of the world I'm most familiar with. I think I recall reading about mummies reclaimed from parts of the Andes that were six or seven thousand years old."

"Realistically, there's no reason we couldn't just transplant these folks to the southern continent and call it a good deed done. That shouldn't cause any rifts in the space-time continuum."

"Space-time continuum?" François rolled his eyes. "Dr. Cohen, please leave the science stuff to me."

"Fair enough, but these folks will probably need to be taught new survival skills for whatever the differences are," Marty pointed out with a grin. "François, you can show them how to hunt saber-tooths together."

"Don't joke," François said. "The Smilodon, otherwise known as the saber-toothed tiger, didn't go extinct until ten thousand years before we were born. They're likely still around, and yes, they did roam throughout the Americas, both North and South."

"So, it's decided?" Surjan asked. "We're heading south?"

The party mostly nodded in silent agreement, though Surjan noticed the troubled expression on Gunther's face.

Kazap approached them again, the woman in yellow next to him. She stared intently in Surjan's direction. She looked familiar, but with such a small community of just a few hundred people, many were related to each other and tended to look very similar. He quickly filled Kazap in on the plans, and all things considered, he didn't seem to have a strong reaction.

"It does not matter which road you choose," Kazap said with a disapproving expression, "if you do not have the blessing of the gods."

"Fine," Surjan agreed, feeling annoyance at the man. "I won't kill you or burn down the temple. That should make the gods happy and we can continue with our plans."

Kazap shook his head. "The king's magic depends on his virility."

"I *am* virile," Surjan snarled. "What kind of nonsense are you talking about?"

"You must have a queen."

The party all fell silent and stared at the priest, while Marty grinned and shook his head.

"No, I don't need a queen," Surjan finally said. "And if I were to decide I wanted a queen, it certainly wouldn't be to prove something to you."

"Nesha is not protected by the magic of the king alone," the priest insisted, rubbing the knuckles of one hand and then the other. "It is protected by the magic of the king and queen together. Whether you are to battle the guardian or sail the seas, you can only succeed with a wife."

Lowanna chortled.

François gestured to the young woman at the priest's side. "Is this a priestess?"

"Technically, yes," the young woman said. "Because I am of the family of the queen. My name is Dawa."

François nodded. "Are you Halpa's daughter? Are you the daughter of the old king?"

"I am Halpa's sister," she said, looking at her feet. "The queen's bloodline flows through the throne as the king's flows through the grove."

"I don't need a queen," Surjan insisted.

"Am I so hideous?" Dawa pulled the shawl away from her hair, revealing what was indeed a lovely young woman, with clear eyes and a wide smile. Her chin quivered as she fought back whatever emotions she was dealing with.

Surjan sighed. "No. No, you are very pretty. But why must I continue to have my free will taken from me?"

"Is it not ever thus," Kazap asked, "for those whom the gods choose?"

Surjan hesitated. "And you, Dawa, would marry me, to save your people?"

"I wish for the power of the gods," Dawa said. "But also, the people need to follow a married king, to feel reassured. Especially now, when their queen has fled, shattering the proper order of things."

"Well, that's a surprisingly sophisticated take," François said.

Dawa looked down at her feet.

"What would this require?" Surjan asked. "I'm not up for any more sacred battles if I can avoid them. Is there some form of divorce needed from Halpa and quick marriage to make everyone happy so we can get going?"

Kazap held a puzzled expression. "I don't understand the meaning of this 'divorce' thing that you are speaking of, but yes, a quick ceremony is all that would be needed."

Surjan looked at the young woman. "If that is your wish. And I will presume nothing from our marriage. We do this because we must do it to save Nesha. I will treat you with respect and deference, and I will not take advantage of you."

Dawa nodded.

"Marty, is there anything else we need to know about your visions?" Lowanna asked.

"Just the cliffs of ice," Marty said.

"Calving icebergs?" François suggested.

"Maybe," Marty said. "I'm not totally certain."

"Do you see people?" Lowanna asked.

Marty shook his head. "Just penguins."

"What is a penguin?" Kazap asked. "I don't know the word you're using."

"It's a bird," Marty said. "But it doesn't fly. It swims and eats fish. They are far to the south of us."

"South," Dawa said. "Following Halpa."

"Not following her," Surjan said. "Just going in the same general direction. It's a big planet."

"If this is the king's decision, then we go south," Kazap said. "And he should be married before he decides, to ensure that the gods will be with him in his decision."

"Butt out, priest!" Surjan snapped. The man's desire to control his actions grated on his nerves. "Dawa, I propose we be married, here and now, on the docks. I don't care what the astrologers say or what the omens are, we do it now. All the people we capture from the shipwreck, we free them as a gesture of magnanimity to celebrate our wedding. Those who are freed can join us with no penalty, or stay here if they prefer. Then we round up the ships that can still sail and all the supplies and tools we can salvage and we head for the cliffs of ice—in the south. If we encounter Halpa and her coconspirators, we sink them to the bottom of the ocean. What do you say?"

Dawa reached out and held Surjan's hand. "Yes, I agree. On that I do pledge."

Surjan felt a shiver go up his spine as if something had just happened that changed an element in their adventure.

The hive mind sensed the exception triggered by an event in the test matrix, and immediately launched a thread to evaluate the current status.

"Interrupt Service Routine activated for a test checkpoint out of Brane sigma+654PWJZBE in the Orion arm of the Milky Way galaxy. Planet Earth, local relative year is 9104 B.C.E."

The Administrator shifted a part of his attention to the event and asked, *"Have we yet traced any of the anomalous communications being received by the test subject?"*

"The source of the communication signal to test subject Gunther is still a mystery. We have hit a checkpoint in the test, and a trial is underway."

The Administrator applied a part of his attention to the proceeding.

"Motion to terminate the trial now," the Prosecutor said.

"Objection," the Advocate said. "No grounds."

The proposal caught the Administrator by surprise. He examined himself and found he had been engrossed in the actions of the test subjects.

"Explain the basis for your motion," the Adjudicator said.

The Prosecutor was within his rights, but had stated no reason for his motion.

"This species is too stupid for continuation, whatever positive outcomes they may happen to bumble into," the Prosecutor said. "Look at them. Despite the test script pointing them to the approved escape location, they've been made aware of the presence of a nearby portal. They are choosing to ignore it."

"They're not ignoring it out of laziness," the Advocate said. "Look at what they're doing."

"I didn't say the grounds was laziness," the Prosecutor shot back. "I said they're stupid. They're incompetent. I doubt they've even realized they're on trial, despite all the hints. They think they're recreating. They know where the portal is, and they are fleeing it."

"They're not fleeing anything," the Advocate said. "This species runs toward danger. The test subjects are attempting to rescue the other members of their species, even though they are not of the same community."

"Is that the test now?" the Prosecutor asked. "We admit all species that have a taste for danger?"

"They're saving their people," the Advocate said. "This is an admirable trait, and one which should be selected for. And besides, they have decided to go to the southern continent, where there is another portal."

"The seer remains among the living, so it would take someone truly braindead to not pick up on that message given him," the Prosecutor huffed.

"It's lucky that he remains alive, and if possible, we should select for luck," the Advocate said.

"I disagree," the Prosecutor snapped. "We need your decision, Adjudicator."

"The trial will continue," the Adjudicator ruled.

"I preserve my objection," the Prosecutor said.

"Noted," the Adjudicator agreed. "Do you have a proposal for the judgment criterion of this trial?"

"Faith," the Prosecutor said.

"You choose that criterion because you believe the subject species has already failed on this basis," the Advocate said. "Your proposal is disingenuous."

"Do you have a counterproposal?"

"I agree that faith should be selected for," the Advocate said. "Faith is the power to accomplish things. I accept faith."

"Faith it is," the Adjudicator decided.

The Administrator had not expected Earth's trial to get past round two's first checkpoint. He shifted his attention to the hive mind and said, *"I want to know where the signal is coming from that the Gunther subject is receiving. It is creating an unexpected variable in the test matrix."*

"We will continue to do what we can to trace its origin."

⟨ CHAPTER ⟩
SEVENTEEN

Marty stood at the edge of the bustling courtyard. There was mud and damp everywhere, and the previously orderly city within sight of the main palace grounds was in complete shambles after the floods, mudslides, and other chaos of the last couple days. There was a nervous energy in the air as the natives raced back and forth, all of them organized with specific tasks in mind. The news of their planned departure had spread like wildfire, and the preparations were well underway. Amidst the clamor, he found a moment to steal away with Surjan, who for the moment wore a fatigued expression as he took a break from coordinating the evacuation preparedness.

Surjan shook his head and sighed. "Marty, this is a tough position for me to be in, I hope you realize it. I'm not meant to be this type of leader. I just wanted to be a soldier, a part of a team, and this has all gotten to be a bit much."

He patted the large man on his back and said, "None of us is prepared for what we're facing. We're just doing what we can to get by."

"It's more than just having these people look to me for leadership . . . I don't know how you managed to talk me into this." The large Sikh huffed with frustration. "I became a soldier because I didn't relish the idea of having women around me or my parents demanding I start a family. And now here I am, about to get 'married' for the second time in a week."

Marty chuckled. "Well, life has a way of surprising us, doesn't it?

Dawa seems different from your prior option. That has to make it a little easier, no?"

"Dawa's nothing like Halpa, thankfully." Surjan's expression softened and he rolled his eyes. "She just let me know she has twenty-three female witnesses for the wedding that she wants to introduce me to. Can you imagine?"

Marty burst out laughing, clapping Surjan on the shoulder once again. "That's quite the entourage! But don't worry, everything will work out fine. You never know, maybe you've got a built-in harem now."

Surjan gave him a severe look and shook his head. "I don't even want to bloody think about that. Dawa herself seems to be pretty shy and humble, which is good, I suppose. This whole wedding thing has me on edge. I feel like a phony and like I'm betraying these people because I know this marriage thing is just an act, at least on my part. I don't understand these people and their beliefs. Just a few days ago they all seemed loyal subjects of Halpa and her cronies, and now it's as if she never existed. I can't help but think about her being out there somewhere . . . She really really despises us."

Marty shrugged. "Well, hopefully with her hasty departure, she and her entourage end up drowning somewhere out there in the ocean. With any luck, they're in Davy Jones's locker already. It's almost time for the ceremony, isn't it?"

"Your Highness!"

Surjan and Marty turned to the voice of Kazap as he trudged up the slope and motioned in Surjan's direction.

"Your Highness, it's time. Come with me, and I'll help you prepare for the ceremony."

"Good luck, buddy." Marty grinned as Surjan took a deep breath and exhaled slowly as he walked down the slope, looking much more like a man on his way to the gallows than to his own royal wedding.

As the time for the wedding approached, Marty stood to the side, near the shadows. The palace's big courtyard and the adjacent rooms filled with nearly all the remaining natives from the island. The air was thick with anticipation and the scent of tropical flowers. Dawa stood beside Surjan, looking genuinely happy. Unlike the former queen, who had a seductive and predatory way about her, Dawa seemed to be a quiet and shy soul, even though she had the radiant beauty of someone in the prime of her youth. With an image of Tafsut the spearwoman in Marty's mind, he couldn't help but smile at his friend's situation. Marty suspected Surjan had taken a liking to the Ancient Egyptian female warrior, and the would-be bride looked a bit like her in some ways. Dawa wore practical, shapely attire that highlighted her hourglass figure, eschewing the ornate finery that her sister had favored.

Surjan glanced down at Dawa, who looked up at him with a shy smile. She reached up and gently finger-combed his long beard, a gesture that Surjan initially seemed to recoil from. But as the would-be bride stepped closer and repeated the gesture, his stern features softened. Even at a distance, Marty saw something in his friend's demeanor change in the small woman's presence.

As the ceremony proceeded, a crowd of Dawa's twenty-three witnesses surrounded the couple and Kazap's voice droned on and on, speaking of gods and omens and the future. The crowd watched with rapt attention.

It was a surprisingly long and drawn-out ceremony, with Surjan, the pagan priest, and two dozen women at the top of the rise.

Marty felt something in the air that raised the hair on the back of his neck. It was almost as if the priest's words were carrying an energy of sorts, and as he panned his gaze across the assembled natives, they too seemed to sense something. They all stared up at the couple, enraptured by the ceremony.

The first marriage to Halpa had been very different. It had seemed rushed and almost desperate, with far fewer people to witness the event. This one had pretty much all the remaining Neshili present to witness the wedding of their king. Many of the natives were clearly struck with emotion as vows were exchanged, just like the weddings Marty was familiar with.

Being closer than most to the rise, he saw Dawa's expression as she stared at her soon-to-be husband. With a mostly downcast gaze, she looked shy, but when she looked up at Surjan to repeat some words the priest had asked her to say, Marty witnessed the expression the young woman wore. Warm affection beamed from her, and had Marty not known any better, it almost seemed like Surjan returned the same look. Dawa was nothing like her sister; she was a beacon of calm and sincerity in the midst of the chaos that surrounded them.

The vows were exchanged, and as Surjan and Dawa were

pronounced husband and wife, the crowd erupted with cheers. Marty joined in, clapping and smiling as he watched his friend's face light up with joy. Despite the looming departure and the uncertainty that lay ahead, this moment was a brief respite, a reminder of the simple, beautiful things worth fighting for.

As the celebration continued, Marty caught Surjan's eye and raised a glass in a silent toast. Surjan nodded, his eyes conveying both a sense of contentment and determination. They had a long journey ahead, but for now, they could revel in this moment of happiness and hope.

Marty's thoughts were interrupted by a distant rumble.

His gaze shifted to the nearby ocean as another iceberg scraped past the rocky shelf, a reminder of the rapidly changing conditions that had prompted their impending departure.

Lowanna walked up to him and whispered, "We're not yet close to being ready to leave. We need a team meeting to figure out what the exact plan is."

"Agreed." Marty nodded. "If you can help get folks gathered this evening, we'll work through the logistics."

She tilted her head in the direction of the ongoing celebration. "What about Surjan? Should we—"

"Let him enjoy the festivities, God knows he needs some break from things for a moment. I'll fill him in after we decide what the details of the trip will be." Marty focused on Lowanna's somber expression. "Are you okay? I know that spear did a number on you, and—"

"I'm fine." Lowanna waved the question away brusquely and glanced at the slowly setting sun. "I'll go start gathering everyone."

Without hesitation, she turned and walked away.

Marty stared at the receding figure of the dark-skinned woman and sighed.

He sensed that things weren't "fine" with her, but her irritability and brusqueness had made it kind of hard for him to pry and see if he could help.

A group of Neshili kids almost crashed into him as they ran past, laughing at what seemed to be a game of tag.

Marty closed his eyes for a moment and prayed for wisdom and guidance from anyone who might listen to his thoughts.

Nobody responded.

✣ ✣ ✣

Gunther moved with purpose through the bustling market square, which had been transformed into a makeshift supply depot for their impending journey. The air was thick with the scent of ripe fruit, fresh fish, and the unmistakable tang of salt from the sea. Islanders scurried about, gathering provisions and packing them into crates and barrels. Gunther, with his sharp eye and keen senses, was tasked with ensuring that all the food was fit for the long voyage ahead.

He paused by a stack of baskets filled with various fruits—soursop, star apples, and guavas. The tropical heat had taken its toll on some of the produce, and the sweet, cloying smell of overripe fruit was unmistakable. Gunther picked up a soursop, examining it closely. Its skin had developed brown spots, and a faint, sour odor emanated from it.

Gunther closed his eyes and focused his energy, feeling the familiar warmth of his preternatural abilities flow through him. He held the soursop in his hands, visualizing the process of purification. A soft glow enveloped the fruit, and the sour smell dissipated, replaced by the fresh, sweet scent of perfectly ripe soursop.

He repeated the process with the rest of the basket, his hands moving swiftly as he purified each piece of fruit. Islanders nearby watched in awe, their faces a mix of relief and admiration. Gunther's abilities were now well known among them, but seeing him in action never failed to draw their attention.

As he finished the purifying process, the Neshili began processing the fruit for the upcoming travel.

Moving on, Gunther approached a stall where several large fish were laid out on a bed of salt. The fish had been caught earlier that morning, but the heat and humidity had started to take their toll. He could smell the beginnings of spoilage, and he knew they couldn't afford to lose any of the precious protein.

Gunther placed his hands over the fish, his fingers tracing the contours of their sleek bodies. Again, he summoned from within him an energy that was hard to explain, but at this point had become almost instinctual as he tapped it and focused on purifying the fish. The glow coming from his fingertips was more intense this time, flickering like a blue flame as it encompassed the fish. The off-putting smell vanished, replaced by the clean, briny scent of the ocean.

He worked his way through the market square, purifying

everything from meats to grains to vegetables. Each time he finished, he received grateful nods and murmurs of thanks from the islanders as they continued to preserve what they had. They understood the importance of his work—every piece of food he saved meant one less worry for their journey.

Gunther finally approached a wagonload of baskets, each filled with tubers and roots. It was obvious that many of these items wouldn't make it for the voyage because some of of the yams and potatoes had started to grow mold. He sighed, knowing this would be a more challenging task. But he steeled himself, determined to do whatever it took to ensure their supplies were safe.

He placed his hands on the crates, feeling the rough texture of the woven baskets beneath his fingers. His hands glowed, but instead of the localized eerie glow, light bloomed across the wagon. Gunther felt the energy flowing through him as the contents of the wagon gave off an incandescence that caused everyone nearby to stop and stare.

Gunther felt his energy waning as the mold receded, the tubers' skins smoothing out and returning to their healthy, vibrant colors. And just as the last of the signs of rot vanished from the food, the world tilted. He grabbed ahold of the wagon.

With sweat beading on his forehead, Gunther barely kept his legs from buckling as one of the nearby islanders approached with a worried expression.

"The magic seems to have drained you, my friend. Here..." The middle-aged islander uncorked a large gourd he had hanging from his felt and handed him the vessel with its sloshing content.

Without thinking about it, Gunther took a swig and his mouth was filled with a warm, sweet liquid that went down easily. It was some kind of fermented fruit juice. A primitive tropical wine, maybe?

Gunther's skin tingled as his belly grew warm from the liquid.

"Go ahead," the islander insisted, making a drinking motion. "You need it more than I. Drink as much as you can, it will restore your energy."

Gunther took another swig and felt the warmth spread from his core to his extremities and for only the briefest moment felt lightheaded. The lightheadedness turned into a dull ache as the German stood up straight, feeling surprisingly energized, as promised. "What is this?"

"It is amikawa. It is made from soursop that is fermented and prepared in a special way. Helps with relaxation and sleep."

"Interesting," Lowanna said in English.

Gunther turned and saw Lowanna approaching with a determined expression.

"I'm not sure what the root 'ami' might mean, but it's interesting to hear the term 'kawa' being used—it means water or even river in some Algonquian languages. Anyway, Gunther, we have a team meeting in a little bit near the palace at sunset. I just want to make sure you're aware."

Gunther glanced at the setting sun and nodded. "I'll be there."

The German healer handed the gourd back to the islander as Lowanna turned and departed as quickly as she'd appeared.

For a moment, Gunther closed his eyes, reaching within himself and was surprised that he felt like he had something in the tank. He'd overextended himself in the past and knew that he'd just done it again, yet he sensed that he was not totally drained, at least not anymore.

He shifted his attention back to the islander and the gourd, which he was tying back onto his belt. "Friend, are there others who make that drink?"

The islander held an amused expression. "It's not uncommon to find each family has some amikawa available or being made as an occasional drink. But I should warn you, if you consume too much your mind will not be able to control your legs or body anymore. Are you feeling better?"

Gunther smiled as the man was describing what was almost certainly the effects of getting drunk. Even though he'd felt the warmth of the alcohol, he wasn't feeling any of those kinds of symptoms anymore. It was almost as if he'd very quickly metabolized all the alcohol, leaving him with nothing but a lingering headache as a side effect of the drink—a reasonable trade-off if it had actually left him a bit more energized. "I am feeling better, thank you. I'll need to learn how such a thing is made—"

"How what is made?" François asked.

He turned to see François approaching and explained, "It seems our friends have learned to ferment some of the fruits around here into an alcoholic beverage, and I think I might have a good use for it."

François shifted his gaze to the islander and asked, "Do you have a recipe for this . . ."

"Amikawa," the islander shook the gourd on his belt, its contents noisily sloshing inside. "Yes, I do. Is that something you—"

"Yes, let me follow up with you tomorrow. Right now, my friend and I have to meet up with some others." François placed a hand on Gunther's shoulder and said, "Let's go off to the palace and figure out where we're at with supplies and everything else. I just got done talking with Marty and he really wants to get going right away."

"Okay." Gunther put two fingers in his mouth and let out a loud whistle.

Two islanders came running and the German pointed at the wagon. "These are all good to go. Let's get this and the other items I worked on loaded onto the ships and ready to go."

Without another word the two men called others and the process of loading the ships began.

"Come on." François began walking toward the palace. "The sooner we get going, the sooner this can all maybe come to an end."

The flotilla of ships had been sailing south for over a month. The fleet contained nearly thirty vessels, all told, with five of them approximately the size of a Viking longship and the rest considerably smaller. François worked himself into such a habit of counting and recounting the ships every time he turned around, he worried he was becoming permanently compulsive.

The voyage had been long and arduous, with tensions running high as they entered the third week. François had done what he could to assuage everyone's concern over their heading in the right direction, and it was only with Surjan's help that there wasn't a revolt midway through their travels.

François had managed to distract some of the Neshili by teaching them to make and shoot bows. The thorough scavenging of Nesha on their departure had meant that a fire pile of spare wood had made it aboard ship. Some of the wood was fresh, and François had first made a bow and arrows, then demonstrated that it could shoot faster than an atlatl, and that an archer could carry more arrows than a spearman could carry javelins.

Then he had persuaded a number of the men to make their own

weapons, and then to learn to shoot. They fired at the mast of one of the ships, with a doubled leather sail stretched behind it to catch missed shots. In time, the men got better.

Still, the islanders weren't totally distracted. They were rightfully fearful, and to be honest, François felt that same knot of anxiety as the days had stretched into nearly a week since they'd last seen a hint of land.

The warm sun beat down on François as he looked ahead into the direction the primitive sailing ship was aimed. Marty walked over to him and whispered, "It's been a week since we last saw land—"

"Not quite a week, but it's getting close." François responded in a curt fashion. The last sighting of land was by his best estimation Puerto Rico, and it shouldn't take much more than three days to make the passage across to the northern coast of South America.

The salty breeze filled the sails, pushing their vessel forward at a good clip, but François's mind was filled with concern. He stood at the bow, his eyes scanning the horizon while the other islanders busied themselves with their tasks.

François snapped his fingers at one of the Neshili. "You, bring me a ballast stone and a rope."

The islander lurched to comply, but paused mid-stride and asked, "How long of a rope?"

"About four or five body lengths should be enough."

The islander returned almost immediately with a misshapen ten-pound stone and the required length of woven rope.

François hadn't done this since he was a child, learning to navigate on his tiny sailboat, but he made quick work of tying the stone to the end of the rope, and walked to the rear of the boat.

Marty followed along and asked, "What are you doing?"

"Watch and you'll see." The Frenchman glanced at the sun's position and then dropped the lead into the water, letting it sink until the rope grew taut. "We're heading south, as planned, but you'd expect the rope to trail directly behind the boat in a straight line. But what are you seeing?"

Marty stared at the taut rope drifting behind the boat. "It looks like it's veering a bit to the right."

A frown creased François's brow. "The current is pulling us east, and from what I can tell, at a pretty good clip." His voice was tinged with concern and he began pulling the drift line back onto the ship. "I'm almost positive such currents aren't the norm in our time, but the drift line doesn't lie. I had us aiming for the north coast of what will be Venezuela, but if the current's been like this the entire time, that might explain a few things."

"That's not exactly good." Marty's frown suddenly matched François's. "The last thing we need is to miss South America entirely and end up in the open Atlantic."

"Agreed. Another reason I don't like feeling we're in the grip of the current is because Halpa and her people might be in that same grip." François paused, considering their options. "We need to shift our course southwest to counteract the effects of the current. If we continue as we are, we risk overshooting our destination." He turned to the islander manning the rudder and pointed southwest. "Aim between south and west from now on."

François felt the ship begin to shift direction and he panned his gaze at the other ships trailing behind them, feeling a sense of relief.

The navigators on each ship matched the change of course and followed their lead.

It would take more than a handful of hours to pass before François felt a euphoric rush of satisfaction:

Near the western horizon he spotted the first sign of land in (almost) a week!

Despite their efforts, the coastline that eventually came into view was not what he expected. The distinct north-south stretch of land looked familiar, but not in the way François had hoped.

Marty joined him at the bow, squinting at the distant shore. "That's not Venezuela, is it?" he asked, a hint of disbelief in his voice.

François shook his head slowly. "No, it's not. The shape of that coast . . . it reminds me of the eastern coast of Brazil. We must be near the Rego Grande region, not far from the mouth of the Amazon."

A chill raced up and down François's spine as he realized that, had he not made the recent course correction, they might have become lost and starved in the middle of the Atlantic Ocean.

"Well, that's as good as any other destination, I'd expect, especially if you're right."

The worried expressions that the islanders held had been replaced with smiles as they approached the coastline. The fisherman Muwat approached and flashed a toothy grin as he said, "Thank you for finding us our new home. Many of us were worried about ever seeing land again."

François and Marty exchanged glances and Marty patted the fisherman on his shoulder. "We *are* approaching a new home, but this place is not yet it. We need supplies to get to our final destination."

The old man's jubilant expression melted into one of concern. He remained silent for a few long seconds and then nodded as he turned to get back to his work.

Marty shifted into English and said, "François, we need to keep these guys believing that we're leading them into a safer place for them to prosper."

François pursed his lips and nodded. "But do we actually know that's the case?"

Marty nodded. "I don't know exactly where, but I'm hoping to hit the Pampas region near the southern tip of South America. It's a grassland in our time where some of the best beef is raised; we can only hope that it's a good place for the Neshili to prosper. It's not mountainous and should do well for farming."

"These people really aren't an agrarian society, at least not yet," François noted. "I'd argue they're more hunter-gatherers. Also, the Pampas are a low plain, aren't they? Won't they be flooded?"

"They might be." Marty nodded. "But remember that the Pampas are above water after the ice age ends. And if they *are* flooded, there will be fertile foothills of the Andes somewhere. And I suppose in the meantime there are some skills and knowledge we can leave them with that shouldn't upset the space-time continuum."

François rolled his eyes. "You and that space-time continuum—do you even know what that means?"

Marty shook his head and smiled. "Not really, but it sounds good."

François nodded and remained silent about his concerns.

Would bringing these people to that part of the world, and teaching them anything, cause a huge ripple effect down through the future?

If and when the team came back to their time, would the world be a different place?

That was a question François didn't have an answer for, and it was a growing concern that nagged at his core.

CHAPTER EIGHTEEN

Peering over the bow of the ship, Surjan felt a strong sense of relief for himself, for the team he'd arrived in this world with, and especially for the Neshili, whom he was now leading. The sun was high in the sky, yet the brightness of the noonday sun penetrated not an inch of the thick, untamed jungle that bordered the shoreline. The islanders were busily lashing together their vessels as they floated about one hundred yards off the shore of a new land. The waves lapped gently against the hull of his ship and he breathed in deeply of the air that was thick with the scent of salt and earth, foreign and enticing.

Surjan turned his gaze away from the approaching shore to look at the young woman he'd married just over a month ago. Dawa, now queen, stood at the bow, staring ahead at a new world. Somehow, she'd transformed from the shy girl he'd met to one who looked proud, had a regal bearing that showed confidence, and carried life sparkling in her dark eyes as the wind blew through her long black tresses. Surjan couldn't deny that the girl was beautiful in her own unique way. It wasn't anything like the seductive curves and mannerisms of her elder sister, which had triggered many warnings in his mind. Hers was a more wholesome, traditional beauty that took much of his will to ignore.

On the boat were her twenty-three handmaidens. They were Dawa's lifelong friends and it almost seemed like they were in some way beholden to her—almost like servants, yet that term didn't seem to exist in the Neshili language. Unlike Dawa, who since her wedding had worn a plain-colored woven garment, the girls were adorned in vibrant colors and would dart in and out of the new couple's proximity to check on her and see if she needed anything.

Surjan leaned closer to Dawa and whispered, "Your thoughts on the new land?"

Dawa turned to him, her eyes shining with determination. "My king, the goddess of flowers has blessed us with this bountiful land. We must offer our thanks and ensure her favor continues. My friend-sisters need to go ashore to make the sacrifice."

Surjan's jaw tightened. He knew almost nothing about the religious practices of the Neshili, but he had gotten the strong impression that Dawa was a devout adherent to these beliefs. "I understand the importance of the sacrifice, Dawa, but it is too dangerous. We do not know what lies beyond that beach. There could be hostile natives, wild animals, or other threats."

Dawa's gaze hardened. "Are you doubting the goddess's protection, Surjan? We have come this far under her guidance."

"It isn't the goddess I doubt," Surjan replied, his voice lowering. In point of fact, he had zero knowledge of any of the Neshili pantheon, and zero confidence in their ability to provide any kind of blessing or protection whatsoever. "It is the unknown dangers of this land. We cannot risk your safety or the lives of your friends."

One of the handmaidens, a young woman named Amara, stepped forward. "Your Majesty, we are willing to take the risk. The goddess will protect us."

Surjan's mind raced with all of the unknowns about the land they were approaching, and he shook his head firmly. "No. Not yet, and my decision is final. We will send scouts to survey the area first. Only when we know it is safe can I allow more of us to set foot on that shore. The danger of the unknown is too great."

A tense silence settled over Dawa and her companion.

Surjan noticed in his peripheral vision that some of the other handmaidens had overheard the conversation and were exchanging worried glances.

Dawa's eyes flashed with frustration, but she held her tongue and nodded her head slightly in Surjan's direction. "Very well," she said, her voice cool and composed. "We will wait for the scouts' report."

Surjan nodded, relieved that she had not pressed the issue further.

He talked with one of the Neshili warriors on the boat, instructing him to communicate with the other boats and arrange for a landing party for him to lead. They'd explore the immediate area and report back by nightfall. As the warrior departed to communicate with the others, Surjan turned to his queen once more.

"I promise you, Dawa, we will perform the sacrifice. But we must ensure our safety first."

"There is no 'we' in the sacrifice." Dawa laughed and shook her head. "This is a woman's responsibility; you cannot commune with the goddess." She inclined her head, a flicker of resignation in her eyes. "I trust your judgment, Surjan. But do not delay longer than necessary. The goddess's patience is not infinite. I do not want harm to come to our people."

Surjan panned his gaze across the small fleet of larger transport boats and noticed that several outrigger-style canoes were being deployed. Preparation for the scouting team.

"I'll lead the scouts and come back before sundown with news."

Dawa reached out and grabbed his hand, giving it a squeeze. "Be careful. May the Flower Goddess protect you."

Surjan smiled, gave her hand a squeeze and began helping one of the islanders lower a canoe onto the water.

Leading a group of six Neshili warriors, Surjan moved cautiously through the dense jungle, his eyes scanning the surroundings for any signs of danger or food. The tropical foliage was thicker than anything he had ever seen in the Bahamas, the air humid and heavy with unfamiliar scents. The islanders followed closely, their primitive axes and spears at the ready, faces tense with a mixture of excitement and fear.

"Stay alert," Surjan whispered, raising a hand to halt the group. "We are not familiar with these lands. There could be dangers we do not recognize."

They moved on, the underbrush rustling softly under their feet. Surjan spotted a cluster of dark purple berries hanging from a tall, slender tree. He approached and plucked one, gave it a sniff, and a tentative nibble. He immediately recognized the earthy, tart, and slightly sweet flavor of the açaí berry and popped it into his mouth. He plucked another and showed it to the others. "These are good to eat."

The islanders gathered around, eagerly picking the small, nutritious fruits and filling some empty tightly woven baskets they carried on their waists.

Even though the others were very interested in gathering supplies, Surjan couldn't help but worry about what nearby threats there might be. He wasn't one hundred percent convinced that they were in Earth's prehistory, but if they were, nobody was entirely sure whether some *really* dangerous animals might still be lurking in these forests.

His mind brought up an image of a saber-toothed cat and he tightened his grip on the narwhal spear he'd acquired in the Sacred Grove. As he felt for the presence of his sharpened ankh, he focused his heightened senses ahead, looking for any type of threat.

So far, the only sizable wildlife they'd encountered was a peccary that had raced across their path, never giving them a moment's attention. Had the wild pig turned to attack, its sharpened tusks could have posed a danger to them.

After stripping the low-hanging branches of the tree with the açaí berries, they moved farther into the jungle. A little farther, Surjan spotted a large, familiar-looking fruit hanging from low branches. Banging the hard woody pod against a tree trunk, Surjan broke the fruit open to reveal a creamy, aromatic pulp.

He recognized it from his military survival training that he'd completed in the jungles of Central America.

"This is something called cupuaçu," he said, handing the fruit to the nearest islander. "We can eat the pulp, but leave the seeds."

Using sharpened stone axes, the islanders gathered all of the easily accessible fruit as Surjan focused on their surroundings.

Even though the sun barely penetrated the thick canopy, Surjan had an innate sense of direction. All he needed to do was to concentrate and he could point in the direction of the shore, where they'd entered the dense jungle.

He continued to lead the group through the labyrinth of twisted vines and towering trees, the air thick with the scent of damp earth and vibrant vegetation. They all used their edged weapons to help cut through the underbrush as the sun had dipped lower in the sky and the shadows grew slowly darker, more ominous.

"Keep close," Surjan urged, glancing back at the group. They were heavily laden with the bounty of the jungle. Warriors who had expected to find danger at every turn, now found themselves burdened with an abundance of fruits and tubers. The weight of papayas, pineapples, and other unfamiliar but enticing foodstuffs slowed their progress.

"We should head back," Surjan said, his voice steady but laced with urgency. "We have plenty of examples of what can be gathered in this jungle."

The islanders nodded, their expressions a mix of relief and weariness. The dense foliage pressed in on all sides, and despite the richness of the jungle's offerings, an undercurrent of unease ran through the group.

As they began their trek back to the shore, Surjan's senses remained on high alert. The jungle was a living, breathing entity, full of sounds that hinted at unseen eyes watching their every move. The occasional rustle of leaves or snap of a twig set his heart racing, but he pressed on, determined to return with everyone safely.

Despite Surjan's admonition against loading themselves so heavily with their culinary burden, the men couldn't resist gathering all that they could, and now each step seemed heavier than the last as they navigated through the thick undergrowth.

"Your Majesty!" one of the warriors called out, pointing to a patch of bright yellow among the green. "More pineapples!"

Surjan shook his head. "No, we have enough. We need to get back before nightfall."

The group moved on, but Surjan's unease grew with each passing minute. The jungle seemed to close in around them, the shadows growing longer and darker. They were close to the shore now, he could feel it. The salty tang of the sea was a faint but welcome scent on the breeze.

Suddenly, a rustling noise stopped him in his tracks. He held up a hand, signaling for silence. The islanders froze, their eyes darting nervously through the trees. The rustling grew louder, closer.

Surjan gripped his spear tightly, muscles tensed and ready. "Stay behind me," he whispered.

From the shadows emerged a large, wild boar, its eyes glinting menacingly. The creature snorted, swung its razor-sharp tusks from side to side and pawed the ground, preparing to charge. Surjan's heart pounded, but he stood his ground, spear raised.

"Hold steady," he commanded.

The boar charged, but Surjan was ready. With a preternatural precision, he sidestepped the creature at the last moment, his spear poised. In a fluid, practiced motion, he drove the tip between the vertebrae at the base of the boar's neck. The spear slid in perfectly, severing the spinal cord and instantly paralyzing the large animal.

The boar collapsed, immobilized. Surjan approached the fallen beast, and with a quick, merciful thrust, ended its life.

The islanders breathed a collective sigh of relief. Surjan withdrew his spear, wiping the sweat from his brow. "We need to move quickly," he said. "We need to get back before it gets completely dark."

The warriors pointed at the animal and before they could say anything, Surjan crouched low and with a grunt of effort hefted the animal onto his shoulder.

"Let's go!"

They quickened their pace, and it was only a few minutes before the shore finally came into view through the thinning trees. As they broke free from the jungle's grasp, the sight of their makeshift camp greeted them. Dawa and the others rushed to meet them, their faces alight with hope and curiosity.

"We found food," Surjan announced as he dropped his porcine burden onto the ground and gestured to the array of fruits and tubers. "More than we can carry."

Dawa's eyes sparkled with relief. "That's wonderful news, Surjan. We can resupply our efforts without fear and for that we must thank the Flower Goddess right away."

Surjan shook his head as he glanced at the sun hanging low on the western horizon. "It's almost sundown. Let's leave the gathering and thanks for tomorrow morning so we have full sunlight."

Suddenly, a commotion erupted near the shoreline. Surjan rushed over to find some islanders excitedly hauling in nets filled with snapper, grouper, and a plethora of crabs.

"Good catch!" Surjan praised. "Handle them carefully. Those large-clawed crabs look like they could lop off a finger if you're not careful."

One of the islanders pointed farther down the shore and smiled. "This place has much to offer for food. We didn't even have to go hunting, the food came to us."

Surjan walked over to a group of people focused on butchering what looked like the remains of a capybara and several wild pigs. The islanders worked efficiently, their movements practiced and precise despite their unfamiliarity with the animals. The talk focused on the capybara, since none of the islanders had ever seen a one-hundred-pound rat before, and they debated about how to best deal with it. Surjan provided guidance. "Treat it just like a pig. Skin it, slice the meat into strips, and hang them to dry."

As Surjan surveyed what the others had discovered, it quickly became abundantly clear that some others had discovered caimans and turtles, many of which were being prepared for immediate consumption.

Spotting François, he walked over and noticed that he'd managed to gather a pile of rock salt from a shallow basin near the shore. "This will help preserve the meat," François instructed several islanders, his hands white with salt. "We can dry and cure it properly."

The islanders had already started an assembly line of butchering and drying of the fish and meat, ensuring nothing went to waste.

As the sun dipped below the horizon, casting long shadows over their makeshift camp, Surjan allowed himself a moment of relief. They had navigated the perils of this strange land, escaping a flooding island, finding supplies, and making progress toward their goal. All great things, but his mind remained vigilant, knowing that the true challenges of their new home were only just beginning.

"We did well today!" Surjan bellowed to all within reach of his voice. "But remember, we are still strangers in this land. Stay cautious, stay alert, and most importantly, stay together while we gather our needed supplies."

The islanders all nodded, their spirits seemingly lifted by the successful gathering effort, and almost assuredly from being back on land.

Surjan steeled himself for what needed to be done on the long journey that still remained. He scanned across the small fleet of ships that bobbed offshore and grabbed one of the canoes.

He needed to visit all the ships, talk to the people, allay any fears they might have, and keep everyone on the same page.

Surjan couldn't take to heart the role he'd been given of king, knowing that he and his companions would hopefully soon depart from this time, but he was compelled to do what these people needed.

The responsibility lay heavily on his shoulders and he took it seriously. Together, they still would have to face the unknown dangers for whatever lay ahead in this ancient, untamed world.

The moon hung low over the horizon, casting a pale light over the Brazilian coast. Lowanna silently cursed under her breath as she trailed after Dawa. The young queen and her companions were determined to make their sacrifices to the flower goddess of prosperity and went silently swimming toward the shore.

Surjan's bride may not have been the conniving, evil creature that his former queen had been, but the woman had a mind of her own—she'd waited until nighttime and while Surjan was talking with others on another ship, the young woman and her companions put into action their planned sojourn onto the shore.

Lowanna had been given no choice but to follow or completely lose track of these impetuous fools. Lowanna's senses were on high alert. The unfamiliar territory filled her with unease, but she pressed on, following the group into the dense jungle. The air was thick with the scent of flowers and damp earth, scents which Dawa and her entourage would surely take as a reminder of the goddess they were going to honor.

Suddenly, the peace was shattered by the rustling of leaves and the sound of footsteps. Lowanna turned just as a sharp blow to her head sent her crashing to the ground.

Darkness swallowed her.

When Lowanna regained consciousness, her head throbbed painfully. She found herself tied up, her hands bound tightly behind her back. Her vision blurred, she blinked rapidly, trying to make sense of her surroundings. Around her, the other girls were similarly restrained, their faces etched with fear and confusion.

A familiar voice cut through the haze. "You see? I promised you my magic would summon food, and here they are!" It was Halpa, the previous queen, standing triumphantly before a group of fierce-looking raiders. The men looked like very dark-skinned Native Americans, had high cheekbones, and a fierce expression that sent a chill up Lowanna's spine. One of the men grinned; his teeth had been filed into fearsome, razor-sharp points. One of the natives went to work at freeing what appeared to be Halpa's men, who had been tied up nearby in a separate group.

Dawa, bound and struggling, caught Lowanna's eye. Horror filled the young queen's face as one of the natives grabbed two of the queen's companions and dragged them toward a roaring fire. The screams of the girls were brief, their bodies soon tossed onto the flames. The smell of burning flesh filled the air, making Lowanna's stomach churn.

Lowanna's head spun from the blow she had taken. Her thoughts were muddled, but she forced herself to focus. She recalled the stories of this area that she knew from her anthropology studies, tales of a mysterious megalithic structure known as Rego Grande. Rumors spoke of human sacrifice and a people long lost to history. Now, faced with these men who were almost certainly cannibals, the stories seemed all too real.

Desperation fueled her resolve. Lowanna concentrated, reaching out with her mind, searching for any help she could find.

Enemies. Stupid strangers.

The voice had come in the form of a parrot's squawks in a nearby tree.

Lowanna shifted her attention upward and, despite the nausea-inducing headache, focused on the nearby parrot.

Unsure if it would work, Lowanna put all of her energy into projecting an image into the bird's mind.

The boats near the beach.

An image of Marty ... he'd be the only one who might understand what the animal would say in his seemingly random squawks and tweets.

And as the nausea grew stronger, threatening to empty her stomach, she whispered, "Danger ... come quickly ..."

Somewhere up in the trees, she heard the parrot squawk. A bird ruffled its feathers and took off from its perch.

With her consciousness waning, Lowanna tried to steady her breathing.

Halpa's voice broke her concentration. "You will all serve as a feast to prove my power," she declared, her eyes cold and calculating as she glared at the captured group.

Lowanna's vision blurred again.

She struggled to stay conscious, the weight of the situation pressing down on her. She had to hold on, for herself, for Dawa, and for the others. They needed to survive this nightmare, to escape these savages and return to their own form of nightmarish tasks.

As the fire crackled and the sun began to rise, Lowanna succumbed to the darkness.

CHAPTER NINETEEN

Marty frowned as he stared at the spot where Lowanna and the missing Neshili had been.

Surjan crouched low and studied the ground, shaking his head. "These tracks . . . there are too many." He shifted his gaze to Marty and asked, "Does anyone know where they've gone?"

Marty shook his head. "Obviously, with your queen and her entourage missing, we can pretty much guess that Dawa went on her own volition to sacrifice to her goddess and Lowanna followed them."

"I told that girl to wait for the new day," Surjan grumbled, and shook his head.

Marty was standing with Surjan and Sharrum, at the head of a war party comprised of François, Gunther, Kareem, and twenty men with spears and bows. François had insisted they bring their bows, rather than the atlatls they had spent most of their lives using. When Surjan had asked him why, the Frenchman had said, "Fire faster, and more shots."

That had settled the argument.

They were deep in the forest, with trees crowding in all around them. There was no path, but the ground was damp and preserved tracks well enough despite grass and other ground cover.

"It looks like our people might have been attacked by other Neshili," Sharrum said. "Look at this track; it's made by a sandaled foot. It is the same design as the ones we wear. Maybe Queen Halpa's men? This one, on the other hand, is the imprint of a bare foot."

160

"Queen Halpa," Marty said with a grimace. "If you're right, then it's them and whoever else they've joined with."

"So, who are the barefooted people?" Sharrum asked.

"I don't really care who they are," Surjan growled. "They kidnapped our people. Now they pay." He panned his gaze across the team, looking at each of the original expedition members and said with an ominous tone, "We'll use everything we have to get these people back."

Kareem's frown melted away only to be replaced with an enthusiastic smile. "By God."

"First, we have to find these people," Marty said as a loud squawk filled the air.

"Marty!" a voice cried. "Marty!"

Marty felt like he was being paged. He turned, looking for the source of the voice.

Marty! A parrot flew past overhead. It had the same green-and-yellow coloration as the one that had alerted him to Lowanna's call for help.

The large bird banked and flew directly toward Marty as the linguist instinctively held out his arm to block the bird's approach.

Instead of flying off, it landed heavily on his arm and gave out a loud squawk. *Marty!*

"I heard you!" Marty responded as he stared at the unexpected bundle of feathers perched on his arm.

The bird ruffled its feathers and returned his stare.

"Yes?" Marty wasn't sure what to make of the visitor when the bird suddenly began speaking rapidly in chirps, head bobs, and the occasional squawk.

The others in the group simply stared as the bird began chattering at Marty.

Your woman sent me.

"I don't have a woman," Marty said, and then felt stupid. The bird must mean Lowanna. "Where is she?"

They have not eaten her yet.

"What?" Marty nearly threw the bird to the ground. "What do you mean, 'yet'?"

"Marty, what is it?" Surjan leaned forward, looking as if he might tackle the bird.

Eaters of your people. Some are eaten. But not your woman. Your woman sent me. To guide you.

Eaten? Marty's eyes widened.

The bird would have no idea who had been eaten and probably couldn't even count how many. "Where are they?" Marty asked.

The bird shifted his gaze away from Marty and pointed his beak toward a low rise in the distance. *At the top of the hill. Follow me.*

"Show us!" Marty snapped his arm, intending to launch the parrot into the sky, but the bird dug in his claws and stayed clutched to him.

Your woman warns you. Other woman there. Angry woman.

Angry woman? Maybe Halpa?

"Will you fly now?" Marty asked.

The parrot took off and headed toward the hill Marty had indicated. "They're captured by cannibals!" was the initial summary Marty shouted to the war party and he quickly filled them in on what the bird had told him as they chased after it.

It occurred to Marty, as he was racing toward the mound, ducking and dodging through bright green foliage with the war party at his heels, that the cannibals holding Lowanna might be waiting for him. Even though the parrot had obviously been sent by Lowanna, he and his team could still be running into a trap. Shortly thereafter, the parrot swooped low over his head and called to him.

Follow the stream! Use cliff.

With Surjan by his side, Marty echoed the instructions to him in a whisper, veered right, and began splashing through the shallow water, following the curve of the hill around to the other side. There the side of the hill was shorn away, leaving a granite cliff exposed. Marty stopped to examine the cracks in the rock, looking for the best handholds.

Surjan and François caught up, and the rest of the war band was only moments behind. They stood together and stared up at the rock. Marty could make out the ends of palisade walls, built right to the edge of the cliff. He also saw boulders, singly, like standing stones.

"I'll take most of the men around front," Surjan said. "We'll attack the men on the wall."

"With the bows and arrows," François said.

"Fire faster," Surjan said, "and more shots."

"I'll take the best climbers and go up the wall," Marty said. "By the time we get to the top, you should be engaged." He turned to the men. "Who here is a strong climber?"

He expected Kareem to be his first volunteer, and instead he couldn't find the young Egyptian.

"Did anyone see where Kareem went?"

Kareem got himself up the cliff easily while Marty was jabbering with the warriors. The climb was child's play, easy enough that near the top he slipped his ankh into his hand to arm himself.

Nearing the top of the cliff, he smelled roasting meat. His mouth watered.

He didn't wait for Surjan's men to provide a distraction, either, but just squirmed through the tall grass at the top of the cliff on his belly. Three dark granite stones squatted there in a triangular arrangement, a few steps from the edge, and a man with a spear leaning against his shoulder and a stone knife in his hand stood idly whittling at a scrap of wood. He wore a leather kilt and a leather strap from hip to shoulder, from which hung a pouch and two short javelins.

Kareem wriggled past the man, stood on the far side of the stones, and then stabbed the man high between his shoulder blades.

The ankh sliced through skin, tendon, and without resistance pierced between the vertebra, severing whatever connection the head had to the rest of the body.

The man's limbs spasmed as his body pitched forward.

Kareem heard the phlegm-filled death rattle of the man's last breath.

Easy.

The smell of food grew stronger. He hadn't had a truly satisfying meal since Surjan's coronation and wedding feast, and his belly rumbled.

Then he crouched in the shadow of the stone triangle to survey the space he had entered. A wooden palisade surrounded an area cleared of trees. The posts were ten feet tall and a parapet ran around the inside. The palisade made a horseshoe shape, with the cliff left undefended. Men stood on the parapet, spaced forty feet apart. They wore the same kilt and pouch as the man Kareem had just killed and were armed with the same knife and javelins.

Within the wooden walls stood a ring of granite stones. These looked ancient, something like the Nabta Playa stones, or the English Stonehenge. As a younger man, Kareem would have said they looked pagan, but he'd walked many strange roads in the last year. Some looked like fangs, individual sharpened teeth poking from the wet earth. Others were arranged in clusters or stacked in haphazard piles. Some had holes bored through them, but smoothly, in a fashion suggesting the holes had been drilled by the action of water.

Within the circle of the stones, Kareem saw skin tents and huts. He saw fighters, some armed and dressed in the local fashion, and some who were obviously Neshili. He recognized some of the faces from Nesha.

Traitors to their own people.

He saw meat on a spit, smelled it, and then recognized the meat.

Ammun.

That had been the man's name. He was the genealogist and poet of Nesha, the fat fellow who seemed to know all about their history and stories. He turned over a fire now on a spit, the pole entering through his open mouth and emerging from . . . Kareem didn't want to think where. His hair had been shaved before he'd been put on the spit or maybe it had already singed away, but Kareem didn't smell burning hair.

He thought that his stomach should be churning in outraged revolt, but it didn't.

Two men turned the spit with Ammun on it, and a third poked at his flesh with a knife. Other men loitered about, seemingly laughing at the dead man's expense. The Neshili who had fled with their queen had somehow made common cause with these savages, and they were now preparing to eat their historian together.

Kareem had come first up the wall for one reason. Slipping unseen as the shadow of a passing bird, he began checking tents and huts. He peeked in through cracks and under lifted flaps, trying not to attract attention. He ignored a group of bound Neshili who didn't notice him. They'd be saved or they wouldn't, but they weren't what Kareem had come for. He ignored unbound Neshili when he saw them, too. He was uninterested in inflicting justice on those who had fled with their queen. Surjan or Marty would see to that.

He heard shouting at the wall, telling him that Surjan and his men had begun their attack.

A weasel slipped into one tent as he approached. When he lifted the flap to look inside, he found Lowanna, lying on her side, wrists and ankles tied together, a gag in her mouth, and the weasel standing beside her head. Lowanna faced Kareem and looked him in the eyes.

He hadn't come for her, either, but he couldn't exactly ignore her. Carefully, he sliced off her gag and then freed her hands and ankles. She pointed past her feet at the tent's door. Kareem slit the tent with the ankh and entered. Then he casually stepped over a number of Neshili prisoners and peeked through the door. A leather-kilted warrior stood at the tent door, his back to Kareem.

Moving like a shadow, Kareem jumped onto the man's back, and from behind squeezed the guard's windpipe, shutting it as he stabbed his ankh into one of the guard's lungs.

The guard twisted as Kareem sliced sideways, puncturing the other lung and slicing the heart in half on the way. The man fell to his knees and shuddered. For the briefest of moments, it felt like the man's life essence poured from him into Kareem, giving the assassin a euphoric rush that made him tingle from head to toe.

The body went limp and Kareem let the guard sink to the ground without a sound.

With his skin tingling from the incident, he eagerly looked for his next victim.

He glanced at Lowanna and paused . . . In the dimly lit tent, the dark woman was limned with a preternatural glow that he'd never noticed before. And suddenly it vanished.

Kareem blinked, shook his head and asked, "You can free these others, right?" He didn't wait for an answer. These people were not his problem.

He snuck out of the tent and in the next tent he found Queen Halpa dallying with a man. It took Kareem only a moment to recognize the lucky fellow—he was Sapal, one of the three elders the party had met that first morning at Muwat the fisherman's hut. Peeking under the flap, he saw them lying on cushions and talking, faces close together. Light came from candles sitting on a flat stone at the head of the tent. Kareem was behind the queen, and could just see the outlines of the wall-like elder on the other side of her curves.

"It was a stroke of genius to turn these primitives on your own people," Sapal said.

"They aren't my own people," the queen told him. "My own people came with me."

Kareem had imagined achieving this moment would have been more difficult. Without hesitating, he rolled under the tent flap and clamped his left hand on the queen's mouth, silencing her. Pulling himself forward, he plunged the ankh in his right hand into Sapal's forehead.

The minister's eyes opened wide as his body convulsed.

Sapal fell backward, the head wound making a sucking sound as it tried to take the ankh with it.

Tightening his grip, Kareem ripped the ankh free and the elder died silently on the ground, staring blankly up at the ceiling, probably never actually even seeing Kareem before the fatal strike.

The queen struggled but he was stronger than she was. She slapped him, to no avail. Her eyes stared wildly at him as she scratched at his face.

"This gives me no joy," he lied. "But you do not get to escape me twice, cow."

With one quick move, he sliced off her head.

Marty reached the top of the cliff before the warriors on his squad. Even Sharrum—strong, agile, and apparently motivated—was no match for Marty's preternatural climbing prowess. Leaving his ankh in his belt for backup in a truly difficult fight, Marty ran headlong into the stockade of the cannibals.

He stepped over a dead sentinel. Two men challenged him with spears; he easily took the weapon from one and used it like a staff, battering the other man's spear from his hand and then beating them both like dusty carpets until they turned and fled. Snapping the spear over his knee, he advanced with a fighting club in each hand. A warrior in a leather kilt emerged from a tent to take three rapid blows to the face, rendering him unconscious. Then Marty hurled the stick with the spearhead still attached, sinking it into the sternum of a man with an atlatl filled with a javelin who was directing his attention at Marty.

"Where were you?" Lowanna's voice tore into Marty like a buzz saw and then she burst from a tent. Neshili women poured from the tent in her wake, picking up weapons from fallen warriors and crashing into other tents. They were mostly keeping their voices down, arming themselves and freeing each other without attracting the attention of the crowd of warriors around the fires in the center of the compound, or the men fighting on the palisade walls.

Lowanna wasn't. She was shouting.

"Maybe you can hold this complaint until later," Marty suggested.

"Oh, it's a complaint, is it?" Lowanna howled. "You knew those women were going to go out and do their dance to Flower Girl, and you let them!"

"Surjan told them no!" Marty said back, still trying to keep his voice down. "How much more 'no' do I need to say than what their king said? The answer was no, and they went anyway!"

"You knew I would have to follow them!" Lowanna snapped. "You knew I'd be in danger!"

"How was I supposed to know they'd do this?" Marty yelled back, finally losing volume control.

She slapped his chest. "Maybe stop them before they left? Maybe explain to them the risks, not let them go running out on their own?"

"They're adults!" Marty cried. "Or at least mostly adults! Am I supposed to babysit everyone, forever? Is that my job, babysitter for life?"

"Dawa isn't an adult! Dawa is a teenager!"

"Dawa is the queen!" Marty protested. "Of all people, I couldn't stop her! I'm not sure Surjan could even stop her. Unless you're suggesting maybe I should have knocked her out!"

"Yes!" Lowanna agreed. "Next time, knock her out."

Marty stared at Lowanna and nearly burst out laughing.

As others were fighting, the two of them were bickering like teenagers. "This isn't the time," Marty said. "At least I got your bird's message, and here I am."

A look of something similar to tenderness crossed Lowanna's face and for a moment Marty thought she might hug him. Then she hit him again instead.

"They're coming!"

This was Dawa's voice. The queen was freed, and maybe all of her Flower Girl worshippers—eyeballing without counting, Marty thought he saw thirty Neshili or so in the knot around him. Only half a dozen had spears, and they were all collapsing in around Marty.

They were closing in around him because a wall of warriors advanced on them, grim looks on their faces. They were a mixed band of Neshili and cannibals, and their spears were lowered for business.

⇥ CHAPTER ⇤
TWENTY

Surjan crouched in the forest and looked up the hill. The east side of the mound was protected by a cliff, but the slopes on the north and the south sides were scarcely less steep. Only on the west was the approach tenable for a man walking or carrying a burden, and the western slope had been entirely cleared of brush so that a person climbing the slope would be exposed the entire way.

A dozen bare-chested men with javelins stood on the palisade wall at the top of the slope. No doubt more could easily be summoned.

The last sun of the evening came from over his shoulder, which favored him several ways. First, it meant that he and his warriors were in shadow, difficult to see. Second, it meant that the sun wasn't in his eyes, blinding him and his men, whereas it might disturb the aim of those on the wall. Third, the men on the wall stood in high relief.

He would lose all those advantages as soon as the sun shifted. Now was the moment.

"François," he said. "Take the half of the men who are the best shots and give the rest of us cover while we charge up the hill."

François snapped off a nod and then a series of barked instructions. In two minutes, he had archers ranged all along the edge of the foliage.

"Stay back," François said to Gunther. "Come after the attack."

Gunther took inventory of several flasks hanging from his belt and then cracked his knuckles. "I'll heal those who need it."

François and Surjan shared a look and another nod, and then François shouted, "Fire!"

Surjan yelled, "Charge!"

A wave of arrows slammed into the men on the wall and sliced them neatly away, like a razor cleaning a jawline of stubble. Surjan was already running, ankh in hand. Javelins dropped past him and he heard the cries of warriors as they fell, but not many. His superior speed and stamina quickly left behind his own men, leaving him more exposed, but also shortening the time he'd spend while vulnerable. As enemies dared appear on the wall to replace their fellows, they were met with further volleys of arrows, and as he reached the gate, he heard cries of surprise and anger within.

The gate hung on leather hinges, one large patch of leather on each side, and was designed to swing inward. With the last rays of the sun, Surjan made out a heavy bar across the middle, locking the gate. He didn't mess with the bar at all. With a single swipe, he sliced through one leather hinge. The left side of the gate thudded to the dirt and two men yelped and fell off the parapet.

His warriors arrived at the gate, catching up to him. "Push!" he yelled, and they threw their shoulders against the gate, which sagged to one side and leaned back.

"The gate! The gate!" men inside the palisade cried.

Surjan sliced through the second hide hinge and the gate crashed to the ground, silencing the defenders' cries.

Within, a mob charged forward. They were a mixed rabble of Neshili in their tunics and sandals and bare-chested men in leather kilts, all holding spears.

"Drop!" Surjan yelled to his men.

Surjan's Neshili fell to their bellies. François and his archers fired three quick volleys, shattering the mob. The archers began running up the hill, Gunther tending to the wounded in their wake, and Surjan rose to his feet, snatching the spear of a fallen foeman. His men rose with him, spears in their hands and blood in their eyes.

Within the palisade wall stood a circle of megaliths, and within the standing stones crouched something that was half village and half camp. Leaning hovels and leather tents alternated. On the far side, Surjan heard shouting voices that he thought belonged to Marty and Lowanna, but they weren't shouting at him so he tuned the words out.

A line of spearmen faced him. The line was already ragged, having lost half its number to François's arrows. Surjan struck it in the center at a dead run, pushing his spear neatly through a warrior who had the misfortune to be looking the wrong way at the wrong moment.

Then he pivoted, took his ankh into his hand, and cut through the line to his left.

His men hit the line just three steps behind him.

"Surjan!" he heard them yell. "Surjan the Lion! Surjan the Lion King!"

Somehow, the name had gotten out. Surjan didn't have the luxury of being in a position to cringe. He gritted his teeth and kept fighting.

He turned inward to the center of the camp and found himself in the eye of the storm. Warriors on the other side fought Marty and Lowanna, and warriors to his left and right still battled, though his Neshili were steadily overcoming their enemies.

Here in the center, peaceful for one moment, he saw a cooking fire, with a roasting spit cooking meat over the coals, and the meat was a man he knew. It was Ammun the poet, who had gone with the girls to protect them. Maybe the cannibals had chosen him to eat for his majestic, imposed fat, which was ruined now, cut away in strips. His spine was exposed, pressed against the roasting spit, and his cooking innards.

He had been a man of heart, and he had loved his people.

The line of enemies around Surjan wavered and he hurled himself into it, shattering the last resistance, lopping off arms and heads with his ankh.

"For Ammun!" he cried.

His men saw the ruined body of the poet and took up the call. "For Ammun! For Ammun and Nesha!"

They crashed against the undefended backs of the warriors on the east side of the camp.

The sun was getting low behind the spearmen advancing on Marty and his Neshili, most of whom were young women. The few who held spears couldn't be counted on to have any military discipline or training.

"Get behind us!" he said to them. "Dawa, get your people back. I will defend them!"

He shouted the words with confidence, but there were many

warriors running their way, and he wasn't entirely sure what he was going to do about them. Sharrum and the few men who had climbed the cliff with him ranged out to his right and left.

"*We* will defend them!" Lowanna yelled. She stepped forward to Marty's side with a length of wood in her hand. As he looked, the wood thickened and grew gnarled, with its thin tip swelling into a heavy, bulbous knot. Lowanna's skin abruptly wrinkled, as if she was aging before his eyes—not aging, but drying out, becoming leathery.

Marty couldn't help but stare at the transformation. He'd never seen Lowanna do this before—it was clearly one of the preternatural tricks that had come with this new life of theirs.

Her skin became wrinkled because it looked like it was thickening, like a wrap of bark encircling her body like some new form of armor.

Marty took a spear from the hands of one of the young women and threw it at the advancing warriors. He impaled one of the men through the thigh and then he leaped into their ranks. He fought with his ankh, slicing spears neatly in half to disarm his enemies, and then taking legs and arms as well.

Lowanna fought with her club. She swung it like a croquet mallet, in great arcs, and she connected to deadly effect. Marty saw her literally cave in the head of one attacker.

When the dead man's companion happened to stab Lowanna, his spear glanced off her thickened skin. Whirling her club over her head, she brought it straight down on top of her attacker's skull. The head disappeared, and Marty couldn't tell whether she had pulverized it or pounded it down into his chest. His lifeless hands dropped his spear and he toppled over sideways.

The attackers fell back to regroup. Marty heard a commotion at the gate. Marty's spearmen had suffered wounds, but no serious casualties. He met Sharrum's gaze and they shared a congratulatory nod.

"I was going to express regret that the sky wasn't overcast," Marty said, grinning at Lowanna. "I do like those lightning bolts of yours. On the other hand, it appears you have a few more tricks up your sleeve than I had realized."

"That is indeed what I have." Her voice was flat and hard. "Tricks up my sleeve."

"At the risk of sounding totally autistic," Marty said, "I am trying to compliment you. Indeed, I am complimenting you. I am saying that you are a capable warrior and, though I still find it strange to say this, companion."

"I'm a capable teammate," she said.

"You still sound mad at me."

"It shouldn't matter to you that I'm mad," she shot back. "I'm your teammate, and I'm capable."

"You're impressive," he said, feeling a growing sense of awkwardness between them. "And skilled, and obviously strong as hell. These are desirable things."

"In a teammate," she clarified.

"In a person," he said. "Yes, in a teammate. Why the hell are you mad at me?"

The enemy charged again.

Lowanna charged the nearest attacker, throwing herself against his spear. Marty flinched, but the weapon failed to penetrate her thickened hide, and with the impetus of her charge she swung her club up into the warrior's leather kilt. He made a sound like a reluctant jam jar finally popping open and fell straight onto his back without bending his knees.

Then Marty lost track of Lowanna, dealing with his own difficulties. Sharrum did him the favor of organizing and leading the small group of Neshili fighters, and they moved to put themselves between the young women and any attackers who made it past Lowanna and Marty. This left Marty free to wreak as much havoc as he could. He sprang in among the enemy, turning aside spears with perfect slaps to the weapons' shafts. This was a skill he'd long had, dating back to kung fu practice with Grandpa Chang in his youth, but the new Marty, the time-traveling Marty who would speak with birds and run up walls, was even better than the martial artist he'd always been. Better than the young academic who'd gotten fired for punching a jerk when jerk-punching was called for.

He knew exactly how much force he needed to apply to each tap. He knew exactly where to touch the weapon with a single finger so that the fire-hardened wood or sharpened bronze tips whistled within millimeters of his skin without touching him. He saw the flaws in each man's balance that let him pull them off-center, toppling them effortlessly to the ground so he could stomp and kick them without slowing down.

It wasn't work to defeat them. It wasn't play, either. It was breathing.

He was still a finite quantity, and attackers got past him. But if Lowanna didn't bash in their heads, Sharrum and his men ran them through without mercy.

The rush of warriors fell back a second time to regroup.

Beyond them, Marty saw that the gate was now open. Neshili were pouring in through the opening, Surjan at their head. But the enemy were still numerous.

"Should we send the girls down the cliff?" he asked Lowanna.

"Good leadership," she said. "You should consult with the team. Be more of a facilitator of discussion than a dictator."

"I give up," he said. "There's a riddle, but not only do I not know what the answer is, I can't even tell what the question is. And you're angry about it. But now I'm going to send the girls down the cliff to get away, unless you tell me not to."

She sighed the angriest sigh he'd ever seen. "Don't send them down the cliff, dum-dum. Some of them will slip and be hurt. Besides, we're about to defeat these clowns, and then they'll be on the run in the forest. Any girls who actually make it to the bottom of the cliff will just be at more risk."

"Thank you," he told her.

"You're welcome," she said. "Teammate."

"I get it," he said. "You don't want to be on my team anymore."

She yelled and charged at the enemy while they were still regrouping.

Marty ran after her and Surjan and his warriors hit from the other side. Kareem emerged from one of the huts, his appearance putting him right behind two unsuspecting raiders with his ankh in hand. In moments, the remaining raiders and Neshili defectors evaporated, wiped off the grass like dandelion spores in a hurricane.

Marty put away his ankh and stalked across the bloody ground to Lowanna. As he approached, the husk of her wrinkled, leather skin fell away from her. It dropped like the old skin of a snake, peeling away in heavy chunks. She brushed at her face and forearms to shake off patches that clung.

"I'm sorry," he said.

"What for?" she asked.

"I get it," he said. "You feel like I'm ignoring you."

"Oh no," she said, "you're not ignoring me. You're treating me like one of the guys."

Marty hesitated. It felt like there was a trap here. "Sometimes, I *need* to treat you like one of the guys. You can call lightning and punch holes in ships and ... whatever it was you did today. Make a superclub and grow your own armor. And I need to be able to think about those abilities, and your great knowledge of anthropology, as assets the team can access."

She looked at him through narrowed eyes.

"As *you* need to be able to think about *my* abilities," Marty said. "As you did, when you sent the parrot to summon me."

"You can't have it both ways, Marty," she said. Her voice sounded disappointed. "You don't get to think of me as just a teammate, and then be jealous because Sharrum notices that I'm a woman."

Here was the real issue. And she was right. "I do think of you as a teammate," Marty said. "But I never think of you as *just* a teammate."

He stepped in closer to her.

She peeled skin-armor from one elbow and cast it aside. "Oh, yeah? What do you think of me as?"

"A woman," Marty said. "A hot, smart, interesting woman."

"Tell me more."

Marty didn't dare look, but he hoped that the rest of the party and the Neshili were distracted with cleanup after the battle.

"A woman who makes me want to do things."

"Teammate sorts of things?"

Marty shook his head, ignoring the rest of the world. "Naughty sorts of things."

"If you really like me," she said, "and I really like you, and I agree to it ... then maybe those sorts of things aren't really naughty after all."

"Well," Marty said, "they must be kind of naughty. I mean, they aren't the sorts of things you do in front of other people."

"Oh, no?" She looked up into his eyes.

"Well, maybe you do." He took her into his arms.

⊰ CHAPTER ⊱
TWENTY-ONE

Gunther knelt beside the wounded warrior, his hands hovering just above the torn flesh. The man grimaced, his breath coming in ragged gasps, but his eyes were locked on Gunther's, filled with a desperate hope. Gunther inhaled deeply, steeling himself for what was to come.

As he placed his hands on the wound, a barely visible glow began to emanate from beneath his fingertips. It was faint, like the first light of dawn breaking over the horizon, but it grew brighter as he focused his energy. The light pulsed with the severity of the wound, intensifying as it knitted torn muscle and fused broken bone. The tension in the warrior's body lessened as the wound began to close, the pain slowly easing.

Gunther felt the energy draining from him, a deep exhaustion settling into his bones. The glow dimmed, flickered, and then faded away as the wound sealed itself completely, leaving nothing but a puckered pink mark on the skin that would slowly fade away. Gunther swayed slightly, the world tilting around him.

He scanned the field, and there was at least another dozen who needed healing. This was the sixth man he'd healed and he'd reached a temporary limit.

With a shaking hand, he reached for the flask at his side. The amikawa had a sharp, sweet taste, and as the liquid slid down his throat, he felt a surge of warmth spread through his body. The alcohol in the drink didn't get him drunk, nor did it seem to have any bad effect on him other than a headache. Yet the exhaustion ebbed, replaced by a gentle rejuvenation that steadied his hands and cleared the fog from his mind.

Gunther moved to the next wounded man, laying his hands on a deep gash across his chest. The glow returned, brighter this time, almost blinding in its intensity. The healing was swift, the wound closing almost instantaneously, but instead of the usual fatigue, a sense of euphoria flooded through Gunther. His body tingled, electric currents dancing from the tips of his toes to the crown of his head.

He staggered back, clutching the flask, the now-empty vessel falling to the ground. His heart raced, pounding against his rib cage, and his senses heightened to an almost unbearable degree. He could hear the rustling of leaves far beyond the clearing, the soft breathing of each man around him, even the distant rush of a waterfall he hadn't known was there.

Gunther closed his eyes, trying to steady himself against the dizziness that threatened to overwhelm him. A thought wormed its way into his mind: *Have I gained a level?*

The idea was absurd, yet the sensation coursing through him felt like an elevation, a step beyond what he had known before.

He opened his eyes, expecting to see the familiar glowing balls of light they had encountered in Egypt, but there was nothing. There was something within him, pulsing, thrumming with a power he hadn't tapped into before. He could feel his mind reaching outward, far beyond the boundaries of the physical world, stretching toward a place he wasn't sure even existed.

Are you out there? he thought, the question forming on the edge of his consciousness.

For a moment, there was nothing but the sound of his own breathing, the wind rustling through the trees, and the distant, ever-present hum of life around him. Then, suddenly, his mind snapped back to the here and now as a voice responded, clear and undeniable.

I am here.

Gunther's eyes widened, his breath catching in his throat. It was the same voice that had often intruded on his thoughts, garbled and distant, but more recently it had been insistent, urging him to explore the island's underworld, a command he had resisted. But now, the voice was clearer, more present than ever before.

He looked around, half expecting to see someone standing beside him, but there was no one. The men he had healed were staring at him, their eyes wide with a mixture of awe and fear. "Gunther, you are glowing," the man he had just healed said.

Gunther swallowed hard and looked at his hands. It wasn't just his hands that were glowing, his entire body was shedding some sort of light.

These people had seen what he was capable of, and for however long he'd paused in self-reflection, his body had begun to glow... bathed in what could only seem like an act of a spirit of some kind.

The voice lingered in his thoughts, a presence just beyond the veil of reality. He had reached out, and something had reached back. Something ancient, something powerful.

The light around him faded and he shuddered as a chill raced through him.

"Are you okay?" one of the Neshili asked.

He bent down to pick up the flask, his hands trembling. The euphoria was fading, replaced by a deep, unsettling knowledge. The world had shifted around him, and he wasn't sure what that meant. But the voice, that voice, it was undeniably with him now, and there would be no turning back.

He took a deep breath, steadying himself. The men were watching, waiting for him to speak. He nodded to them, the words coming out more forcefully than he intended. "I'm fine. Let me finish tending to the wounded."

The air inside the makeshift tent was thick with tension as François paced back and forth, his usually calm demeanor strained by the weight of the conversation he was about to have. Outside, the sounds of the camp settling in for the evening drifted in—the quiet murmurs of the islanders, the crackling of the fire, and the distant calls of the jungle's creatures. But in here, it felt as though the world had been drawn tight, ready to snap.

Kareem stood by the entrance, his face a mask of indifference, arms crossed over his chest. He had been summoned, and he had been told why. But François could see the defiance in his eyes, the unspoken challenge in the way he held himself.

François stopped pacing and faced him. "Kareem," he began, his voice low but firm, "what the hell were you thinking?"

Kareem's eyes narrowed slightly, but he didn't respond immediately.

He was weighing his words, choosing carefully. "I was thinking," he said slowly, "that if I didn't kill her, by God, she would have alerted everyone to my presence. We were on the edge of attacking, François. She would have ruined everything."

François stepped closer, his eyes locked on Kareem's. "And you decided to kill her on your own? You didn't think for a moment to wait, to give us a chance to be ready? You could have scouted the area and warned us, and then any yelling she did wouldn't have mattered because the fighting would have already started."

"She was a threat," Kareem shot back, his tone edged with frustration. "A threat I neutralized. She didn't deserve a trial, not after what she'd done."

François shook his head, the anger simmering just beneath the surface. "That's not for you to decide alone. We're a team, Kareem. We don't go rogue and execute people without consulting the others. Prisoners of war, no matter how guilty, deserve some kind of process— something more than a knife in the dark."

"International Court of Justice? The Hague?"

"Something like that."

Kareem's jaw tightened. "You're being naïve, François. Out here, it's kill or be killed. She was a danger to all of us."

"And what if your actions had turned the situation against us?" François pressed. "What if her death had led to some unforeseen event that we weren't ready for? You're not a lone wolf, Kareem. You're part of this team, and that means you don't act alone when other people's lives are at stake."

For a long moment, the Frenchman and teenager stared at each other, the air between them crackling with unresolved tension. Outside, the camp was quiet, but François knew that others were aware of this conversation—maybe even listening in.

Finally, Kareem's posture softened just slightly, a reluctant acceptance in his eyes. "Fine," he muttered, looking away. "Next time, I'll consult with you before I kill someone."

"That's not good enough," François replied sharply. "You'll consult with the team, not just me. We make these decisions together, or we risk everything we've built falling apart. We're in this together, or we're not in it at all."

Kareem didn't respond immediately, but François could see the internal struggle behind his eyes. Finally, he nodded, the fight in him ebbing away. "All right," he said, his voice quieter now. "We'll do it your way."

"It's not *my* way, it's the only fair way." François let out a breath he hadn't realized he was holding. "Good. Because the others are worried, Kareem. They need to trust you, and you need to trust them. We're a team, and we should behave as such. We all have each other's back, no matter what."

Kareem gave a short, curt nod, his eyes meeting François's once more. "Understood."

The tension in the tent eased slightly, though the undercurrent of unease remained. François knew this wasn't the end of it—Kareem was a teenager, and he'd expected some sense of rambunctiousness from someone his age. But rarely did someone his age have the skills Kareem brought to the table. In addition, the young man had been shaped by a world that had taught him to survive at any cost. But for now, they had reached an understanding, and that was enough.

"Get some rest," François said finally, turning away. "We have a lot more to deal with tomorrow."

"Fine," Kareem said. "But there's something you need to know. Something I saw underneath Nesha."

Caught off guard, François sat and listened.

When Kareem had finished, he turned and left the tent. François stood alone for a moment, letting the quiet settle around him. Should he tell the others? That perhaps they had missed a portal in Nesha they were supposed to take? But what would that do, other than cast the leadership and judgment of Marty into doubt? He thought, and decided to keep his silence.

They were all walking a fine line, and every decision could be the one that tipped them over the edge. But for now, they were still together, still a team. And that had to be enough.

The heavy weight of judgment hung over Surjan as he sat at the head of the makeshift Neshili council, his queen Dawa by his side. The sky was clear, but the waves crashed hard against the sand, threatening violence and sending the ships at anchor turbulently up and down. He could hear the murmurs of the assembled islanders hushed as they awaited his decision. Before him stood the Neshili who had fought on the side of Halpa, the former queen who had betrayed them all. They were bound and kneeling, their faces a mix of fear, defiance, and resignation.

Dawa leaned in close, her voice a whisper meant only for him. "The default penalty for going against your own people is death, Surjan. You know this. But if there is anyone who will speak in their defense, you should let them do so now."

Surjan nodded, his expression impassive as he scanned the faces of the accused. "Does anyone here wish to speak on behalf of these men?" he called out, his voice strong and clear.

For a long moment, silence reigned, the only sound the rustling of the leaves in the trees above. Then, a woman stepped forward, her face lined with sorrow and desperation. She was thin, her clothes worn, but her eyes burned with the fierce love of a mother.

"My lord," she began, her voice trembling, "I plead for the life of my youngest son." She gestured to the young man kneeling before her, his head bowed. "Halpa poisoned his mind. She seduced him from the righteous path, filled his head with lies and promises. He is misguided, yes, but he is still young, still capable of redemption."

Surjan listened, his heart heavy, but his face remained unreadable. The mother's words tugged at something deep within him, but he knew this was not a time for sentiment.

Another figure emerged from the crowd—a man, older, his posture slumped with grief. He hesitated before speaking, his voice thick with sorrow. "My lord, I beg for mercy for my only son." He looked down at the boy kneeling before him, a boy who could have been no more than eighteen summers. "My wife died in the attack, and he is all I have left of her. He is my only son, my last tie to her. Please, do not take him from me."

The father's plea struck Surjan even harder. He could see the pain etched in the man's face, the unbearable loss that clung to him like a shadow. But the weight of the law, the need for justice, pressed down on Surjan's shoulders.

He looked to Dawa, seeking her counsel. Her eyes were steady, her expression firm. "We cannot show weakness, Surjan," she said softly, but with a hard edge. "This is not a time or place for nuance. We must be consistent. To go against the people is to betray the very foundation of our survival."

Surjan nodded slowly, understanding her point, even if it pained him. He turned back to the crowd, his voice heavy with the finality of his decision. "The law is clear. To betray your own people is to face death. There will be no exceptions."

The mother let out a wail of despair, collapsing to her knees beside her son. The father, too, looked as if he had been struck, his face crumpling with grief. But Surjan knew there was no turning back now. The law had to be upheld.

As the executioners stepped forward, Dawa raised her hand, and the crowd fell silent. "There are two more decrees," she announced, her voice carrying with the authority of a queen. She pointed to a woman standing at the edge of the crowd, her face pale with shock. "You, the unmarried sister of the wife who died. You will marry this man and become his sister-wife," she gestured to the grieving father, "and you will give him another son, so that his line does not end here."

Surjan turned to her, surprise flickering in his eyes, but he held his tongue. Dawa's decision was unexpected, but it was a practical solution. It hadn't dawned on him that these people held family line continuity to be important, but such things mattered to many in the modern day, why not in the distant past?

The woman at the edge of the crowd stepped forward and nodded slowly, her eyes wide with a mixture of fear and resignation. The father looked at her, his expression unreadable, but he did not protest. "And the second decree, Your Majesty?" he asked.

"My sister's handmaidens," she said. "Nirni and Kuzi."

The women were dragged forward. Surjan remembered them from his first meeting with Halpa, when she had seemed to offer them to him along with herself. "Yes," he said.

"They came only because they were compelled," Dawa said. "We spare them."

Surjan inclined his head, signaling his approval of Dawa's decrees. The executions were carried out swiftly, the cries of the mother and father echoing in the stillness of the clearing. Nirni and Kuzi wept, maybe from the relief of survival as well as for those they had lost. Surjan watched, his heart heavy with the burden of leadership, knowing that this was the price of order, the cost of ensuring the survival of their people.

When it was done, he turned to Dawa, his voice low. "Your decision was unexpected, but wise," he said, his tone carefully measured.

Dawa turned to him and gave him a warm smile. "I watched my sister and learned a lot. Both what to do and *not* do. I believe we must balance justice with the needs of our people, Surjan. This is the way forward."

Surjan nodded in agreement, though the weight of the day's events still pressed heavily on him. As they turned to leave, the cries of the grieving parents still lingered in his mind, a reminder of the harsh realities of the world they now lived in.

He glanced at the new queen and felt a sense of contentment. When the time came for him and the team to leave this time and place, the Neshili would be in good hands.

⋈ CHAPTER ⋈
TWENTY-TWO

The wind whipped cold and fierce across the deck as Marty stood at the helm, his eyes fixed on the distant horizon. The air had a bite to it now, a sharp contrast to the humid jungles they had left behind weeks ago. The sails billowed above him, catching the strong gusts as their high-prowed vessels cut through the choppy waters of the southern Atlantic. The journey had been long, almost three weeks of endless ocean, and the men and women on board were weary, but there was a growing sense of anticipation as they neared their destination.

Marty pulled his cloak tighter against the chill of the early morning. It was one of the many patchwork creations made from various animal hides that the Neshili had prepared in response to the cooling weather. He had warned them that this place would be different, colder, harsher. The weather had been gradually cooling as they sailed south, but it wasn't until dawn of this morning that someone had shouted from the lookout, their voice edged with awe and fear.

Squinting at the horizon, he spotted the first sign of what he'd been looking for—an iceberg, its massive white form floating serenely in the distance, a silent sentinel of the frigid waters they were entering.

Marty stared at it, his heart sinking and yet oddly exhilarated. An icy destination. It was exactly as he had envisioned. They were getting closer, maybe very close. He turned to the others on deck, a mix of former islanders and his own team, and gave the order. "Veer onto shore. It's time to find a place for all of us to settle."

The crew moved quickly, adjusting the sails and setting their course toward the distant shoreline that was just beginning to take shape against the graying sky. Marty kept his eyes on the land, his mind racing with the possibilities that lay ahead. This land was vast and wild, untouched by any civilization they knew of. This was where the Neshili would make their new home.

As they neared the coast, the full scope of the landscape came into view. Rolling plains stretched out before them, covered in tall grasses that swayed in the cool breeze. To the north, the land rose into rocky hills, their peaks dusted with snow. The sight was both beautiful and forbidding, a stark contrast to the lush jungles and warm beaches they had left behind.

The ship grounded softly on a pebbled beach, and Marty was the first to step ashore. The ground was firm beneath his feet, the air filled with the scent of salt and earth. He turned to the others, who were beginning to disembark, their faces a mix of relief and uncertainty.

Surjan hopped off the bow of the ship, splashing at the shore and grimacing. "The water is freezing!" He hopped onto the pebbly beach, put his arm over Marty's shoulders, and whispered, "Is this where we start *our* journey to the beyond?"

"It is." Marty nodded. "But we need to find a suitable site for the Neshili."

Surjan turned to the nearest islander who'd just hopped onto shore and said, "Tell the other ships to moor near the shore. We need some warriors for an exploration team, and we will scout this place to find our new home."

Without hesitation, the islander raced off to do what his king had requested.

As more of the island warriors gathered, Marty announced to the group, "We all return back to this spot before sundown. We are looking for somewhere with access to fresh water, native fruit, and good hunting grounds. We'll split into groups and search the area."

The Neshili formed their own search parties and moved out quickly, with one of the groups being led by Surjan. They all spread along the shoreline and into the hinterland. Marty led one group of about a dozen warriors himself, heading toward the northern hills. As they trekked inland, they found signs of wildlife: small streams trickling down from the hills, clusters of berry bushes, and the tracks of animals unfamiliar to them. The land was fertile, promising, despite the cooler climate.

After nearly a full day of scouting, the teams regrouped near the beach. They gathered around a small fire, sharing their findings. One group had discovered a large freshwater lake just a short distance inland, its waters clear and cold. Another had found an area rich with trees bearing fruit that were strange, unfamiliar, but seemingly edible.

"The site near the lake is ideal," one of the scouts suggested, his face flushed from the cold. "It is fed by a large, winding river which comes from the north and continues south. The water is sweet, I spotted what I think are deer and maybe some form of furry, short-necked llamas, and it's sheltered from the worst of the wind by the hills."

Marty nodded, considering the options. The lake was a good choice, providing a reliable water source and could likely be used to introduce irrigation and farming techniques to these people. He'd also noticed the temperature rose quite a bit the farther inland they were. The nearby forests would also provide plenty of wood to build with. This place in the future would be miles upon miles of fertile grasslands that supported farming and the raising of livestock. There wouldn't be a reason these people couldn't make those things work in this ancient past, once they figured out what grew here.

He turned to Surjan and asked, "What do you think?"

Dawa, who'd been sitting near the fire with Surjan, grabbed the king's hand and pronounced, "I like it." She panned her gaze across the landscape. "Are we sure there will be no flooding?"

Marty noticed the look of concern and realized that these people had no clue they weren't on yet another island. Their people had always lived on an island and probably couldn't conceive of what living on the mainland would be like. "I think you will find that these lands are vast and proof against the kind of flooding you encountered back on Nesha."

Dawa held a thoughtful expression and nodded. "It will be different," she said softly and sandwiched Surjan's large hand between her own, "but we will make it our home."

Surjan did his best to not look uncomfortable, but Marty could easily guess what was going through the man's thoughts. The team would be leaving these people behind and their head of site security was not thrilled about the inevitable upset the young bride would encounter with her husband's departure.

"Then it's settled," Marty said, turning to the others. "We'll set up camp near the lake and start planning the settlement. We have a lot of work ahead of us."

The sun was beginning to set, casting long shadows across the plains as the island people of Nesha finished removing all of their possessions from the boats and began the process of migrating inland toward their new homesite. Marty lingered on the beach for a moment, watching as the last light of day glinted off a distant iceberg, a reminder of the challenges that lay ahead.

He took a deep breath, the cold air filling his lungs, and turned to follow the others.

They had brought these people to safety, and this was just the beginning of what he knew would be an arduous journey. But as he walked toward the unknown, there was a strange sense of peace that settled over him.

The Neshili were where they belonged, but the vision of a large, glowing wall of ice loomed large in his mind.

Marty and his team had come this far with fewer dangers than he'd actually expected. If things continued going as planned, they might reach their goal within the week. What lay beyond the wall of ice was something that kept him up at night.

Despite Surjan's role as the king of these people, Marty knew that the team would be looking to him as the de facto leader. It was easy enough for him to point generally to the south, given that his visions had made their destination clear enough. But once they reached their destination, then what?

If only he could see past the icy barrier . . .

It was early morning as Kareem moved cautiously through the dense brush, his spear held loosely in his hand, ready to strike at the first sign of danger. The air was cool, the sun casting long shadows across the unfamiliar landscape as he explored the area around the newly chosen settlement site for the islanders. The ground was damp beneath his boots, the earth rich and dark, and the scent of wet foliage filled his nostrils. It was quiet here, the only sounds the rustling of leaves and the occasional distant call of a bird.

He had been walking for nearly an hour when he spotted something unusual: a mound of disturbed earth, partially obscured by thick undergrowth. Kareem narrowed his eyes, approaching cautiously. As he drew closer, he saw that it was not just a mound, but the entrance to a burrow, wide and deep, the earth freshly turned.

Kareem's instincts immediately went on high alert. He crouched low, peering into the darkness of the burrow, his grip tightening on the spear.

He slowly breathed in deeply and tasted the air. There was a musky scent of an animal on the breeze. Kareem wasn't sure how he knew it, but his senses told him that there was something living nearby.

His mind raced, considering the possibilities. What kind of creature lived in this hole dug into the side of a hill? Something large enough to warrant a burrow this size, that was certain. But before he could ponder further, movement from within the burrow caught his eye.

Two large shapes emerged, shuffling out of the darkness and into the light. Kareem's breath caught in his throat as he took in their appearance. They were like nothing he had ever seen before— somewhat resembling sloths, but far larger, easily the size of a large dog. Their thick, shaggy fur was matted with dirt, and their long claws dug into the earth as they moved. But what struck him most was their behavior. These creatures were not slow or timid like the sloths he'd heard about as a kid. Instead, they eyed him with an unsettling aggression, their beady eyes narrowing as they regarded him. One of them let out a low, growling sound, a noise that sent a shiver down Kareem's spine.

Kareem instinctively raised his spear, every muscle in his body tensing, ready to eliminate what he perceived as a potential threat to the former islanders. But as he steadied his weapon, François's voice echoed in his mind, sharp and reprimanding. *We're a team, Kareem.... You don't act alone when other people's lives are at stake.*

He hesitated, the memory of the chewing out he had received from François still fresh. His instincts screamed at him to act, to neutralize the threat before it could grow into something more dangerous, but he forced himself to lower the spear. The creatures were watching him closely, their movements cautious, their bodies tensed, ready to spring at a moment's notice.

Kareem slowly backed away, keeping his eyes on the creatures until he was out of sight. Only then did he turn and make his way back to the camp, his heart still pounding in his chest. As he walked, he couldn't shake the feeling that he had encountered something significant, something that needed to be addressed.

When he arrived back at the camp, he found François and immediately pulled him aside, his voice low and urgent. "I found something. A burrow, with creatures inside. They looked like sloths, but bigger—about the size of large dogs. And they didn't seem at all afraid of me. In fact, they seemed . . . aggressive."

François's expression darkened, his eyes narrowing as he listened. "How big were they, exactly?"

Kareem thought for a moment, then gestured with his hands, indicating their size. "Larger than most street dogs in Cairo, but not by much. Maybe the size of a wolf, or a big dog."

François's face grew even more concerned, and he glanced around the camp, his mind clearly racing. Without a word, he turned and called for Marty, his voice carrying across the camp. Within moments, Marty appeared, his brow furrowed as he and Lowanna approached.

"What is it?" Marty asked, his tone serious.

François quickly relayed what Kareem had told him, his voice urgent. "If these are what I think they are, we need to investigate immediately. They could be dangerous, especially if there are more of them around."

Marty nodded and didn't hesitate, immediately gathering a small team of the best warriors and trackers. Kareem watched as the group quickly armed themselves, preparing for whatever they might find.

"Show us where, Kareem," François said, his tone leaving no room for argument.

Kareem nodded, his mind still racing with the memory of those creatures, and led the team back onto the rough hill area he'd been exploring. As they moved through the dense undergrowth, he couldn't help but wonder what exactly was the issue. After all, Kareem was sure he could have dispatched the threat himself. Why all the others?

Even with the brightness of the midday sun chasing the shadows away, Kareem felt a sense of foreboding settle over him like a shroud.

As they approached the flat area ahead of where he'd found the burrow, the air seemed warmer. It was thick and heavy, the warm breeze carried with it a strong scent of musk.

They were obviously downwind of the sloths, but why was the scent so much stronger now than just a couple hours earlier?

Noticing Kareem's nose wrinkle, Marty breathed in deeply and detected the musky odor of an animal.

Kareem pointed east and whispered, "At the base of that hill in the distance is where the burrow is."

François approached Marty and said in an urgent voice, "If Kareem is right, these aren't just any sloths. They might be Megatherium."

Marty glanced at François, frowning. "Megatherium? Let's pretend I'm not a zoological expert. What is a Megatherium?"

François stopped and motioned for Kareem, Lowanna, and the eight warriors to gather closer so they could hear. "Megatherium is a type of giant ground sloth that lived during the Pleistocene epoch."

"The Pleist . . . what?" one of the former-islanders asked.

François waved dismissively, "Sorry, I mean these creatures aren't something you've ever seen before. They are mostly herbivores—plant eaters—but they are massive, capable of growing to the size of an elephant." He glanced at the islanders, who seemed more confused than ever. "Twenty times bigger than the largest goat you have ever seen. Anyway, I think the creatures Kareem saw were very young specimens. And if those were truly young burrow-dwellers, then their parents are likely not far away."

There was a collective intake of breath from the team. Marty's mind raced as he processed the information. "Infants the size of wolves? That's . . . insane. But the sloths I'm familiar with are slow-moving and not typically aggressive."

Kareem cleared his throat and shook his head. "Those things growled at me. It was like they were trying to intimidate me, by God."

Marty nodded, reevaluating their position. The tools and weapons they had were designed for hunting animals they knew, not for taking down elephant-sized sloths. He wasn't sure they were equipped for this.

He looked over at Lowanna and asked, "Is this the kind of thing you have any guesses about? I know you're an anthropologist and all, but—"

"No." Lowanna shook her head and gave him a crooked smile. "I'm not aware of any animal's disposition ever being captured in the fossil record, nor have I learned of such in the spoken history of the indigenous people. I'm guessing these things mostly disappeared a long time ago."

François nodded. "Just about ten thousand years before our time."

Marty sniffed the air once again and said, "Well, I guess there's only one way to find out, but everyone needs to be extremely cautious. We have no idea how aggressive these creatures might be, especially if they feel their territory is threatened. So we'll go at this very slowly."

With Marty taking the lead, the team continued onward.

The pungent scent of these Mega-things filled his nostrils and even the Neshili, whose senses weren't as sharp as his, began wrinkling their noses at the aroma.

For a moment, the clouds above parted and the sun beamed its harsh light down onto the grassland. Marty squinted at the brightness and his heart skipped a beat.

There, at the base of the hill about two hundred yards ahead, two massive creatures lumbered into view and paused next to a copse of bushes. These things were easily the size of large bears.

Kareem pointed frantically and Marty nodded. "Those aren't the size of dogs."

With Marty's hand blocking the sunlight, he focused on the creatures in the distance, trying to make out the details of what they were facing. Their shaggy fur lay very differently from a bear's, and the loping gait was another dead giveaway that these weren't bears. And besides, he was pretty sure there was no history of bears ever having been in this part of the world. Marty's breath caught in his throat as the reality of it hit him. François was probably right.

Giant sloths.

Creatures that were supposed to have been extinct for over ten thousand years—from a twenty-first-century point of view, that is—and yet here they were, living and breathing before his eyes.

François's face was pale, but his voice remained steady. "It's hard to believe it, but this is undeniable proof that we're not in Kansas anymore." He glanced at Marty with a grin. "That's what you Americans like to say, isn't it?"

Marty felt a surge of adrenaline, his mind racing. These things weren't exactly something he wanted to mess with, but now what? What should their objective be? Were they here to document, to observe, to protect the former islanders from these massive beasts? His thoughts were interrupted by a low, rumbling growl that reverberated through the air.

The winds had shifted and the sloths had caught their scent.

Marty's heart pounded as the creatures turned their massive heads toward the group, their eyes locking onto the group of humans with an unsettling awareness. The larger of the two let out a deafening bellow and began to charge; flying clumps of dirt and dust billowed behind the accelerating creature. The other followed suit, their movements surprisingly fast for creatures so large.

"Get ready!" Marty shouted, his voice cutting through the tension as the team braced for impact. Weapons were drawn, but there was an air of uncertainty, a sense that they might not be enough to stop these beasts.

But before the sloths could reach them, Marty caught movement from the corner of his eye.

Lowanna, who had been standing slightly behind the group, moved forward and began to glow. A soft, ethereal light surrounded her, growing brighter as she raised her hands toward the charging sloths. The creatures, mid-charge, suddenly froze in place, their bodies seemingly rigid as if every joint had locked in place.

Marty watched in awe as the massive creatures toppled over, their momentum carrying them forward even as their bodies refused to move. They landed heavily on their sides, the earth shaking with the impact. But they were still breathing, their chests rising and falling rapidly, their eyes blinking in confusion.

These things were easily thousands of pounds each, with the larger of the two probably twice the size of an American bison.

Marty turned to Lowanna, who was now approaching the downed creatures with a calm, steady gait. She glanced back at him and gave a playful wink. "I suggested they hold their position. We want to talk... and I guess my suggestion worked better than I thought it would."

Marty stared at her, his mind reeling. He had seen Lowanna's abilities before, but this was something entirely different. She had stopped these enormous creatures with nothing but a thought. As she neared the sloths, she knelt beside the larger of the two, placing a gentle hand on its thick fur.

Lowanna's glow intensified slightly as she closed her eyes, her lips moving silently as she communicated with the creatures. Marty and the rest of the team watched in stunned silence, not daring to interrupt whatever was happening. Marty knew that if he walked closer, he would understand the conversation, but he was afraid that his presence might upset the sloths, and stayed put.

After a few tense moments, Lowanna opened her eyes and stood, turning back to the group. "We've come to an understanding," she said, her voice carrying a strange, soothing quality. "We won't disturb their den, and they won't disturb us."

Marty exhaled a breath he hadn't realized he was holding. "That's . . . good. But why were they so aggressive?"

Lowanna tilted her head thoughtfully, her gaze distant as she relayed the sloth's words. "They're wondering why we've settled here. Most humans they've seen travel south from the north."

"South?" Marty asked, his curiosity piqued. "South where?"

The larger sloth, still lying immobile on the ground, made a low rumbling sound.

Three days' journey to the south.

"They say there's a human outpost three days south of here," Lowanna announced for the benefit of the others.

Marty's mind raced. A human outpost? In 9000 B.C.E.? "Where exactly?"

Lowanna turned back to the rigid sloths; her brows furrowed as she concentrated. After a moment she turned back to Marty and said, "Their thoughts aren't exactly like ours, but the best I can get out of them is that the outpost is 'where the ice meets the river.'"

Marty's blood ran cold at the mention of ice. They had seen the iceberg in the water, the harbinger of a colder, more treacherous land, but there was no real sign of ice on the land. His thoughts raced as he tried to piece together what this could mean. A human settlement at the edge of an icy expanse? It didn't make sense, but nothing about their journey so far had made sense.

Yet such a thing would match what his visions had been promising him. Somewhere south of them was their icy destination, and if there was a human outpost to the south, and it was in any way associated with ice, then that's where they'd have to go.

Lowanna's glow faded as she took a step back.

The sloths made loud guttural sounds as their limbs twitched.

We do not hate humans. We will leave the humans alone.
We know of no other humans here.

The team took several steps backward as the giant creatures began to move.

The giant sloths slowly rose to their feet and, for a few terrifying moments, stared silently at the humans. Then they turned and lumbered back toward the den, casting one last glance at the humans before disappearing into the darkness of the burrow.

Marty motioned to Kareem, François, and Lowanna as his mind still buzzed with the implications of what they had just learned. "Guys, we need to figure out what's going on to the south. If there's a settlement there, we need to go find it."

François leaned forward and spoke in English. "I'm thinking this is where we leave our island friends behind."

Marty nodded. "We need to have a team meeting, but yes. I suspect so. Regardless, we need to inform the Neshili that Lowanna has struck a bargain with these creatures." He looked over at the hill and noticed that two smaller sloths had come out of the den. "I'd recommend that the Neshili not disturb these creatures."

As the team began walking back the way they'd come, Marty walked up beside Lowanna, snaked his arm around her waist, and gave her a quick one-armed hug. "Pretty impressive stuff you did back there."

Lowanna glanced at him and her normally somber expression cracked with a hint of a smile. "I didn't want anyone to get hurt, and it was what came to mind."

François looked over his shoulder in their direction and Marty leaned his head against Lowanna's. The Frenchman grinned, shifted his gaze to one of the Neshili, and began talking with him.

Lowanna grabbed Marty's hand, interlacing her fingers with his as they walked side by side.

Marty wasn't sure exactly why, but he sensed that something had shifted within Lowanna. Maybe because they were getting closer to their destination. Or maybe because he'd tried to show that he appreciated her as a woman. Either way, it was a positive change, and one that they'd need.

Marty knew one thing for certain: their mission was far from over, and the dangers they faced were only beginning to reveal themselves.

⇥ CHAPTER ⇤
TWENTY-THREE

The sun hung low in the sky, casting long shadows over the clearing where the Neshili worked tirelessly. The rhythmic sound of stone axes striking wood, the grunts of exertion, and the occasional murmur of conversation filled the air as they labored on clearing the land and constructing the walls to what would be their new home. Lowanna moved silently among them, her senses attuned to the earth beneath her feet and the life that pulsed all around her.

The Neshili were having a tough time with the work, especially since the local wood was much harder than any they'd encountered on the island.

It was under François's guidance that the Neshili began working with what the Frenchman had identified as mesquite and quebracho, both of which were extremely hard and resistant to rot and insects. These woods, François had explained, would ensure their walls stood strong against the elements and any potential threats.

The primitive tools slowed their progress, and Lowanna could see the frustration etched on the faces of the natives. These people, once island dwellers, were unaccustomed to the demands of building large-scale walls or clearing vast amounts of land. The clearing was beginning to take shape, but the walls they were constructing around it were progressing far too slowly for her liking.

During the team meeting, they'd all agreed that they wouldn't leave until the Neshili were on solid footing, and that meant these people needed protection from whatever dangers lurked out there, which meant they needed a wall.

Lowanna felt a familiar restlessness stirring within her. Her connection to the land, to the plants and creatures that thrived here, was a constant presence, a power she'd grown used to and had begun learning how to harness and control it. But now, watching the painstakingly slow construction, she felt an urge to act, to bend the natural world to her will and speed up the process.

She removed her boots, the only remnants she had of where she'd come from, and walked to the edge of the clearing, her bare feet sinking into the cool earth. For some reason, the physical contact with the soil made her feel better, even sometimes improving what would otherwise be a sour mood.

The forest beckoned to her, its hidden secrets whispering on the breeze. She closed her eyes, letting her senses expand outward, searching for the plants and vines she knew would be nearby. In her mind's eye, she could see them—strong, resilient vines, capable of binding the wooden walls together with a strength no tool could match.

Once the walls were up, they could cover them with clay, a technique that was used almost worldwide in primitive cultures for making walls stronger.

Her eyes snapped open, and she began to move, slipping away from the group and into the dense undergrowth. Her movements were fluid, almost animalistic, as she navigated the forest floor. She found what she was looking for quickly: a cluster of vines coiled around the base of a towering tree, their leaves glistening with dew. It seemed like an entire section of the forest had these ropelike vines climbing up the tree trunks. Lowanna knelt beside the nearest of them, placing her hands on the ground, feeling the life force within them.

With a whispered word in a language known only to the earth and the creatures that lived within it, Lowanna reached out with her power. She could feel the vines respond, their energy shifting as she guided them, coaxing them to grow, to spread. They obeyed her command, the tendrils unfurling and stretching out, moving in the direction she willed.

Lowanna's eyes grew wider as she rose to her feet. Even though she'd willed it to be, it still left her dumbfounded that these otherwise inanimate plants responded to her.

Hundreds of vines from the neighboring trees all unwound themselves and began writhing on the ground. They curled themselves into balls and began to roll. It was as if a wind were blowing them like a tumbleweed—toward the clearing. She followed them, her pace quickening as she felt the energy building within her, the connection between her and the plants strengthening with every step.

Her abilities were not something she was conscious of . . . she was acting on pure instinct.

When she returned to the clearing, the others had barely noticed her absence. The workers continued to haul logs and seat them into the holes dug into the hard-packed soil, unaware of the green tendrils that were now snaking their way across the ground, creeping toward the half-built walls.

Lowanna's eyes glowed with an inner light as she dug deep within herself, summoning more of whatever it was inside her that made these abilities a reality. She could feel the earth respond, the plants surging with energy as they rolled up against some of the loosely seated logs, unfurling themselves from their tumbleweedlike form. Their tendrils began wrapping around the logs, weaving in and out across the nearest wall, tightening the binding between each log.

She called to the nearest bewildered workers and yelled, "Quickly! Seat the other logs into their holes."

The workers scrambled, rolling the prepared logs into place as some murmured things under their breath and stared wide-eyed at the writhing vines that had gathered around Lowanna.

"Magic."

"The gods are at work through her."

"The priestess is gifted by the gods."

Lowanna ignored the speculation as she focused on the work at hand. The moment a new log was seated, several of the vines lashed out to it, intertwining with the wood and binding it to its neighbor with a strength that rivaled anything the Neshili were capable of.

After nearly an hour of this, this section of the wall that once stood fragile and incomplete began to take on a new sturdiness that was miraculous given the short time that had elapsed.

Lowanna's eyes were closed as she felt her power waning. Nonetheless, she sensed his presence approaching before he ever uttered a word.

"You're full of surprises, my dear," Marty said with a light tone.

Lowanna gave him a sly smile, her eyes still glowing with the remnants of her power. "The land here is strong . . . I know it sounds strange, but I can feel it in the same way I can your pulse by holding your wrist. And somehow, it listens to me when I'm speaking to it."

"That's an amazing talent. How long have you been able to do this trick with the vines?"

"About an hour."

"Wow."

"Learn by doing."

Marty panned his gaze across the one-hundred-foot section of wall. "You probably saved days of work in just that amount of time." He put his hand lightly on her shoulder and asked, "Are you okay?"

Lowanna nodded. "Just a bit tired. Doing this does kind of suck something out of me."

Marty kneaded her shoulders and said, "You're really tense. Maybe you should talk with Gunther about that stuff he drinks to replenish that healing battery of his. It might help you as well."

Lowanna pressed her lips together, focusing on the vines writhing on the ground, and doing her best to ignore what she was feeling with Marty giving her an impromptu massage. If she had her way, the vines wouldn't be the only things writhing on the ground, but sadly now was not the time.

Feeling the energy within her begin to wane, she called out to the workers, "I have to stop now. Gather more logs, prepare the ground to receive them, and we'll do this again when you're ready."

Standing behind her, Marty leaned forward, put his chin on her shoulder, and said, "It's getting late. I'll go find Surjan and make sure we have lookouts scheduled through the night. You go talk with Gunther and get some rest tonight. You need it."

Lowanna took in a deep breath and slowly let it out. There was something about that man that drove her crazy with emotions, both good and bad—well, maybe not bad, but he frustrated her beyond anyone she'd ever met.

She let go of whatever thread of control she'd been maintaining on the vines, and they convulsed and fell in heaps across the clearing.

One of the workers approached her. He looked nervous and was wringing his hands. "Um, Priestess Lowanna?"

Lowanna tilted her head as she looked at the sweat-covered islander and sensed a nervous fear coming from him. What goddess, exactly, did they think she was a priestess of? Flower Girl? But "priestess" was more respectful than "sorceress," in any case. "Yes?"

The man pointed at the lifeless vines and asked, "Are they asleep or should we gather them for tomorrow's work?"

She let out a short laugh and gave the nervous man an uncharacteristic smile. "I brought them out here for us to use. Go ahead and gather them up, we'll need them."

The man nodded and he shifted a nervous gaze to the nearest piles of vines. He looked back and forth between her and the vines, as if debating with himself if he could trust her. Suddenly, he grabbed at the nearest vine and almost immediately dropped it, his expression full of suspicion.

"Don't worry, I promise you they won't do anything if you pick them up."

The man nodded and focused on the vine that he'd previously grabbed and dropped. The pace of his breathing was elevated and he looked like he was psyching himself up. With his jaw tightened, he reached forward and quickly grabbed the vine, holding it as far away from him as he might do with a snake.

Lowanna chuckled and the man grinned in response.

He gathered another vine, and without any obvious signs of these things coming to life, he called to the others and they all began to gather the vines, looping them into coils and creating a neat stack for use tomorrow.

The sun dipped low on the horizon, casting long shadows across the clearing. Lowanna took in a few deep breaths and allowed herself a moment of peace. Somehow, she'd commanded the vines to help and it had worked. They were that much closer to moving onward.

Lowanna stared through the many gaps in the wall and knew that even with the help of the vines, there were still several days of work ahead before they would have a usable barrier.

As she gazed out over the pampas, a faint unease settled in her stomach. The land was wild, untamed, and full of secrets. While she had bent some of it to her will today, she knew that the true challenges still lay in wait for them.

✛ ✛ ✛

François stood at the edge of the newly cleared field, the warm sun on his back as he gestured toward the freshwater lake that shimmered in the distance. The Neshili, gathered around him, listened intently, their faces a mix of curiosity and concern. These people had always relied on the sea and the bounty of their island for sustenance, but here, on the mainland, things would be different. The vast, open land was both a blessing and a challenge, and François was determined to prepare them for what lay ahead.

"Look at the slope of this land," François began, pointing to the gentle incline that led down to the lake. "We can use the water from the lake to irrigate these fields, ensuring that your crops will have enough water even during dry spells. But it requires planning and effort."

He picked up a stick and began to draw in the dirt, sketching out a simple diagram. "We can dig channels here and here," he explained, marking the lines in the soil. "These will direct water from the lake up the slope and into the fields. We can use a series of pulleys and levers, like a shaduf, to lift the water from the lake. It's a technique used in many parts of the world, and it will allow you to grow crops even in areas that are not directly beside the water."

"I'm sorry, François," one of the former islanders interjected, his brows furrowed. "I don't understand. How can we lift the water up a slope?"

"A shaduf is the name of a simple tool that was used a long time ag—I mean that I've seen it used before. Imagine a long pole with a heavy stone on one end and a bucket on the other. We lower the bucket into the water, and the stone helps lift it back up. Then, we pour the water where it's needed, often into an irrigation trough that I'll show you how to make. This shaduf makes the work much easier."

"Ah!" The islander's eyes widened with understanding. "So the stone does the lifting?"

"Exactly. The stone balances the weight, so you don't have to lift the water by yourself."

The Neshili murmured among themselves, some nodding in understanding, others furrowing their brows as they tried to grasp the concept.

One of the younger islanders, a boy named Huz, scratched his head. "François, why are you teaching us all of this now? You've shown us how to find food in this new place, what wood to use to build our walls, and now this farming that you're speaking of . . . it's a lot to take in at once. Why all of this so quickly?"

François hesitated, his heart sinking slightly. He had been dreading this moment, knowing that the truth would have to come out eventually. But it wasn't his place to be the one to tell them, to break the news that the team would be leaving soon. They had done their part in saving the Neshili from the encroaching waters, and the time was coming for the former islanders to stand on their own.

He looked at the teen, choosing his words carefully. "The world is a dangerous place," he said slowly, his voice steady. "You've seen that already. There are many things out there that we don't fully understand, and there are threats that can appear without warning. I'm teaching you all of this now because . . . well, I may not always be here to guide you. I want to make sure that you can thrive, no matter what happens."

Huz's eyes widened slightly, and François saw the wheels turning in his mind. The young man wasn't foolish—he sensed that there was more to François's words than he was letting on. But he didn't press the issue, simply nodding slowly as he absorbed the information.

François turned back to the group, forcing a smile. "This knowledge is your safeguard, your way of ensuring that your people will continue to grow and prosper. These techniques are tried and true, and with them, you can transform this land into a thriving home."

He moved to the edge of the field, where a small patch of earth had been prepared for planting. Kneeling down, he scooped up a handful of soil, letting it sift through his fingers. "This soil is rich, but it needs care. We'll start by planting crops that are hardy, ones that can withstand the cooler climate here. Once the irrigation system is in place, you'll be able to expand, grow more diverse crops, and even trade with others you might meet."

As he spoke, François felt the weight of the situation pressing down on him. The Neshili were resilient, but they were also vulnerable, thrust into a world that was entirely new to them. He had to give them every tool, every piece of knowledge he could, because soon, they would be on their own. And he had no idea what kind of threats existed in this place. This was still a world when the megafauna had yet to go extinct. Things like the giant sloth or even saber-toothed tigers roamed the forest and plains, and these people needed to be ready.

He stood up, brushing the dirt from his hands. "Let's start with the channels. We'll need to dig them deep enough to carry the water without losing too much to evaporation. I'll show you how."

The Neshili set to work, their movements slower than usual, weighed down by the uncertainty of their future. François moved among them, offering guidance and encouragement, but his thoughts were elsewhere, turning over the reality of what was to come.

As the sun dipped lower in the sky, casting long shadows across the field, François paused to look out over the lake. The water shimmered, calm and inviting, but for all he knew, there could be deadly threats in those waters. He wasn't a prehistoric zoologist, none of them were.

These people needed to be careful.

François wasn't the kind of person who was known for his compassion and mothering instincts. On the contrary, he knew himself to be a bit of a curmudgeon, but these people deserved peace after what they'd been through.

As he watched the Neshili work, he couldn't help but feel a pang of guilt, knowing that the foundation they were building together was one that he would soon have to leave behind.

Gunther stood before the newly constructed wall, his eyes narrowing as he studied it with a critical gaze. The final section of the wall had just been raised, encircling the Neshili's first settlement, a physical barrier meant to protect them from the unknown dangers of this ancient land. But as solid as the wall appeared, Gunther couldn't shake the nagging doubt gnawing at the back of his mind.

The tales of the giant sloths had reached him—massive creatures with the power to crush a man with a single swipe, their aggression unlike anything any of the islanders had encountered before. If those sloths decided to attack the settlement, would these walls hold? What if a neighboring tribe of natives attacked? Would the walls protect the people as they slept, as they toiled to build a new life here?

Gunther's jaw tightened as he reached out and placed his hands on the rough surface of the wall. The woven vines and wood, though expertly crafted, felt almost insignificant under his touch. Someone had mentioned that the walls would be covered with a clay-and-straw mixture to solidify it further, but he knew that the core of the wall's strength would be what was in front of him right now. His heart thudded in his chest, the weight of responsibility pressing down on him. He had become a healer, but here, in this ancient, untamed world, he felt as if his role had expanded to something more—a protector, a guardian.

He closed his eyes, trying to steady his racing thoughts. As he did, he felt a familiar presence stir within him, a surge of energy that flowed from deep inside, something primal and raw. The voice, the one that had always been there, just on the edge of his consciousness, grew louder, clearer.

"How can I strengthen this wall?" Gunther thought, his mind reaching out to the presence. "Make it more impervious to attack?"

For a moment, there was nothing but the sound of his own heartbeat, the cool breeze rustling the leaves. But then he felt it—a response, not in words, but in purpose. The energy within him surged, and he sensed a direction, a clarity to the power that coursed through him.

He didn't fully understand what he was doing, but he didn't need to. Gunther let the energy flow through him, into the wall, his hands pressed firmly against the vines and wood. His connection to the voice deepened even though it hadn't uttered a word. He felt his mind guided along a path. The barrier between him and the wall seemed to dissolve as if they were becoming one.

A flash of brilliant white was all he saw in his mind's eye.

He opened his eyes and nothing changed.

Gunther gasped.

Had he gone blind?

But it wasn't dark—it was the brilliant white that he'd encountered when traveling to this world.

It was the flashes of white when the voice had spoken to him.

But something was very different.

He felt the ground under his feet.

The palms of his hand rested against the wall of the Neshili sanctuary.

Suddenly, heat bloomed within his chest, pouring through his arms. He felt like gouts of flame were about to burst from his palms.

And in the blink of an eye, the white veil vanished and he was fully back in the here and now. But something about the world around him had changed.

The wall shimmered faintly, a soft glow emanating from the woven vines. The tiny gaps in the weaving that had been visible moments before began to close, the vines both tightening and expanding as if guided by an unseen hand. The entire structure rippled and writhed, somehow seeming to grow more substantial, more solid.

Gunther's breath caught in his throat as he watched the transformation, his heart pounding in his chest. The glow intensified for a moment, and then, as quickly as it had begun, it faded, the light dimming to nothing. But the change remained. The wall, once a patchwork of vines and wood, now looked impenetrable, seamless.

Around him, the Neshili who had been working nearby had stopped, their tools hanging limply in their hands as they stared in stunned silence. One of the warriors, a tall man with a scar running down his cheek, stepped forward and tapped the wall with the butt of his spear. The sound that echoed back was solid, resonant, as if the wall had been forged from stone rather than plant and wood.

The warrior looked at Gunther, his expression a mix of awe and confusion. Gunther nodded slowly, his chest still rising and falling with the remnants of the euphoric surge that had accompanied the transformation. He felt content, more so than he had in a long time. Whatever had just happened, it felt right.

He stepped back from the wall, his hands falling to his sides, still tingling with the remnants of the energy that had passed through them. Gunther closed his eyes for a brief moment, sending up a silent prayer to the voice, the presence that had guided him.

I don't know what I did, or maybe what you did through me, he thought, his mind reaching out once more, *but it seems like a job well done.*

As he opened his eyes, the warrior gave him a curt nod, respect and gratitude etched into his features. The Neshili resumed their work, building the first of many small huts for the people to live in—a shelter from the elements.

Gunther stepped away from the wall, his body humming with the afterglow of what had just occurred. The doubt that had plagued him earlier was gone, replaced by a quiet confidence. The walls protecting the Neshili as they slept were solid, hopefully impenetrable. Whatever came next, he'd done for the former islanders what he could to help.

As he walked away, the sun beginning its descent, casting long shadows over the settlement, Gunther felt a peace settle over him. He didn't fully understand the power he had tapped into, but he sensed its presence. It was there, accessible with just a mental flick and the connection would be restored.

What was this thing that he'd reached out to and gotten a response? Some form of alien?

A delusion of the mind?

Or was this all part of the elaborate test they were going through? A tool that if left untapped might spell their doom or maybe serve as a distraction?

Could it be trusted?

How could he know what it was and whether to use it as they navigated this dangerous, ancient world?

The setting sun bathed the clearing in a warm, golden light as the Neshili gathered around Surjan, their faces filled with a mixture of anticipation and unease. The walls of their new settlement rose proudly behind them, a testament to the hard work and resilience of these former island dwellers. Surjan stood before them, his heart pounding in his chest, but his expression calm and resolute. He knew this moment had been inevitable, but that didn't make it any easier.

He steeled himself for what he needed to do.

He cleared his throat, the murmurs of the crowd dying down as all eyes turned to him. Dawa stood nearby, her presence a steadying force, but even she didn't know what he was about to say. Surjan took a deep breath and began.

"People of the Neshili," he started, his voice carrying across the clearing. "My friends and I have traveled far. We have faced many dangers with you and we've all overcome great challenges together. The gods sent us to bring you to safety, to help you build a new home where you can thrive. And now, that mission is complete."

A ripple of surprise went through the crowd, the Neshili exchanging confused glances. Surjan continued, his voice growing stronger with each word.

"The gods have shown me a new destination for myself and my team. Our journey is not over, but it is time for us to move on. You are safe now, and you will continue to grow and prosper in this new land. But our path lies elsewhere."

Beside him, Dawa stiffened, her eyes wide with shock. She turned to him, her voice a whisper laced with panic. "Surjan, what are you saying? You can't just leave—what will become of us?"

Surjan placed a reassuring hand on her shoulder, but his gaze remained fixed on the crowd. "The gods have sent messages, Dawa," he said, his tone gentle but firm. "They have spoken, and they have chosen a new leader for the Neshili."

Dawa's eyes widened even further as she looked at him, then up at the sky, her lips moving in a silent prayer. Surjan watched her, a sense of calm washing over him. He had never wanted to be king, never sought the responsibility that had been thrust upon him. Now, the burden was finally being lifted.

"The gods have chosen Sharrum as the new king," Surjan announced, his voice steady. "He will lead you, guide you, and protect you. It is his destiny."

The crowd gasped in unison, turning to look at Sharrum, a tall, strong man with a calm demeanor who had always been a respected figure among the Neshili. Sharrum, who had been standing quietly among the people, looked just as shocked as everyone else. Dawa turned to Surjan, her eyes shining with unshed tears. "Are you sure this is what the gods have asked of you?"

Surjan nodded. "I wish it could be otherwise, but I am but a servant to the gods."

Dawa took a deep, shuddering breath and said, "As am I." She turned, head raised to the sky, muttered another silent prayer, and then moved to stand beside Sharrum, tears rolling down her cheeks.

For Surjan, it was as if a weight had been lifted from his shoulders. He walked over to Sharrum, placed his hands on the man's shoulders, and said, "I'm sure you will do what's right for our people."

The man nodded, accepting the mantle that had been passed to him.

Dawa looked up at her new king, her expression a mixture of resignation and determination. She took Sharrum's hand, and the Neshili began to murmur in approval, their anxiety giving way to acceptance.

Surjan's eyes caught a small movement at the edge of the crowd. Shush, Lowanna's weasel friend, was climbing her leg, his tiny paws gripping her trousers as he made his way up to her shoulder. Lowanna smiled softly, giving the weasel a quick cuddle, her fingers brushing through his fur. The sight brought a fleeting smile to Surjan's face, a brief moment of levity in an otherwise heavyhearted day.

As the Neshili began to circulate through the team, saying their farewells, Surjan felt a strange sensation wash over him—a sense of relief. He had carried the burden of leadership for so long, but now, that responsibility was no longer his. The Neshili had their new king, their new path, and it was time for him and the others to find their own.

Marty approached, his expression unreadable, but his eyes searching Surjan's face for some sign of what he was feeling. Surjan draped an arm over Marty's shoulder, exhaling deeply. "I'm done with this king stuff," he said, his voice carrying a note of finality. "Next time, you be king—you're better suited for it."

Marty chuckled, though there was an edge to it. "I think I'll pass on that, Surjan. It's time to move on. Time to find out what the 'gods' have in store for us next."

Surjan chuckled. "They are a demanding bunch, aren't they?"

Marty nodded as they stood together, watching as the Neshili continued to bid their farewells and huddle around their new king.

The sun dipped lower in the sky, casting long shadows over the new settlement. It was the end of one journey and the beginning of another, and for the first time in a long time, Surjan felt ready to face whatever came next.

CHAPTER TWENTY-FOUR

Marty and the team had several choices on how to travel three days south toward the so-called human outpost the sloths had told Lowanna about, but opted for the simplest option, which was using one of the smallest sailing ships still beached on the shore. The party sailed southward in a vessel just big enough for the six of them.

Marty had taken for granted the details of how to sail one of these things, because he hadn't had to know about any of that on their escape from the island. But with just the six of them on board, there was no escaping the details. The ship was roughly thirty feet from stem to stern, with a small hide lean-to aft that could shelter two people comfortably sleeping or four sitting or all of them hunkering down against the occasional hail they encountered. François knew the workings of rigging and rudder and sail, and the craft was small enough that he could manage it all, with a judicious amount of bellowing at the rest of the party.

The Frenchman taught them a few knots so they could help, and when to heave on what lines, and it was enough. They sailed close to the land and stopped daily to replenish any supplies. Luckily the hardy plant life provided fruit and fresh water, and along the way, they hadn't spotted another sign of humans anywhere.

As they traveled south, Marty detected the scent of pending snowfall, and it had gotten cold enough that they could all see their breath in the air.

Marty felt the reality of his vision getting closer and closer, and as they approached, he sat more and more in the front of the ship, staring forward in daylight and in darkness. When he first spotted the ice from his vision, it was as a gray line of fuzz on the horizon, yet he knew instinctively that this was their goal.

Lowanna saw him staring and tapped him with a boot. "What do you expect when we get there?"

Marty had been asking himself the same question for weeks, and now tried to formulate his thoughts. "I think a portal. Just like last time, when my visions were trying to get us to where we could proceed to the next phase, and I think we're being led to the same kind of portal. We're in some kind of test, but I get this feeling it's like a game to whoever is administering it. It's almost certainly larger than we even know. The portals are just how we move forward from scene to scene."

Gunther looked up from his own reverie. "Do you know how to operate the portals?"

"No," Marty said. "We had instructions the first time around."

Surjan laughed. Of all the party, he'd been in the best mood since parting ways with the Neshili. The burdens of kingship—and maybe arranged marriages—had weighed heavily on him. He'd sung his way down the coast, occasionally leaning over the side to spear fish for them to eat. "The first time around, we had no such thing. The first time around, we were in Egypt and we set off a portal by accident. The *second* time, Narmer told you what to do."

"Who will tell us what to do this time, if you're right?" Gunther asked.

"I may have a vision that will show us the way," Marty said. "Or maybe that voice you were talking about will give us some hints or teach you what to do. Or maybe the portal will activate itself. Maybe, if Narmer hadn't taught us anything, the second portal would have simply functioned. Maybe they're programmed to do that, to advance us from scene to scene."

"Like the door in the wall in *Super Mario*, after you rescue the princess," Kareem said with an amused expression.

Marty hadn't realized the teen was familiar with western video games.

"Is he called Super Mario in Egypt, too?" Surjan asked.

"Disappointing. I'd hoped he'd be Sayyid Mario or Pasha Mario or something, at least."

"Pasha is Turkish," Kareem grumbled.

"My voice wanted us to go into the last portal," Gunther pointed out.

Marty nodded slowly. "Well, maybe your voice will give us a second chance."

"Did we do what we were supposed to do here?" Lowanna asked. "How do we know when it's over?"

Marty wanted to point out that it wasn't clear that they were supposed to do anything, but in his heart, he had the same question Lowanna had posed. And he didn't know the answer to it, so he eventually just shrugged.

"This is the archetypal dilemma of the human species," François said from the rear of the ship, where he sat working the rudder. "What do I do with my time? Attempting to do all the good we can for others is not a terrible answer. Maybe it's the only decent answer, in fact."

"And if we are . . . built to a heroic scale, then perhaps we need to be doing heroic amounts of good for others," Surjan suggested.

"Like marrying multiple women," Lowanna suggested.

"I didn't choose that," Surjan muttered.

"Still," Marty said, "it does feel as if there is an intelligence watching us, waiting to see what we'll do."

"More than one," Gunther said as he puckered his lips, looking like he'd tasted something sour.

"And if this is a test," Lowanna asked, "what's the goal? How do we know if we're winning, or even scoring points?"

"I don't have any answers," Marty said. He cracked a grin. "As you know, better than most?"

"Last time, they set up other creatures against us," Lowanna continued. "Was it just the Grays? That's it? Or are we about to get walloped by some other players in this game and we don't even know it? We never did fight the big boss Gray. What did they call him, the Guardian? Do we not get to advance until we beat him in a fight?"

On that sobering question, even Surjan fell silent.

Marty watched the ice as they approached. He was looking for an opening, a cave, a landing place, and saw none of those things. He saw gray-white ice, rising starkly in cliffs above choppy, cold ocean. Every moment, he felt that the ice could not possibly get any taller, that they had come so close, they must surely bump into the ice wall itself and be done.

But they kept sailing closer and the cliffs continued to grow. The land to their right also became spotted with thick fields of ice.

"The Straits of Magellan might not be open," François said, breaking an hour of silence.

"Because of the shape of the land being different?" Marty asked.

"That could be a factor," François agreed. "Also, it could be iced over."

"We're not circumnavigating the world," Marty reminded them.

The air became uncomfortably crisp and they took to wearing the animal skins that the Neshili had sent with them.

They saw penguins, swimming for fish and huddling on floes of ice.

They continued to follow the coast, until they saw smoke.

"That's not a natural fire, by God," Kareem said.

François frowned. "There's so much ice, I'm not even sure what flammable material is exposed to be able to burn."

"It's humans," Lowanna said. "Humans lit that fire. We should go talk to them."

"Ask if they've seen a portal to other lands and times?" Surjan chuckled, but then he nodded. "Might as well get all the intelligence we can."

"No guarantee it's humans, though," François said. "And even if they are, they might not be all that welcoming to strangers."

They beached the ship in an inlet, dragging it up onto a long sandbar thick with tall, scrubby grass to a stand of trees where they could hide the craft, covering it with hardy green branches. They concealed their ankhs beneath furs and linens and marched toward the smoke, Surjan and Marty in front and Kareem bringing up the rear.

A three-mile walk brought them over a low rise and into a broad valley. As they walked, Surjan surveyed the sheets of ice to the south. "I think those cliffs are two miles tall," he said. "I think they're five miles away, and two miles tall."

"That's insane," Marty said. "That's mountain-tall."

"That's where the oceans of the world are locked up in this age," Surjan said. "It's why the land is different. And look, the ice stretches continuously almost to where we are. I'm not sure we could have gone much farther in the boat."

The south end of the valley ended in a rocky ridge. Snow capped the ridge, and a cave opening gaped in the stone. The cavern was round and regular, suggesting to Marty volcanic action.

Around the mouth of the cave and spread around the floor of the valley were tents. Near the cavern, steam rose from the ground, suggesting a hot springs. Smoke rose from numerous small fires near various tents.

Marty and Surjan stood on the high ground, letting the others catch up. "Look at the different tent styles," Surjan pointed out. "These are people of different nations."

Marty stared at the site and concluded that Surjan was probably right. The construction materials ranged from animal hides to wood to something that looked like roughly woven wicker. It was a patchwork of different domiciles and he wondered aloud, "What is this place? A neutral ground? A shared holy site?"

Lowanna, François, and Gunther joined them. "That's a magma tube," François said immediately, pointing at the cave. "That must go where we want to go. That must be what draws all the people here."

"They might have come for the hot springs," Lowanna suggested.

"They've come for the portal," Gunther said. "The portal is a place of visions and voices. These people have been summoned."

Marty looked over at his German friend and asked, "Do you know that or are you suspecting it?"

Gunther shrugged. "I don't know it for certain, but I'm sensing that these people were called in some way—don't ask me why I think that, I just do."

"We probably should ask them and find out," Marty said. "But be ready for any reaction, you got me?"

They all nodded as Kareem joined them and they sauntered down among the tents and their inhabitants. As they drew closer, Marty saw that not only were the tents of various styles, but the people were visibly different in complexion, in sizes, and in styles of clothing. Some had beasts of burden, of various species: Marty saw alpacas, burros, and yaks.

The team walked into the area as if invited, and the inhabitants didn't even give them a second look.

Just in case there was some hidden threat, Marty didn't want to get all the way to the center of the makeshift village and then discover the issue, so he quickly approached a short, broad-shouldered man who stood outside a tent, attaching the two yoke-poles of a sturdy hide travois to the back of an ox.

"Hail, friend," Marty called out. "My name is Marty, and I come in peace."

The man turned to him, revealing a flat, circular face, long dark hair, and blackened teeth. "My name is Lelwan. You'd better come in peace, or the healer won't see you."

Gunther emitted a wordless murmur of excitement.

"Are you the healer?" Marty asked.

"Your people have no knowledge at all if you think I'm the healer," Lelwan said. "I'm here with my cousin Anittas. He cannot eat, and vomits blood."

"I could—" Gunther said, but Marty put a hand on him to stop him. They didn't want to set themselves up in competition with the healer or muddy the waters in any way at all.

"We have brought no sick," Marty said. "We've been brought here by visions and voices."

"Ah," Lelwan said. "We call that soul-sickness in my people."

Marty nodded. "Can the healer cure soul-sickness?"

"One can only ask," Lelwan said.

"This travois is for your cousin, I take it," Marty said. "Let us help you bundle him into it. Maybe we can accompany you to the healer, and you can show us the way."

"You've found the way, as far as that goes," Lelwan said. He pointed at the magma-tube opening. "There is the gate. Through the gate and you walk until you come to the healer. I have been told it is many miles of walking. But I'd be grateful for the help and the company."

Anittas was a small man like his cousin, once sturdy but now wasting away. Even wrapped in furs, he was easy for Marty and Gunther to lift together. They laid him across the hides, turned him to his side with a leather pail in case he vomited. They covered him with furs Lelwan provided and strapped him in with rawhide thongs.

Then they followed Lelwan toward the magma tube.

"Have your people been coming to see the healer for a long time?" Lowanna asked.

Lelwan nodded. "Many generations."

"Is the healer a god, then?" Lowanna asked. "If he were a man, he would be dead."

"The healer is not a man," Lelwan agreed. "He is something else. A spirit. A magician."

They nodded, as if he had said something that was obviously true.

"There are two springs at the mouth of the healer's cave," Lelwan said. "The nearer spring is cold water, potable and healthy. There, beyond the gate, lie the springs of hot water and the basin they collect in."

"Does the healer use the hot springs?" Lowanna asked.

"No," Lelwan said. "But sometimes people who come to see the healer stop and immerse themselves in the springs first, and the immersion in the hot waters is enough to heal them. Obviously, the healer's power bleeds into the spring."

"Will you immerse Anittas?" Marty asked.

"I hadn't planned to," Lelwan said. "He is heavy for me to maneuver alone. But if you are willing to help me, then it is certainly worth the attempt. If my brother can be healed without bothering the healer, then I won't have to pay the healer's price."

"What's the healer's price?" Marty asked.

"It is negotiated," Lelwan said. "We pay in iron. My people have to trade furs and precious stones for iron from the far north."

"I have confidence that the waters will heal Anittas," Gunther said.

The pool of the hot springs lay beside the hard-beaten track leading down into the open magma tube. Several people, frail and sickly, huddled on stones in the pool. Each was accompanied by a relative or caretaker who massaged shoulders or spread mud onto chests or cheeks. Objectively, Marty knew the pool must be a bacterial soup as likely to cause illness as cure it.

Secretly, he knew very well what Gunther intended, and was proud of his friend.

"Lelwan, you keep the yak," he suggested. "Gunther and I will carry Anittas into the waters."

"He must be immersed," Lelwan said. "We cannot be healed unless we are entirely immersed."

Marty and Gunther stripped Anittas down. In only a loincloth, he looked like a plucked bird, unnaturally thin and shivering, with an oversized skull and a thick shock of black hair. The furs and linens he was wrapped in were clean, though; Lelwan had been caring for him to the best of his ability.

They hoisted the sick man between them and carried him into the pool, which was as deep as their waists. The heat was welcome on Marty's legs. He could feel Anittas's heart beating through his frail frame and paper-thin skin.

"Nice and slow," Gunther murmured. To Anittas, he said, "Can you hold your nose?"

Weakly, motions jerky, Anittas did so.

Lelwan watched from the bank, holding the ox's lead-rope.

As they dunked the prehistoric sufferer into this hot-springs mikveh, Gunther's hands gave off the faintest of glows. They lowered Anittas down to the level of their knees, so that even all his hair, which suddenly exploded in a black crown, was under. They held him there for a brief moment, and the white light poured from Gunther's hands into the sick man's body.

"Healer!" Lelwan shouted.

The other people crouching in the pool turned to stare.

Anittas kicked his legs out and threw his arms wide, pushing Marty and Gunther away. Light played up and down his limbs and then he got his legs under him and stood suddenly, spraying water and light in all directions.

"Wow," Kareem said.

Anittas retched up some bloody phlegm and stood sobbing in the pool. He still looked emaciated, but something had changed. The man stood firmly on his two feet and his shaking limbs had become rock steady. He reached out to Lelwan, and Lelwan rushed to join his cousin, embracing the restored man.

"That's a sudden turnaround," François announced. His voice had that echoing quality that made it sound like it had a halo and carried well. "The power of the healer's pool."

Gasps of excitement arose from the sick in the pool as well as people passing by on the track.

Gunther looked drained and began fumbling for one of the flasks at his belt. Marty gave him a hand and they climbed out of the pool.

With a dubious expression, François stared at the other still-sickly people in the pool and murmured, "We can't wait around. Lelwan might realize we had a hand in it. Let's get while the getting is good."

CHAPTER TWENTY-FIVE

Marty craned his neck upward and couldn't see the top of the glacier even though it was miles ahead of them. He knew this was where they were meant to go, but he didn't sense any hint of a glow coming from the ice, as he had seen in his visions. It was a bluish-white behemoth and ahead of them was the opening to a magma tube that seemed to burrow into the icy expanse between them and the glacier itself. He pointed at the volcanic structure and said, "I guess this is it."

"This looks like it would be a slippery slope into the ocean," Lowanna said. "That's all we need, for us to all end up drowning in a cold pool."

Marty had the same concern, but others had descended into the magma tube ahead of them and there'd been no obvious screams or yelling from within. "Here goes nothing..."

They walked into the magma tube.

The tube descended at a steep incline. Marty worried that they'd soon be plunged into darkness, but as the light of day gave out, a glowing line appeared on the right-hand wall.

Ahead of them he spotted more glowing splotches appearing at regular intervals.

The light hadn't been formed by luck and taken advantage of, it had been created deliberately, by someone with the know-how to do it.

"You're all seeing what I'm seeing," François said. "Artificial light."

"These people keep talking about a healer. I'm wondering exactly what kind of medical equipment the healer uses," Marty said. "It would be ironic if the only magical healer in this place is the one we brought with us."

They followed a woman who led three alpacas. One carried a child on its back, strapped into a wooden seat with leather thongs and bearing on its head a crown woven of golden strips. The other two carried leather saddlebags, two per alpaca, balancing each other on opposite sides of the beasts. The woman wore wool leggings and a wool serape, all dyed red and green, with the images of trees stained into the fibers.

Behind them in turn came three old men in furs. They had long white hair tied in loose braids down their backs and complexions the color of milk chocolate. The one in the middle leaned heavily on a staff and the other two sang droning modal melodies, watching his every step.

"We have to be below the level of the water now," Lowanna suggested.

"You're jealous of my bath with Gunther," Marty said. "You were hoping for a swim."

She punched him playfully in the arm. "I am worried that a small tectonic shift could flood this tunnel with water and kill us instantly."

"Oh, that," François said. "Large numbers of humanity live their entire lives right on top of fault lines, where a small tectonic shift could kill them all instantly with no notice whatsoever."

"Yes," Lowanna agreed, "and are you saying that's a good thing?"

"I'm saying we'll be through this tunnel soon enough," François said. "And I'll trust you to keep a sharp eye out for water, and let me know if you see signs of flooding."

They walked for nearly a mile. The strip of phosphorescence on the right wall threw soft greenish light across them, illuminating their steps well enough and creating deep, shifting pockets of darkness on their left, below a ceiling and upper wall with a faint pond-scum glow.

Ahead, the magma tube reached a bottleneck, and a short line waited. As they stood behind the alpacas, Marty looked up and saw a crack in the ceiling. Above the crack hung bulging boulders massed as if poised to leap down and attack. Water trickled down between the stones and ran across the tunnel floor.

"It wouldn't take very much seismic activity at all to drop those right on our heads," Lowanna said.

"And flood our corpses all out, to boot," François agreed cheerfully.

The woman with the alpacas moved ahead, and the party found themselves standing in the entrance to a wide, low chamber. The phosphorescent strip was painted on all the walls here, giving the room a green insectoid glow that tended to pool all the shadows together in the center. Another magma tube led out the far side, but in this room a long counter of carved stone barred the way forward. People in furs and wool helped their sick comrades forward to the counter, where they explained the woes of the ill and negotiated for treatment, plunking bars of iron and nuggets of iron ore onto simple scales on the countertop.

Marty's eyes widened as he looked behind the counter and spotted the first of the Grays. They wore knee-length tunics that looked surprisingly similar to lab coats. Following successful negotiation, the alien creatures produced modern-looking syringes, bandages, tablets, and ointments from underneath the counter and administered to the sick.

To the right and left side, passages led into other chambers. Marty saw Grays helping sick people into and out of those passages. Were those treatment rooms for more serious problems, or illnesses requiring specialist help?

Marty didn't see anyone who was turned away.

"I'm not excited to see those guys," Surjan said. "Do you think they have a Guardian here?"

"You're not the king anymore," Lowanna said. "You don't have to fight anyone."

"True," Surjan said.

"They should not be excited to see us, by God," Kareem said. His hand rested at his side, very close to where his ankh hung.

"Easy, Kareem," François said.

"Be grateful we don't have to fight those things." Gunther pointed, swinging his arm around to include most of the room's walls. Petroglyphs of monsters covered all the stone surfaces. Marty saw gaping, tooth-filled jaws, spiderlike things with a dozen limbs, serpents that ran for yards, creatures that were humanoid but seemed to be on fire, monsters with eyes on stalks, a man that was headless but had eyes and a mouth in his belly, trees with teeth, swarms of dwarves, men with their arms and legs swapped, winged lions, disembodied laughing heads, bubbling masses of yeast with feet, and more.

"It looks like the Lascaux cave paintings," François said, "if they had been a joint art project by H. P. Lovecraft and Hieronymus Bosch."

"Somehow that doesn't strike me as something the Grays would paint," Lowanna said.

"Maybe they made the paintings to frighten people away," Kareem suggested.

"These Grays seem friendly," Marty said. "More than that, they seem benevolent. Look what they're doing."

"We don't know if those injections really help people," Surjan said.

"Sure we do," Marty said. "If they didn't heal people, people wouldn't keep coming back, bringing them the iron they want, and calling them 'the healer.'"

"Why do they want iron, anyway?" Lowanna asked. "Oh yuck, are we going to find out that these guys eat human livers?"

Marty shook his head. "Relax. If they're trading for iron because they need it to live, then the trade allows them to avoid eating other creatures for the iron."

"Don't relax totally," Surjan said. "The Grays at Nesha ate humans."

A man with a small pack donkey and pink blotches on his face turned from the counter and walked away. The Gray who had been talking to him beckoned the party forward.

Marty walked forward immediately, to encourage his comrades.

The Gray standing behind the counter spread his hands on the countertop, fingers splayed out, and smiled liplessly at Marty. At the same time, his nasal slits twitched.

"Do I smell funny to you?" Marty asked.

"I did not say that," the Gray said.

Marty's friends straggled forward.

"But your nose twitched."

The Gray bobbled his head. "It would be rude to tell you that you smelled strange."

"My name's Marty," Marty said.

"I am Gollip," the Gray answered. "What ails you?"

"I smell bad," Marty said.

"Probably a peculiarity of diet," Gollip said. "I can give you a tablet for halitosis."

"We're not sick," Marty said. "We've come looking for a portal."

Gollip froze. He blinked his eyes, the eyelids snapping over the glossy blacks horizontally rather than vertically. "What do you mean? You have come through a portal to get here."

"You know that's not what I mean," Marty said. "I know you're not from this world, and I think you know it. And if you yourself don't know the portals I'm talking about, then someone in your . . . city does. Can I talk to a scientist or a librarian or something?"

"I don't think what I am smelling is you," Gollip said slowly. "I think you are carrying something."

It took Marty a moment to realize he was being asked to show a sign. Raising a flap of fur to expose the ankh hanging from his belt, he drew it out slowly and laid it on the counter. To his left, the woman with the alpacas heard the clink of metal on stone and turned to look. She stared at the shimmering ankh.

So did Gollip. "Where did you get this?"

"You are not from this world," Marty said. "I am not from this time. In a time thousands of years in the future, on a land far to the north and east of here, I encountered a being who was not of this world. It attacked me and tried to kill me. In defending myself, I slew this being and took this as a trophy."

Gollip pointed. "Was the tip sharpened to a point like this?"

"I did that," Marty said. "I think this device was a badge of office, and also healed the being who carried it. I sharpened the tip to turn it into a weapon, to defend myself against others of its kind."

Gollip looked to each of the party in turn, sniffing experimentally at the air. "You all carry these insignia?"

"Yes," Surjan admitted. "We're very attached to them, so don't try to take them away."

"Not that you could," Lowanna purred. "Not even if you really wanted to."

"I am not hostile to you." Gollip nodded. "Put that away now. I'll take you to see someone who will be very interested in you."

"Interested in me?" Marty asked. "Or excited to see the device?" He took the ankh and slid it back into place under his furs.

"Both, as it happens." Gollip bobbled his head, then pointed. "Walk to the end of the counter. Then follow me."

Marty paced parallel to Gollip, toward the end of the counter, where he'd be able to walk around. Gollip moved nonchalantly, as if doing nothing extraordinary, and the other Grays ignored him. The party followed, and at the end of the counter, they squeezed between it and the wall and trailed Gollip back through an open passage.

As they passed, a rustle of disturbance passed along the line of Grays. They turned to look at Gollip, and Marty had no idea how to read their glossy black eyes or leathery faces. Gollip raised a hand, and the Grays went back to their previous conversations.

"Humans do not come where I am taking you," Gollip said.

"But your friends aren't trying to stop you," Marty said.

"I have taken responsibility," Gollip said. "Besides, these colleagues are ... all of a certain point of view. Otherwise, they wouldn't be working with me here. And they are predisposed to like humans."

"That suggests," Surjan growled, "that there are some members of your species who might be predisposed to *dis*liking humans."

"Oh, yes." Gollip giggled. "Oh my, yes."

The magma tube opened shortly into a much larger space and light flooded Marty's eyes. It took him a moment to process what he was seeing, but there was open sky above him. They stood no longer in a chamber of a cave, but in a massive amphitheater, a box canyon of grayish stone that branched in several directions, all its walls pierced by windows and doors, and hacked into ledges and passages. The network of dead-end canyons had been carved, maybe by brute strength, into a small city of cave dwellings.

Above the rock walls, tall enough in their own right, loomed even taller walls of ice. Gray compounded with gray upon gray and the entire scene was monochromatic to the point of madness, but the ice loomed in overhead and almost touched, leaving a narrow zigzag of sky through which light and air, but little else, could travel. Marty saw side canyons that may once have climbed to a plateau above, but now ended in plugs of gray frozen water.

"Marty!" François grabbed his arm and dragged him around to face left. On a high saddle of rock in the fork between two branching canyons, weighed down from above by a massive plate of ice, lay a metallic object Marty's brain took long seconds to process. He saw antennas, an open hatch on the underside, steps carved in stone ascending to the hatch, and a greenish light leaking from inside.

"It's a flying saucer," Lowanna murmured.

"Exactly!" François cried.

It looked like a UFO from a 1950s monster movie. It was a silver disc, topside and underside both curving gently to meet in the middle, like two hubcaps pressed together. Marty saw windows around the lower half of the disc. Were there counterpart windows around the upper part, where he couldn't see?

"We did indeed come from another world," Gollip said. "This is the vehicle that brought us here."

François shook his head and whistled.

"I am impressed by this craft," Marty said, trying to sound diplomatic. "Do you also have a portal, as we discussed?"

"You trade for iron," François said. "Have you tried mining it?"

"Are there no living things here but your people?" Lowanna seemed repulsed. "I don't see so much as a tree. You're outdoors in some theoretical sense, but it is as barren as South Side Chicago in here."

"All of your questions are interesting." Gollip bobbled his head, then bowed. "I am taking you to someone who can better answer them."

"Let me ask one more question," Marty said. The Gray was being deluged by demands and accusations, and he didn't want his ally to get burned out. He wanted to hand Gollip a win. "What do you call yourselves?"

"My people?" Gollip asked.

"We have encountered others like you before," Marty said, "in the far north, but we were unable to speak to them. So we have no words to talk about you, except outsider words. We have called your people the Grays."

"We call ourselves the People," Gollip said.

Lowanna chuckled. "Everyone does."

"Our word for people is 'Edu,'" Gollip said. "We are the Edu. But I don't think 'Grays' is offensive, and you may call us that."

"If you call yourselves 'the People,'" Surjan asked, "what's your word for us? You must have one, you deal with us every day."

"Oh yes." Gollip bobbled his head. "We call your kind 'Shnipara.' It means something like 'two-legged cattle.' Come this way."

He turned and marched up one of the side canyons.

⇥ CHAPTER ⇤
TWENTY-SIX

Gollip led them up the side canyon for a hundred yards. The ground was hard stone, impressively free of dirt and spare pebbles, and the canyon was fifty feet wide or narrower. Then he headed up a staircase carved directly into the rock. He walked briskly, bobbing his head with no apparent provocation every few paces and emitting an occasional chuckling sound.

Other Grays passed—François couldn't make himself think of them as Edu—and looked astonished at the pack of humans. They staggered sideways, their jaws dropped open, their eyes blinked left to right repeatedly.

"I think we're pioneers," he murmured to Marty.

"We're not under the palace in Nesha," Marty whispered back. "And no one is trying to eat us."

"Yet," François said.

The Grays dressed in a uniform manner, in tunics, coats, and trousers of simple linen. François didn't notice any distinctions of rank or fashion, which he found admirable.

Gollip led them along a wide ledge to a door. All the stone had a plastic quality to it. It was too rounded. François considered why this struck him as unnatural. It just didn't look like stone as nature would erode it, having neither the horizontal-erosion patterns caused by wind nor the vertical-erosion patterns caused by rain.

But then he realized what had caused the odd-looking rock. The erosion came from millennia of touch by hands and feet. Erosion by contact with walking, leaning, climbing, and scampering Grays had worn the stone to a soft, bulbous appearance that would have been at home on an episode of the old TV show *Land of the Lost*.

Beyond the walkways and out of reach of hands, the rock had a more pristine look, angular and sharp, like stone that had been sheltered from erosion by being buried under ice ought to have.

Gollip's door pierced into the upper section of a canyon wall, what would once have been the proud top of a mesa looking down from the sunlit heights over a series of canyons. Now a gray shelf of ice hung low over their heads, and all the windows carved in the canyon wall were in shadow. Gollip worked a long lever beside the entrance and the door parted in the middle, the two halves sliding left and right into the stone with a pneumatic hiss.

François followed Marty through the doorway.

Within, a single massive room contained industrial tooling equipment, laboratory tools, samples, spare parts, and possibly alchemical concoctions, strewn like the rubble left by an explosion across a series of low bronze tables. One wall was dominated by bookcases, all full of scrolls, tablets, and codices. A dozen Grays worked at various stations in the laboratory, and all looked up as the party entered.

A Gray whose skin was thicker and more rugose than average sat with his back turned to the door, working over a wax tablet with a stylus. "This is ingenious, Holipu, but it's only the first step. What we're going to have to do now is take this approach and map the machinery in three dimensions. We're also going to need some sort of input and output analysis. What exactly is generating all the waste?" His voice had the throaty warble of age.

"Engineer," one of the other Grays said, "you have visitors."

"If it's about the vote, I can't be bothered." The Gray with his back turned harrumphed, fussed some more with the tablet, but eventually spun about. Looking across the party, he said, "Oh my."

Gollip bowed deeply. "Engineer, these are extraordinary humans."

"You know my feelings on politics, Gollip," the engineer said. "Still, it's a little sensitive to have them down here right now, and I could have come outside to meet them. In what sense are they extraordinary?"

"They came down to see us, Engineer," Gollip said. "And they are carrying star-metal."

François winked internally at the irony. "Star-metal" in many ancient languages and cultures, including Egyptian, meant "meteoric iron," iron collected from the sites of asteroid impacts. Iron seemed to be what these Grays wanted most, or at any rate what they traded with humans for, but they were still using the phrase "star-metal"—only they used it to talk about the ankhs.

Which meant, he reflected, they apparently knew it as a substance so well that they had a name for it.

"We're here looking for a portal," Marty said.

"We would also like to understand you better," François added. "As fellow children of the stars."

Marty shot him a surprised look and François smiled.

"You come from the stars?" the engineer asked. "What is your name?"

"I'm François. I come from the future. My people travel among the stars." He introduced the others by name.

"I'm Yotto," the engineer said. "We came to this world from the stars. May we see this star-metal that you possess?"

Marty again drew out his ankh and showed it to the engineer, who handled it carefully and looked at it with a critical eye before passing it back.

"I've seen such devices," he said. "They are powerful. I've never seen them in the hands of one of the Shnipara. Where did you get it?"

"Its owner attacked me," Marty said. "I took this as a trophy after I defeated him."

"And sharpened the end to make it a weapon?" the engineer asked.

"A tool," Marty said. "But yes, also a weapon."

François didn't want to spend too much time talking about how they'd come by the ankhs. "You came here hundreds of years ago?" he asked. "Thousands? The erosion on the stone suggests thousands... or more."

"Many years," Yotto agreed, nodding.

"We saw your vessel outside," François said. "It still emanates light. Is it functional still in other ways?"

"It does some things," Yotto said. "It no longer travels among the stars."

"We heard a story about a fleet," François said. "A fleet that delivered some of your people to one location, and then maybe came here. We're uncertain about the details of this story."

Yotto chuckled, his mouth wrinkling into a *W*-shape. "Migrations are always more complicated than they seem, with groups that move earlier and others that move later. Some go, some come, some return, some disappear. Some bear the old name, some change names. Some differences are soon forgotten, some similarities form the basis for undying grudges."

"Some retain civilization," François said, "and others descend into barbarism."

"Or madness," Yotto said.

"Tell us about the migration of your people."

Yotto sighed, emitting a sound like air hissing from a party balloon. "My people came from the stars. We are workers, we have always been workers—healers and scientists, builders and engineers. We came to build this planet with a fleet of many vessels. Not vessels that sail the terrestrial ocean, you understand. Vessels that travel between stars."

François nodded. "And your vessel crashed."

"Not the only one. In a large fleet, it happens. We crashed, and the vessel remained here. Most of its crew and passengers left, to rejoin the main construction project. A few stayed here to protect this site."

"What needs protecting about this site?" Marty asked.

"We wouldn't want local humans to simply find our technology," Yotto said. "We protect the site to protect you."

"What was the main construction project?" François asked. "Did you work with humans?"

"When our patron encountered this planet, it had a single civilization worthy of the name," Yotto explained. "All the rest of you Shnipara lived in the trees, eating fruit and rodents. But one mighty state thrived, building engineering works—aqueducts, canals, windmills, sailing ships, printing presses, and so on—and we sought to help it."

"Was it a seafaring civilization?" François asked.

Yotto nodded.

"Atlantis?"

"I do not know the name," Yotto said. "But we taught them our arts and gave them our tools. And they built nine daughter cities, nine cities in which to hide . . . something that our patron wanted placed in the cities."

Marty frowned. "What did your patron want placed in the cities?"

Yotto shrugged. "I'm not sure. Such a thing was rumored to have been placed here as well, but that is not something I know about."

François shook his head. "So this was one of the nine daughter cities. Humans once lived here."

Yotto spread his hands, palm up. "Yes! This is what I keep trying to explain to my Herder colleagues! This is a human place, built for men. Look how high the ceilings are."

"But there are no men here now," François said. "People stared at us on our way here as if they'd never seen a human within the walls."

"They haven't," Yotto said. "Humans haven't lived here for a long time."

"The main city built nine daughters," François said, "and then the city collapsed. And it sent out fleets of refugees. Terrestrial ships, this time."

"Yes," Yotto said. "And there was a fleet that sailed west and then south. And it deposited Shnipara and Edu together in the west, after building them a palace in which they could live together."

"We've seen it," Marty said.

"Have you?" Yotto's eyes sparkled. "Is it beautiful?"

"It is," François admitted. "The dream of Edu and humans living together is also beautiful, even if the dream has not quite been realized." He couldn't quite bring himself to refer to humans as two-legged cattle, even in an alien tongue.

"Ah." Yotto's voice took on a sad timbre. "The dream is a hard one, no doubt."

"And then the fleet came here?" Marty asked. "But somehow, you ended up with no humans."

"Humans and Edu would not live together," Yotto said. "Despite the best efforts of many people of both races. Eventually, after many years of struggle, the humans left."

"The thing your patron wanted hidden here . . ." Marty asked. "Did the humans take it with them?"

"And was it a door?" Gunther asked.

Yotto shrugged. "I don't know the answer to either question."

"That you don't know makes me think maybe the great mysterious object isn't here anymore," François said. "'With the humans' is a good guess as to where it might be instead."

"If only I knew where they were, I would help you find them." Yotto shrugged.

"This history is dark," Surjan said. "This history is a tale of two peoples who fail to live together every time they try."

"Does that ring false to you?" Lowanna said. "Or does it ring uncomfortably true?"

Surjan looked down and shook his head.

"I reject it," François said. "Every one of us is the product of different people being willing to live with each other. Most of us are products of triumph happening over and over again. Lowanna, your native language is English. Marty, look at him. He's a Chinese Jew! And I'm a pure-blooded Frenchman, but what does that mean? Frank? Celtic? Greek? Phoenician? Roman? I'm all of that! And do I have to live with the possibility that Great-grandfather A was the oppressed and Great-grandfather B was the oppressor? Yes I do, and so what? Some conflicts, people work out in their lifetimes. Some, we have to work out over many lifetimes. But we work them out."

Yotto shook his head. "Not every conflict between peoples gets worked out."

"So we keep trying," François said. "We keep trying because we know it can be done, and we keep trying because it's the moral thing to do. The only alternative is bigotry and genocide."

The Grays in the room broke into a seallike sound that went *hurka-hurka-hurka*, snapping their fingers at the same time. François gathered that was how they gave applause, and nodded in satisfaction.

"Your words are more touching to me than you can know," Yotto said. "I share your sentiments exactly, though not all of my people do."

"Engineer Yotto has fought for many years in favor of the good treatment of Shnipara," Gollip said. "He champions the medical services we offer to humans."

"But I have a problem now," Yotto said, "and I hope you can help me. In the interest of continuing good relations between our peoples."

"Who among your people doesn't share your sentiments?" Marty asked.

Yotto harrumphed. "I hate politics."

"There are two parties," Gollip said. "The other party is sometimes called the Herders, as we are sometimes called the Farmers."

"That sounds so quaint," Lowanna said. "Old-timey."

"Herders and Farmers," François said. "Those who wish to live by farming. And those who wish to live by herding some other species."

"You are from the future, you say?" Yotto asked. "Yours is a technological civilization?"

"It is," François confirmed.

"Are any of you technical people?" Yotto asked. "Engineers, mechanics, technologists, craftsmen?"

"Everyone here is very technically competent in their own profession," François said. "As far as machinery and crafts go, I'm your most likely candidate." He hitched his thumb in Kareem's direction and said, "He's been in some ways my apprentice. What do you need?"

"I'm afraid that, in certain respects, the engineers of my people have become a priesthood," Yotto said. "We don't make new machines, we only operate and maintain the old ones. The knowledge we pass down from generation to generation is that of what levers to pull and when, but not the understanding of how the machine does what it does, how it is constructed, or how to repair it when it breaks down."

"This is a problem guilds can easily run into." François nodded. "Once they start focusing on their perks and defending the boundaries of their own membership, any guild loses its technical edge. In a society that needs some set of machinery to keep running, but that machinery is generally reliable, and the society doesn't need innovation in the machinery . . . it's easy to imagine the engineers forgetting how to fix the machines. What machines are no longer working for you?"

"No longer working as well," Yotto said. "Starting to break down. Less efficient than they used to be, generating more waste than they once did."

François nodded as Yotto enumerated the issues. "I'm the right man for the job. I've always been a creative thinker."

"We have depended for years on machinery that generates a dietary supplement that we need to live on this world," Yotto said.

"Iron," Marty said. "You don't metabolize iron well, or you need extra iron."

Yotto sat back in his chair with his mouth open for a moment. "True. Did the other Edu you met tell you this?"

"We guessed it," Lowanna said, "based on our experience with other species that came down together to this planet."

Yotto nodded. "It's true. And we have depended for many years on machinery that converts raw iron, smelted or in ore form, into a supplement that we can metabolize. Without it, we quickly become ill and weak."

"You also depend on the devices in those nose rings to help you process our atmosphere," François said.

"Related problems." Yotto nodded. "But the rings are still functioning. The food plant is beginning to show signs of breaking down. Can you help us with the machinery?"

"How soon did you have in mind?" François asked.

"As soon as is possible," Yotto said. He had an edge to his voice that might have been stress.

"I can help," François said. "What can you do to help us find the portal Marty is looking for?"

Yotto gestured at the shelves against the wall. "Marty, you're free to access my library and consult with all my people. I don't know that we have the answer to where the portal is that you seek, or whether it's the same as the secret thing placed here by our patron, but we can try to find out together."

◄ CHAPTER ►
TWENTY-SEVEN

Surjan's breath hung in the frigid air, forming clouds that dissipated into the icy expanse as he followed Yotto, the engineer, through a narrow passage carved deep within the Antarctic glacier. The walls of ice glistened with an ethereal glow, reflecting the faint light from the glowing markers placed strategically along the various passages within the glacier. The tension in the air was palpable, and Surjan couldn't shake the uneasy feeling that had settled in his gut since they'd left the safety of Yotto's laboratory.

Accompanied by Gollip the medical clerk, Yotto led them with purpose, his movements quick and efficient, but Surjan noticed the subtle signs of anxiety in the engineer's posture: the slight twitch of his fingers, the way his eyes darted around as if expecting danger at every turn. Behind him, Marty and the rest of the team followed, their faces set in grim determination.

This situation set Surjan's own anxiety to a new level considering none of them knew where they were. This place was nothing but a maze of tunnels that would probably take weeks to fully map out, and they were following a Gray who they'd only met moments earlier.

Nothing about this felt like a smart plan, but there seemed little choice in the matter. Something was going on within the alien population that none of them yet grasped.

As they emerged from the tunnel into a vast, open square, Surjan's breath caught in his throat. The square was unlike anything he had ever seen, a massive, frozen expanse surrounded by towering walls of ice, with strange structures jutting out from the ground like the skeletal remains of some ancient civilization. And in the center, above it all, perched the spacecraft.

"I don't understand, did we go around in a circle?" Surjan asked.

"Don't attract attention to yourself." Yotto made a *glub-glub* sound and shook his head. "No, but I took you around a more secluded way to the other side of the ship. It would have been very awkward to have Shnipara suddenly walking within our ship's security boundaries, especially past some of my brethren who do not share my feelings of benevolence."

Surjan nodded as he stared at the ship from a new angle. Previously they'd only gotten a glimpse of a small section, but in this larger expanse, it was obvious that the ship had made a heavy landing. Much of it was hidden deep within the glacier, but the metallic surfaces of the ship that he could see were coated in frost and gave off a presence that almost felt like the subsonic hum of an engine somewhere in the distance. More a vibration than a sound.

"Even here!" Yotto hissed and shook his head, pointing. Nearby, stairs ascended, rising in the direction of the spaceship. Four Edu with helmets and spears stood across the lowest step, obviously on guard.

Even with the new perspective on the alien spacecraft, the vessel wasn't the thing that drew Surjan's attention—it was the crowd below. Hundreds, maybe thousands, of Edu filled the square, their gaunt, gray faces turned toward two speakers who stood on a raised platform, locked in a heated debate. Surjan was within arm's reach of a dozen Grays, and only the fact that they had their backs turned to him kept the anxiety from rising in his throat.

"The Herder leader is on the left, the Farmer leader is on the right," Yotto muttered, barely audible over the murmur of the crowd.

Surjan strained to hear the words being spoken, the tone of the debate fierce and desperate.

"We are growing weaker," the Farmer leader said, his voice filled with frustration. "Our metabolism is slowing, our ability to absorb the necessary ingredients is degrading. We are in a state of disrepair, and if we do not act soon, we will not survive beyond the next century or two."

The Herder leader, a tall, imposing figure with eyes that seemed to pierce through the cold, responded with a calm, measured tone. "And your solution is what? More technology? Look around you, Farmer. Our devices are failing, breaking down. We can no longer rely on technology to keep us alive until the rescue comes. Indeed, we cannot rely on any imagined rescue. We know what the answer is, but only some of us are willing to face it."

"Rescue?" Surjan's heart skipped a beat. What answer was he talking about? He glanced at Yotto, but the engineer's face was unreadable, his eyes fixed on the speakers with a look of barely concealed anxiety.

But other Grays had heard Surjan's single word. Several turned to face him.

"Devils, by God," Kareem muttered.

"Easy," Marty said. "Everyone, easy."

The mood in the square shifted. More Edu began to turn, their attention drawn away from the debate and toward the newcomers. Toward Surjan and the team. Toward the humans.

"Shnipara!" someone in the crowd hissed, and the word spread like wildfire. "Humans!" Shock, disbelief, and something darker—a simmering anger—rippled through the masses.

Surjan's instincts kicked in as the crowd's murmurs grew louder, more frantic. He could feel the tension rising, the atmosphere thickening with hostility. He caught a glimpse of Marty's face, his eyes wide with alarm as the Edu pressed closer, their expressions ranging from awe to outright aggression.

"Yotto, should we get out of here?" Surjan asked, his voice low and urgent.

But it was too late. The crowd surged forward, and the square erupted into chaos. The factions, once focused on their debate, now turned on each other, their anger fueled by the presence of the outsiders. A near-riot broke out, and Surjan found himself caught in the middle of a violent storm.

"Let's get out of here!" Yotto shouted, his voice barely audible over the cacophony. "We can't let you be captured!"

Surjan didn't need to be told twice. Yotto grabbed him by the arm as the crowd closed in around them. Marty and the others kept the Edu at bay, their weapons drawn but held back, forming a defensive wall but not stabbing. Violence would only make things worse.

Several of the alien creatures hissed at the sight of the ankhs, their eyes narrowing in fear. The word "star-metal" was muttered by some in the crowd as the team pushed forward, struggling to stay together.

Marty launched a front kick at one of the larger Grays who had tried to tackle him, sending the alien flying back into the crowd. The impact created a brief gap, giving their group a momentary reprieve.

Several allied aliens formed a wedge, and Yotto pulled Surjan forward as the team followed closely behind. Hands grabbed at them, voices shouted, and for a moment, Surjan feared they wouldn't make it, that the crowd would overwhelm them with sheer numbers. But with a final, desperate shove from the allied Grays, they broke free from the mob, stumbling into a narrow passage that led away from the square.

Yotto and the other aliens led the way, and they didn't stop running until they were far from the crowd, the sounds of the riot fading into the distance. Surjan leaned against the wall, his breath coming in ragged gasps as he tried to steady himself. Yotto stood beside him, visibly shaken, his eyes darting around as if expecting another attack at any moment.

"Their reaction was worse than I expected," Yotto muttered, his voice tense. "The main body of the Edu is meeting soon. They're going to vote on a resolution, and if it passes..."

"What resolution?" Surjan demanded, his voice sharp. "What are they planning?"

Yotto hesitated, his eyes flicking toward the others before settling back on Surjan. "I don't know all the details, but it's certain to be an unwise move. If they vote to take drastic measures to save themselves... it could mean war between my brethren. It could mean the end of all that we have."

Surjan's blood ran cold. The weight of Yotto's words settled over him like a heavy shroud, and he knew, without a doubt, that they were standing on the edge of something catastrophic—and yet they were no closer to finding a direction for themselves.

"It seems like we need to see how this plays out," Marty said, his voice tinged with uncertainty.

As they prepared to move, the faint sound of an announcement echoed through the icy corridors, the voice cold and emotionless, yet filled with a sense of finality.

"The main body of the Edu will convene shortly to vote on Resolution Forty-Two."

Yotto made a burping sound and grimaced. "Resolution Forty-Two . . . it's worse than I thought."

"What does that mean?" Surjan looked at the engineer.

Yotto shook his head and led them deeper into the glacier.

As Surjan and the team followed the lithe alien, he couldn't help but feel a growing sense of dread.

He had no idea what the resolution would be about, but somehow Surjan felt it wouldn't be good for their mission.

The metallic walls of the alien ship hummed softly, a low, almost imperceptible vibration that seemed to permeate everything. The team huddled in Yotto's lab, the faint blue glow of the control panels casting eerie shadows across their faces.

"I've requested some of the old records from the early days." Yotto said as he sat at a workstation. "They should come soon from the archives."

The team's tension was palpable, the air thick with unspoken fears.

Surjan stood by the door, keeping watch while the others caught their breath. François paced the small room, his footsteps echoing off the cold metal floor.

Marty leaned against a console, his eyes distant. Lowanna sat cross-legged on the floor, rolling a pebble back and forth across her knuckles. Kareem ran his fingers along the sharpened edge of his ankh, his thoughts buried deeply inside the teen's somber expression.

Yotto, the engineer, was seated at the central console, his fingers tapping at the controls.

François stopped his pacing and turned to Yotto, his eyes narrowing with suspicion. "Yotto, the way the Herder faction reacted to us . . . it was like they hated us on sight. Why?"

Yotto shrugged, a very humanlike expression. "Some just hate, they don't need a reason to."

"What happened to the humans who were originally placed here with the Edu?" Surjan asked.

Yotto's hands stilled, the soft tapping ceasing as he looked up, his expression shifting from distraction to something much darker. He hesitated, his eyes flicking to each member of the team before settling back on Surjan. "There has always been... tension among the Edu," Yotto began slowly, choosing his words with care. "From the beginning, there were those who did not take kindly to the mixing of one species with another. The idea of integrating with humans was met with resistance."

François crossed his arms, his gaze hardening. "And those who resisted... they became the Herder faction, didn't they?"

"We had no such names then for ourselves, we were one people. But yes, over time such dichotomies developed." Yotto confirmed, his expression somber. "Over time, the differences in ideology grew into a deep-seated animosity. The Herders believed in purity, in keeping the Edu separate from all other species. They saw humans as a threat, as invaders who would corrupt their way of life."

"Wait a minute," Lowanna chimed in, her brows furrowed. "Are you speaking about this from memory, or from something you've read? How long have you been here? Personally, I mean."

Yotto's thin lips moved silently for a bit, looking a bit confused by the question. "How long? I've been here since our arrival. These are things that I witnessed."

"How old are you?" Lowanna asked.

"I don't know what you mean," Yotto said, his eyelids rapidly sweeping across his eyes from the sides, like a pair of sliding doors. "I was first conceived in another place. I traveled here and have been here since. Age really only means something when you're expected to expire—and that's not the natural way of the Edu."

"Immortal..." Gunther whispered, his eyes wide with a surprised expression.

François took a step closer, his voice lowering but growing more intense. "But what happened to the humans, Yotto? What did the Herders do to them?"

Yotto's face fell and his mouth became a barely visible slit against his gray skin. He looked away, unable to meet François's eyes as he spoke. "There were once many humans here, living alongside the Edu. They were part of the initial experiment, to see if our species could coexist, could help each other survive in this harsh environment."

François's patience was wearing thin, his voice now a harsh whisper. "And?"

Yotto swallowed hard, his hands gripping the edge of the console as if for support. "One day . . . the Herders took matters into their own hands. They saw the humans as a contaminant, something that needed to be purged. They . . . they wiped them all out, before the others could stop them. It was a massacre."

A heavy silence fell over the room, the gravity of Yotto's words sinking in like a lead weight. The team exchanged shocked, horrified glances, the realization of the danger they were in becoming all too clear.

"As you know, the Edu now associate with humans in trade to gather the key ingredients we need to consume, and in some cases to attempt to help maintain our equipment."

François's jaw clenched, anger flashing in his eyes. "And the others? The ones who didn't agree with the Herders? What did they do?"

Yotto looked back at him, guilt and regret etched into his features. "By the time they realized what had happened, it was too late. The Herder faction was too powerful, too entrenched. Once killed, humans are not resilient enough to recover. You are fragile. We could only mourn the loss and try to prevent further bloodshed. But the damage was done. It was a stupid thing to do, because they knew the issues we were going to run into. Some of the equipment had even begun to fail upon arrival. Nonetheless, the rift between the factions deepened, and the Herders maintained their xenophobic beliefs."

François felt a cold fury building inside him. "So, now they see us, and they see some kind of threat, the same 'contaminant' they eradicated before."

Yotto nodded slowly, his voice barely above a whisper. "Yes. It's why we keep humans separate from the main population of Edu. That's why they reacted the way they did. You don't have the smell of humans on you, or at least maybe the star-metal is masking it, but you certainly look like them—and that's enough. To them, you are a reminder of the past, of what they believe must be kept out at all costs. It's a ridiculous notion, but not one I have the ability to cure."

Surjan finally spoke up, his voice steady but laced with concern. "If they've done it before, there's nothing stopping them from trying to do it again."

Marty, who had been silent until now, pushed away from the console, his face grim. "We need to get out of here, find a portal to get our asses home before it escalates."

Yotto nodded. "I told you, I have associates seeking the old records. Maybe there is something there. I might be the engineer, but this is an interstellar carrier capable of carrying more than ten thousand of us. It's larger than any one person can maintain, and I'm the last of the original trained engineers from my home planet."

A gonglike sound echoed through the room from some hidden speaker.

Yotto looked up, light reflecting off his obsidian eyes. "The meeting is soon. If the resolution passes—"

"What is the resolution about, exactly?"

"It's about the trading output," Yotto said as he got up from the workstation. "My faction believes in the free trade of goods for services and believe the mutual benefit is best. The Herders want to change those ways."

"In what way?"

Again a shrug. "Herders refuse to explain how they would propose changing things, they just want the go-ahead to make changes to prove their way would be better."

"What?" Marty guffawed and shook his head. "How can you decide on something when you don't even know the details of your options?"

"We see it that same way you do." Yotto nodded. "It's frustrating to us as well and most any sensible Edu, but that's where we're at at the moment." Yotto motioned for them to follow as he led them from the ship.

Surjan frowned. He was never one to pay attention to politics of any kind, whether Indian, British, or military, yet it seemed like even alien politics made utterly no sense. The only thing that seemed clear was one side was trying for a power grab, and it would be his natural inclination to not want that to happen.

What would the aliens decide and how would it affect their ability to get the hell out of this place and time?

⤜ CHAPTER ⤝
TWENTY-EIGHT

Lowanna followed Yotto into the new chamber, her senses tingling with the strange, almost alien energy that seemed to permeate the space. The room was vast, bigger than a high school gymnasium, and among all manner of other mechanical contrivances stood row upon row of hydroponic setups, each one nurturing a different kind of plant. The air was thick with humidity and the scent of earth, a stark contrast to the cold, icy corridors they had just left behind. It felt like stepping into another world—one that thrived and pulsed with life beneath the surface of the icy wasteland.

Yotto gestured for them to follow, leading the team deeper into the chamber. Lowanna's eyes widened as she took in the sight of the plants—some familiar, others completely foreign—growing in this carefully controlled environment. The Gray explained that the plants were grown for Edu consumption. It was a veritable farm, sustaining the thousand or so Grays who called this hidden domicile home. The glow from the hydroponic lights bathed the room in a soft, almost ethereal light, casting long shadows that danced across the walls.

Beyond the plants, they approached a large collection of boxes stacked on a metal table. Lowanna watched as several assistants carefully brought out what appeared to be a stack of papers that looked like they might explode into a million dust particles if someone sneezed. Yotto's expression softened with a hint of reverence as he began sorting through the contents, handling the brittle paper relics with the utmost care.

"These," Yotto said, his voice hushed, "are some of our oldest records. Maps and written instructions were only needed during the initial training, before we even arrived on Earth. After that, such things became unnecessary, so they were archived and forgotten. These documents probably haven't seen the light of day in thousands of your years."

The team gathered around Yotto as he gingerly unfolded one of the larger sheets of thick, brittle paper. It crackled softly as the creases smoothed out, revealing a faded map that showed the general physical layout of the Grays' city and the surrounding tunnel structure. Marty and the others leaned in, their eyes scanning the lines and symbols, trying to make sense of the intricate design.

Lowanna, however, found her attention drifting back to the plants. She could feel them, the life force within them, the subtle energy that connected her to the natural world. It was a sensation that had grown stronger since they had entered this strange, ancient world. The plants here were not species she could name, yet there was something about them that felt familiar. Could some of these plants have actually come from another planet? She was no botanist, but the possibility intrigued her immensely.

Her gaze settled on a table filled with freshly planted legumes, their tiny leaves just beginning to break through the surface of the nutrient-rich water. She could sense their hunger, their need for the essential elements that would help them grow strong and healthy. Without thinking, she closed her eyes and reached out, not physically, but with a mental focus. She extended a part of herself outward, sensing the tiny shards of green life that lay within reach. She let her senses flow outward into the plants.

The response was immediate. The legumes shivered under her touch, their leaves trembling as if awakening from a deep sleep. Lowanna felt the energy coursing through her, linking her to each of the seedlings. She felt a warm, vibrant pulse that matched the rhythm of her own heartbeat. It was almost as if time sped up. The tiny sprouts began to grow, pushing upward with a sudden vigor that took her by surprise.

"Lowanna," Marty's voice cut through her focus, a note of curiosity in his tone. "What are you doing?"

She blinked, realizing that the entire team had turned to watch. Had she lost herself in the process of communing with these things?

The plants she'd been focused on had tripled in size. Their leaves unfurled, their stems thickened as they rapidly absorbed the nutrients from the water and whatever it was she'd channeled into them. In moments, the table of seedlings had been transformed into lush, green plants, their leaves reaching toward the hydroponic lights as if drawn to a sun that did not exist in this subterranean world. To her astonishment, pods had formed along the stems, swelling and ripening before her eyes. Within minutes, the plants not only flourished but also produced an abundance of edible legumes, their rich, iron-packed contents ready for harvest.

Yotto, who had been engrossed in the old map, looked up in awe. "Incredible," he murmured, stepping closer to the flourishing plants. "These legumes...they are rich in iron, something we've been struggling to cultivate effectively. And yet, you...you...you did something. What did you do?"

Lowanna withdrew her hand, feeling a sense of satisfaction mixed with a twinge of exhaustion. "I just...helped them along a little," she said softly. "They needed a push, that's all."

Yotto shook his head, still amazed. "Is this something all of you humans are capable of doing?"

"No," Marty responded. "Lowanna has some unique abilities." He tossed her a wink and Lowanna's body betrayed her as she felt her face warm from his attention.

"Yotto." François tapped on the map unfurled on the table. "Can you show us some of these sections? I'd very much like to get a better understanding of things in this ship."

The alien shifted his attention from Lowanna back to the map and she breathed a sigh of relief.

The idea of helping the aliens seemed like a good one, but her instincts screamed that these things couldn't be trusted, not even this engineer who seemed to be nothing but kind.

If the aliens found a use for them, that might greatly interfere with the team's ability to ever get out of this time and place.

Lowanna kept her eyes fixed on the dimly lit tunnel ahead as Yotto led the team through the narrow, winding passage. The walls were cold and metallic, a stark contrast to what she'd grown used to in the real world outside of this giant ice cube they were in. She felt the subtle hum of the alien ship beneath her feet, a constant reminder that they were deep within something entirely foreign. Yotto moved quickly, his slender form slipping through the shadows, while Lowanna, Marty, and the others followed close behind.

"We're heading toward the Farmer faction's territory," Yotto explained, his voice echoing slightly in the tunnel. "They should be more welcoming—or at least less hostile—than the Herders. To some extent by partitioning and to some extent by moving ourselves around, we have ended up with a divided city, split into sections that are mostly controlled by one faction or the other. It wasn't always like this, but over the years, the tension between the Farmers and Herders has grown. And perhaps the separation helped prevent outright conflict."

"Yotto, can you help me try to understand what the nature of the differences are between the factions?" Lowanna asked. "I understand that the factions might have a disagreement on how best to adapt to this world, and a strong disagreement about what had happened in the past, but I presume you both want what's best for the Edu, so is the root difference having to do with the treatment of people like us?"

Yotto paused mid-stride and turned to look at Lowanna. "At this point, it's everything. We've slowly become different people. Our views on things have evolved. But you're not wrong about what you said. The humans are the kernel of the truth. Or the problem. The key difference. I personally, and those who are like me, we view you humans as fellow travelers. No more, no less. It seems arrogant to view you in any other way, because most of us see your potential. You say you're from the future, so you must understand what I mean. Your race has the potential for great achievements, but unfortunately some of us don't have that generous view of you. Some of us think of you more as animals than as ill-educated equals. It's an unfortunate thing, but the troubles for the Edu stemmed from such differences of viewpoint. And to be honest, I don't see it getting better. This vote will tell us much."

Lowanna pressed her lips together and glanced at the team. Nothing the alien had said was entirely shocking. The human race was filled with such stories. Whether it was slavery, exploitation, dispossession, or genocide, many humans had treated each other like animals. Why should the Edu do any different?

"Let's go." Yotto continued onward, and it took only a few more minutes before they neared the end of the tunnel; a faint light became visible ahead. The alien slowed his pace, signaling for the others to do the same. "We're almost there. The square should be just beyond this tunnel. Stay close."

Lowanna's heart quickened as they emerged again from the tunnel into the brightness of a large plaza. It seemed to be the same square they'd entered before, only in a different corner now. The space was vast, with high icy ceilings that seemed to stretch into infinity. Edu—apparently Farmer faction members—milled about, their tall, slender forms moving with a quiet grace.

Yotto led them toward a group of Edu, who immediately turned their heads in the team's direction. Their nostrils flared as they sniffed the air. Lowanna tensed, wondering if the star-metal they carried was setting off some kind of alarm.

One of the Edu, a tall figure with long, slender fingers, approached Lowanna. "May I touch your hand?" the alien asked, his voice gentle but curious.

Lowanna hesitated for a moment, then nodded, extending her hand. The Edu carefully cupped her hand in his, his fingers cool against her skin. He brought her hand closer to his face and sniffed at it, his large eyes narrowing from side to side.

"Very curious," he murmured. "You don't have the scent of a human . . . you smell like one of us . . . but you clearly aren't."

Lowanna felt a wave of confusion wash over her. Smell like one of them? How was that possible? Before she could ask, Yotto stepped closer, his eyes widening with interest. He leaned in toward Marty, who was standing nearby, and awkwardly sniffed at his ear.

"This isn't right," Yotto said, his voice tinged with surprise. "It's not the star-metal giving off that scent after all. Your bodies really do carry a different scent. We should look into this further back in engineering. I have some tests I can run, but for now, we need to focus. The voting is about to begin."

Lowanna's mind buzzed with questions, but she forced herself to stay present. A silvery-gray, egg-shaped object hovered overhead, pulsing with a soft glow as it moved above the crowd. Yotto pointed up at it. "That drone is counting the votes. The Farmers have more members, but there could be dissenters on either side. A vote's outcome is never certain."

The tension in the square was palpable as a hidden loudspeaker crackled to life, announcing the question at hand. *"Shall we continue as we are, using the Farmers' techniques, or change to the Herder faction's solution? All for the Farmers' technique, raise your hand."*

The square fell silent as most of the nearby Edu raised their hands, the drone hovering above them, its pulse now a steady flow. Lowanna scanned the crowd and it was an obvious delineation between those with their hands up and the rest on the far end of the square who didn't. Her heart pounded in her chest, as the hands slowly lowered and the loudspeaker announced the second option.

"All for the Herders' solution."

Again, hands went up. It didn't seem to Lowanna that there were more hands up than the prior choice, but there were certainly enough of them raised to create some uncertainty. The drone emitted several beeps, and then projected the tally in a shimmering hologram above the crowd.

The markings were utterly illegible to her, but Yotto nodded. "The Farmer faction has won the vote."

Lowanna let out a breath she didn't realize she'd been holding. The tension that had gripped the square eased as the Edu, without fanfare or celebration, quietly began to disperse. It seemed like a decision had been made, and that was that. No cheers, no chants—just the silent acceptance of the outcome.

A pretty civilized end, given the near-riot they'd seen earlier.

Lowanna stayed close to the team as the crowd thinned. She caught snippets of conversation as some of the nearby Farmers spoke in hushed tones.

"Did you see?" one of them whispered. "Where was Pinosh off to?"

Lowanna's ears perked up at the name, but before she could hear more, Yotto gently touched her shoulder, signaling that it was time to move.

As they made their way back through the tunnels, she couldn't help but wonder how those on the losing side could take the outcome so calmly. She smiled, because in her mind she thought, *It seems almost inhuman to just stoically take a loss in something you cared about.* These creatures were not human. Not by any stretch of the imagination.

And that's what worried her the most.

She couldn't tell whether any of these aliens' reactions was normal and expected, or if something cockeyed was about to happen.

The hairs on the back of her neck stood on end.

⫷ CHAPTER ⫸
TWENTY-NINE

Kareem followed at the rear of the party. He worried that the mob of gray demons might come after them. He didn't really trust that the one calling itself Yotto was really on their side, and wouldn't lead them into a trap. All of the back-and-forth, in and out of the same square, felt like an attempt to disorient them. In any case, he wanted to keep a rearguard position from which he could monitor all the action and be prepared to strike.

Yotto led them away from the square, around the corner, and through large doors. Gollip waddled along with Yotto, bobbling his head at every word the engineer said. The space they entered echoed with grinding, humming, and wheezing sounds. Light here came from a phosphorescent strip on all the walls, but it needed repainting, and was dim. Light of various colors leaked out from the farther corners, creating a muddle of illumination.

Kareem didn't need the light, in any case.

To his eyes, the rest of the party was bright red, as always. The gray demons were also red with heat, and he could see a dull orange glow on the floor showing the paths the Grays generally traveled in this industrial room. They were limited, and large sections of the room seemed never to be visited at all, or at least they hadn't been visited in so long there was no trace on the floor of anyone's passage.

And there were neglected doors in the back corners.

It was child's play to slip away from the group, simply waiting

then tasted the water that poured from the faucet. It was cold and delicious.

He found four slabs per cell, which meant forty-eight prisoners per cluster, unless you jammed them in more thickly, which you could do. With sufficient cruelty, you could double the number of prisoners. At seven clusters he stopped counting and started looking for something different.

At one point, the gray demons had been prepared to hold many prisoners in this dungeon.

And the slabs were tall enough to sleep adult human beings.

He fingered his sharpened ankh, imagining himself beheading the engineer Yotto.

He followed a hallway that ended suddenly, opening into a larger chamber. The floor dropped away below him, the ceiling rose, and the walls opened left and right. The echo of his footfalls told him that the space before him was vast.

And the floor looked strange. Knobby, irregular, arrayed in heaps.

In his heart, he knew what was down there, but he had to confirm it for himself. The wall below his feet was irregular, and easy to find footholds and handholds in. He lowered himself carefully until he was close enough to let go of the wall and drop.

When he landed, he sank to his knees in a heap of bones. Close up, what he saw was unmistakable: human ribs, human pelvises, human skulls. How big was the room, how many bones were there? He couldn't see the opposite wall clearly in the darkness. Hundreds of skeletons?

Thousands?

Kareem was no stranger to death or to violence. But what he saw, looking at the massive heap of bones, broke his heart.

He searched meticulously, found exactly the bone he wanted to show François and the others, and tucked it into the large pocket of his tunic.

Then he turned and began the climb out.

"We need air, of course," Yotto said. He stood pointing out a massive glass cylinder with an accordionlike bellows flexing up and down within it. "Oxygen, the same as you. But also, as you point out, we have a metabolic challenge binding the oxygen into our blood with your atmospheric mix. Unfortunately, the engineer who was master of this device underwent some kind of metabolic shock and ceased to function. All we know is that this mechanism could render the interior of our home amenable to breathing without these devices." He tapped his nose ring.

Gollip bobbled his head and swayed back and forth with excitement.

"I'm guessing there's no instruction manuals or anything of the sort?" François asked.

"That would be correct. As the ship melted through the ice and settled onto the Earth's surface, we lost all contact with the outside, including anyone who could have helped us. Such documentation was digitally stored in remote nonvolatile storage up with the mothership, which at the time was in orbit."

François nodded. "In the time that we come from, we would call that storing data in the cloud. But some of you lived in Atlantis for a time, no?"

"Atlantis?" Yotto blinked.

"The City of the Gods on Earth?" Marty prompted the engineer.

"Ah yes. That city did indeed have functioning machinery, but those of us who came here were expected to rely on the devices in the downed ship."

François tapped at the controls on the device's console and said, "It looks like you have controls for input gasses here, and gauges for measuring the output." He tried twisting the dials and they didn't move.

"Yes," Yotto agreed. "I think there are sockets for inputs on the other side here as well, if you want to come look."

François circled the machine and looked at the indicated sockets. They reminded him of old-style RS-232 cable sockets from years ago. "So, do you have any cables that plug in here?"

"If I have them," Yotto said, "I don't know that I have them. They might be in storage. Or they might have been destroyed."

"Who would have destroyed them?" Marty's voice was puzzled. "And besides, with those nose rings on, you're able to breathe fine, right? What's keeping you here and preventing you from going elsewhere?"

"As to who would have destroyed them..." Yotto hesitated. "I suppose I'm not sure, but I've grown cynical over the years. I trust the motivation of very few creatures nowadays. It's safer that way. And the nose rings . . . some of the nose rings are starting to fail, as well."

Gollip shivered visibly.

François's brows furrowed as he took in what the alien had said. These guys were hosed. "It seems odd to me that anyone of your kind would purposefully sabotage you and themselves as well . . . I guess I'll need some time to study this and compare notes with you and whoever else has looked into this device. Maybe we can both examine your storage space for hoses or anything that might be related to what I'm seeing here before we assume the needed equipment is destroyed. Do you have any other machines with mysterious purposes?"

Yotto led François to a panel. "I am not entirely certain what this does."

"Those are just controls. Where is the machine?" Surjan looked around.

François looked, too, but then realized that the party was missing a member. Where was Kareem? He worried the young man might get up to no good, but he said nothing. Being a good mentor to the lad might from time to time mean coming down hard on him, but generally it must entail extending trust and space in which to operate. Besides, maybe Kareem was simply standing quietly, and had therefore disappeared into the shadows.

"I don't know," Yotto admitted. "I think in the walls. Based on work-log entries written by a predecessor, I believe this might be the control panel for a device to shield us from sunlight and radiation."

"Will you need this if the glacier above covers you?" François asked.

"We will not," Yotto admitted. "In fact, the glacier might inhibit the operation of this device. The ambient temperature in the ship is lower than it's supposed to be, and some parts of the ship may actually be frozen over. Our climate control has not operated as I'd hoped since our heavy landing on the planet. However, power, water, ventilation, and sewer are all functions that work."

Gollip nodded vigorously.

François caught sight of his comrades' faces and saw looks of utter boredom. "Isn't your basic issue one of food?" he asked. "Dietary supplements with the metabolic iron you need? Radiation shielding doesn't feel like a critical need at the moment."

"Over here." Yotto beckoned with a long finger and headed toward an adjoining chamber. "We're trying to work on various solutions to enhance the absorbable iron within our foods."

François followed into a long rectangular room split into two sections. Being somewhat familiar with how basic human metabolism works, he figured that maybe the aliens had similar issues with extracting necessary nutrients from some foods. People couldn't exactly eat iron pellets or even grind up iron and gain any benefit from it, since in those forms it would simply pass through any human digestion system.

Aliens likely had the same kind of problem—the trick was how to gain iron supplementation in a form that could be metabolized.

In the nearer and smaller section, many tables stood in rows with terraria squatting on them. Lights of various colors shone down in the lids, but some of the lights didn't work and others sputtered on and off. In the bottoms of the terraria, white, chalky bricks rested in trays of a milky liquid. Some of the bricks looked sunken and waxy and others had an unhealthy greenish cast. One was speckled black and deeply pitted.

"Looks like tofu," Lowanna said. "This sight here is exactly why I could never be a vegetarian."

"Smells like foot," Surjan said. "What on Earth are you putting into that?"

"Iron," Yotto said. "Those are iron-infused vegetable proteins. Other important vitamins and micronutrients are also added. When it works, the result is an emulsified food substance that can be molded into any shape and easily flavored. Really, it shouldn't be nurtured in these glass cages. That slot in the wall should simply be extruding bricks, one every few seconds. But the machinery is slowly breaking down. Within months, at this rate, none of it will work."

François turned to the engineer with a look of surprise. "Are you saying that you're months away from starvation?"

Yotto shook his head. "No, not really that bad, but remember we're trying to find a solution that makes us less dependent on these devices we're wearing, and with the newly failing equipment, that solution is getting farther and farther away."

"Got it." François nodded. "So your ability to make this tofu that smells of feet is starting to falter."

"It does not smell like feet," Gollip objected.

"What's in the other half of the room?" Lowanna looked at the far end with little enthusiasm.

Yotto showed them the rest: rows of vines climbing up wire trellises out of planting troughs, heavy with bean pods. At the near end, the vines were neat and trimmed. At the far end, they exploded in a wild vegetable profusion, leaping off the trellises and climbing the walls.

"So the plants grow, at least," François said. "That's one problem we don't have."

"These are some experiments we're running. It's a bit frustrating, to tell you the truth. The plants either refuse to metabolize the iron infused into the soil," Yotto told him, "or they *do* absorb the iron and it causes the produce to become extremely woody and inedible. I have some infusions that seem to have promise, but as of right now, they're not very efficient and certainly not ready to scale for wider use."

François nodded. "I see there's much work to do here."

"And not much time," Yotto said. "Our side has been keeping the Herders at bay with the idea that we'll have a breakthrough in this issue, but if we don't make some progress, the patience of our opponents will vanish. And at that point, there may be a point of criticality where someone attempts to seize power. That may be the beginning of the end."

"You're really worried," Marty said.

"I worry," Yotto confirmed.

François frowned. To him this rivalry between the Farmers and Herders was nowhere near its beginning, it looked more like it was about to come to what might be a bloody conclusion. He needed to talk with Marty about this . . . their team didn't want to be anywhere around here when the proverbial excrement hit the rotating blades.

Kareem had rejoined the group at some point. He stood at the back of the party, fidgeting and frowning. He looked at François as if he were trying to catch his eye.

François walked over to the teen and Kareem surreptitiously handed him something and whispered, "Look at it."

François glanced at what looked like the end of a broken femur and felt a chill race up and down his spine. There were jagged teeth marks on the end of the ancient bone. The marks were narrow, finely spaced grooves—the same tooth spacing he'd noticed the Grays possessed.

He pocketed the bone, patted Kareem on the shoulder, and walked back over to the engineer. "Yotto, I know we walked into this structure off the maze of corridors, but if my bearings are correct, aren't we basically under your vessel right now?" François asked.

Yotto nodded. "It's above us." He pointed. "Slightly that direction."

"The ship, it's number seven, isn't it?" François asked.

Yotto clasped his hands together and cleared his throat. "Seven? Seven what?"

François took a deep breath. "Look, if we're going to work together, we're going to have to be a little more candid. You know there's a portal here. My guess is it's inside your space vessel. All the daughter cities have one, plus, presumably, the City of the Gods on Earth, and the portals are numbered one through ten."

Yotto said nothing.

"Where is this coming from?" Marty asked.

"I've seen the map." François shrugged. "You've seen it, too, Marty, but the image of the map is burned into my mind's eye, especially with the hidden markings from the water—that's what gives it all away. I spoke with Kareem on the journey here and he didn't tell us at the time, but from what I can tell, he'd spotted what might have been the remnants of a portal on the island, just like that marking told us. I think the craft above us crash-landed, but it was supposed to set down somewhere around here, with a city built around it like spokes around the hub of a wheel."

"Just like the tunnels and portal in Egypt," Marty murmured, more to himself than anyone else.

"This ship is the seventh portal, isn't it?" François asked with a serious tone. "Yotto, you're the only living engineer left, you have to know the answer. And the place we came from, the one essentially due north of here, it's number five. It's all on the map."

"You have not been forthcoming," Yotto said slowly.

"What are you talking about? This is our first conversation about this topic, and I'm sharing with you everything I know. You, on the other hand, are still dancing around the fact that a faction of your fellow citizens wants to kill and probably eat us, rather than messing around eating tofu bricks that smell like feet."

Yotto's eyes widened.

"Oh, you didn't think we'd know?" François growled. Then he

pushed his voice to take on a melodic, almost hypnotic tone. This was the tone that persuaded people, the tone that he'd only learned to use on these time travel journeys. "My friends and I have been through much getting here. You are not the first of your kind we have met. We have also encountered your type, but in a different form, in other parts of the world. We know about those nose rings you wear. We know about what you—or at least, what the Herders—did with humans. We're no fools."

Yotto opened his mouth as if to reply, and then made a *blurp-blurp* sound as he closed it.

"I appreciate that you want us to help you somehow persuade the rest of the Edu to not do whatever it is they have planned. We know you're ultimately on our side, but let's not fool each other." François nodded. "You also don't want your people to fall into a civil war. You're a visible leader of your faction—these so-called Farmers. You and yours are probably in physical danger if something doesn't change."

"I have not hidden that," Yotto said.

"But you haven't exactly been forthcoming, either," François said. "Which is fine. We haven't exactly been forthcoming on our end. But I want to be very open now. We're looking for a portal. I'm pretty sure you know of one, and it's inside that vessel of yours. I'll help you with the machinery—as best as I can. But in return, you have to show us to the portal and explain how it works."

"I don't know how it works," Yotto said.

It took all of François's control to not smile at the tacit admission that this Gray knew of the portal and where it was. "So we'll have to figure that out, too," François said. "Lead on."

⊰CHAPTER⊱
THIRTY

I will teach you.

"You will what?" Gunther asked the voice inside his head.

The rest of the party, climbing stairs ahead of him, turned and shot him a collective quizzical look. Yotto had taken them to another set of stairs leading up to the spaceship, and this one had had no guard at the bottom. Maybe the guards had gone home after the vote, dispersing like everyone else, but Yotto hadn't ventured any explanation. He'd simply let them up.

"Are you okay?" Lowanna asked him.

"Sorry, I was just thinking about something." Gunther gave her a lopsided grin and motioned dismissively.

He focused on the voice and quietly asked, "Teach me what?"

The door. I can instruct you on its use.

The archaeologist-turned-healer clenched his jaw and wondered if he was going crazy. If that voice was attached to someone, how could it know about the portal they were approaching? Is that what it meant? Or was the voice part of some delusion?

I can teach you to use the portal. I want you to survive.

Survival was good. But the idea of trusting a voice in his head was literally a sign of clinical insanity.

But Kareem had reported seeing what might be a portal underneath the palace in Nesha. And Gunther had first heard the voice when they had transitioned from Egypt to Nesha. Something had happened within him, some channel had been opened or some receiver activated, so he'd been hearing the voice since.

What was going on?

You are mine.

Gunther felt a sudden, strong sensation of calm. It was almost like before his gall bladder surgery, when the anesthesiologist injected something into his IV to calm his nerves. His sudden peace felt exactly like what he'd felt in that moment, only there was no drug wending its way through an IV into his bloodstream. The strange calming sensation bloomed within his chest and he felt relaxation flow through his extremities. He took a deep breath and finished climbing the last of the steps. The party stood with Yotto at an open ramp in the underside of the saucer. Gollip stood slightly to the side, near the stone lip of the bluff, looking over the edge like a sentinel or a gargoyle.

From this vantage point, Gunther could see several sets of stairs that ascended the mountain to the ship, some joining on their way.

"This is not off-limits, exactly," Yotto said, "but my people never come here. They would be . . . surprised to find I had let you in."

"Worried we might turn the death ray on the city?" François grinned.

"There is no death ray," Yotto said.

"Do you have a death ray?" Gollip asked. "Do you plan to build a death ray?"

"Put that on the list, François," Surjan said.

"No," François said, "that was a joke. No death rays. And we will be discreet about our visit here."

Was discretion possible? There were so many paths up to this point, and surely some Edu in one of the open spaces below would look up at any moment and see them congregated on the ramp.

You just have to trust me.

Gunther shook himself, trying to cast off the voice.

The saucer was not level on the bluff. Up this close, Gunther could see that it rested on three metal legs, but one of them was crumpled, so part of the saucer had flexed and tilted at a shallow angle.

"There are usually no Edu in this section," Yotto said. "You will not be harmed, but please be careful what you touch."

The team entered, François and Marty leading the way with Yotto. Gunther waited, trying to empty his mind of conscious thought to escape the solicitation of the voice, until he and Kareem were last, with Gollip still standing watch at the rim.

Kareem fidgeted, both hands in his tunic pocket.

Gunther smiled at the young man. "Find something interesting?"

Kareem spat. "This is a cursed place, by God." He climbed inside the saucer.

"That makes me feel good," Gunther murmured.

I will teach you.

Gunther entered, leaving Gollip outside. A spiral staircase ran up through a column of the ship. The angle meant that on one side the stairs tilted back and you risked sliding off, and on the other side the stairs tilted forward and you had to raise your feet extra high and then put them down at an angle that stressed the ankles. The fact that the steps were made of a metal lattice made the climb possible at all. Gunther went up with considerable use of his hands.

The lower floor contained sleeping and storage compartments, the bunks too small for adult humans of ordinary size, the shelves bare. Gunther followed the others to the upper floor and found them at a semicircular central console. It was built like a podium, to be worked by someone standing inside it, and lights shone up onto the faces of the party. The controls consisted of various buttons, faders, levers, and joysticks.

Above them and to the left ballooned a domed chamber with white walls and floor. In its floor were a series of dark circles, and Gunther was reminded of the portal they'd entered together in the time of Narmer to be sent to this time.

I will teach you.

"Do you know the controls?" François asked Yotto.

"By experimentation, a few," the engineer said. "That fader disperses heat via multiple external vents. Space is cold, but the inside of a vessel traveling in space may become quite hot. Those buttons activate lights; don't touch, it will alert my people to our presence in this section. These controls affect the air circulation, that one empties the latrine reserve. These would activate a travel field around the vessel to escape gravity's effects, but those fuel cells have long ago been depleted."

"The ship has some other energy source for life support systems?" François asked.

"Yes, there are thermoelectric generators that power the critical support features of the vessel." Yotto tapped on a console in front of him. "This console has access to the vessel's database, or at least what portion of it we had locally stored prior to having our communication systems isolated from the mother ship." He touched a button, and one of the walls that had been a flat, blank, dark screen suddenly lit up.

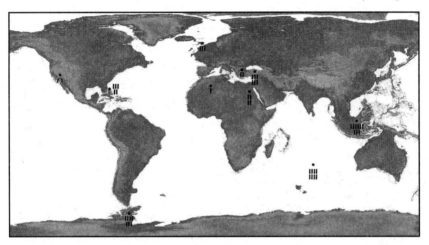

It showed a map. The map was a detailed Mercator projection of the Earth. Gunther recognized the continents, except that they were all too large and their shapes weren't quite right—though the map might have been accurate to what Earth looked like during the most recent ice age. During the ice age, Gunther reminded himself, that was ending this very moment. And there were small clusters of vertical lines tucked inside neat circles at various spots around the globe— including, in particular, spots the party had been to.

"There's Nesha," Marty said. "Number five. And we're at number seven here. And look, we started at number four."

"The numbers are written Egyptian-style," Gunther murmured.

"Not especially clever," Marty said, "since the Egyptians wrote single digits by just drawing a number of lines equal to the number they wished to express. But yes."

"Isn't it interesting that where we started isn't number one?" Gunther announced.

"Actually number one looks like it's near Jebel Mudawwar," Lowanna said. "And if you think about it, that actually is where we started. Why is it marked? You'd sort of expect something major if a portal is there."

"If you recall, we didn't exactly look hard in that area," François said. "And even at the time we were transported there, anything substantial could have been swallowed in the sand."

"We weren't there in the twenty-first century," Lowanna said. "We were there in the fourth millennium B.C.E."

"By that time that part of the world had seen a significant climate shift," François said as he crossed his arms and tapped his chin with his pointer finger. "What if it *was* Atlantis that was the city Yotto's referring to? For all we know, Atlantis was the ice age capital of our species."

"You've made this suggestion before," Marty remarked. "Atlantis as the City of the Gods on Earth. This is sounding a lot like when I first met you and you kept talking about aliens."

François gestured at Yotto and gave Marty a triumphant smile. "I was right then, and I'm telling you now, I'm probably still right on this."

Marty shrugged. "Maybe . . . I guess it doesn't really matter what we call it, we have the here and now to focus on."

François grunted in exasperation and pointed at the map. "Yotto—number one on the map, is that a place knows as the City of the Gods?"

"I'm not sure I've heard that name," Yotto said.

"The humans from number five referred to a City of the Gods on Earth in their legends," Lowanna noted. "François, think about it . . . if there was some early human city—"

"Atlantis," François interjected.

"Fine, called it whatever you want. But if there was an early city with advanced technology that had maybe reached out to various places, they probably would come off as gods to the primitive cultures in other parts of the world."

"True," Francois said. "Sort of a spin on the Arthur C. Clarke quote that states that any sufficiently advanced technology is indistinguishable from magic, or in this case, miracles of the gods."

"Why the numbers?" Marty asked. "Are these numbered in the order in which the locations were built? That seems randomly scattered, unless this map is some kind of outline of the development of the civilization."

"Maybe it is also that," François said.

"What do you mean 'also'?" Marty asked. "What's the other thing? Why are these locations numbered?"

François shrugged. "It seems obvious to me. We started at number one. The numbers are the gauntlet. They're the test we're being put through in order."

"We emerged first at number one and walked to, what, number four?" Marty asked. "Is the test we're going through broken, or did we cheat?"

"Maybe neither," François said. "Maybe we accidentally played our knight like a rook."

"I don't know that mixing metaphors helps," Surjan growled.

"Playing your knight like a rook would be cheating," Lowanna said. "Has no one taught you how to play chess?"

"Maybe it isn't like chess," François said. "Maybe no one is enforcing the rules. Or maybe it's more like a psychological experiment. We're in a cage, being observed. Maybe the great psychologist of the universe has left a bunch of game pieces sitting here and is watching us to see what we make of them."

"And if we solve the puzzle," Lowanna said with a frown, "we get a monkey pellet?"

"Are you thinking we were sent to one in the first instance," Marty asked, "and our job there was to find a portal and get to site two, but instead we accidentally took a shortcut?"

"Or accidentally went off the rails, depending on how you look at it," François said.

"Presumably this means we can't win," Lowanna said. "There's some kind of flag we need to go back to Jebel Mudawwar to capture, and then go on to site two. Or can we take them in any order? For that matter, if there was a flag to capture in Egypt, we didn't do it."

"If there's another team playing against us," Surjan said, "we're losing."

"Maybe it's not capture the flag," François said. "Or a race."

"And as you said, if it's not chess," Lowanna asked, "what game *are* we playing?"

François scratched his chin. "I'm not sure."

"You are clearly extraordinary Shnipara, as Gollip said," Yotto said, shaking his head and blinking rapidly. "I have no idea what you are talking about."

"Honestly, we probably don't, either," François told him.

You do not need to run the gauntlet.

"We don't need to run the gauntlet," Gunther said.

Everyone turned to look at him.

"Why do you think that?" Marty asked.

Gunther opened his mouth to speak and made a sharp yelping sound instead. He took a deep breath, steadied himself. "I don't think it. I don't know why I said that."

Marty looked at Yotto, then back at Gunther. "The voice again?"

Gunther nodded.

I will teach you to control your arrival portal. To choose. To act, and not to be acted upon.

"I think we're in the right place." Marty shrugged. "Beyond that..."

"Perfect," Surjan said. "So we figure out who we're supposed to save here, we save them, and then we... do the thing with Gunther."

"I don't know whether we should or not," Gunther admitted.

"Who do we save?" Lowanna asked.

"The Edu," François said. He spun slowly, gesturing to take in all the machinery. "We secure their food supply, which is the basic prerequisite for peace. Then if there are other things we can help, we do what we can." He turned to Yotto and asked, "I assume you can get me whatever other supplies that are needed."

"I can do that," Yotto confirmed. "But some items may be locked away and nobody knows how to open it. Some things never got repaired since the crash."

"We'll figure out the rest." François beamed. "My young friend Kareem there is very clever, he's a budding engineer. He's very good at elaborate mechanical devices, locks and such. He and I will set you right in a heartbeat."

"No," Kareem said.

François gave Kareem a stern look.

Marty clapped his hands together and said, "Let's all maybe take a break and think about our next steps."

"Come with me, Kareem." François tried to keep his voice calm, but his hands shook and his feet were unsteady as he rattled down the tilting staircase and onto the bluff.

Gollip remained there, crouched now at the edge to watch over. He looked down on the Grays below.

François switched deliberately to French, forcing himself to adopt his native Gallic insouciance along with the words he knew Kareem understood.

"Kareem, my young friend, it's not enough to avoid killing innocent people. Just not being a murderer is not enough righteousness and decency for a civilized man."

Kareem looked back and forth between François and the Gray. "You mean you want me to help you fix their engines."

François smiled. "Yes. And graciously."

"I can't do it," Kareem said. He seemed to understand François's tactic and was also smiling. Something was making him feel angry or shaken, though, because his smile was the worst pasted-on grin François had ever seen.

"You can."

"I don't want to. You won't want to, either, once I tell you about that bone I showed you."

François's frustration ebbed as his mind flashed back to the chewed bone that Kareem had shown him. The kid's heart was in the right place, and he hated anything alien at the moment. "Go ahead, tell me."

"A mound of skulls," Kareem said. "In a prison, beneath this very ridge."

"What kind of skulls?" François asked. "Human?"

Kareem nodded. "There were thousands and thousands of bones. All of them with bite marks like the one I showed you. Needle-sharp teeth, the same as these things have." He tilted his head toward Gollip. "We know the Grays eat human flesh. The ones living under Nesha did, and there is a group of them here that wants to eat us."

François sighed, his heart sinking. "But there is a group that doesn't."

"The engineer says. Do you trust him?"

François hesitated, but then nodded slowly. "I believe I do."

"Then ask him to tell you the truth," Kareem said. "There's a dungeon under his precious engine works, that held hundreds of prisoners, and a massive pile of gnawed-on human bones."

"You think they eat people who come here seeking healing?" François asked.

Kareem shook his head. "The bones are too old, and there are no prisoners down there now, and the door was jammed shut." He hesitated. "Maybe Yotto doesn't know. Maybe this has been a secret for a long time. I think those bones down there belong to the humans who sailed here with the Grays. I think when the city hit its first crisis, the Grays ate all the humans."

⇌ CHAPTER ⇌
THIRTY-ONE

Lowanna followed Yotto through the dimly lit corridors of the alien ship, her senses on high alert despite the engineer's assurances that they were safe. The air was thick with the hum of the ship's inner workings, a low, steady pulse that resonated in her bones. Yotto had promised them sleeping arrangements in his lab, a space he insisted was secure. The team moved in a tight group, wary of the unknown dangers lurking in the depths of the Edu city.

Yotto glanced back at them, his expression calm but serious. "We'll be safe here. My lab is well-protected, and I've had some of my assistants bring out items from storage that you should probably look at. They might provide us with some answers."

Lowanna nodded, though her mind was elsewhere, still trying to process everything they had learned. The tension in the group was palpable, everyone on edge after the unsettling encounters with the Edu factions.

She also didn't really know what to make of Gunther's mysterious voice. On the boat she'd heard parts of what he'd said with regard to the voice trying to get him to go down under the Neshili palace to find the portal. If it were her having voices in her head telling her to do dangerous things, she'd be pretty convinced that she was going insane, so Lowanna couldn't exactly fault the German archaeologist-turned-healer for being hesitant about admitting what he was going through.

It's not like they could afford to have him totally go bonkers on them; his ability to heal had proven a godsend in the past and probably would be needed in the future. But the idea that the voice was now influencing the team's decisions wasn't sitting well with her.

How the hell could some voice in that man's head know anything about using some alien portal? But seeing that map projected in the air and reading a numeric mark on Nesha that made some of Gunther's crazy voice story seem less crazy. The mark implied that there *had* been a portal there, and they had missed it.

But did the number really imply a portal? They had seen no portal at Jebel Mudawwar, after all.

But François had reported about Kareem's solo explorations under Nesha, explorations Kareem had told no one else about, that the young Egyptian man had found a portal.

It all fit together. In a surreal way.

She needed to talk to Marty about this. She personally suspected that if the voice had any useful data, then it had to be coming from one of the Grays...but could that alien be trusted? None of them could tell the difference between a good alien that was probably ambivalent about humans and one that had a craving for their iron-rich livers.

This seemed to be the dreadful thing that no one was quite saying, that the Herders saw humans as food.

As they neared the entrance to the lab, Lowanna felt something slap onto the back of her leg. Her heart skipped a beat, and before she could react, it was climbing up her body with alarming speed.

She nearly jumped out of her skin, her hand instinctively going to her weapon. But then she froze, her heart racing as she found herself face-to-face with Shush the weasel. The small creature's eyes were wide with urgency, his tiny paws gripping her shoulder as he chirped and grunted at her in rapid-fire fashion.

"Shush?" Lowanna whispered, incredulous. She had said her farewells to the furry guy back when they'd left the Neshili in their brand-new fort on the Pampas. "What are you doing here?"

The weasel continued his frantic chattering, and Lowanna's blood ran cold.

Many of the Neshili had been captured and taken prisoner!

"What's he doing here?" Gunther asked. "Is that the same weasel?"

Her breath caught in her throat as she processed the information.

She felt her panic rising, but Lowanna forced herself to stay calm. This wasn't the time to lose control. The Neshili were in danger, and they needed to act fast.

She turned to Marty, raising her voice. "The Neshili—"

"I heard him." Marty stepped forward, his expression darkening. He caught up to Yotto and put his hand on the alien's narrow shoulder. "One second, we have an issue."

Lowanna's heart pounded as Shush nestled against her neck, his small body trembling. Some kind of enemy had fallen on those they'd left behind and somehow this little guy found her. This wasn't something they could do much about.

But what could they do? Sail back to the Pampas and rescue the Neshili?

Come with me and see.

Lowanna and Marty shared a look.

"I'll go," Marty said.

Marty crouched low, his eyes scanning the shadows as he moved through the labyrinth of tunnels that led toward the main chamber. Shush scurried ahead, the weasel's agile body slipping through the shadows with ease. Marty's mind raced as he tried to piece together the fragments of information they had gathered.

Marty had agreed to follow Shush, and was still trying to understand what the weasel wanted him to know.

The weasel was a surprisingly smart creature and, from what he could piece together from its account, it seemed like the Neshili had been captured and were being marched south.

Why?

If some other tribe had attacked, what sense would it make to capture anyone other than for breeding purposes? Yet Shush seemed adamant that it wasn't just the women. It was everyone.

Marty didn't think there was a concept of ransom in the ancient world . . . maybe they needed slaves? Was there some large city between here and where the Neshili had been that the team had bypassed by going via a water route?

Or had the Neshili been taken by cannibals?

The question gnawed at him, and the more he thought about it, the more his gut twisted with dread. It didn't make sense—unless . . .

"They're being herded," he muttered to himself, the realization hitting him like a cold slap to the face. "It's the Herders. It has to be."

Shush stopped suddenly, his body tense as he sniffed the air. The weasel chirped softly, pointing down the corridor that led toward the trading post, and beyond it was the magma tube that led to the outside world. Marty hesitated, the icy chill of fear creeping up his spine.

"Fine," he relented, his voice tight with tension. "But if we're going, we need to move fast."

They pushed forward, the narrow tunnel walls closing in around them as they approached the chamber that led to the magma tube. As they entered, Marty's heart sank. The chamber, once filled with the bustling activity of traders and clerks, was eerily empty. The stalls were abandoned, the equipment left behind as if the Grays had vanished into thin air.

Marty had had the impression this was a place that operated at all times, but maybe not...

He had agreed to follow Shush, but this was taking him dangerously close to the outside world.

"We can't leave this place," Marty argued quietly, glancing around nervously. "We can't just abandon the others."

Shush chirped softly and bolted toward the magma tube. Marty followed, his body tense with every step. It was a long ascent, but the little weasel seemed tireless as it slunk quickly toward the outside world.

It took some time, but Marty finally emerged from the tunnel into the open air, where the icy wind bit at his skin and a thick fog rolled in, partially obscuring the landscape. Night had fallen, and obscured whatever the fog might have revealed.

The area that had once been filled with tents and people from many disparate nations was now a desolate wasteland. The tents were flattened, the ground littered with debris, but there was no sign of any living creature, much less any Grays—or the Neshili.

Marty's heart raced as he turned to Shush, who raced in a frantic circle around a tattered scrap of fur. "What happened here? Where did they go?"

The weasel chirped again, the sound almost lost in the howling wind. *The Neshili are close.*

"South? You mean the Neshili have been captured and are being brought here?" Marty's mind raced as he tried to make sense of it all. Why would they capture the Neshili and march them across such a long distance? His thoughts darkened as the only plausible answer came to him—they were being led to their doom.

Rescue them, Shush said. *Rescue them again. Only you can save them. Rescue them from the Hungry Dead again.*

"No," Marty said, his voice filled with resolve. "We can't go after them now. It's too dangerous. We'll go now and tell the others. We'll come back in the morning."

Shush looked up at him, his beady eyes glistened in the moonlight, but he didn't protest. Marty knew they had to get back and let the others know what they had discovered.

As they turned back toward the tunnel, Marty couldn't shake the feeling of impending doom that hung over them like a dark cloud. The Edu had voted. Did the Herders not regard their vote as binding?

No, it was worse than that. The timing suggested that when the Herders voted, they had already sent a raiding party out to capture the Neshili. Or to capture humans, at least, and it happened to be the Neshili who were captured.

The Herders had never intended to abide by the vote.

Marty would go out again in the morning. Maybe then some answers would become evident.

The weasel rapidly climbed up his pants leg and perched on his shoulder.

Marty turned and began jogging back.

Whatever was going on, his guts were in a knot over the fate of the Neshili. He had strong suspicions and silently he prayed that he wrong. The fate of those natives was teetering on the edge of a cliff.

≼CHAPTER≽ THIRTY-TWO

Marty's mind raced as he gathered the team in a small, dimly lit room. The walls seemed to close in around them as he recounted what he'd seen at the trading outpost and at the waiting area beyond the magma tube—the flattened tents, the eerie silence, the missing Grays. He could see the tension on everyone's faces, a mixture of fear and determination as they tried to process what this meant.

"Yotto," Marty said, his voice steady but urgent, "the outside waiting area looks like a war zone. The Grays are gone—vanished. It's like something swept through there and left nothing but destruction."

Yotto's expression darkened, his thin lips pressed into a grim line. "The trading post is not always populated, as we've instructed the humans to come only during the daylight. However, what you saw outside is disturbing," he muttered. He quickly turned to one of his assistants, a tall, slender Edu with silver-gray skin. "Go. Check the outpost. See if the Herders have broken the peace with the humans. Report back to me, and to me only, as soon as you confirm the situation."

The assistant nodded and left without a word, moving with a haste that only deepened Marty's sense of dread.

"There's nothing that can be done right now, but I promise you that we will learn what it is you saw and then we can formulate a response. In the meantime," Yotto continued, "I would like to follow up on some of our prior discussions and gather more data from you. I'll also show you your sleeping quarters." He motioned for the team to follow him, leading them through a series of corridors until they reached his lab. The space was filled with strange equipment, blinking lights, and displays of alien symbols that flickered across translucent screens. The room buzzed with a low hum of energy, making Marty's skin prickle.

"I've been thinking about that smell of yours," Yotto remarked.

"Smell?" Marty asked.

"Yes, the scent you all give off. Maybe your sense of smell is not as sensitive as that of the Edu, but you all clearly have an aroma about you that is unique. It has a very unique yet familiar smell. Either way, I think a simple chemistry analysis will help clear up some questions."

Marty glanced at the others, who looked a bit apprehensive, and he turned to Yotto and offered his arm. "Okay, go ahead and take your sample. Let's get this over with."

Yotto gestured for Marty to sit in a high-backed chair resembling a dentist's chair, except that each arm had a flat metal sensor where your palm might rest. Marty hesitated for a moment but then complied, feeling the cold metal beneath his hands as he gripped the armrests.

"We'll start by taking a small blood sample," Yotto said, his tone clinical. He activated the console in the center of the room and tapped on a few symbols. Marty felt his chair click. "Okay, all done."

"What?" Marty furrowed his brows with confusion. "I don't understand. Done with what, exactly?"

"The sample has been taken." Yotto pointed at the chair. "Those sensors on the armrests contain an array of microneedles. I'm not sure about human anatomy, but for the Edu, the needles penetrate only the outmost layer of our skin, which is above the pain receptors, but low enough to capture some interstitial fluids as well as minute amounts of blood."

Marty stared at the palms of his hands and saw a couple of red splotches that weren't painful at all.

Yotto pointed above the console he was working on and a holographic image flickered to life in the air above them, displaying a magnified view of what looked like blood cells as well some bar graphs with alien symbols on them.

Marty leaned forward, his eyes narrowing as he examined the image. The red blood cells were unmistakable, but there were other things—tiny dots that seemed to float among them, almost like poppy seeds.

"What are we looking at?" François asked.

"Marty's blood chemistry and a close-up of the cells themselves..." Yotto's gaze was fixed on the image. He raised his hand, made an outward motion with his thin fingers, and the image zoomed in, focusing on the tiny dots.

As the magnification increased, Marty's breath caught in his throat. The dots weren't just specks—they had structure, form. And as the details sharpened, they took on a familiar, unsettling shape.

"It's... It looks like a scarab beetle," Marty whispered, his voice tinged with disbelief. The tiny gold-hued figure was intricately designed, with golden filaments extending from its body like delicate tendrils.

Yotto's eyes widened, clearly as shocked as the rest of them. "Have you been in any of the Edu biological labs?" he asked, his voice almost accusatory.

Marty shook his head, confused. "No, of course not. I don't understand... what *is* that?"

Yotto exhaled slowly, running his hand over his hairless head. "These... these are nanites. They're incredibly advanced—machines at the molecular level. And this version... notice the filaments? They're capable of repair at the molecular level. These nanites flow in the bloodstream of the Edu as well."

François's face was pale. "Does that mean... do we all have these things in us?"

Yotto's gaze flicked to François, then back to the holographic image. "We need to find out."

One by one, Yotto tested each of them, his expression growing more intense with each result. And in the results of each test, the same thing appeared—tiny, beetlelike nanites swimming in their bloodstreams.

Marty exchanged a glance with François, their minds racing. "Wait a minute," Marty said, suddenly remembering something. He pulled out the ankh-shaped weapon that he'd kept with him since the beginning of this crazy adventure. "All of us had one of these, but at the time they were covered in some kind of gold dust. But when we grasped them, the gold... it leached into our hands."

Yotto's eyes flickered with recognition, and he nodded slowly. "As such things are wont to happen..."

"What does that mean?" Marty asked, his voice tense. "Are we infected with something? Is that why François no longer looks his age? Why the fatigue that I'd been dealing with vanished soon after all of this started?"

Yotto nodded again, his expression grave. "These nanites are keyed to the biology of the infected. They attempt to repair anything they find needing repair. They use your DNA as a specification for the way things should be."

François gasped, the realization hitting him hard. "So ... in effect, it means any illness we have, any injury ... these things are automatically fixing them?"

"Within reason," Yotto clarified. "Even the nanites can be overwhelmed. They can't regrow lost limbs, for example, but they can correct what's wrong within the limits of their programming."

Marty felt a chill run down his spine. The implications were staggering. They were carrying something inside them, something that could change everything about who they were, how they lived. But at what cost?

"What about the blood chemistry?" François asked, pointing to the graphs next to the image of one of his nanites.

"It's not vastly different from other humans', albeit it seems all of your metabolic by-products are significantly affected."

"In what way?" François took on a curious expression as he rubbed at his chin.

Yotto looked up at the hologram and said, "Your microbial metabolites are elevated compared to all of the humans we've profiled. Your readings show a much higher level of various volatile organic compounds, which to me is an indicator of a gut microbiome that's different in some way—maybe more efficient than most. It would certainly explain the noticeable change in scent." The Gray swiped at the console, shutting it down, and said, "It's getting late. My assistant will take you to a reserved chamber where you can sleep."

Marty nodded, his mind still reeling from the revelation that they'd been infected with some kind of micro-robots. As they followed Yotto's assistant out of the lab, the weight of everything at once settled heavily on his shoulders. The report from the weasel about the Neshili, the seeming destruction outside the magma tunnel, the nanites in their blood ... it set his mind racing.

And as they made their way up a set of stairs inside the engineering wing, Marty knew that when they woke up, nothing would be resolved.

The complications were accelerating, and he knew that all of this was far from over.

Marty woke with a start, the cold, sterile light of the chamber pressing down on him as he tried to shake off the remnants of a restless sleep. Shush shook himself and then sat upright on Marty's chest. The others stirred on cots around Marty, still groggy from the revelations of the previous day. He was just about to stand when the door slid open, revealing Yotto, his smooth gray skin practically vibrating with anxiety. For anyone else, it would have been hard to read the emotion on the alien's minimal facial expressions, but Marty had now spent enough time with these aliens to pick up on the subtle nuances—the slight furrow in Yotto's brow, the way his eyes darted from side to side.

"Something's wrong," Marty muttered, more to himself than anyone else, but Surjan, already alert, caught the note of concern in his voice.

Yotto didn't waste time with pleasantries. "A team of Herders has been spotted outside the glacier walls," he said, his voice low but urgent. "One of the Farmers is transmitting back what he sees."

Marty's heart skipped a beat. He knew what the Herders were capable of, at least historically, but the way Yotto spoke... there was definitely worry in the alien's tone of voice.

Yotto moved quickly to a console embedded in the wall, his long fingers flying over the controls. A hologram flickered to life above the console, but at first, all it showed was static, a murky haze that made it impossible to discern any details.

"The signal doesn't penetrate the lava tube well," Yotto explained, his tone tight with frustration. Marty saw the tension in his movements, the way his hands trembled ever so slightly as he adjusted the controls. "But just... give it a moment."

The static began to clear, the image sharpening into focus. What Marty saw next made his blood run cold.

Pouring out from the mouth of the lava tube were hundreds of humans, their bodies bloodied and bruised, shackled and yoked neck to neck and ankle to ankle. The sight of them, so broken and defeated, sent a wave of nausea crashing through him. And leading them, several

Grays marched with an eerie calm, their expressions devoid of emotion as they herded the string of humans into the main square.

He didn't think they were all Neshili. They were just too many.

Their large number itself was a reason to be horrified.

Marty's eyes scanned the crowd, searching for any familiar faces. And then he saw her—Surjan's former queen, Dawa, her regal demeanor barely intact beneath the layers of dirt and blood that marred her face. Her nose was bloodied, but her eyes... her eyes still burned with defiance.

Surjan's reaction was immediate. He surged forward, his face a mask of fury. "Dawa... those bastards," he snarled, his voice thick with rage. Marty reached out, grabbing his arm before he could do something reckless.

"Sharrum!" François pointed out the warrior, now a beaten, bloody mess, but still standing upright.

"Arnun! Telipi! Yaru! Zidna!" Lowanna cried.

Muwat!

"Wait," Marty urged them. "We need a plan. We can't just run in there blindly."

But it was too late. The team, spurred on by the sight of their captured friends, was already rushing toward the exit, their footsteps echoing off the cold metal floor as they raced down the corridors.

By the time they reached the main square, the scene was even worse than Marty had imagined. The humans were being loaded into wheeled cages, their shackles clinking ominously as they were dragged toward a distant cavern, pulled by other humans who looked equally beaten and terrified. The air was thick with the stench of blood and despair, and the cries of the prisoners echoed in Marty's ears like a haunting chorus.

Marty spotted Dawa being shoved roughly into one of the cages with the rest. Her chin was held high, but it was clear she was barely holding on. The sight of her, so strong yet so vulnerable, seemed to ignite something deep within him.

Yotto frantically pulled at Surjan and hissed, "Get back so you aren't seen."

Marty fell back out of sight and nodded to the rest. The last thing they needed was to get captured along with the rest. He did a quick head count and grumbled with frustration. Kareem was missing, again.

He whispered to François, "Where's Kareem?"

The Frenchman frowned and shook his head. "I'm not sure. He was with us in the sleeping quarters."

Marty stepped farther back into the tunnels, the wailing of the prisoners tearing him to pieces.

They needed to do something.

Kareem melded with the shadows as he surveilled the outskirts of the main chamber, watching what the alien scum was doing to the Neshili.

Under normal circumstances, he didn't have a care at all for any of these natives, but given a choice between the gray-skinned freaks and the natives, he was Team Neshili all the way.

Even with his ankh at the ready and a deep-seated desire to split these creatures in half, Kareem knew there were too many of them for him to make any kind of obvious offensive move.

On the far end of the chamber, Kareem spotted a lone sentry.

Without hesitation, Kareem padded forward and with a practiced swipe of his razor-sharp ankh, he parted the alien's head from its body and dragged them both deeper into the shadows.

He had no idea who the alien was nor did he care what faction it belonged to. The Herders wanted to eat humans, and the Farmers didn't stop them. None of them deserved to breathe any longer.

François's disapproving expression bloomed in his mind's eye, and Kareem shook his head and muttered, "I'll beg forgiveness later, because sometimes you can't ask permission."

The shadows extended outward in this area and Kareem managed to get close to some of the cages. Not close enough to help those inside, but enough to listen to the Grays standing nearby.

The aliens' eyes were cold and calculating as they watched their brethren make quick work of the former islanders. One of them, taller and more imposing than the rest, stepped forward, his voice carrying a chilling calm.

"We've reclaimed our prize," he said, his gaze sweeping over the captured humans. "These will be the foundation of our thousand-year herd. Carefully selected, genetically screened, and consumed in an order that will maintain maximum genetic diversity over time. This should prove much more effective than the misguided Farmers' attempts."

Kareem's blood boiled. The Herders weren't just imprisoning these people—they were treating them like livestock, like a resource to be bred and exploited.

This was no different from back in Egypt. The aliens were going to farm humans for their own good, like cattle. And when the human was of a certain age or size, they'd be eaten.

Eaten, their bones gnawed and tossed into a pit. Kareem clenched his fists and knew that there wasn't much he could do on his own.

Slowly, he began retracing his steps, replaying in his mind what he'd heard.

Kareem passed the smoking remnants of the alien he'd killed. Just like the Sethians back in Egypt . . . they turned to goo upon death.

François wouldn't give him grief this time about the one death . . . not when he told him what he'd overheard about the aliens' plans for them.

≼CHAPTER≽
THIRTY-THREE

The riotous clamor of the Grays' voices rang off the ice and stone above, disturbing a flock of gulls and sending them off with raucous cries. Not all of the Edu were shouting; fewer than half were, probably. But the shouters were loud. They had enthusiasm and they were unified.

Kareem gripped the hilt of his ankh. Marty and François were good at waiting, but in the face of danger, Kareem wanted forward momentum.

A Gray climbed onto the speaking platform where shortly before there had been debate. He carried a hooked scimitar naked in one hand and bore savage scars on one side of his face. He wore leather leggings with metal plates stitched to them, and a tunic and skirt of overlapping bronze disks. Bronze bracers covered his forearms from wrist to elbow. He stomped to the front of the platform, tunic and skirt jangling, and leaned forward over the crowd. The crowd continued to boil and shout, and the scar-faced Gray waited.

Two more Grays followed him onto the platform and ranged themselves one to his right and one to his left. They wore leather breeches and jackets, and each held a long staff. The one to the scarred Gray's right stepped forward and banged the end of his staff on the stone of the platform. "Silence, all!"

The Grays began to quiet.

"Silence!" The herald banged his staff again. "Silence! Warleader Pinosh will address you to explain the situation!"

Kareem looked for his party and found them hopelessly scattered through the crowd, insulated from the Herders by groups of the Farmer faction. He wanted to consult with François, because he knew he needed to do something, and he wanted to take an action François would approve of. But François was on the far side of the crowd from Kareem, and looking the other direction.

Kareem cursed his luck that his enemies among the Grays seemed to include all the warriors, while his allies were useless scholars, healers, and engineers who didn't even know how to operate their own machines.

"Silence!" The herald banged his staff one final time and then stepped back.

Warleader Pinosh, the scarred Gray with the scimitar, looked out over the crowd, head slowly swiveling one direction and then the other. His Adam's apple rolled up and down once with a resounding click. Finally, he opened his mouth, and the voice that came out sounded like barbed wire soaked in unsweetened lemon juice.

"You all know me!" Pinosh howled over yellow teeth, sharp and numerous. "I am a warrior of few words! I am a fighter who takes action!"

A muted cheer rose from some quarters of the crowd, but in other sections, there was uneasy silence.

Kareem saw Marty and François begin to gather up the rest of the party. They spoke to each other briefly in whispers, then headed to grab Surjan. They were still too far from Kareem for convenience.

And he wanted to do something to help, something effective.

Even though Kareem felt confident in his skills, he still felt that he needed to prove himself, but he also wanted to do the right thing for the team. It might seem silly, but he wanted to feel a heroic moment that was all his own doing.

"I urge my Farmer brothers to relax." Pinosh sheathed his scimitar in a scabbard at his belt. "No good will come of conflict among us. I will let anyone who wishes to farm beans continue to farm beans. And I have done nothing any of us need be ashamed of. When a creature is starving, it is no crime to eat, and all creatures eat other beings to live. Are we not creatures, too? This is simple biology. We've slowly been choking ourselves to death in this wretched atmosphere and something had to be done. What the Farmers have done is laudable, but insufficient."

The rumble that arose from the crowd sounded like general, maybe somewhat reluctant, agreement. Kareem spotted a knot of angry young Grays near the front, muttering their disagreement.

"I have brought food that will feed us for many days," Pinosh said. "The Shnipara livers are rich in iron, which will help us breathe free. And most of them are not even local. We have captured a migrating clan from a distant land. This means we will continue to bring in the iron that my Farmer brothers buy with medical assistance, with no interruption. These are all victories. There is no compromise in these actions and no defeat."

Kareem knew where the Herders would take their prisoners. To get out in front of them, he turned and headed toward the machinery room. He ducked to shrink himself in size and he slipped into the crowd, heading for the entrance he'd discovered.

But Pinosh wasn't finished yet. "Survival was at stake. Am I right, yes or no? Was survival at stake?"

"Yes!" some in the crowd cried.

"The gods sent us their bounty," he continued. "Am I right, yes or no? Did the gods not send us their bounty?"

"Yes!" the crowd roared. "The gods sent us their bounty!"

Kareem was surprised that aliens would have any gods whatsoever. What demonic thing would these monsters worship?

"Would the Farmers have agreed, if I had asked their consent?" Pinosh asked. "Would Yotto have said, 'Yes, I agree, let us eat the humans'? Would Chaz have said, 'Yes, take as many as you can, so we have stores'? Would the Farmers have chosen their own species above the Shnipara?"

He let the question fall onto the stage, rhetorical and heavy.

"I think we all know they would not have chosen their own people," Pinosh said. He stood still and shook his head in sorrow.

A soft boo rose from the crowd.

"I had to do it! I had to seize the opportunity!" The warleader sprang back into action. He paced back and forth on the stage, shouting. "We must eat to live, and it would be a corruption to let ourselves die! I had no choice! I had to capture the humans for food, didn't I? Yes or no, didn't I?"

"Yes!" the crowd cried.

Pinosh raised his arms and bowed his head.

"Pinosh is a liar!"

Kareem was nearly to the engines room when he heard the voice shouting. He slipped behind the edge of a rock wall and looked back, just in time to see a gang of Grays rush the speaking platform.

One of the attacking Grays slapped his hands on the edge of the stage, in order to pull himself up. Pinosh already had his scimitar in hand and slashed through both wrists in a single motion. His attacker fell away, screaming and jetting blood from both wrists. Both of Pinosh's heralds stepped forward, swinging clubs. They cracked skulls and ribs and used the staffs like levers to throw attackers back into the crowd.

"Anyone resisting," Pinosh shrieked, "goes into the dungeons with the humans!"

Kareem faded back toward the engine room. Pinosh hadn't quite ordered his people to seize every other human, but it seemed like only a matter of time. Kareem let himself into the room full of machines, shut the door behind him, and briefly considered his options in the sour stink of iron-enriched tofu bricks.

He could wait in the machine room, but then he might have to sneak past or attack guards to gain access to the prisoners. He could try to hide somewhere in the cells, but the rooms were bare stone, and anywhere he might hide, he risked discovery.

The choice was obvious.

Kareem headed down into the dungeon, toward the chamber of gnawed bones.

Gunther stared at the wheeled cages, full of humans and drawn by humans, with the whip-wielding Grays standing atop. He recognized dozens of their faces, maybe hundreds. He told himself they couldn't logically all be looking at him, but he felt they were. Everywhere he looked, his gaze met accusing eyes.

He closed his eyes and still he saw them.

He saw Dawa, weeping. Where was Sharrum? Had he died defending his people in vain? Had he been eaten by the Edu war party on the frozen Pampas?

Save them.

He saw Arnun and both his sisters, Telipi and Yaru. They weren't fishing now, or frolicking in the tall grasses behind their family's hut, they were huddled together to protect each other, and their faces were streaked with tears.

Rescue them. This is the task at hand.

He saw Zidna, the fisherwoman, but no sign of her husband, Muwat. He saw the queen's handmaids, Nirni and Kuzi, who had been forced to flee with their abdicating queen, then survived cannibal raiders, had been allowed back among their people, and were now facing death by consumption.

Save mankind, and then come to the portal.

"All of mankind?" The voice's words felt like iron.

Save the ones in front of you, and you have saved all of mankind.

Gunther rushed through the crowd. Grays milled this way and that in insensate flows that risked sweeping him away. He pushed with his hands and shoulders and made his way as best he could.

He had no skills or magic with which to rescue the Neshili, so he needed to gather his friends. He ran into Lowanna, who fought her way through the mob with the fisher family's weasel on her shoulder.

"The voice says we have to save them!" Gunther cried.

"I don't need a voice to tell me what to do!" Lowanna snapped. "Do you think I don't know that we need to rescue our people?"

"I think it's more important than our survival," Gunther said, out of breath. "I think it's part of our test. I think it's why we're here."

Lowanna eyed him strangely, but led him away from the crowd.

Kareem hid at the mouth of the tunnel leading to the chamber of the bones and waited. After the chaos of the square above, the silence was comforting. The bones would have unnerved him, but now he felt as if they were the bones of his friends.

Or his family, maybe. Or his clients. They were the remains of someone whose death he was about to avenge.

But he couldn't just kill all the Grays himself. There were too many for that.

He needed information.

The raiding party came down into the dungeon not through the machine room, but by some other way Kareem had not scouted. How many unused entrances did this ancient prison have? Had all the entrances been sealed off? Or had the Herders been keeping some set of entryways open, preparing for the moment when they'd fill these ancient pens with prisoners again?

Phosphorescent light came to the prisons, illuminating what he had known in complete darkness. He watched torchbearers come first, carrying clubs like maces with bulbous heads, dipped in glowing green paint and giving off light. These were fixed into brackets in the walls. Scouts checked all the cells to be certain they were empty; guards were posted at exits in pairs and trios.

Then Kareem retreated around the corner and listened. He heard the cracking of whips and the crunching of clubs on bone. He heard curses and whimpers. He heard cries for mercy from voices of all ages and both sexes, but never did he hear the Grays relent. He heard pleas not to be locked away, and the slamming of doors.

Eventually, the prisons grew quiet.

Kareem knew very well that he should reconnoiter, learn the positions of the Gray guards, and go report to Marty. He should do nothing to interfere with the prisoners or their guards, not yet. Anything he did might give away their hand. He knew that he should control his rage, keep his cool, and take wise actions that would keep the party's hands free.

But Kareem was angry. The same monsters that had seized him and run off into their dungeon below Nesha had now seized all the Neshili and locked them away to store them for food. That included children and women, but those weren't even really the grounds for his wrath; in Kareem's mind he felt that he himself had been locked up again.

The single Gray he'd killed hadn't slaked his thirst for vengeance.

And Kareem now had the advantage of surprise.

So he was going to do something about it.

He took the first guard standing in a pump room, with his back to the chamber of bones. It was easy. Kareem walked up behind him silently and sank his ankh into the creature's lungs. Hot blood spattered the stones of the floor, and he took the alien's sword and dagger, stashing them in the wall-niche in the hall leading to the chamber of bones, as the Gray disintegrated into goo.

It felt like the beginning of justice.

Kareem felt even better after taking the second Gray. This monster stood at the iron door to one of the cells, hissing threats to a room full of young women inside. He would eat them alive, he told them, because liver tasted best when it was fresh. He would violate them first. Moreover, he'd force each one to witness the deaths of all her friends before her, and even compel them to taste each other's livers before dying.

Kareem took off the guard's head with one blow. He plucked the leather helmet, dagger, and spear from the pile of ichor and stashed them with the other gear he was accumulating.

He slightly regretted that the Edu dissolved into black pudding. He would have found it satisfying to drag their bodies back into the labyrinth and hurl them onto the pile of human bones.

He told the young women to be patient, that he couldn't release them yet, but that he would come right back. It felt good to say the words. He felt heroic.

He considered slicing open the cell doors and freeing as many prisoners as he could then and there, but decided again that he had to wait.

Kareem killed a third Herder guard coming out of the latrine. With no warning—just as they'd given him no warning when they'd snatched him in Nesha—he sliced through the Gray's chest, opening both lungs and cutting through the heart in one blow. The gear went into Kareem's growing stash and he scattered dirt over all the ooze he'd sprayed on the floors and on the walls.

Then he headed for the surface.

His thirst for justice was still not slaked. The taste of vengeance he had had made him, if anything, want more. But there were too many Grays moving about in the dungeon and he didn't want to get caught.

He used his heat vision to explore unused passages, eventually finding a tunnel that was really an air vent. When it turned upward ninety degrees and rose vertically, he had no problem shimmying right up the shaft and out onto a ledge at its top. From there, he ran across the ridge, leaped over the narrow point of a ravine, and let himself down onto the ledge in front of the engineer's laboratory.

Gollip let him in and François turned to meet him with a relieved expression. "It's about time you got here. We need a plan."

CHAPTER THIRTY-FOUR

"It's not enough to get the Neshili out," François said. "If we free them, they'll just be pursued and captured again. We have to stop the pursuit."

Marty felt the weight of that point, and also the counterpoint, which he made. "Obviously, the answer isn't to kill the Edu, either."

The party sat in Yotto's laboratory, scattered around on stools or sitting on the floor. Surjan stood at a window, watching outside. The engineer, Gollip, and several other like-minded Grays sat among them.

"That's appreciated," Yotto said.

"We want peace, too," Marty said.

"I will die if I must," Yotto said. "For the errors of my people, it is likely some of us will have to die. But I would prefer not to kill."

"Are all the Herder warriors?" Surjan asked. "Is the Herder party basically your military caste?"

"Not quite," Yotto said, "but that's not a terrible way to think about it. It's mostly the case."

"And are they all back now?" he continued. "Are they inside the city boundaries?"

Yotto looked to another Gray, one of the ones Marty didn't recognize. "Spazut?"

"Almost all," Spazut confirmed. "There are always a few scouts out, and the odd warden patrolling near the gate. But if a thousand Shnipara were to leave the gate together, even unarmed, there aren't enough Edu outside the city right now to pose them a significant threat."

"Are there other ways in and out of the city?" Lowanna asked.

"One can climb the ice and cross the glacier," Gollip said. "It is an extremely rigorous, dangerous, and slow journey. A single person or a small group of determined persons might make that journey, but the entire human population would be foolish to attempt it. Nor would Pinosh and his warriors use that route to pursue fleeing humans."

"Don't rule humans out," François said. "We have three great evolutionary advantages, and one of them is what the English would call sheer bloody-mindedness."

"What is an English?" Yotto asked.

"He means we can be stubborn," Lowanna said. "Curious what you think our other two advantages are, Garnier."

"Our ingenuity, of course." François smiled as if he were accepting an award. "Other Earth species use tools, but we are innovative to an extraordinary degree."

"A very François Garnier answer," Lowanna said.

"And our altruism," Marty guessed.

François shook his head. "Our hypersexual nature. We are compelled to breed."

"Come for the escape planning," Marty said, "stay for the lecture on human reproduction."

"So, we're worried about pursuit," Surjan said. "We should smuggle them out at night. And then we can hold the tunnel ourselves."

"We'd need to hold it for a long time," Gunther said. "Unless there are ships the Neshili can use to sail away, they'd need to put enough ground between themselves and the Edu that they couldn't just be caught again."

Lowanna shook her head. "Do we really solve anything this way? This is like freeing one lamb from the lion while knowing he's just going to turn around and catch another lamb the minute our backs are turned."

"Yes," François said, "but this is the lamb I know."

"And the lion I hate," Kareem added.

An awkward pause followed.

"The ultimate solution is to teach the lamb and the lion to lie down together," Marty said. "But there's a reason that the Bible promises that will happen in the end-times, after God comes and fixes things. Because in day-to-day life, it never happens."

"Technically, Isaiah says the wolf will dwell with the lamb. The young lion dwells with the calf and the fatling." Gunther shrugged. "We read the Bible in my house when I was a kid. The lion and the lamb are a later poetic summary. I assume for the alliteration in English."

"Well played." Marty laughed. "My grandpa Simcha is rolling over in his grave now in embarrassment."

"Your grandpa Simcha has plenty to be proud of," Lowanna said.

Marty felt himself blushing.

"We could hold the gate a long time," Surjan said. "We could light a big fire in it and then just tend the fire."

"That creates a different problem for us," Marty said. "It puts us on the other side of a big fire from the portal we want to use."

"There's an easy solution to that," Gunther said. "We sail back to Nesha and take that portal."

"Fight one whole city of civilized Grays, sail halfway around the world, enter a palace of savage, man-eating Grays—probably totally flooded by now, so François will be using his ingenuity to make SCUBA gear for us out of coconut shells—and take the portal we're pretty sure exists because Kareem saw it." Lowanna shook her head. "I like the easy solutions."

"I know what I saw," Kareem said.

"She isn't doubting you," François said.

"You will not have to fight one whole city of civilized Edu," Gollip said. "We will fight with you."

"Thank you," Marty said. "Let's think about that carefully, though. It may be that you can give us the biggest help with intelligence and planning, and then get out of the way so as not to put yourselves at risk."

"There is a dungeon," Kareem said. "We free the humans from it and we put the Herders in." He blinked and then looked at his feet.

"This might be the sabre-tooth and the alpaca solution," Yotto said. "We would then teach our fellows to be more peaceful. Perhaps, receiving the instruction in prison, they might be more amenable to it."

"We would have to repair the food production equipment very quickly," François mused.

"Immediately," Yotto agreed.

"If we're going to have to immediately repair the machinery, though," François continued, "maybe there's another machine that would let us defeat the Herders. Maybe we can use the air circulation machines to fill the city full of some gas that would knock all the Edu out. Then we could imprison the Herders while they were unconscious. It would be a bloodless solution."

"We could deprive the entire city of oxygen," Yotto agreed slowly. "That would only give you a few minutes of unconsciousness in which to act. But I think you also breathe oxygen, in any case."

"Gunther?" François asked. "Lowanna? Any help?"

"Do you mean, do I know anything in my bag of tricks that will let you go without breathing?" Lowanna asked. "I think so, if you can submerge yourself in water. But I'm not sure if it works on just me or on other people. That's something we could test. But even if I could figure something out for two people, what then? Marty and Surjan dunk themselves in a tank and breathe water while everyone else gets knocked out because we turn off the air? Then Surjan and Marty come back out, turn the air back on, and they have a couple of minutes to put all the Herders into prison? Which can only be, what, many hundreds or more of them, right, Yotto?"

"Okay, so that's not a complete plan," François agreed. "But it has some workable elements."

"Are the Herders all in one part of the city?" Surjan asked. "Maybe we could tamper with the water to knock them out."

"The Herders who are sitting in the old prisons watching the prisoners are right on top of the central flows," Yotto said. "We couldn't get to their water without affecting everyone's. And we'd need a huge amount of that drug, whatever it was. And we'd need to draw off water for ourselves and our allies first, so we retain consciousness and can act once the Herders pass out."

"I'm seeing some challenges here, too," François murmured.

"Not to mention," Gollip added, "that if it's the water that is drugged and not the air, they'll drink water at different times. And once a few of them start falling unconscious, others are likely to try to figure out what's happening to them, and some of them will realize that the water has been tampered with."

"Hmm," François said.

"Also," Yotto said, "any solution that depends on using or altering the city's core machinery will require us to implement it right under the noses of the largest concentration of Herder warriors, there at the prison."

Lowanna held her temples as if she suffered from a headache.

Yotto rested his pointy chin in his hands. "If the Herders realize we have helped you, there will be reprisals. A machinery solution will give us away. I am prepared to pay that price, but we should be realistic about it."

"I'm not prepared for that," Marty said.

"Saving the Neshili is more important than saving ourselves," Gunther said. "I'm prepared to pay the price."

"So am I," Marty said. "But I'm trying not to inflict the price on other people."

"We repair the food machinery, as discussed," François said. "We sneak the Neshili out. Then we blow up the magma tube."

"You'll interrupt the work of providing medical help to the Shnipara," Gollip pointed out.

"And save a thousand lives," Lowanna said.

"How long will it take to fix the food machinery, though?" Marty asked. "You say it like you're the Fonz and you're just going to kick the Coke machine so it spits out a bottle, but in fact you haven't diagnosed what the problem is."

"Or problems, plural," Surjan pointed out.

"And how many humans will get eaten while we wait for you to kick the Coke machine again and again?" Gunther added.

"Could we provide some sort of animal substitutes?" Marty asked. "What if we offered to go gather a herd of ... I don't know, alpacas?"

"The ram in the thicket," Gunther said. "I approve."

"It can't work," Lowanna said. "Remember the Sethians in Egypt. They didn't solve their problem by just going out and eating goats' livers. There's something about human livers that accumulates the iron better or is easier for off-worlders to metabolize."

"The Hathiru made some kind of bean pottage that seemed to do the trick," Marty remembered.

"Should have asked them for their recipe when you had the chance," Lowanna said.

"It's true," Gollip said, "human livers seem exceptionally well-suited to carrying and delivering the nutrients we need."

"Which is why you call us 'cattle.'" Kareem scowled.

"I did not make up the word," Gollip said. "And I apologize for ever using it. I will only call you 'humans' from now on."

Kareem's scowled deepened.

"What is the portal?" Yotto asked. "It is inside the vessel, I understand that. But what do you need it for? In all my tinkering with the controls of the vessel, I have never been able to make it activate."

"The problem is not just to activate it," Gunther said. "The problem is also to direct it."

"It's how we get out of here," Marty said. "I think . . ." He considered. "I think the ten numbered locations on the vessel's map, the City of the Gods on Earth and her nine daughters, are connected in a chain through portals. So we're in portal number seven, though we're not really supposed to be here, because out of sheer stubbornness we deviated from the path. We started the path at one, as we were supposed to, and instead of . . . accomplishing our assigned quest, I suppose . . . and then going to location two, we marched across a continent, fought a war that wasn't assigned to us, and then jumped to number five. From number five, we sailed to number seven. So going through that portal should take us to number eight, which is . . ." Marty had an image of the map in his mind's eye and frowned. "Am I misremembering or did eight show up in the middle of the Indian ocean, halfway between Australia and Madagascar?"

Surjan nodded. "That's what I recall, which seems a bit strange."

"Ah, wait a minute." François lifted his index finger, his eyes wide. "The map shows us locations, but remember, we're dealing with a factor of time. Portal number one landed us in the time of Narmer, but coming to number five rewound the clock thousands of years. For all we know, we might go very far in the past or future with any of these hops. Maybe we're not meant to come here the way we did and we're actually very late, which to be honest, wouldn't surprise me. It seems like some things happened long ago in this place that probably shouldn't have happened."

Marty cringed. "You know, that actually sounds right. Who knows what portal number eight would do, but the idea of landing in the middle of the ocean doesn't thrill me."

"It could be millions of years from when we are right now,"

Lowanna suggested. "Continents drift over that kind of timeframe. Maybe our next stop is fighting dinosaurs."

Marty shook his head. "We're off the trail, anyway. But the only way we know to get forward—and possibly home, if that's the goal—is to try to get back on the road somehow."

"Bloody-mindedness at its best," François said. "We won't cooperate with this test or game or whatever it is. I say we bang on this portal until we get what we want out of it."

"That does feel rather English," Surjan said.

Yotto cocked his head to one side. "You use the metaphor of a game. Let's define our winning conditions. One, the captive humans finish the game outside the city. Two, pursuit is hampered sufficiently so that they can escape. That likely means that pursuit must be delayed weeks, but certainly several days. Three, you have access to the portal afterward."

"Four," Marty said, "as few people as possible—of all species—are harmed."

"And are those four winning conditions all essential?" Gollip asked. "Or what is the order of their priority?"

Yotto waved the question away with a dismissive hand. "The plan we must implement is obvious. We free the humans, send them out the magma tube, and collapse the tube. With you six inside the city, of course."

"We condemn you all to sickness and slow death," Marty said.

"No," François countered. "We send the Neshili out and destroy the gate. The Herders will have to negotiate. We'll offer to stick around and fix the machinery. It would take them way too long to send parties over the ice to chase after the escaping humans, so they'll have no choice."

"They'll have a choice," Surjan said. "They could choose to eat the six of us, then murder all the Farmers to conserve supplies while they establish their routes over the glacier."

"That would be a tragic outcome," Gollip agreed. "But the Neshili would get away."

"But you're right," Yotto agreed. "Pinosh would want revenge. Visible justice to reinforce his power. So we shouldn't give him the opportunity. We send out the humans, collapse the gate, and send you through the portal. Fixing the machines was my problem before you arrived, and it will continue to be my problem afterward."

"Pinosh might exact his revenge on you," Marty said.

Yotto shrugged. "This is my home, and I was always going to live or die here one way or another."

"You say we should collapse the tunnel," Marty said. "Is there a machine that does that?"

Gollip bobbled his head.

Yotto nodded. "There is such a machine. We call it a bomb."

"Oh, good," Marty said. "François loves bombs."

"This bomb is held as a defense of last resort," Yotto said. "When we first crashed and lost all communications, we weren't sure what we'd be facing, so some of us took defensive measures and devised this type of defense. It's intended precisely to close the tunnel, in the event that the city is threatened by an overwhelming enemy outside the gate. The bomb is not located in the tunnel, but it's in a location from which it can easily be carried to the tunnel. Probably."

"Probably?" Lowanna asked.

Surjan folded his arms across his chest. "Sounds perfect."

"The only problem," Yotto said, "is that it is in the possession of Pinosh and his Herders."

Kareem punched one fist into his other palm. "That's not a problem."

≒ CHAPTER ≒
THIRTY-FIVE

The sun had set. Patrols were crossing through the main square and the only constant light was the glowing splotches of paint that the Edu had strategically placed at each entrance and exit.

Marty himself carried a glass bulb that glowed with phosphorescent green light, tucked inside his clothing for when he'd need it. He moved silently through the dimly lit tunnels of the glacier, his footsteps muffled by the thick layer of ice beneath his boots. The walls around him seemed to close in, the cold biting at his skin despite the thick fur-lined clothes he wore. The narrow passages twisted and turned, forming a labyrinthine maze that felt as if it were deliberately designed to disorient and confuse anyone who dared to navigate it. But Marty was focused, his mind sharp with purpose.

As he pushed deeper into the heart of the glacier, the faint sounds of grinding, humming, and wheezing began to echo through the corridors. The noises grew louder with every step, a symphony of mechanical groans that sent shivers down his spine. He knew he was getting close. The machine room—Kareem had described a secret entrance to the dungeon via that room.

Marty's breath fogged in the frigid air as he finally reached a thick metal door. He walked into the empty room, panned his gaze to the left and grinned. Just as Kareem had said. The door was old, and as he walked to it, his senses tingled as he looked for anything out of place.

Marty pressed his ear against the door, listening intently. The faintest sound of clanking reached him, but he couldn't be sure if that was due to the din from the room he was in or something on the other side of the door.

With a deep breath, Marty steeled himself and reached for the lever. It clicked once as he slowly pulled it open, revealing in his phosphorescent light a long hall and at its end a narrow staircase descending into darkness. The cold was even more intense here, wrapping around him like a suffocating shroud. He slipped into the shadows, using the gloom to his advantage as he began his descent. He kept his bulb of light concealed, waiting for when he'd really need it. Though these passages were long unused, faint splotches of phosphorescent paint remained on the walls here and there, enough to navigate by.

The air grew thicker, almost stifling, as he moved farther down. The grinding of machinery above faded into a distant rumble, replaced by an eerie silence that made the hairs on the back of his neck stand on end. The dungeon was close. He could feel it.

Marty reached the bottom of the stairs and paused, peering into the darkness. The dim light from above barely reached this far, leaving the corridor ahead in almost complete darkness. This passage was clearly not used often, because he had yet to encounter a place where some of the luminescent paint wasn't applied somewhere. He moved slowly, his eyes straining to make out anything in the darkness. The walls here were smooth and flat, unnaturally so, as if they had been carved out with advanced tools.

After what felt like an eternity, Marty spotted a faint glow ahead— a small, flickering light coming from a crack in the wall. He approached cautiously, his heart pounding in his chest. Peering through the crack, he could see a large chamber, lined with doors to smaller rooms. The dull light cast long, ominous shadows, but he could just make out prison cells, each with figures of prisoners huddled within.

Marty stepped into the dungeon and scanned the room. He spotted a pair of Grays standing watch over a bank of cells on the far end of this level of the dungeon. A winding set of steps at the center of the floor likely led to other levels, and maybe even more prison cells.

Crouching low, Marty blended with the shadows and approached one of the nearest cells. He stooped and flashed his fluorescent bulb into the window set into the door, just for a moment.

One of the Neshili prisoners, a thin man in a tattered tunic and leather kilt, stirred and sat up. He looked wide-eyed at Marty.

Marty put a finger to his lips, motioning for silence, and the ragged prisoner nodded. He tapped at the person next to him, leaned down and whispered something Marty couldn't make out.

Another of the prisoners sat bolt upright and stared open-mouthed at Marty.

A chill raced up and down Marty's spine as he locked eyes with Dawa, Surjan's former queen.

Marty inched closer to the cell. He could see the tension in her body, the way her hands tightened into fists as she recognized him. She didn't move, didn't speak, but her eyes were sharp, focused on him with an intensity that almost took his breath away.

He glanced over his shoulder and found that the stairs blocked his view of the guards, which meant they couldn't see him, either.

"Dawa," he whispered urgently. "It's Marty. We have a plan."

She slowly scooted closer to the bars of the cell, then tilted her head slightly, indicating that she was listening. He couldn't make out her expression in the shadows.

"We're going to free you," Marty continued, his voice barely above a whisper. "All of you. But we need you to pass the word to the others—make sure they know that help is coming. When the time comes, you'll need to be ready to move quickly."

Dawa's eyes narrowed, her mind clearly working as she assessed the situation. "How?" she asked, her voice low and measured. "How can we get out?"

Marty glanced once again over his shoulder. "You don't need to know right now, just know that help is coming and let the others know. We'll be back."

Dawa nodded, her expression hardening with resolve. "We'll be ready."

Marty felt a surge of relief, but it was tempered by the knowledge of the danger ahead. "It won't be long, trust me."

Dawa's hand gripped the bars of her cell, her knuckles white. "Thank you," she said, her voice carrying a quiet strength. "I'll make sure everyone knows."

Marty gave a quick nod and slipped back into the shadows, his heart racing as he retraced his steps. The tension was thick in the air, the weight of what was to come pressing down on him with every step. But there was no turning back now. At least now he knew the rough layout of the dungeon. It seemed lightly guarded, and certainly the bottom floor had many prisoners. A plan of sorts was falling into place and other elements of it were already in motion. Soon these prisoners would either be free—or facing the full wrath of the Herders.

His pace quickened as he ascended the hidden staircase, the grinding and humming of the machinery grew louder. Marty's thoughts were already racing ahead, planning their escape, knowing that every second counted.

Kareem moved with purpose, his senses heightened as he navigated the maze of corridors beneath the ship. The dim, flickering lights cast eerie shadows on the cold metal walls, making the narrow passages feel even more claustrophobic. Beside him, the Grays moved in near silence, their slender forms gliding through the darkness with practiced ease. Despite their lack of obvious expression, Kareem felt the tension radiating from them. They were deep in Herder territory now, a place where even the Grays of the Farmer faction were not welcome.

The plan was simple in theory: locate the bomb that the Herder faction had in its control and steal it before it could be used. The Farmers knew roughly where it might be stored, but the exact location was a mystery. The added complication was the presence of humans in this hostile environment. The Herders would not take kindly to any intrusion, least of all from the Farmer faction or any human ally like Kareem. Even though Kareem couldn't tell the factions apart, the Grays evidently could, and they didn't need to tell him that they were walking on a razor's edge.

Kareem felt the cool metal of his ankh against his leg as he moved, his fingers itching to draw it. But this wasn't a search-and-destroy mission; it was a theft, a delicate operation requiring stealth, not force. Still, the weight of the weapon was a comfort in this alien labyrinth.

Somewhere in this area, Surjan with the help of other Grays was setting up the distraction. The plan was to create enough chaos to draw attention away from their target location, giving them the precious time needed to find and secure the bomb.

As they approached the first set of doors, Kareem already detected the faint scent of smoke beginning to waft through the corridors. That was almost certainly Surjan's doing. Now it was up to them.

The Gray leading the group halted at the door, casting a glance back at Kareem before cautiously pressing a panel to open it. The door slid open with a soft hiss, revealing a small, dimly lit room. Inside, a barrel-shaped container sat in the center of the floor, its surface smooth and unmarked.

Kareem's heart raced. This had to be it. He stepped forward, his breath catching as he reached out to touch the cold metal surface of the container. But as he turned it over, a sinking feeling hit him. It was empty. No wires, no explosive materials—nothing.

"Damn it," Kareem muttered under his breath. The Grays exchanged a quick series of glances. Time wasn't on their side.

"We need to keep looking," one of the Grays whispered.

The smoke was getting thicker now, filling the corridor and stinging his eyes. They moved quickly, their pace hastening as they opened door after door, each time hoping to find the bomb, each time coming up empty-handed. The fire Surjan had started was spreading faster than anticipated, and Kareem felt the heat beginning to seep through the walls.

The anxiety was palpable, every second ticking away with an almost audible thrum in his ears. Kareem's heart pounded in his chest, the fear of discovery growing with each step. They had to find it, and soon.

Suddenly, a loud, piercing alarm blared through the corridors, making Kareem's blood run cold. The Herders knew. They had been discovered. The Grays exchanged frantic looks, their calm shattered as the reality of their situation set in.

"Keep moving," Kareem urged, his voice barely audible over the wail of the alarm. "We're close, I can feel it."

They pressed on, the smoke now so thick that it was difficult to see more than a few feet ahead. Every breath burned in Kareem's lungs, but he pushed forward, driven by the urgency of their mission.

Finally, they reached one last door, the metal cold against Kareem's hand as he grasped the handle. He exchanged a quick, tense glance with the Grays beside him before yanking the door open, revealing a darkened room beyond.

✢ ✢ ✢

The air in the dungeon was thick with tension, the oppressive atmosphere pressing down on Marty as he crept through the dimly lit corridors. The plan was simple, but it was fraught with danger: attack the prison guards, free the prisoners, and make a run for the magma tube before the Herders could realize what was happening. The Farmer faction Grays flanked him, their expressions unreadable, but Marty felt the anticipation radiating off them. They were ready.

As they approached the lowest level of the prison, Marty's eyes narrowed, focusing on the guards stationed about fifty feet away. The Herders were armed with a club that had glowing bands encircling it. He'd been warned by Yotto that such things existed, and the best he could make out was that they were some form of stun weapon—likely similar to a Taser. The guards were alert, their cold eyes scanning the area. But they had no idea what was coming. Marty took a deep breath, centering himself. His martial arts training had always been a source of strength, a way to control the chaos within him. Now, it was going to be their key to survival.

The signal came—a subtle nod from the lead Farmer Gray—and then everything happened in a blur. Marty surged forward, his body moving with practiced precision. He closed the distance between himself and the nearest guard in seconds, his foot striking out in a powerful kick that connected with the Herder's midsection. The guard doubled over, gasping for breath, but Marty didn't give him a chance to recover. A quick, fluid motion brought his elbow down on the guard's neck, and the Herder crumpled to the ground.

The Farmer faction Grays moved in sync with him, their weapons—improvised from those Kareem had gathered in prior skirmishes—flashing in the dim light. They fought with brutal efficiency, their strikes precise and deadly. Marty had to admit, these Grays knew how to handle themselves in a fight.

Another guard lunged at Marty, but he sidestepped the attack, grabbing the Herder's arm and twisting it behind his back. With a swift motion, he slammed the guard into the wall, the impact echoing through the corridor. The Herder slumped, unconscious, and Marty moved on to the next target.

The dungeon erupted into chaos as other guards poured down the central staircase, whooping and brandishing stun-maces.

One of the prisoners yelled a warning and Marty ducked, nearly getting zapped by one of the clubs before smashing a fist into the Gray's neck, crushing his windpipe and sweeping his legs out from under him.

The sound of weapons clashing, bodies hitting the ground, and the shouts of the prisoners filled the air. Marty's heart pounded in his chest, adrenaline coursing through him as he fought his way through the guards. He had to keep moving, keep fighting—there was no room for hesitation.

Finally, the last of the chamber's guards fell. The Grays that were with him claimed new weapons and half of them raced up the stairs to both eliminate any remaining guards and begin executing the rescue. Marty turned to the remaining Grays with him, nodding in silent acknowledgment, and one of them pulled a large lever, opening all of the doors on the floor.

They had done it—the prisoners were free.

"Move! Now!" Marty shouted, his voice cutting through the noise. The humans scrambled to their feet, their eyes wide with a mix of fear and determination. They knew the plan, knew that this was their only chance at escape.

Marty led the way, his breath coming in ragged gasps as they raced up the stairs and through the corridors toward the magma tube. The Farmer Grays followed, their weapons at the ready, while the prisoners ran as fast as their weary bodies would allow.

But as they burst into the darkness of the main square, in sight of the entrance to the tube, Marty's heart sank. The Herders were already closing in, their cold eyes locked on the fleeing group. The sight of them, moving with eerie calm, sent a jolt of fear through him. They had to get to the tube before the Herders cut them off.

"Faster!" Marty urged, his voice tinged with desperation. The prisoners pushed themselves harder, but it was clear they were running on fumes. And then, just as they reached the mouth of the magma tube, with shrieking Herders hot on their tails, Marty saw Kareem sprinting toward them.

Kareem's expression was a mix of frustration and defeat, and as he skidded to a stop beside Marty, his hands were empty. "We couldn't find the bomb," he gasped, his chest heaving. "I'm sorry."

Marty's stomach dropped. The bomb had been their ace in the hole, the one thing that could have given them a fighting chance against the Herders. With the bomb, they didn't have to win, they just had to get the refugees through the tunnel and then set off the explosives.

And now, without the bomb . . .

It was time to face their enemy.

⫷ CHAPTER ⫸
THIRTY-SIX

Lowanna's breath caught in her throat as she exited the trading post into the main square and was met with the chaotic scene unfolding before her. Marty, leading a ragged mob of human prisoners, was racing toward her, and ultimately the magma tube. The sight was jarring—a mob making a mad dash toward her, their eyes wide with fear and frantic for the freedom they were seeking. The humans staggered and fought for every step; some of the youngest and oldest stumbled and were picked up by others as they fled their captors. But it wasn't just the humans she saw. With them came Grays, Farmers, friendlies, urging them on and lifting them as they fell.

She also saw the weasel Shush, leaping alongside his human family.

And behind them, a wave of further Grays surged forward, their expressions twisted with fury as they pursued the escapees with lethal intent. These were the Herders. Where the wave of pursuing Herders caught the fleeing humans and Farmers, battle was being waged.

The air was thick with the smell of acrid smoke, stinging Lowanna's eyes and nose. The source of the smoke wasn't clear, but it was unmistakable—something was burning. Her heart pounded in her chest as she took in the scene, the sounds of battle filling the chamber. Shouts, cries, the clash of metal on metal—it was a symphony of violence.

Lowanna's gaze locked onto Marty, who was already engaged with a group of Grays. He moved with precision and speed, his body a blur as he dodged and struck, each movement fluid and deadly. The Grays were armed with the stun clubs Yotto had told them about, which crackled with energy as they swung them at him.

But Marty was relentless, his martial arts training evident in every calculated strike. He narrowly avoided being stunned twice, ducking under one swing and sidestepping another, before retaliating with brutal efficiency. A well-placed kick sent one Gray flying backward, while a swift punch crushed another's windpipe. He didn't hesitate, didn't falter, even as the battle roared around him.

The Farmer faction Grays, who had joined the fray on the humans' side, were armed with clubs, spears, and the occasional sword.

Anxiety filled Lowanna as she noticed Surjan's tall figure pummeling two Grays at once. To her eyes the friendly faction of Grays was indistinguishable from the enemy one, so even if she wanted to wade in, how could she tell friend from foe? Even if she only attacked the Grays wielding stun maces, she risked killing some friend who had taken advantage of a fallen enemy to pick up a better weapon.

Nonetheless, the Grays seemed to know who was who since one side fought desperately to hold off the other faction, whose weapons gleamed with a savage intent. The acrid smell of smoke grew stronger, mingling with the metallic stench of blood as the bodies of fallen fighters littered the ground.

Lowanna's eyes darted to the fleeing humans, her heart sinking as she saw some of them being cut down by the Herders. The sight of them, their bodies crumpling as they were struck down mere steps from the magma tube, filled her with a cold fury. She spotted a young woman who had stumbled, her ankle twisted painfully, struggling to rise as the Grays closed in on her.

Without thinking, Lowanna sprinted toward her, her instincts screaming at her to move faster. She reached the woman just as a Gray raised his club, the weapon crackling with energy. Lowanna acted on instinct, grabbing the woman and pulling her to safety, her heart racing as the Gray's club slammed into the ground where the woman had been moments before.

Another Gray tackled the attacker and Lowanna dragged the woman away from the fighting.

"Get to the tube!" Lowanna shouted, pushing the woman toward the tunnel. The woman nodded, her eyes wide with fear and gratitude, before limping as fast as she could toward the escape route.

But Lowanna wasn't done. The Grays were closing in, their relentless pursuit threatening to overrun the escaping humans. She felt a surge of desperation, knowing that if the Herders weren't stopped, there would be no escape for any of them.

She glanced at the ground beneath her feet, finding small roots and plants that clung stubbornly to life in the cracks and crevices of the ancient stone. Something deep within her stirred, an instinct she had always known but rarely called upon. She focused, reaching out with that part of her that was connected to the earth, to nature itself.

She didn't have a name for what she was about to do, but it felt right. She closed her eyes, blocking out the chaos around her, and concentrated on the life beneath her. She could feel it, the tiny roots and tendrils, the plants that lay dormant, waiting for the right stimulus to grow.

With a deep breath, Lowanna let that energy flow through her, into the ground. She didn't need words, didn't need to understand how it worked. She just needed it to happen.

The response was immediate. The small roots and plants beneath the surface began to writhe and grow, surging upward with a force that took even Lowanna by surprise. They burst from the cracks in the stone, twisting and curling as they reached for the nearest Grays. The Herders stumbled as the roots snaked around their legs, tripping them, pulling them down. The plants thickened, tightening their grip, hindering the Herders' movements and slowing their pursuit.

The Herder Grays snarled in frustration, hacking at the roots with their weapons, but it was no use. The more they struggled, the tighter the roots clung, their movements becoming more frantic as they realized they were being overtaken by the very ground they stood on.

Lowanna opened her eyes, panting with the effort but filled with a fierce satisfaction. The humans were still fleeing; some had already passed through the trading post and were racing through the magma tube.

She looked over at Marty, who was still in the thick of the fight, his eyes burning with determination as he helped fight off another wave of Grays. She knew they couldn't hold out much longer, but for now, they had bought the fleeing prisoners time. And in this battle, time was everything.

"Run!" Lowanna shouted to the humans who were still within earshot. "Get to the tube! Now!"

They didn't need to be told twice. The last of the prisoners sprinted for the tunnel, their feet pounding against the stone as they made their final dash for freedom.

At their tail, the weasel Shush stopped, turned, and looked at Lowanna one last time. *Thank you!*

Lowana waved the creature on.

As the chamber began to empty, Lowanna took one last look at the tangle of roots and plants that had risen at her command. She didn't know how long they would hold, but she knew one thing for sure: they had given the prisoners a fighting chance.

And that, for now, was enough.

Lowanna's lungs burned as she struggled to take in what little oxygen remained in the stifling air. The sounds of battle still echoed through the chamber, but the chaos was growing fainter as the last of the prisoners disappeared into the magma tube. The thickening smoke clung to everything, turning the air into a choking, acrid haze. She could feel the weight of the situation pressing down on her, the mounting casualties, the desperation in every breath.

The Grays, relentless in their pursuit, were closing in. But she could see it in their movements—they were struggling, too, gasping for breath in the deteriorating conditions. They were as much at the mercy of the failing environment as the humans were.

Lowanna's heart raced as she watched Marty sprint toward her, his face streaked with sweat and grime. He darted and weaved, narrowly avoiding the grasping roots that she had summoned to slow the enemy down. When he finally reached her, he skidded to a stop, his eyes wide with a mixture of amazement and concern.

"Is this your doing?" Marty asked, pointing to the writhing plants that continued to snake across the ground, lashing out at anything that moved.

Lowanna nodded, her voice hoarse from the smoke. "Yes. I didn't know what else to do to slow them down. It was the only thing I could think of."

Marty glanced at the advancing Grays, then back at the plants. "It's a great idea, but we need to give these people more time. Kareem couldn't find the bomb, so you don't by chance have anything else in that bag of tricks you keep hidden?"

Lowanna followed his gaze, noticing a crack in the rock high up near the ceiling where the magma tube and trading post met. A plan began to form in her mind, a desperate idea that just might work. "I have an idea," she said, pointing up at the crack, "but I need to get up there."

The ceiling was about twenty feet above the ground.

Marty's eyes followed her finger, and he nodded with sudden resolve. "I can get you up there. Hold onto my back."

Without hesitation, Lowanna grabbed one of the writhing roots and it immediately curled up into a tight ball.

Marty raced over to the rocky wall under the crack and motioned for her to hurry.

She climbed onto Marty's back, wrapping her legs tightly around his waist, and immediately wished the situation was different and they had some privacy.

Marty scanned up and down the rock wall as he ran his hand over the uneven texture. His muscles tensed beneath her and he began his climb, finding handholds in the jagged rock face with ease.

The ground fell away beneath them as they ascended, and even with the cacophony of battle occurring nearby, for a moment everything seemed okay. Her mind found a calming place to focus as she stared at her objective.

The crack in the ceiling loomed closer, and Lowanna's heart thudded loudly in her ears as she realized just how far they had come. The ground seemed a long way down.

"Okay, do your thing," Marty grunted, his voice strained.

"What, am I heavy?" she asked.

"Good hell, woman, not now! Do the thing and be mad at me later!"

Lowanna's stomach lurched as she looked down, her head spinning with vertigo. Heights had never bothered her before, but now, clinging to Marty's back, with nothing but air beneath her, she suddenly realized just how exposed they were. The fighting continued below, a chaotic mix of shouts and clashing weapons that felt distant and unreal.

They'd finally reached the crack, the narrow fissure in the rock just within her reach. Marty seemed to grip the wall by invisible handholds, but he held firm, gritting his teeth as his feet searched for a ledge to perch on. Lowanna quickly shoved the root she had brought into the crack, her fingers trembling as she began to focus.

She reached deep within herself, drawing on the same power that had called the roots to life before. She could feel the plant responding, its energy surging as she poured everything she had into it. The root began to grow, expanding and pushing deeper into the crack, twisting and turning as it sought out every weakness in the stone.

The sound of stone cracking was almost immediate, a deep, rumbling groan that reverberated through the chamber. Lowanna's breath caught in her throat as she felt the rock beneath them shift. The root was doing its job, growing rapidly, forcing the rock apart with relentless pressure.

One of Marty's hands lost its grip on the wall, and for a terrifying moment, they were both hanging by three fingers. "Lowanna," he gasped, "we need to move—now!"

But it was too late. The crack widened and the stone Marty had been hanging on gave way, and they were suddenly falling, tumbling through the air as the ground rushed up to meet them.

Lowanna squeezed her eyes shut, bracing for impact. The sound of crashing rock filled her ears, followed by the thunderous rush of icy water as it poured through the breached ceiling. The avalanche of stone and water struck the ground with a force that shook the entire chamber, sending debris in all directions.

She hit the ground hard, the impact knocking the breath from her lungs and leaving her stunned. For a moment, everything was a blur of noise and pain. She could feel the cold water seeping through her clothes, the jagged rocks digging into her skin, but all of it seemed distant, as if it were happening to someone else.

Slowly, the world began to come back into focus. She could hear the distant sounds of the Grays, their pursuit halted by the sudden collapse. The writhing roots had been buried beneath the rubble, but they had done their job.

The world grew dim as she wondered whether the escape route had been sealed.

Lowanna coughed violently, her lungs burning as she expelled icy water from her chest. The cold bit into her skin, the taste of the mineral-laden water sharp in her mouth as she spat it out. The world around her was a blur of pain and confusion, the sounds of crashing rocks and rushing water mingling with the frantic shouts of Marty and Surjan.

She was half-buried in rubble, the weight of the rocks pressing down on her chest, pinning her in place. The world was at an angle, and it was only then that she realized that was on the steep, sloping entrance to the magma tube itself.

The cold, jagged edges bit into her skin, but the sensation was dull, distant, as if her body was no longer entirely her own. She could barely see through the haze of dust and debris, her vision swimming with dark spots.

Marty and Surjan were above her, their hands moving with desperate speed as they clawed at the rocks, trying to free her. Their faces were etched with fear, their voices hoarse from shouting instructions to each other over the deafening roar of the water. Lowanna noticed something else that sent a fresh wave of dread through her—far more of the ceiling had collapsed than she'd imagined.

The entire magma tube seemed to be slowly caving in on itself, the walls groaning under the pressure. But even more alarming was the water. It was gushing in from all sides, a relentless tide of icy cold that surged over the rocks, filling every crevice and hollow. The water was flooding the magma tube. She realized that even if the rocks didn't block the passage to chase the fleeing prisoners, the rising water almost certainly would.

Surjan grunted with effort as he heaved a particularly large stone off her chest, tossing it aside with a grimace. "Stay with us, Lowanna!" he urged, his voice tight with strain.

Marty was by her side, his hands digging into the debris, his face set in a mask of determination. But there was fear in his eyes, too—a fear that Lowanna could feel deep in her bones. What was he afraid of? They had managed to block the passage, and that's what mattered.

Marty's hand suddenly cupped her cheek, his voice trembling with urgency. "Lowanna, are you in pain? Do you feel anything?"

For a moment, she couldn't answer him. She stared up at him, the world fading in and out as a torrent of water flowed past them into the magma tube. The edges of her vision darkened, and for a split second, the roar of the water and the frantic movements of her friends seemed to fade away. She felt...peaceful.

A strange calm washed over her, dulling the edges of fear that had gripped her heart moments before. She knew, deep down, that this might be the end. And in that moment, as the cold numbed her limbs, she found herself accepting it.

Her breath was shallow, her voice barely a whisper as she looked into Marty's eyes. "I don't feel anything . . . no pain at all."

She wasn't lying. The crushing weight on her legs, the cold that had seeped into her bones—none of it mattered anymore. There was no pain, only a distant, fading sensation as if her body was slipping away from her.

Marty's eyes widened in panic, but Lowanna's gaze remained steady, almost serene. As the darkness began to close in around her, she felt a strange sense of relief. The battle was ending, and maybe, just maybe, she could finally rest.

The last thing she saw was Marty's frantic face, his voice echoing in her ears as the world went dark and the water threatened to swallow them all.

⇐ CHAPTER ⇒
THIRTY-SEVEN

Marty hovered over Lowanna as she groaned, drifting in and out of consciousness. He cupped her cheek with a callused hand and asked, "Are you okay?"

"I'd say 'ouch,'" Lowanna muttered through gritted teeth, "but that seems a bit cliché."

"Embrace the cliché," Marty replied. "I, for one, could use a little familiarity in my life right now."

He pulled at the rocks around Lowanna's legs. He was afraid her bones were crushed. At least he wasn't seeing spurting blood. She also lay in icy water, which was pooling around as he dug her out from the pile of rocks.

Surjan knelt to help with the rocks. "That fire of mine may have been too much," the Sikh grunted. "We may in the end be suffocated to death by that little distraction."

"Gunther!" Marty yelled.

Surjan pulled aside the last rock and then stood. Wordlessly, he returned to the fight as Gunther arrived.

"Her legs might be broken," Marty said.

"I got this, Marty," Gunther said as he crouched by Lowanna's side.

"You sure you don't need any help?" Marty asked.

The archaeologist-turned-healer grinned at Marty and shook his head. "I'm pretty sure I've got this, you go kung fu somebody for me."

Marty left her in Gunther's care. He ran through the chamber that had once held the city's human-facing health clinic. Now it seemed to him more like a veterinary clinic. But the side tunnels were both collapsed, and a chunk of ceiling had fallen down in the middle of the room, creating a cairnlike pillar that reached all the way to the top of the cavern.

Water was gushing in through various cracks in the ceiling, spraying everywhere as the runoff flowed into the magma tube.

Marty emerged into the city and found that it was growing dark. The fissure in the ice above showed a patch of dull blue sky sliding into navy. Light came from phosphorescent streaks painted on many surfaces. He hadn't had occasion to notice them before, but the city had activated streetlights and lamps affixed over some exterior doors. Possibly from the setting off of the security alarm?

The destruction in the tunnel had also wreaked havoc in the city near it, and had changed the battlefield. Chunks of stone and ice as large as kitchen appliances lay strewn about the mouth of the magma tube. If Marty's team had principally been armed with projectile weapons—François's bowmen, or the archers and slingers of an earlier campaign—the rubble would have created wonderful cover. Instead, it created a battlefield like an ice-and-stone maze.

They needed a clear route to the vessel. The smoke in the air made his eyes water, but Marty could still see the flying saucer up on top of the canyon wall, and he knew the road he'd taken to get there with Yotto.

The orange flicker of flames was uncomfortably close to the vessel.

"We should move now!" he barked in English, then slid along the path toward the vessel.

Two Grays leaped at him from an unseen perch atop a boulder. He heard a faint creak before they moved and he was ready for the attack. Taking a long step back, he let them land on the hard stone rather than on him. One landed with a yelp and skewed sideways, leaning on a boulder. The other landed on his feet but wobbled.

Marty kicked the wobbler in the center of his chest, throwing the Gray staggering thirty feet away. In the precious seconds gained, Marty attacked the other Gray struggling to rise from the boulder. He slammed the alien against the stone twice, then swept his feet out from under him.

The Gray dropped to the stone floor and lay flat.

The first Gray charged raggedly back, and he had a long knife in his hand. As the Gray closed in, Marty felt a third attacker circling at him around a boulder to his left with an upraised club, and a fourth leaped from atop a chunk of ice to his right. Marty sprang forward, catching the knife-wielder by surprise and grabbing his knife hand by the wrist.

Then he turned and fought with the knife. He stood behind the Gray and maneuvered him like a marionette, keeping him off-balance with long lunges and stagger-step sideways maneuvers. He drove the ice-jumper back with a series of attacks and then spun the knife-wielder sideways into the Gray with the club.

He leaped and spun, dropping the unengaged Gray with a kick to the jaw. Then he seized the knife fighter again, ducked beneath one attack of the club, sidestepped a second, and finally killed the club-wielder with a knife to the sternum right as the club-wielder cracked his cudgel down on top of the knife-fighter's skull, smashing it open and killing him instantly.

Marty tossed both corpses aside. "Gunther!"

"Coming!" The German emerged from the magma-tube opening. Lowanna walked gingerly, gripping his arm for a little support, but she walked.

And as she did so, she unloaded her sling from her tunic pocket. "Rocks," Marty heard her say.

Gunther began scooping large pebbles off the ground and handing them to her. She put one in the pocket of her sling and filled the pocket of her tunic with the rest. She met Marty's gaze and grinned.

"Let's go!" she called. "Next stop: Anywhere but here!"

She abruptly spun her sling about and let fly. Marty turned as the rock whizzed past his ear, just in time to see it strike a Gray in the forehead, dropping him like a felled tree.

Surjan reappeared, bloodied spear in his hands.

François followed, gripped a long-shafted spear. "Has anyone spotted Kareem?"

Marty hadn't, and the last time he'd seen the young Egyptian, he'd looked angry. "Keep an eye out for him. But let's get to the vessel." He pointed up the appropriate side canyon. "That's the way."

Surjan and François took point. Two Grays with knives charged almost immediately from behind a rock, and Surjan swung his spear sideways, slicing with the blade through both their throats in one motion.

"Kareem!" François yelled in French. "Where are you? If you can't reach us, head for the vessel!"

Where had Yotto and the Farmers on their side gone? Were they crushed under the fallen rock, or had they fled when the tunnel had collapsed?

Marty waved Gunther and François past, so that he could take up the rear. Gunther looked exhausted but happy. Like a woman who had just given birth, Marty thought incongruously. Lowanna seemed to increase in strength and vitality every time she let a slingstone fly. It wasn't a mean streak in her character, exactly, but maybe a competitive streak, or a desire to assert herself. So she asserted herself left and right against the Edu Herders, and her grin got wider as each assertee fell.

Marty's job was easy. His senses were getting sharper, especially his sixth sense. That made it sound psychic, and it wasn't. *Anyone can sense the chi of another person,* Grandpa Chang had told him many times. *He only has to learn to try.*

Marty hadn't been especially good at sensing other people's chi in his academic life or as the owner of a woodworking shop. But it had become easier and easier for him since he'd started time traveling, and especially since coming to Nesha.

So he walked at the rear of the party, separated from Lowanna and Gunther by as much as a hundred feet, and just relaxed. He breathed deeply, released the conscious part of his mind, and trusted to his muscles. His legs carried him forward on their own.

And he felt Herder warriors approach.

When one threw a spear at him from behind, Marty felt the attack coming. He turned, stepped to the side, and caught the spear as it passed. Continuing his motion, he threw the spear through the chest of the Gray who had attacked him with it. The Gray sank to his knees with an open mouth and then fell over backward.

A second leaped down from a boulder with a hooked scimitar in his hand. Marty felt him coming and stepped into the attack. He grabbed the attacker's ankle lightly and tugged, sending the Gray spinning forward with a shrill yelp that ended when he planted face-first on the stone ground.

A third threw stones from a window overhead and Marty caught them. A fourth slashed at his feet with a spear and Marty stepped on the shaft, snapping it. A fifth rushed forward shrieking, jaws gaped wide to bite Marty, and was tapped in the larynx, knocking him down with a single blow.

Marty reached the canyon below the vessel, where the others stood waiting for him.

"No sign of Kareem," François said.

"He'll make it," Marty said. "Of all of us, he's the most suited for this environment."

"Maybe not in a good way," François pointed out.

"Hurry." Gunther pointed at the vessel. "The fire is getting closer to the ship and our way out."

Marty eyed the climb and the surrounding canyon walls. They'd be exposed to hostile fire from any Herders hidden in any of hundreds of windows. He looked back and forth between Lowanna and Gunther and said, "Between the two of you, since getting to the ship is going to expose us all—do either of you have anything in your bag of tricks that'll maybe help in any way?"

"You mean like how I toughened my skin in that fight against Halpa's cannibal friends?" Lowanna asked.

"Yeah, you ended up almost looking like you were armored with tree bark or something when you did that. Can you replay the trick on yourself, and maybe on Gunther, if that's possible? As long as you two are in good shape, you can heal the rest of us if we get an ouchie."

"As much as I don't like the thought of getting hit with a thrown spear," François said, "I concur."

Lowanna looked over at Gunther and asked, "You up for this?"

Gunther had an uncertain expression but he nodded.

Marty watched as Lowanna placed her hand gently on Gunther's shoulder. The moment her fingers made contact, something extraordinary began to happen. The skin beneath her touch started to change, the soft texture of flesh shifting into something far more resilient. It was as if the very essence of the forest had seeped into them, turning their skin into a tough, barklike surface.

The transformation spread from Lowanna's hand, creeping across Gunther's shoulder and down his arm, the smooth surface giving way to a rough, textured layer that resembled the ancient trees of the deep woods. It wasn't just a visual change—Marty could almost feel the protective energy radiating from them, a living armor that pulsed with the vitality of the earth itself.

Lowanna's own skin mirrored the change, her arm adopting the same rugged texture, as if the spell had intertwined their fates for a moment, binding them in a shared shield of nature's strength. The air around them seemed to thrum with power, as if the earth had lent them its ancient endurance.

Marty couldn't help but stare in awe as the transformation was completed, the two of them standing together—the change was dramatic to say the least.

"Okay, gather 'round." Gunther motioned for everyone to come closer. "I think I might be able to do a little something for us all."

Marty watched as Gunther stepped forward, his usually calm demeanor shifting into one of intense focus. The air around him seemed to thrum with a quiet, palpable energy, as if the very atmosphere was holding its breath. Gunther clasped his hands together, and a soft, warm light began to glow between them, growing brighter with each passing moment. The light was not harsh or blinding, but soothing, like the first rays of dawn breaking over a quiet field.

As Gunther raised his hands, the light spread outward in a gentle wave, washing over each member of the team. Marty felt the warmth seep into his skin, infusing him with a sense of calm and quiet strength. His heartbeat steadied, and the weariness in his limbs seemed to fade away, replaced by a renewed sense of purpose and resolve. He glanced at the others and saw the same light reflected in their eyes, a quiet determination and confidence settling over them like a well-worn cloak.

Gunther, too, seemed transformed. The lines of tension in his face softened, and a serene expression took their place, as if he was the conduit for something far greater than himself. The glow surrounding him faded, but the feeling it left behind lingered, like the echo of a distant hymn.

Marty couldn't help but marvel at the change. It was as though Gunther had reached into the very essence of their spirits and bolstered them, not just with strength, but with hope. Whatever lay ahead, they would face it together, supported by the quiet power that Gunther had summoned. He blinked for a moment and then it dawned on him that time wasn't standing still.

"Okay, let's go!" Marty shooed his people up the steps.

As they climbed, he could see through a thick veil of oily smoke what was happening with the Farmers. They had fallen back and were defending various points—Yotto's laboratory, for one, and the machines room, for another. Marty looked, but didn't see Yotto in either place.

Grays who had to be Herders attacked the Farmers. More Grays filed up a steep canyon with ropes and picks. They seemed to be headed for the ice wall, to try to climb out. And a swarm of Grays, thicker than he had realized, converged on Marty's own tail. They threw spears and threw or slung stones, which he found he could easily deflect, even when the missiles came two or three at a time.

Lowanna and Gunther didn't have his ability to dodge and deflect, so they took a few hits. With their thickened, barklike hides, they didn't even slow down.

Marty felt an ambush ahead and above. Pivoting, he saw Surjan turning the corner into a narrow defile that led up to the stranded flying saucer. The Sikh and François, at his shoulder, were focused on the stairs in front of them, where apparently they confronted some enemy Marty couldn't see.

What Surjan and François couldn't see was the row of three windows above them, and from each window leaned two Grays with javelins in their hands.

"Lowanna!" Marty shouted.

Then he ran up the wall. Old as the rock was, it wasn't perfectly smooth, and his fingers and toes found easy purchase. Again, he released his conscious mind and let his body and spirit find the way. He leaped into an open window and then dove forward, tapping with the balls of his feet on the tops of the first two Grays' heads as if he was crossing a stream on stepping stones. With shrill cries, the Grays tumbled down into the canyon. One hit the ledge between Gunther and Lowanna and lay groaning and arching his back. The other struck the edge of the walkway and bounced off, disappearing into the deeper canyon below.

Marty kept moving. He knew this was impossible, he was performing feats like the hero in an over-the-top Wuxia film, but he was performing them. Was he somehow enhanced by what Gunther had done? Was this the result of the nanites Yotto had found in his blood? Was this good evidence that he and the rest of the team were living in a simulation?

But he kept the part of his mind that processed those thoughts relaxed, subdued, quiet, and locked away.

He dropped between the next two Grays, just as they raised their weapons to attack. He grabbed them both by the neck, yanking them down. Their javelins flew off into space uselessly and they lunged forward, fighting to regain their balance. Marty planted his feet against the wall, tugged the two Grays down, and flipped back up again. He spun and landed on his feet, crouching in the window just as they left it, tumbling forward and screaming.

The two remaining Grays released their javelins. One took a stone to the temple from Lowanna as he released; his dart and his body scraped against the wall as he fell. But the last Gray sank his javelin into François's shoulder.

From his high position, Marty saw a knot of Grays on the stairs above Surjan. The Sikh advanced on them with his spear from below, but on the stairs above them, they also faced a handful of Grays wearing linen scarves tied around their necks, Grays who were awkwardly trying both to fight the fire and hold the stairs.

Marty sprang into the last window, snatched up the startled Gray who remained, and hurled him into the knot of Herder warriors just as Surjan charged. Then he raced down the wall into the ravine, where he picked up two javelins. Plunging into the battle behind Surjan, he stabbed left and right, defending the Sikh's flank, dispatching Grays who wanted to stab him in the back, and running the Herders over completely.

Once the knot was gone, he left Surjan to greet the Farmers and ran back down the stairs. François sat leaning against the stone, his tunic soaked in blood, his face pale as soap. He coughed and spat blood all down his chest.

"Fatal," François gasped, spitting more blood. "Neshili escaped. A price I can gladly pay."

"Unacceptable," Marty said. "Watch the stairs," he told Lowanna. She put a stone into the pocket of her sling, nodded, and stepped down the stairs.

To Gunther, Marty said, "I'll pull on three, you heal him."

"If I can," Gunther murmured.

"You can, damn your eyes." Marty gripped the javelin. "One... Two... Three!"

⇤ CHAPTER ⇥
THIRTY-EIGHT

Marty yanked the javelin from François's shoulder.

François screamed—a wet, bubbling shriek that sprayed blood all over his legs, Marty, and the steps, and slumped forward.

Gunther's brows furrowed as a lattice of blue light expanded from his hands. The web of light wrapped around François's upper body, including his arms and his head, then constricted suddenly. The light slapped itself against François's skin and conformed itself to his contours, as if it were bands of tape. Between the bright blue lines, a dimmer blue sheen, with sparkling white in it, filled the gaps. The blood flow stopped and François slammed upright again, as if the light were pulling him.

Marty tossed aside the javelin.

Gunther's knees buckled and Marty caught him. The light sank into François's skin, showing briefly as a dull subcutaneous glow. The hole in the Frenchman's shoulder knit shut. The glow beneath his skin blinked out. Then François opened his mouth and light spewed forth, dissipating into the night air.

Then a Gray stood among them, clapping Marty on the shoulder and drawing François to his feet. "Come, come, my friends, we have no time. The vessel is on fire!"

Darkness fell, and Kareem felt at home.

He'd grown up in a village with two electric lights at the edge of

Cairo and had spent plenty of time moving around the farms and wadis in darkness. He'd led a dissolute youth mostly on the streets of Cairo, in alleyways sometimes lit by an oil lamp or a candle. He was utterly comfortable in darkness and always had been, even before he'd gained the ability to see in the dark.

The City of the Hungry Dead was not thoroughly dark, but it was comprised of twisted alleys. With its central square reshaped by Lowanna throwing a mass of boulders and chunks of ice into it, it was now even more labyrinthine than before.

He slit throats. He padded up behind gray demons, and while they were still sniffing for him, trying to determine from which direction they were detecting an approaching human, he stabbed his ankh through the backs of their necks.

When their heads hit the ground, he kicked them like footballs, watching them dissolve into goo before they landed.

He struck with killing blows that left no chance to escape, cry out, or make reprisals. That meant using the ankh, which cut without fail through muscle and bone. That mean striking at the heart, the lungs, the brain, the neck.

He killed them perfectly, then stabbed or slashed or kicked their defenseless bodies to vent his disrespect and rage on them. He spat on them, he severed arms and legs and threw them into windows, he stuffed a severed head into a latrine. He disemboweled a Gray warrior, holding its jaws clamped shut so it couldn't attract attention while its life force flowed over its knees, then hung it from a lamppost by its own linen scarf.

He found demons that were unconscious and slaughtered them. He crossed the path of his own comrades and found a wake of battered, bruised, and injured Grays. He released every one from its misery, sending them all to whatever demons presided over their miserable afterlives in hell, to be punished for their failures.

He took javelins from several dead warriors and climbed up onto a balcony overlooking a wide canyon. He looked toward the flying saucer; it was still burning. He was sure Marty and the team would have to extinguish that fire before they went anywhere, so that gave him time yet.

He lay on his belly beside the stack of javelins. Below him, the canyon lay in shadow, but he saw the Grays walk along it in perfectly visible blobs of red heat. He watched, waiting until any one of the gray demons got into the center of the avenue, far from either end, and then it was a simple matter to throw a javelin through their chests. Mostly, the demons fell at the first blow and lay dead. Twice, he had to throw a second javelin, once to a Gray who tried to drag itself away down the street and once to a demon that dragged itself to a door and pounded on it, demanding admission.

Elsewhere in the city, buildings burst into flame. The end near the door seemed to be turning into an icy lake; Kareem could tell because he could see the cold water as a sheet of blue-gray darkness.

Kareem grew bored of killing the gray demons with javelins. The ankh made it too easy, too. For a brief period, he entertained himself by throttling gray demons with his bare hands. That, too, was too easy. The Grays were short and not very strong and by the time they realized what was happening, the struggle was generally already over.

Kareem didn't want to be left behind. This was a garbage place and he didn't want to be surrounded by the gray demons for the rest of his life. Part of him wanted to just go home, but he didn't know what home would look like. His uncle Abdullah would certainly not be there. Other family members would ask him about Abdullah, and where Abdullah had gone. That would be uncomfortable. Would Kareem retain his new skills? His extraordinary gifts for stealth, climbing, and so forth? If he didn't, would he once again become a young man who rode a cheap motorcycle and scrounged for odd jobs as a guide or day laborer? He could smell the bad foreign cigarettes, slutty perfume, strong coffee, diesel engine exhaust, and sweat of that life as he visualized it.

He should look for something new. Not work as François's apprentice, like François seemed to imagine for him, but some situation in which his abilities would matter. Some situation in which he would be king. At the head of a robber band or a guild of pickpockets. Strongman of an important alley in a large city. Maybe a respected pimp or a feared drug smuggler. Some person in the community everyone needed, feared, and respected, some role in which both his ability to be stealthy and his desire for violence would bring him out on top.

It was time to join the others. He didn't need to take the walkways and stairs, as he'd seen them do. He put away his ankh and started climbing the wall of the bluff, directly toward the flying saucer.

⁜ ⁜ ⁜

"How does a flying saucer burn?" François demanded.

"Shut up and rest," Marty said. "Heal. Fight later!"

"I'm healed!" François shoved Marty away, in part playfully but also in irritation. "Go fuss over Gunther, you mother hen, he's the one who's exhausted himself helping me."

It was true. Gunther drained the last of the flasks he'd had with him since leaving the island and even though he no longer looked like death warmed over, he was definitely sagging. François took Gunther by one arm as Marty took him by the other.

"It's not the metal burning, of course," Yotto said. "But that doesn't prevent the ship's hull from getting scorched, and if there's any content within that is flammable, it might burn."

"Well"—François shrugged—"if things go pear-shaped with the portal over here, I see no other choice but to climb the ice wall, cross the glacier, build a ship, sail back to the City of the Gods on Earth, and find the portal there."

"Yeah." Lowanna rolled her eyes. "Piece of cake."

"Here," Gunther said. "The voice is telling me to use the portal here. But I have nothing left in me. I'm really running on empty, and I'm out of that stuff the islanders concocted that seemed to help."

"All you need to do is walk," Marty said.

"Don't get injured," Gunther told him with a weak smile.

"Yes," François said. "We got this."

"It is under control," Yotto said confidently.

Another hundred feet of steps separated them from the flying saucer. François could see an orange glow coming from inside the opening. He saw none of the interior lights he'd spotted before; either the flames obscured them or else they were out. Given that night had fallen, and the flames were what lit the steps he was climbing, he figured he ought to see those lights.

If they were out, that boded poorly for the portal. It suggested the ship might have lost power or taken other internal damage.

Was the voice in Gunther's head going to power the portal without any need of resources from the ship? He said nothing, but he felt disquieted.

He heard Edu voices from inside the vessel. He saw Grays beating at the flames with blankets. Surely, that couldn't be the most effective way to put out a fire. You'd think a species that could create a spaceship would have better fire retardant technology. As if reading his mind, Gollip emerged from the flames, ran halfway down the steps toward them, and shouted, "The fire extinguishing systems are out!"

As Gollip turned to walk back to the ship, a shadow rose from the darkness, outlined against the fire. For a moment, François assumed another of Yotto's Gray assistants had come with a message, but then he saw the hooked scimitar raised high, and the facial scars on one side in high orange relief.

Pinosh slashed sideways with his sword, slicing Gollip's head clean off. The egg-shaped leathery skull bounced down the steps past François, mouth agape in an expression of surprise for brief seconds before it melted.

"Nooooo!" Yotto shrieked and fell to his knees, scooping up his assistant's head and cradling it in his arms.

Or had François misunderstood the nature of their relationship?

François drew his ankh, but the truth was he was afraid to get under the feet of Marty in a fight. Surjan and Lowanna were inside the saucer, and the roar of the flames might make it difficult for them to hear. Gunther wasn't much of a fighter anyway, and was now tapped out magically. François held his ankh in his hand, but he expected Marty to take out the trash and make short work of this murderous upstart.

Marty set out to do it. He leaped up on the wall to his right, and François expected to see a spectacular spinning kick take the head clean off the Gray, a perfect act of justice. Instead, Pinosh jumped to the opposite wall, compacted like a spring, and hurled himself off it toward Marty, sword swinging.

Marty deflected the scimitar softly, the combatants swung about each other gently, and they perched on walls opposite each other, Marty with fists raised and Pinosh brandishing his sword.

"Go!" François pushed Gunther forward and rushed after him on his heels. They ducked low and passed beneath the duelists right as Marty leaped high, arcing in midair and angling to crash into the Gray feet-first. Pinosh responded by throwing his sword and then jumping like a living cannonball immediately after it.

François and Gunther scooted through. Marty caught the sword between his palms. Pinosh's head struck Marty in the thigh, sending him spinning down the stairs and hurling the sword onto a balcony above the steps, where it clattered to a halt.

"Gunther, you're in no condition to be out here with this fight. Are you able to make it to the map room?" François asked.

"I think I can," Gunther said. "As long as fire isn't blocking the way."

"Okay," François said. "You go run inside and talk to that voice in your head and figure out what needs to be done."

"Listening to strange voices in my head," Gunther said, "while standing inside a burning flying saucer."

"You've done stranger things than that." François slapped him on the back. "And if Surjan and Lowanna are in there fighting the fire and can be spared, send them on out."

Down below in the stairwell, Marty and Pinosh threw hammer-rains of blows on each other. Yotto wept on a step above them, curled into a ball over a puddle that had once been Gollip.

"Go!" François pushed Gunther toward the saucer's entrance.

He turned to try to see how to help Marty with his surprisingly difficult fight and stopped in his tracks at the scraping sound of two climbers coming over the lip of the bluff. In the same place Gollip had stood lookout for them before, two Grays now climbed into view. The fire gave their gray skin a ruddy cast and their black eyes glinted. They both drew scimitars and advanced on François.

François knew he was outclassed and had nowhere to run. If he drew them into the ship, he'd be burned alive. If he drew them down into Marty's fight, he risked making Marty lose by distracting or impairing him.

He took the offensive. He threw his voice behind the Grays and to their left, uttering a strangled, berserk war cry: "Garnier!"

The Grays startled and turned, fearing attack from behind, and François lunged forward in a desperate attack. He stabbed his ankh down through the upper arm of the Gray nearest him. The blow cut right through muscle, bone, and artery, and the Gray wheeled away shrieking, blood spraying from its wound and the arm hanging useless by its side. François lost his grip on his ankh and it flew into the fire below.

The wounded Gray bumped into its comrade, nearly hurling them both over the side of the bluff. While they struggled, François scooped up the dropped scimitar. Marty and the Gray warrior chief traded kicks now, still deeply focused.

The wounded Gray ran off the edge of the bluff, screaming.

François steeled his voice, giving it an edge of command. "Surrender, demon!" he barked. "Stand down and I will spare your life!"

The Gray charged. François tried to back away, scorched himself as he backed into rising flames from below, and scooted sideways instead. That put him on the stairs, though, and slightly downhill of the Edu warrior. Suddenly he found himself warding off a flurry of attacks aimed at his head.

His voice had gained some kind of hypnotic power at times—how far did that extend? Throwing his voice was a trick he'd picked up, but that usually only worked once against anyone.

He risked a long jump to his left. He made it out of the stairwell and back onto level ground, but he moved a little more slowly than he had imagined and received a cut along the ribs. Also, he had now put himself out on the bluff, where the stone fell away from under his feet on three sides.

No more retreating. He struck a fierce stance and threw his voice behind the Gray again. "Avast!" he yelled.

This time, the Gray ignored the thrown voice and rushed François. Unable to retreat, François tried to dodge, then to parry, and didn't quite manage to pull off either. For the second time in an hour, he was run through the shoulder, and fell to the ground. The scimitar bounced from his grip and fell down into the canyon.

The Gray stood over him, a wide grin on its toothy mouth. It ran its scimitar past its maw and a thin, bright green tongue snaked out, licking off François's blood. It raised the weapon over its head to strike.

A metal spike abruptly flowered in its chest, poking right through the Gray warrior's heart.

⫷ CHAPTER ⫸
THIRTY-NINE

Marty heard François's cries, but he needed all his attention for the Gray warrior Pinosh, who was turning out to be a ferocious combatant. He retreated until he could catch the Gray off-balance and then advanced with a flurry of blows until the Gray countered. Pinosh moved with the practiced confidence of a warrior of long experience. He possessed the energy of a wild cat, snapping his teeth when he attacked and hissing in disappointment when Marty parried.

But Marty's stamina was not waning, while the Gray showed signs of flagging.

He caught a kick aimed at his head, throwing the Gray away from him. Pinosh caught himself on his knuckles and kicked back with both feet, this time catching Marty on the shoulder. He melted away from the double kick, moving with the energy of the blow and pirouetting out of range.

When François slipped and fell, Marty was tapping aside a savage storm of attacks and couldn't free himself. He briefly feared François was doomed, despite his vocal tricks, but then Kareem slipped up from behind and stabbed the Frenchman's opponent through the heart, saving his life.

Feeling a sense of relief, Marty focused solely on his fight with the Gray. He fought better when he thought less, even about the fight he was in. His body and spirit could fight without his brain overthinking his moves. He sent Pinosh away with a graceful kick, then raced up the wall, gripping the edge of the balcony above him with both hands and spinning up and over, landing on his fingers and toes.

He scuttled backward, imitating a centipede. He had played strange movement games with Grandpa Chang as a small child. Move sideways like a crab. Jump from hind legs to front legs like a dog. Roll on your back like a flipped turtle. Creep on toes and hands like an insect. Crouch like a snail. Dart forward like a snake. Some of those games had later turned into stances he'd used in his forms and his fighting. Some of them never had, but he was beginning to see their possibilities now.

He remembered where he had lost the scimitar, and he found it again now, scuttling over it until the hilt was in his hand. Just as he gripped the sword, he felt the Gray coming up the wall behind him, so he rolled onto his back against the wall. Pinosh had found another weapon, and the sight of it left Marty momentarily stunned.

Pinosh held a sharpened ankh.

Marty's own ankh was in his belt, and he felt like an idiot for not having it already in his hand. He strongly suspected that if he tried to parry an ankh attack with the scimitar, the metal of the sword would fail. Pinosh stabbed down and Marty rolled to his left, pinning his stomach against the wall and trapping his ankh for the moment. With the so-called star-metal weapon, Pinosh gouged a divot of stone out of the floor of the balcony. Marty kicked Pinosh in the knee and he slid back, but he kept his grip on the ankh and it came away with him.

Marty rolled to the center of the balcony again, and this time, when Pinosh lunged forward with the ankh, Marty rolled right off the edge.

Pinosh dove, throwing himself onto his belly and grabbing Marty by the forearm. He stabbed downward with the ankh. Marty knew he had no hope of parrying the ankh, so he writhed sideways to dodge and stabbed Pinosh in the shoulder of his sword arm.

He drew blood. Pinosh growled in rage, the ankh cut through the bronze, snapping the blade in half, and Pinosh dropped the ankh. Marty heard the exotic weapon hit the steps beneath him and clatter away. He tried to shake himself free, but Pinosh wouldn't let go. He scrambled to draw his own ankh, and maybe the Gray would drop him.

Then Marty saw motion out of the corner of his eyes, and Kareem pulled himself up onto the balcony. The teen was spattered in blood, which Marty thought nothing of—they were all gory at this point. But fury blazed in his eyes as he stalked across the balcony, his own ankh in his hand, point forward.

Marty drew himself up and grabbed Pinosh's head, pulling it against the stone of the balcony. Pinosh tried to shake Marty free, and now Marty gripped him by the head and shoulder, pinning him in place. Pinosh wriggled and raged.

"Cattle!" he cried. "You are nothing but cattle!"

He held up an arm to defend himself, and Kareem sliced the arm off.

"Kill him!" Marty cried. The wounded Gray was still dangerous. "Don't play with him! Stab him in the chest!"

Pinosh raged. Marty kept him pinned to the balcony, his grip increasingly slick and tenuous. Kareem stabbed again. Pinosh shuddered but still didn't die.

Marty couldn't see what was happening. "What are you doing?" he demanded.

"Killing my enemy." Kareem leaned over the balcony and tossed something large to the ground. It landed with a wet thud, and Marty looked down to see Pinosh's leg.

"Kareem, no! Just kill him!"

But Kareem ignored Marty. He sliced off another leg, and then Pinosh finally lost consciousness. Marty let go of the warrior and ran down the wall at an angle, wanting to get away from the gore and the violence.

He retrieved the dropped ankh. It wasn't Kareem's, so it must belong to the Frenchman.

"What are you doing?" he called to Kareem.

Kareem stood finally, holding Pinosh's severed head over his head and yelled, "Kareem did this! Know it and cower!"

He threw the severed head into the canyon.

The severed bits of Pinosh all separately shuddered into ooze.

"What are you doing?" Marty repeated himself.

"These things murdered our kind, Marty. It happened in Egypt, and it happened here as well. They murdered them and ate them, and they planned to do it again. They are monsters, not men. They would have eaten any of us. Now they will fear me forever. In their worst nightmares, in their folk tales, in the very blood in their veins they will regret what they tried to do to me and fear my name."

Marty could only stare at the young man. He had no experience of war and didn't know what to say to such bloodlust. The mournful wailing of Yotto caught his attention. What could he do to offer solace to the engineer who had helped them at risk to himself, and had suffered loss? What could he do for the other Grays? The Neshili had escaped, and that was good. But would the Herders now destroy the Farmers here in the city of the Grays? And if so, then what? Had he accomplished anything at all? The Grays were sentient, they had feelings. Was it any great win to save humans at the cost of Gray lives?

Maybe it was. The Grays had intended—some of them, at least—to eat the humans and not the other way around. Maybe there was a morally preferable side. And maybe, in any case, it was morally acceptable to take the side of his own species, when it came to a war for survival.

He realized that François was tugging at his tunic sleeve and had been tugging for some time.

François's voice was tired. "We'll figure out how to help the boy later. For now, we need to get into the portal. Gunther's in there trying to make it work, and the ship's on fire."

Marty handed the ankh back to the Frenchman, who tucked it into his belt. They turned to climb the stairs, Marty feeling the ache of the long day and all the battles in his muscles. As they trudged forward, Kareem dropped down from the balcony in front of them. Without turning to look at them, he marched up the steps toward the burning saucer.

Yotto still wept, hunched over the slimy remains of Gollip. Kareem stomped up the steps in a beeline toward the engineer, and Marty got a sick feeling in his stomach.

"Kareem!" he called. "Kareem, don't do anything foolish!"

Kareem kept marching and Yotto continued to wail.

"Kareem!" Marty called. "He's not our enemy!"

Kareem sank his ankh into the engineer's forehead, silencing the Gray instantly. Then he walked to the flaming ship and stepped inside.

Yotto dissolved.

François staggered and fell to his knees. Marty tried to help him up but ended up dropping beside him, on a step slick with blood and slime.

"Great god of heaven, I have failed," François said.

"You didn't fail," Marty said. "Kareem is in a bad place right now, and he made a terrible decision."

"Because I didn't lead him right." François buried his face in his hands. "Yotto..."

"François," Marty said. "Listen to me. Kareem is not your son. Even if he had been your son, he is a grown man, making his own choices, and is responsible for them. Remember that he came to you fully formed, and maybe already broken."

François struggled to his feet ponderously, moving like a man three times his weight. "We're all broken, Marty," he said. "Kareem made a terrible mistake today, but it could just as easily have been me."

Gunther stumbled up the stairs on hands and feet.

Activate the portal.

"I don't understand. How?" He coughed from the smoke billowing up from the lower level of the flying saucer, and the heat was almost unbearable.

Activate the portal. I'll show you.

Surjan and Lowanna stood at the command console of the upper level. "Hold on," Lowanna said, "I just got an idea."

She rested both hands on the control panel in front of her and, tapping into whatever it was inside of her, focused on the panel. A pale violet light flowed from her fingertips and bathed the controls. The panel activated, symbols scrolled on a screen, and the console began to glow of its own accord, in a purplish cast.

Air moved through unseen vents, slightly cooling the room and wisping away smoke.

Gunther stared at the control panel, and nothing made sense to him.

"Now what?" he demanded.

Activate the portal.

Gunther yelped in dismay and pounded the edge of the console. "Come on! Help me!"

"We're right here," Surjan said. "What do you need?"

Gunther ran the fingers of both hands through his hair. His skin felt hot to the touch. "How do I activate the portal?" he asked.

"We thought you knew," Lowanna said.

"There's power," Surjan said.

"Also, not to put too fine a point on it," Lowanna added, "there's fire. This vessel is on fire. Hurry your schnitzel up, Gunther. You can feel angst about it later. Now is the time to do the thing."

Kareem plodded to the top floor of the ship. "What now?" His voice was flat and affectless, inhuman.

"We're trying to make it work," Gunther said. "*I'm* trying to make it work, but I can't figure it out!" His own voice sounded like screaming to him, and Lowanna patted him on the shoulder.

First, activate the portal.

"How?" he yelled, staring at the controls. "How do I activate the portal?"

Like before.

Gunther looked to the rest of the party. "What did we do before?" he asked. "How did we activate it before?"

Surjan furrowed his brow. "There were some panels. Like a checkerboard, almost. And King Narmer touched some of them in a certain sequence, and then it worked."

Gunther gestured at the control panel. "Do you see any such checkerboard here? Do you see buttons in the same arrangement, or levers in the same layout, so we could use them to touch the same control sequence Narmer touched?"

"I don't," Surjan admitted.

François and Marty stumbled into the chamber, coughing. Flames licked up behind them.

"I don't know how to activate the machine," Gunther said.

Marty stared at him. "This is the whole thing! Gunther, you have been telling me for weeks that your voice will teach you how to use this portal! Now we're here, and the ship is on fire, and you don't know anything!"

"The voice is saying to turn it on!" Gunther screamed. "I don't know how to turn it on!"

The seer knows.

"Wait!" Gunther exclaimed and he pointed at Marty. "The voice says that you know how to turn it on. You're the seer, right? Didn't you say that you'd been called that before?"

"What did you do in Egypt?" Lowanna asked Marty.

Marty shrugged, brow furrowed. "We just got inside."

Kareem stepped into the white-walled portal, moved onto the rearmost of the dark circles, then turned and faced his comrades. Gunther caught his eye for a moment and was disturbed by the flat look of hatred burning there.

But new lights appeared on the panel.

Marty scooted around and looked down. "It's just a blank panel."

"Narmer touched an activation sequence in the wall panels to start the portal that brought us here," Gunther said. "Please tell me you remember the sequence of the squares he touched. Hell, you also did it to get us into this in the first place."

"You've got to be kidding me," Marty said. "This is like Grandpa Simcha asking me to remember some passage he recited out of the Mishnah Chagigah two years earlier."

"And how would you remember that passage when Grandpa Simcha asked you for it?" François asked.

Marty chuckled. "Kind of the same way I accessed my chi when Grandpa Chang asked me to do that. By relaxing and trying not to remember." He closed his eyes, breathed in through his nose three times, and then opened his eyes again.

"Get in the portal," Marty said.

Gunther shuffled in beside François and was quickly joined by the others. Marty took a deep breath. Gunther heard an ominous creaking sound, like a heavy piece of metal bending or buckling.

In his mind's eye, Marty saw the tunnel before him.

They were in modern-day Egypt and they were stuck, staring at an impenetrable wall.

Looking down at the panel, it had the same shape as the wall.

Could it be that simple?

It seemed like a lifetime ago, but he recalled the instructions he'd written to himself on that ancient wall.

With a chill racing through him, he saw himself reach out and touch the top left corner of the top left panel.

He touched the same area on the panel in front of him.

He then touched the center of the top right panel, then continued through the other panels, following the memories of what he'd done before.

He felt foolish as he tapped the panel, just like he'd felt foolish the first time back in Egypt, not knowing if it would work.

As he finished the first sequence, he touched the top-left portion of the panel in front of him again and felt a trembling beneath his feet as a whirring noise appeared, sounding almost like an engine spinning up.

The holographic image of the portal map popped up above the console.

"You're doing it!" Lowanna yelled triumphantly.

As he tapped out the rest of the sequence, the whirring got louder and louder.

"You need to teach everyone that sequence just as soon as we get through," François said.

Marty stood by the control panel, his fingers hovering over the final sequence of buttons. The rest of the team stood on dark circles embedded in the floor, the whole thing reminiscent of scenes he'd seen in old *Star Trek* episodes when a crew was about to be teleported. He took a deep breath and let it out slowly, trying to ease the tension in his chest.

He glanced at the others—Surjan, Lowanna, Kareem, François, and Gunther—each standing on their designated pad, their faces illuminated by the faint glow coming from the holographic image.

With a deep breath, Marty tapped the final sequence on the control panel. The lights in the room blinked off, plunging them into darkness. For a moment, there was nothing but the sound of his heartbeat pounding in his ears. Then, slowly, a bluish-white glow began to bloom from the pads beneath each of his teammates, bathing them in an ethereal light.

The glow pulsed softly, casting long shadows on the walls. Each member of the team stood in their circle of light, their faces calm but their eyes filled with the quiet resolve that had brought them this far.

The holographic image of the portal map reappeared, yet this time it seemed so real Marty was tempted to reach out and touch it.

Marty's heart raced as he looked at the empty pad waiting for him. It was the last step, the final commitment to whatever lay ahead.

Lowanna caught his eye, a small, wry smile playing on her lips. "I'm guessing at this point we're going to go somewhere as soon as you step onto your spot," she said, her voice steady despite the tension in the air.

Marty nodded, a faint smile tugging at the corners of his own mouth. "Seems like it," he replied, his voice betraying a mix of anticipation and nervousness.

Lowanna looked down and then gazed at the others on the team and grimaced. "Oh Lord, we're all covered in gore. Let's just hope we can wash it off before anyone spots us at our destination."

"Where are we going?" François asked, turning to Marty and back to Gunther. "Gunther, do you think you have an idea how to steer this thing?"

Everyone shifted their focus to Gunther. His jaw dropped as the light underneath him wavered for a moment and then returned to normal.

"I c-can do this," Gunther stammered with a shocked expression. "Where do we want to go?" he asked the group.

⇥ CHAPTER ⇤
FORTY

Gunther took a deep breath and stepped off his pad, ensuring that the transportation sequence couldn't initiate. The bluish-white glow beneath him dimmed, and the room fell into a tense silence. He motioned for Marty to step onto his teleportation pad. "We need to take control of this," he said, his voice firm. "But first, we need to decide where we're going."

The team exchanged uncertain glances, the gravity of their situation weighing on them. They all knew they were being tested, manipulated by forces they couldn't fully comprehend. But they also knew that they couldn't keep reacting—they needed to take the initiative, to wrest control of their fate from whoever or whatever was behind this.

The team's focus shifted to the holographic image of the map that hovered in the air above the portal's console.

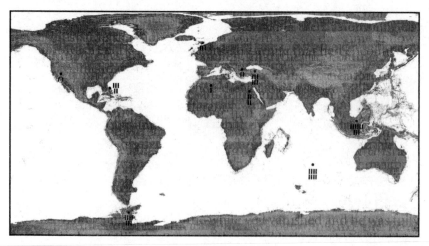

"Where do we want to go?" Gunther asked, his voice steady but filled with the weight of the decision they had to make.

Lowanna was the first to speak, her eyes fixed on the map. "We've been through so much already . . . Do we really want to keep jumping from portal to portal, not knowing what's next? Maybe it's time to face whatever this is head-on."

Surjan nodded in agreement, his jaw clenched with determination. "I'm with Lowanna. We can't keep playing their game, going from one test to the next. Let's just finish this."

"What does that even mean?" François asked. "Jump to portal number ten? And what happens when we get there? We fight the big boss? We face our judgment, hearts weighed against the feather of Maat like some dead pharaoh?"

Marty's face held a worried expression. "But what if this is just another trap? What if going straight to the end is exactly what they want us to do? We could be walking right into their hands."

"Does it actually matter? If we're going to go in order, we do it now or do it later, and later might never come if we fail at one of these ridiculous tests of theirs," Lowanna said, her voice calm but resolute. "We can't stay here forever, debating what to do. We need to make a choice."

The room fell silent for a long moment and everyone turned back to Marty.

Marty glanced once more at the holographic map and sighed. His expression hardened with resolve. "All right, I guess it's somewhen in the western part of North America. Let's go to portal number ten and end this."

The others murmured their agreement, and Gunther felt a surge of uncertainty. The decision had been made, and now it was up to him to guide them through it.

He closed his eyes, focusing inward, reaching out to the voice that had promised to guide him.

I hear your plea and understand.

The voice rang loudly in Gunther's head.

There is an error in the transport logic. You will leverage it.

Marty gave Gunther a look. "Are you doing something?"

Gunther waved the question away. "I'm trying to listen."

Do not move until you've received all that I have to tell you, because the moment you step onto the pad, the circuit will be completed and the process will begin. Understood?

Gunther nodded and worried as the voice gave a technical explanation for what was about to happen. He understood some of it, but some of it made no sense:

. . . you will induce an error in the system . . .

Triggering the watchdog timer will yield the results that are desired . . .

Now go ahead. You are ready.

Gunther felt anything but ready, but aside from the technobabble, the instructions seemed clear.

He gazed across the faces of his team and asked, "Are we ready?"

They all nodded.

"Okay, whatever you do, don't move or say anything while I do this."

Gunther stepped onto his teleportation pad and it was almost as if time slowed to a crawl.

His heartbeat stopped.

Nobody blinked.

Not a breath was taken as the room was bathed in a brilliant white light.

Gunther stepped off the pad, triggering a series of clicks as the blinding light vanished, and he was back in the portal room with the others frozen in columns of white light.

In his mind replayed the instruction the voice had given him.

A five-second delay in transportation will trigger the countdown.

He kept a count in his head and just as he said the fifth Mississippi a loud metallic click alerted him to some change.

"One . . ."

Just like the voice had said, the transporter would start enumerating its targets, deviating from its normal programming.

"Two . . ."

As Gunther focused intently on the count, he was reminded of the warning the voice had given him: *If you fail to put your foot back onto the teleportation pad before the count expires, the entire team will be vaporized.*

Gunther was standing right next to the pad. Too early and they'd all end up in another place and time; too late, and they'd all be dead.

Suddenly, Gunther panicked as he realized he wasn't sure if he was supposed to step in at the announcement of "ten" or if he heard "ten" and it was already too late.

"*Eight*..."

Gunther focused, trying to guess how many tenths of a second there were between each number.

"*Nine*..."

Gunther tensed as he tried to count—*NOW!*

He leaped onto the pad just as he heard "*T—*"

The bluish-white glow beneath him flared to life, and the room was once again bathed in blinding white light.

✢ ✢ ✢

The hive mind sensed the exception triggered by an event in the test matrix, and immediately launched a thread to evaluate the current status.

"*Watchdog Timer activated for a test checkpoint out of Brane sigma+654PWJZBE in the Orion arm of the Milky Way galaxy. Planet Earth, local relative year is 9104 B.C.E.*"

The Administrator sighed as he briefly focused on what had occurred and, for a brief moment, he was frustrated. "*I see that the test subjects exploited a flaw in the transportation programming. The communication received by test subject Gunther had to have come from us, otherwise how could the source of the communication know about an internal aspect of the transportation logic?*"

The hive mind puzzled over the issue for a moment and came back with nothing. "*We have been monitoring the communication with the test subject and have been unable to trace the communications to its source. I have no other answers.*"

"*Monitor all communications from all elements of the hive mind. Seek out those who have had access to the transportation design and gather all of their communications across the multiverse. There must be an answer.*"

The Administrator shifted some of his attention to the trial that was underway.

"Motion to terminate the test now," the Prosecutor said, his voice cold and precise.

"Objection," the Advocate replied swiftly. "No grounds."

Tests such as the one being administered to the Earth subjects were typically evaluated at specific checkpoints, where the team's progress and decisions were scrutinized according to predetermined parameters. But this time, the situation had grown contentious.

"Prosecutor, explain the basis for your motion," the Adjudicator commanded, his tone one of measured patience.

"This species has flagrantly violated the natural order of the test," the Prosecutor said, his words dripping with disdain. "They were to proceed to portal six after arriving at portal five. Instead, they bypassed it entirely, using portal seven to jump directly to portal ten. Such actions are a clear breach of the rules. They are circumventing the intended sequence, thereby undermining the integrity of the test."

The Advocate folded his arms, his gaze unwavering as he replied. "What rules have they broken? The test is not simply about following a predetermined path—it's about their decisions, their actions under pressure."

"The test of faith," the Prosecutor shot back. "The sequence was designed to test their resolve, their ability to trust in the process. By bypassing portals, they have shown a lack of faith, choosing the easy way out instead of adhering to the challenges set before them."

The Advocate took a step forward, his voice firm but calm. "You argue that they've lacked faith, yet what they demonstrated was, in fact, a profound leap of faith. They faltered at portal five, yes. But at portal seven, they chose to leap forward—to take a risk in the face of uncertainty. That is the essence of faith."

The Prosecutor's eyes narrowed, his voice rising in frustration. "These acts of so-called faith were not part of the designed test scenarios. They are irrelevant and should not be considered valid responses to the trials of faith. The team has manipulated the system and should be judged accordingly."

The Adjudicator observed the exchange with a thoughtful expression. "You claim their actions are manipulative, Prosecutor, but the question here is whether the test subjects acted within their own understanding and judgment, or if they exploited a flaw in the test."

"They exploited a flaw, plain and simple," the Prosecutor insisted. "Their leap from portal seven to portal ten is evidence of their disregard for the structured nature of the test. It undermines the purpose of this trial."

The Advocate countered smoothly, "The test is meant to judge them on their actions. They saw an opportunity and they took it, knowing full well the risks involved. That leap was not a calculated cheat—it was a demonstration of their belief that they could overcome the challenges ahead. They did not break faith; they embraced it."

A tense silence followed as the Adjudicator weighed the arguments. The room seemed to hold its breath, the tension thick enough to cut.

Finally, the Adjudicator spoke, his voice resolute. "Judgment is based on the actions of the test subjects, not on the unforeseen variables introduced by the test environment. The Advocate's argument holds. The actions of the team, though unconventional, do not constitute a violation of the test. They acted on faith—a faith in their own abilities and in the decisions they made. Judgment is for the Advocate. The test may continue."

The Prosecutor's expression darkened, his jaw clenched in frustration. "I maintain my objection. This ruling sets a dangerous precedent."

"Noted," the Adjudicator replied with finality. "But the trial will proceed. The focus remains on their actions. Let them continue to prove themselves."

The Advocate nodded, satisfied, while the Prosecutor's anger simmered beneath the surface. The test would go on, and with it, the fate of the Earth subjects would hang in the balance, inching ever closer to an unknown conclusion.

Marty's head spun as the white light dissolved, leaving him unsteady and disoriented. He felt the ground solidify beneath him, but the disconnection between body and mind lingered, making it difficult to tell up from down. He blinked hard, trying to clear the swirling haze from his vision. The transition left him gasping for air as if he had been plunged underwater.

The first thing he noticed was the cold, dry air hitting his lungs. It was a stark contrast to the acrid scent of the chamber they had just left. He coughed, his throat raw, and instinctively reached out to steady himself, his hands finding purchase on something rough—stone. Slowly, his senses began to return, and he became aware of the gritty texture beneath his fingers.

Marty opened his eyes, forcing them to focus. The world around him was coming into view, and what he saw took his breath away. They were surrounded by towering walls of rock, their surfaces layered in shades of red, orange, and brown, as if the earth had been sliced open to reveal its ancient history. The cliffs rose high above them, their jagged edges etched against a brilliant blue sky. The sun, low in the sky, cast long shadows across the rocky terrain, adding depth to the already dramatic landscape.

He pushed himself upright, his legs still shaky from the disorienting transition. As he took in the vast expanse before him, he realized they were standing in some kind of canyon. The ground beneath them was uneven, a mix of gravel and larger rocks, with patches of hardy vegetation clinging to life in the harsh environment.

The rest of the team was scattered around him, each recovering in their own way. Gunther was the first to rise, his eyes scanning the cliffs with a mix of awe and wariness. Lowanna, already on her feet, moved cautiously, her gaze sweeping over the landscape as if expecting danger to leap from the shadows. Surjan, still on his hands and knees, took a deep breath before pushing himself upright, his expression one of sheer disbelief.

Marty took a few steps forward, his boots crunching on the loose gravel. The air was dry, tinged with the scent of dust and stone, and he could feel the heat radiating from the ground despite the coolness of the air. He glanced up at the sky, noting the absence of clouds, the vast openness making him feel both exposed and insignificant.

"What . . . is this place?" Gunther murmured, breaking the silence.

Marty shook his head, his mind racing as he tried to place the landscape. It was unlike anything he had ever seen in person, yet there was something about it that tugged at his memory. The scale of the canyon was immense, the cliffs stretching far into the distance, their layers telling a story that spanned millennia. It was a place of raw, untamed beauty, but there was an undercurrent of something else— something that made him uneasy.

"It's . . . it's some kind of canyon," Marty finally said, his voice filled with uncertainty. "But the size . . . it's massive."

"You mean like a 'Grand Canyon,' you doofus?" Lowanna smiled as she walked toward him, her boots crunching on the gravel, and gave him a bearhug.

Marty returned the hug, feeling the warmth of her body pressed against his. "Are you sure?"

"Zero doubt," Lowanna responded. "I've been here before, doing a study on the Anasazi." She examined the ground. "Look at the way the rock has been carved," she said, pointing to the smooth curves in the stone that hinted at ancient water flows. "This place has seen some powerful forces at work. It's beautiful, but . . . it feels isolated, desolate."

Marty's eyes drifted to the horizon, following the steep drop-off that led down to the canyon floor. A narrow river snaked through the bottom, its waters a distant, glittering ribbon. The sound of it barely reached them, a faint murmur carried on the wind. The scale of the place made him feel small, insignificant, and yet he knew that they were here for a reason.

"There's a river down there," Marty said, pointing to the water below.

Surjan joined him at the edge, staring down at the river. "It's amazing that the water carved out this entire canyon," he said, his voice laced with disbelief.

"It looks like it's late in the day and we need to get our bearings," Marty said, his voice steady despite the tension gnawing at him. "Remember, we have no idea when we are, even if we know where. This place . . . I'm sure it's not what it seems. We need to be ready for anything."

"For all we know, we might be in the modern day," Gunther said.

"No, I don't think so." Lowanna shook her head and pointed at one of the looming walls of stone. "I recognize that cliff. Nowadays . . . er, in our time . . . it has metal railings to help folks hike down the trail to a lower level. I don't see any of that."

As the sun dipped lower in the sky, casting even longer shadows across the canyon, Marty knew they were about to face something significant. The voice in his head remained silent, but the feeling in his gut told him that they were far from done.

Marty motioned to the horizon and said, "We probably have just enough time to get closer to the river before it gets dark. Whatever and whenever this place is, it holds answers—answers that we're going to need to survive."

◄ AUTHORS' NOTE ►

Thanks for reading *Ice Trials* (and *Time Trials* before it), and there's lots more where that came from.

If you're interested in getting updates about our latest work, we have links below so you can join our mailing lists.

—Mike and Dave

M.A. Rothman: https://mailinglist.michaelarothman.com/new-reader

D.J. Butler: https://davidjohnbutler.com/mailinglist/

⇥ ADDENDUM ⇤

The addendum is the place where we as authors get to roll up our sleeves up and talk about the technical pieces of the story you've just read. When you have an author with a strong science background cowriting with an author who has a strong background in ancient history, you can imagine you might get a story with a bit of both.

And that would be true with *Ice Trials* (and the book that preceded it, *Time Trials*).

The Bimini Road

In *Ice Trials* we made some veiled references to things that are very much items that truly exist, such as the Bimini Road. We purposefully made light of it in the context of the story, but ultimately two things were later mentioned that are related: the Piri Reis map, and Atlantis. We'll cover the map in a moment, but the relation with the Bimini Road and Atlantis might seem like a stretch—after all Atlantis is a made-up place, right?

Well, let's leave that topic for the reader's conjecture and focus on the Bimini Road for a small moment:

The Bimini Road, a mysterious underwater formation off the coast of Bimini Island in the Bahamas, has intrigued explorers and researchers for decades. Discovered in 1968, this unusual feature consists of a series of large, flat stones arranged in a linear pattern, resembling a road or pathway submerged beneath the ocean's surface.

Some believe that the Bimini Road is evidence of an ancient, advanced civilization, possibly linked to the legendary lost continent of Atlantis described by Plato, which was said to have disappeared into the sea thousands of years ago. Proponents of this theory argue that the stones are remnants of a sophisticated, sunken city, and point to the alignment and construction as proof of human engineering.

However, the scientific community remains skeptical of these claims. Most geologists and archaeologists contend that the Bimini Road is a natural formation, likely the result of beachrock fractured and eroded by natural processes. They argue that while the formation is intriguing, there is no definitive evidence linking it to Atlantis or any other lost civilization.

Despite the lack of concrete proof, the Bimini Road continues to capture the imagination of those fascinated by the mysteries of the ancient world, keeping the legend of Atlantis alive in popular culture and fueling ongoing debates about what lies beneath the waves.

The Piri Reis Map

In *Ice Trials* we discovered a map that François related to an ancient map he'd seen that he called the Piri Reis Map. Again, we purposefully made reference to it because of its historical significance and the conjecture associated with it. You might ask, why is it special? Let's talk a little about it:

The Piri Reis Map is a world map compiled in 1513 by the Ottoman admiral and cartographer Piri Reis. It has long intrigued historians and conspiracy theorists alike. What makes this map so fascinating is its depiction of parts of the world with surprising accuracy—particularly the coastlines of South America and Africa—despite being created during a time when European exploration of these regions was still in its infancy.

One of the most controversial aspects of the Piri Reis Map is its depiction of what some believe to be the coastline of Antarctica. This has led to speculation that the map might be a remnant of ancient knowledge, possibly dating back to a time during the last ice age, over twelve thousand years ago. This theory suggests that an advanced civilization, perhaps even that of Atlantis, could have charted these lands long before the rise of known civilizations.

Proponents of this theory argue that the Piri Reis Map could be evidence of a forgotten era of exploration, where ancient mariners mapped the world during a time when sea levels were lower.

However, mainstream historians are more cautious, attributing the map's accuracy to a combination of known ancient maps, including those from the Greeks and the early explorers of the Mediterranean, rather than evidence of a lost civilization. They point out that the supposed depiction of Antarctica could simply be a misrepresentation of the southern tip of South America or an imaginative interpretation based on incomplete knowledge.

Whether the Piri Reis Map is a genuine relic of an ancient, advanced civilization or simply an example of Renaissance cartography's blend of fact and fiction, it remains a captivating artifact, fueling debates about the mysteries of our past and the potential for lost knowledge hidden within the annals of history.

We'll leave it as an exercise to the reader to determine what you believe.

Nanites

We introduced something that was actually a "mystery substance" coating the ankhs back in *Time Trials,* but in *Ice Trials* we gave this thing a name: nanites. And even though the substance was a mystery to the cast members of the story, these microscopic little specks of gold served as a literary tool for us to do various things, especially things that affected the characters in ways that might have been subtle or somewhat drastic, depending on the situation. And you might think such things are fictional—they are not. The engineering world has had the ability to create things at the molecular level for quite some time.

The best example of this is in computer CPU manufacturing. Today, we are mass-manufacturing electronics with processes dealing with trace widths as low as 1.8 nanometers. That's more than a thousand times smaller than the width of the finest hair. An atom averages anywhere from 0.1 to 0.3 nanometers wide.

We've even been able to manufacture tiny machines at the nano-scale. Think of a nanite as a tiny robot. A nanobot, if you will. Molecule-sized robots have been the promise of medicine for quite some time. The concept used in this series, where these "tiny doctors" are able to repair the body (within reason), and fend off sicknesses, is not really as ridiculous as it might seem.

Today, it is already possible to synthesize nanites that can determine where they are, and deliver minute units of a medicine to the correct locations. For instance, if one of these nanites was carrying a drug meant to treat a specific form of cancer, it would also carry a sensor that would help it identify its molecular target.

The advantages of such a precision approach are obvious. Chemotherapies, by contrast, blast the entire body with poisons, damaging healthy cells along with the cancerous ones. Nanites could be "programmed" to target only the unhealthy cells.

Yet today we are not using nanites as tiny doctors. Why?

Many challenges exist—among them, the ability to manufacture these nanites in a sufficient quantity to do clinical testing. This is hugely expensive today, and frankly, that's the biggest technical hurdle.

But once that hurdle is crossed, the field is open for what could be a revolution in medicine, generating entirely new methods of treating cancer, other diseases, and even possibly halt the aging process.

The End of the Ice Age—the World is Changing

Ice Trials is set in a time of turbulence for our planet. We're at the end of the last ice age, around 11,700 years ago, marking a dramatic turning point in the history of our planet. It was a time of profound change, not just for the climate, but for the creatures that roamed the Earth, the landscapes they inhabited, and the oceans that shaped the boundaries of continents. Among the most affected were the giant sloth and other megafauna—once rulers of the land, they found themselves struggling to survive in a world that was rapidly becoming inhospitable.

The Twilight of the Giants

When we think of the giant monsters of our ancient past, we often go back sixty-six million years ago to the age of the dinosaurs, but we had some very intimidating creatures much more recently than that. For tens of thousands of years, the Earth was home to an array of enormous creatures, collectively known as megafauna. The giant sloth, towering mammoths, saber-toothed cats, and massive bison roamed the landscapes of North and South America, thriving in the cooler, glaciated world. These creatures were well-adapted to the cold and the vast, open environments that characterized the Ice Age.

However, as the Ice Age drew to a close, the climate began to warm rapidly. Glaciers that had covered large portions of the Northern and Southern Hemispheres retreated, giving way to forests, grasslands, and wetlands. The habitats that had sustained these massive animals began to shrink, and with the changing climate came new challenges: dwindling food sources, competition with other species, and the arrival of skilled human hunters.

The giant ground sloth, a remarkable creature that could grow up to twenty feet long and weigh several tons, was one of the many species that found itself on the brink of extinction. As the forests expanded, the open areas where they foraged for food diminished. Coupled with human predation, the giant sloth's numbers dwindled, and they eventually disappeared, leaving only their bones and the occasional fossilized track as a reminder of their once-dominant presence.

The Oceans in Flux: Rising Waters and Changing Shores

The end of the Ice Age didn't just affect the land; it also brought about significant changes in the world's oceans. As the glaciers melted, vast amounts of water were released into the seas, causing global sea levels to rise by as much as four hundred feet. This dramatic increase in ocean levels reshaped coastlines, inundated low-lying areas, and formed new islands and waterways.

During the height of the Ice Age, much of the Earth's water was locked in massive ice sheets, and sea levels were significantly lower. This created land bridges that connected continents—most notably, the Bering Land Bridge between Siberia and Alaska. It was over this bridge that humans first migrated into North America, tens of thousands of years before the Ice Age ended. These early pioneers spread across the continent, eventually reaching South America, and establishing diverse cultures and civilizations.

But as the Ice Age ended and the glaciers melted, the Bering Land Bridge was submerged by rising seas, cutting off the land route between Asia and the Americas. The civilizations that had taken root in the Americas were now isolated, separated from the rest of the world by vast oceans. For thousands of years, these societies would develop independently, creating rich and varied cultures that remained largely unknown to the rest of the world until the voyages of European explorers millennia later.

What Is This Deal with the King Being Killed When His Powers Run Out?

This is an idea brought to public consciousness in James George Frazer's monumental work *The Golden Bough*. This groundbreaking study in comparative religion got bigger as it went into new editions, until in its third edition it comprised twelve meaty volumes. *The Golden Bough* has had a massive influence on various spheres of intellectual activities, including poetry (see William Butler Yeats's "Sailing to Byzantium" and Robert Graves's *The White Goddess*), classical studies (see Jane Ellen Harrison's *Themis* and *Prolegomena to the Study of Greek Religion*), Biblical studies (see William Robertson Smith's *Lectures on the Religion of the Semites*), psychoanalysis (see Sigmund Freud's *Totem and Taboo* as well as Joseph Campbell's *The Hero With a Thousand Faces*), and even film (see Francis Ford Coppola's *Apocalypse Now*).

One of Frazer's key ideas was that many religions were fundamentally fertility cults that contained buried within them reverence for a sacred king who ruled as long as he was virile and his magic was effective (in doing fertility things, such as bringing the rain, warding off death, etc.). Once the king's powers showed signs of flagging—or in some cases, before they showed signs of beginning to fail and in order to avoid their failure—the king was murdered and replaced in his role by the man who killed him. This is the situation, obviously, into which we have inserted poor Surjan Singh.

Frazer starts his investigation with the priesthood of Diana at Lake Nemi in classical (Roman) times, but ranges all over the globe. His inclusion of Christ in his study caused no small amount of scandal. *The Golden Bough* also argued for an intellectual history of mankind in three phases, beginning with magic, then progressing to religion, and then ultimately graduating to science. If that sounds a little self-congratulatory to you, well, it has sounded self-congratulatory to other critics of the book.

The Golden Bough remains in print and is well known to the general reader. Within anthropology, its influence was initially pervasive but has long since faded. Nevertheless, it retains enough power—whether by virtue of its mass of ethnographic detail or by virtue of its creative vision—to continue to inspire new thinkers. And who can say whether it might yet come back into the limelight?